Also by Jack Viertel

The Secret Life of the American Musical.

BROADWAY MELODY

BROADWAY MELODY

A Novel

JACK VIERTEL

BENZINGER & FRANK
NEW YORK

Book design by Edwin A. Vazquez

Broadway Melody is a work of fiction, though a number of real people and events appear throughout. In a few cases I have played a bit fast and loose with when things happened, and even how they happened or if they happened at all. I've tried to be at least approximately accurate in many other matters, though I do admit to having invented a fictional trumpet part in the original orchestration of *Sunday in the Park with George*. As to the activities and attitudes of the characters bearing the names of real people, they are, for better or worse, also entirely my own invention. My apologies to the descendants of Max Meth, if he has any.

For Seymour "Red" Press
1924–2022
Maven, Mentor, and Mensch

Everyone said to be nice to the people you meet on the way up because you'll meet the same people on the way down. But I have to tell you—I haven't met any of the same people.

Jack Searles

No man ought to have to die while his heart was still young enough to love beauty.

John Galsworthy

The only trouble with getting to be my age is that breakfast comes every fifteen minutes.

Kitty Carlisle Hart

PART ONE

1

The Winter Garden

T*his is not the Broadway I remember*.

As he turned the corner of 44th Street and looked up at the huge illuminated Coke sign he realized he had said it aloud. He hadn't said it to anyone in particular; he'd just said it. This was beginning to occur with some frequency. Four months short of his ninetieth birthday, Zachary Harris, born Itzhak Horowitz and still called Ike—but that's another story—was beginning to let his thoughts escape from his mouth for no reason. He was coming to understand that certain things just happened to you. You weren't supposed to control them anymore. It was too late.

It bothered him, though; it shook his confidence, and especially on this morning, when he feared he might be called upon to handle a crisis. Moments before, he'd had a call on his cell from Aurora Shelton, with whom he had been in love for over half a century. Her husband had apparently left his bedroom at the Actors Fund Home in Englewood early that morning and had not been heard from since. Vincent Donnelly was not known to be much good at following rules or doing things by the book, but this was the first time he had ever run away. His condition was perilous, and no one knew where he had gone or how he might have found the money for transportation to wherever he thought he was going. Ike promised Aurora he would check in with her as soon as he got done at the Winter Garden, and not to worry. This would all be okay, he said, though why anyone should be comforted by such talk he had no idea.

He pulled his coat around himself, a small man in an old parka, and began to trudge north toward the Winter Garden, where he had once held down the first trumpet chair in the pit orchestra of *West Side Story*. That was in 1957—a long time ago. Everything from those days was gone. The Hawaii Kai restaurant, once nestled in the basement, with the entrance under the theater's marquee, was gone. Colony Records, across Broadway and down a block, was gone. Bond Clothing Store, where he had purchased his first Broadway pit tuxedo, had become a restaurant, and now the restaurant was gone too, moved to the other side of Broadway. Even the Coke sign had once said Coca-Cola, with a picture of a real glass bottle. No more. Now the signs morphed from one advertisement to another right before your eyes, each of them a gigantic LED video screen. One moment it was promoting a soft drink and the next a new cable series starring people Ike had never bothered to learn about. The first time he had seen the new signs he thought he was hallucinating and began to hyperventilate. But now they were just a regular feature of the district, as neon had once been, and multicolored lighted bulbs before that. It was 2016, and he assumed that time would continue to march on, with him, and soon enough, without him.

What bothered him, though, was that he could still see it all, then and now, like a double exposure.

"Double exposure," he said aloud. Even Kodak film was gone, and maybe his eyes were going too, cursing him with double, and sometimes triple vision. But he, himself, was not gone, not quite.

Back when he left his final big-band gig to take his first job in a Broadway pit, it was considered mediocre employment. The great musicians played in the last of the big bands, and if they insisted on staying home in New York, as he had decided to do, they aimed for one of the television orchestras. NBC had one. CBS had one. The record companies had them—house orchestras: RCA, Columbia. Those were the good jobs, steady jobs, with new material to master every week. The New York Philharmonic, the Metropolitan Opera, the best and most prestigious of all, were generally out of reach, except for subbing for a sick or missing player. Broadway was a glamorous place for an audience, but in the hierarchy that the players believed in, the pit band was a third-rate gig. The same score eight times a week. If you were lucky the show ran, and you got paid, but the tunes began to drive you crazy. Besides, there were no guarantees that the show would run. And nobody could see you.

He hadn't started with *West Side Story* but with a semi-turkey called *The Vamp* in late 1955. That was the job he could get after he had subbed for a while at *Plain and Fancy*. The trouble really started in 1960. It was while playing for the out-of-town tryout of a disaster called *Nowhere to Go But Up* on a wintry half-empty night in Philly that he began to believe that—with the aid of a Harmon mute—he could make a sound that would melt the coldest of hearts, that could change lives forever. This, as it turned out some time later, was a risky thing to believe, even if you never told anyone about it. It was a thing that, if you really believed it, could nearly kill you. The show ran only a week and a day on Broadway. But the damage had lasted fifty-seven years.

When he thought about it now, as he did, leaning into the

weather and making it past the Szechuan-and-sushi place on the corner of 47th Street, it was amazing that he still worked at all in this alien landscape, never mind melting hearts, or breaking them.

The network orchestras and the record company orchestras, all gone. Still, Ike Harris had friends in the business on Broadway and they continued to hire him. But the trumpet? No. Even in a lousy Broadway show, there's only a certain number of clams you can hit before the music director will come to you and gently suggest that maybe it's time. The union will fight for you as best it can—they don't always care what the music actually sounds like as long as your job is protected, but who wants to look around at twenty-three other pit musicians eight times a week and see it on their faces? They are in the company of a venerable veteran trumpet player, a man of great passion and musical distinction, whose lip has turned to shit right in front of their eyes and ears. His teeth are going and can't support the pressure from the mouthpiece. He's outlived his usefulness. What the hell is he still doing here? It's going to happen to each of them one day, which is why, quite naturally, they don't want it in the room with them.

So, he quit playing at eighty-two because he couldn't play anymore. It seemed like a logical next move.

He had become a contractor long before—he suggested the best people for each job, hired the musicians, filled out the paperwork, made sure the work rules were being followed, navigated disputes between management and the union, and hung out in the room, for the pure pleasure of listening. A dull job in theory, but he was organizationally minded, and he'd learned the nuts and bolts of it in the army, of all places. This way, he could do more than one show at a time and spread the risk, since he didn't have to show up and play every night, and maybe the flops balanced the hits sometimes. If you had a good year, income came in weekly from various sources. He could walk into any Broadway theater and be welcomed. He could stand in the back or sit in the pit. He could work well into his eighties—no one was there to stop him. True, even after all this time on Broadway, no one outside the business had the slightest idea who he was, which might have seemed odd in such a public business. But he had no regrets. In fact, most days he thought to himself that it had been a good run, full of quietly satisfying moments, when the music lifted him up and made him whole.

But eventually, as the sounds changed and the composing, if you could call it that, became almost unrecognizable to him, he realized for certain, and for the first time, that he actually no longer had the slightest fucking idea what was happening on the street he had grown to love with such unrestrained passion. It was just like every kind of love he had ever experienced: incomprehensible, all-consuming, potentially fatal, an addiction, a source of joy and bewilderment and hope that also contained the certainty of death.

And yet, sometimes there was a good show.

No matter what, he told himself, that's all a show is. A good show. Or not such a good show. At the moment, he had hope for the one coming into the Winter Garden, but mainly he just wanted to get out of the wind and the snow and into the damn building.

The Winter Garden had been good to him, more or less. Back in the fifties, each theater had its own union players—four of them in each, usually strings, but in his case first trumpet—who were guaranteed employment when the theater had a musical show in it that used those instruments. The rest of the time, you scrambled. In those years the Winter Garden had been home, and a venerable one, if not always a steady source of income. It was said that the year before *West Side Story* opened, Leonard Bernstein himself, in the middle of composing it, had come to see a flop called *Shangri-La* there, and found the house viola players in the pit so lousy that he directed his orchestrators to write the musical charts for his new show without violas. There went two jobs out the window, and there have never been any viola parts in the *West Side Story* score. But there was always plenty for the trumpet.

He pulled open the stage door, that same stage door, for perhaps the ten thousandth time, nodded at the doorman, whose name he could never learn, and made his way up onstage, through the pass door that led to the house, and out into the auditorium. The stage doorman was in his twenties, with a shock of bleached blond hair, a tattoo of some Eastern deity on his neck, and a single red fingernail. It was a Russian name, but the kid no doubt came from one of the outer boroughs. He had no accent to speak of. Ike tried to remember when it had happened that old guys in derby hats smoking cigars had been replaced by fake Russian punkers with fake blond hair as Broadway stage doormen. Not that it mattered—he would have been happy simply to remember the kid's name. Vlad? Probably not.

It still thrilled him, however, to look around the Winter Garden, empty except for a small production staff gathering in the aisles. The wide, elegant low-arched proscenium, the widest on Broadway, held promises and secrets, and, over the course of the twentieth century, had contained multitudes. Ziegfeld girls in their scanties, or less, declamatory Shakespearians including a host of great English knights and Lords—Gielgud, Richardson, Olivier, and the others. Al Jolson, Bert Lahr, Mary Martin, Bea Lillie, and, somewhat more depressingly, actors dressed as cats—all kinds of cats—not to mention, in the late fifties, the Jets and the Sharks. Jerome Robbins had stormed up the theater's aisles in various states of rage and made great art here. Irving Berlin had no doubt sat on the stairs leading to the mezzanine during rehearsals, his head in his hands, trying to find a better rhyme. Risks had been taken, resulting in triumph or humiliation. Audiences had had their lives changed here or had dozed off. It was the Winter Garden.

Currently restored and featuring a rich brown coffee-and-cream décor, the auditorium itself was also unusually wide and commodious, reflecting its origins as one of the two flagship theaters of the all-powerful Shubert Organization, which for much of the twentieth century had controlled the street. Their other flagship was the Shubert Theatre itself, which Ike had hiked past on 44th ten minutes before. The Shubert Theatre couldn't hold a candle to this place, he mused, even though it had been the domain of the smarter of the two Shubert brothers back in the day.

Empty, in work light, the theater lacked much of the romance Ike associated with the experience of playing shows there. A theater bereft of its lighting, of its hum of anticipation just before curtain time, of its noodling musical instruments and the vague but unmistakable certainty that there were actors behind the curtain transforming themselves into characters other than themselves, invented people whose history and passion and fate had to be retraced with each performance—a theater lacking all of that was really a barren place, an old lady in the morning, reaching for her teeth and the coffee cup that might begin another day's crossing into evening.

But when evening came, the singular theatrical events that graced the stage were often things of grace, full, ornate, emotionally stirring.

And history is made at night, Ike thought, looking around the vast empty space.

As a finished experience, a performance was all one thing,

indivisible. Yet he knew that each one was manufactured by fulfilling a thousand mundane requirements, which, looked at in the cold light of day, could reduce the grandeur of the ultimate achievement to splinters, each as ugly and potentially painful as a bedbug. In some ways the theater was an unending parade of problems to be squashed underfoot before they made your life hell. *How could it be both?* he wondered. The great thing itself and the infested mattress on which it had been conceived? How could this paradox sustain itself? How, after all this time, could one give oneself over to the illusion of theatrical revelation when the mechanics were plain to see? He'd been wondering this for an awfully long time, and time was surely running out.

Today's meeting concerned the band for the new show. After the policy of each theater maintaining its own house players had been abandoned in the 1960s, the union had settled for the concept of theater minimums. Each theater had an assigned number of musicians who had to be hired for each show that played there—the minimum at the Winter Garden was currently twenty-four. The show could choose the musicians (the policy came too late for Bernstein and his absent violas), but once a musician was hired, he or she held down the chair for the life of the show.

And then came rock and roll. The soon-to-be tenant at the Winter Garden was based on the collected work of an eighties rock band, now long disbanded; none of their records had ever used twenty-four musicians. So there was going to be an argument with the union about the minimum. Why should the production hire them if there was nothing for them to play? This was Ike's bread and butter, a *vonce deluxe,* and a long way away from whatever the finished event would be.

Gathered in the aisle was the music director, a bearded kid-wizard named Tino Flores, whose parents had fled Cuba in the nineties. Next to him was the show's corpulent producer, who'd made a fortune syndicating TV sitcoms in Asia; and the painfully antisocial, weak-chinned orchestrator, who, along with Tino Flores, would figure out how many musicians were necessary and then try to defend their choices. The producer wanted as few players—as few salaries—as possible. Flores and the orchestrator wanted as many as they could find reasons for. Ike just wanted a number he could go argue with the union about. They were waiting for the band's attorney, who would undoubtedly have many confident and widely uninformed opinions on the subject.

"How long do we wait?" Ike asked. He wanted to check in with Aurora. But it was warm and dry in the Winter Garden, and he was grateful for that. He was shrugging off the old parka when someone called his name—shouted it, actually. The assembled group looked toward the back of the house, where a disheveled old man was limping down the aisle. His thinning gray hair reached in all directions as if the house was somehow magnetized around him and the gray strands were made of iron. As he approached, Ike realized it was Vincent Donnelly, drenched, in an old coat that failed to conceal the fact that he was wearing a pair of striped pajamas underneath. He came toward them, a wreck of a man, carrying a cheap wooden cigar box in one hand. The other was clenched in a kind of misshapen fist that he waved at the group as he limped closer.

"Ike Harris," he shouted again. Ike took a half step back from the crowd, the better to be the target of whatever it was that Vincent Donnelly was coming after him for. As he made his way down the aisle, Vincent flung the cigar box toward the center section of the auditorium. A few knickknacks went flying as the box let go of its contents. Then Vincent stopped moving, a few feet from Ike.

"Can you fix this?" he asked in an accusatory tone.

"Vincent," Ike said consolingly. "Vincent, what's up?"

"I'm supposed to be the one who can fix anything!" he bellowed. "But I can't fix this! You're Mr. Music." His voice was poison. He raised his fist, but before he could reach Ike, he froze. His body turned to stone.

"I'm all right," he practically gurgled, but it was as if whatever electrical impulses had been coursing through him a second before had somehow blown a fuse. He was still, silent. Then he began to heave, and a red thread dripped from his mouth, down the front of his soaked overcoat and onto the plush fleur-de-lis carpet of the Winter Garden. His eyes rolled once and he went down, like a marble statue knocked from its pedestal, a heap in the aisle, leaking blood and bile. His entire circulatory system had apparently broken down. Everything that could come apart in a man's body seemed to have ruptured.

His body began to jackknife back and forth, and with each seizure he patted Ike's hand with his balled-up fist, as if to reassure him, to calm him, to claim that this might all end well, that everyone could go back to what they were doing—the victim comforting the comforter. And then, as blood leaked everywhere from his nose and mouth onto Ike's shoes and the cuffs of his slacks, the man fell still. Vincent Donnelly, once a master of the lighting grid, and then possibly the most powerful stagehand in New York, whom Ike had met in this very theater almost sixty years earlier, lay just inches from his shoes, lifeless.

The thought that came to Ike's mind was one he hadn't expected to arrive at so quickly or clearly, and, later, when he remembered it, he was grateful that he was sure he hadn't spoken it aloud: *I wonder what this means for me now.*

2

INVENTION

VINCENT *DONNELLY*, until that moment, had been part of a dynasty. His father Big Vin, his brother, and his two sons had all been loyal members of the International Alliance of Theatrical Stage Employees, the stagehands' union, and worked in various theaters in the district. Such dynasties were by no means unusual. Generations of family members looked out for one another and prospered, sometimes, like Vincent, beyond reason. It was true of the ushers and the box office treasurers as well. Once a foot was in the door, the door could be pried open, and the family would rush through like the backfield of a football team, creating a union within the union.

Big Vin had come off the boat from Ireland back in the thirties, with a pregnant wife and a letter of introduction, and gotten a job in an electric plant that manufactured stage lighting equipment. The boy Vincent was born four months later in an austere shack behind a two-family house on a grim little street somewhere between Long Island City and Maspeth, near the factory.

Before Vincent was old enough to notice, his mother's eyes

had begun to recede into their sockets, as if searching behind her for some escape. And soon there was a baby brother, Pat, and barely enough to eat. Vincent, who was too quick of mind to spend much time studying, nonetheless made it through school to the age of fourteen, at which point he looked old enough for Big Vin to take him to work, with a nod and a wink from the foreman, who had come from Galway, just like the Donnelly clan. He was tall and lanky, and his black curls and dark eyes marked him as a descendant of the Vikings, or so all the Donnellys believed. They were mostly inclined to lighter complexions and red or dirty blond hair, and always felt that Vincent must have been carrying an invader's genes, which might come in handy—or be fatal. It was too early to tell. Either way, he was handsome and a natural magnet for women. The local wives found it hard not to touch him when families gathered for communal suppers or outside of church. There was nothing to it, but it was hard to resist.

Vincent, who never used anything other than his full name, had spent his last year of school running with a bad crowd, which resulted in his learning a number of useful skills that would serve him well for a time. He had an uncanny ability to avoid getting caught, while his schoolmates were perpetually finding themselves in all kinds of petty trouble with shopkeepers, scrap metal traders, pushcart vendors, and the law. Vincent somehow knew when it was too dangerous, or when it was time to bolt. He had been blessed with a God-given talent for staying just barely out of harm's way. And at fourteen, when his best confederate Mike Callahan had been hauled off to reform school for a third offense, Vincent suddenly grasped that whatever he had gleaned from the experience of running the streets was liable to keep him on the streets forever, so he begged Big Vin to take him to work. He was that kind of survivor.

Once there, he learned fast and worked hard, resisting the

myth that there was some kind of easy street on the other side of the factory walls. He resisted it in the face of long hours and repetitive, soul-crushing work. He resisted it even as his friends peeled away, and the opportunity to make new ones dissipated. He knew he was waiting, and he knew he was learning the discipline of doing something he had very little interest in doing.

Only his Sundays belonged to him, and it was on the first warm spring weekend of his fifteenth year that Big Vin decided to take him to Breezy Point to enjoy the water. It was an exclusive enclave that was already known as "the Irish Riviera," out at the end of Rockaway Peninsula. By subway and bus, it took them more than an hour to reach it, but Big Vin wanted to show Vincent what was possible, even for a first-generation Irish American. The two were granted semi-legitimate access because Big Vin knew a waiter at Kennedy's, a restaurant and dance hall at the entrance to the point. The guard at the gatehouse, who happened to be the waiter's brother, winked at them, and by walking through the parking lot and the front door, skirting the bar and passing through a beaded curtain out onto the beach, they were free. Vincent looked ahead of him and was stunned. The view took in Rockaway Bay; beyond it lay Brighton Beach, and, farther off, the Manhattan skyline shone in the sun, tiny and distant but visible, an irresistible land of plenty. Behind Vincent, house after house receded toward the ocean side of the point, each on a tiny lot, each with a deck that offered a view of the bay and relief from the blistering heat of the city.

"That one," Big Vin explained, pointing to the largest of them, "belongs to Eddie Foy. The one next to it belongs to the head man at Local One."

Vincent was uncomprehending. He knew who Eddie Foy was—a great Irish vaudevillian who carried his family and his heritage on his sleeve. Local One meant nothing to him.

"The union," Big Vin explained. "The men who run the lights we make—they're in the union. They make the money. They have a chance. They don't have to sneak into a place like this."

Big Vin's primary interest, once that message was delivered, was in spending an afternoon at the bar at Kennedy's, where the same man who served him a Rheingold also sold ice cream to the children and tea to their mothers. After buying his son a cone, Big Vin settled down on a stool and Vincent took himself off across the sand to explore the two piers that led out into the water. Looking down, he was amazed to see half a dozen mackerel darting under the pier and back out again, chasing after huge schools of tiny minnows that shone silver in the sun as they approached the surface. It seemed like wonderful sport—at least for the mackerel. As he sat with his legs dangling over the side of the pier, he noticed a small rusty nail sticking out of the timbers, and he idly began working it out of the wood. Once he had it in his hand, he examined it and an idea came into his head. He bent it against the edge of one of the planks of the pier until it resembled a misshapen hook. He got himself up and tore loose a thin ribbon of fabric from inside his swim trunks, threading it in circles until he had a couple of feet of it in his hand. He tied the fabric to the bent nail and went in search of something resembling fish food. His first thought was the bottom closed end of the ice cream cone, but it crumbled as he tried to put the rusty nail through it. He tossed it into the water and wandered down the pier, expanding his horizons. At the end of the pier, in a trash can next to the clam shack, he discovered a discarded piece of a raw cherrystone clam that had stuck to its shell and been tossed away by an impatient diner.

Fixing the morsel of seafood on the bent nail, he returned

to the place on the dock where he had seen the mackerel, but they were gone. It took him two or three passes up and down the pier to locate them, but when he did, he sat quietly and let his shadow settle over them for some time before he risked lowering his homemade rig into the water just below the surface.

Almost immediately it was attacked, and by some formerly unrecognized instinct he played the end of the nail into a fish's mouth and hauled it up onto the dock. His heart raced as he detached the frantically desperate fish from the nail. This was, without a doubt, the most magnificent thing fifteen-year-old Vincent Donnelly had ever done. He found a discarded paper bag to hold the fish, which flopped around wildly, and then repeated his feat three more times. There was now free dinner. But there was more: As he was carrying the bag toward Kennedy's to proudly display the fruits of his ingenuity to his father, a certain unfamiliar peace descended over him. A bit of the world had opened up to him at that moment, and he put a name to it. *If there's a fish*, he thought to himself, *I can catch it*.

FROM THIS MOMENT ON, he understood that his future was going to be entirely up to him, and nothing, he believed, could advance his cause other than a good idea that could make money. A couple of days before his sixteenth birthday, he had one.

The issue surrounding stage lighting was heat. Lights were large and intense and follow spots in particular grew almost overwhelmingly scorching as performances played themselves out. In the days immediately following the arrival of electricity, a number of theaters had burned to the ground. For the men who operated spotlights it was a kind of wilting torture, and there was an ever-present danger, which they were responsible for guarding against: Who knew at what moment an errant sheet of tissue, or a piece of cigarette paper, might brush past the lights or into them and ignite?

Vincent had been home on a Sunday night in July when the oppressive heat of the house was enough to drive him to plunge his head into a sink full of cold water every couple of hours. When not soaking his head, he was assembling a toy motor that was built into a model boat. He had detached the motor from the boat, disassembled it and rebuilt it, purely for the pleasure of understanding how it worked, hooking it up to a battery and running the propeller in front of his face, basking in the tiny amount of wind that it created. The wind cooled his brow, and then his brain, just enough to allow it to move from one idea to the next. If one small propeller could create a tiny cooling breeze, what would happen if you manufactured a metal ring that fit around a lighting instrument, on which might be mounted a dozen or so small propellers, powered by the same electricity that was powering the light itself, and dispersing the heat? The ring would have to be soundproofed a bit—silence was a valuable commodity in the theater he had been taught, though he'd never actually seen a play. But that could be achieved with a little insulation. All he needed was a few dollars for some spare parts, and a few evenings at home to build it.

The time he could make. The money was out of reach.

It took him a week to steal eight more model boats, two each from four different hobby shops in three boroughs. It was a popular toy, what with the war and all. He had to call in sick to do it, and Big Vin was immediately suspicious that something was up. Vincent didn't deny it. He told his father that they'd all be rewarded and grateful one day, and that sometimes it was necessary to take the law into your own hands. That was as much as he would confess. Big Vin's reaction was admonitory but philosophical.

"Taking matters into your own hands is one thing," he told his son, chewing on a perpetually moist but rarely lit cigar. "Taking the law into them is something else entirely. The main thing in life, as I make it," he said, "is to stay out of jail."

Vincent explained that there was no risk of jail, even though that wasn't true, strictly speaking. But how would the hobby shop owners ever find him? He surmised, correctly, they never would. He scavenged the local vacant lots in the long evenings of waning sunlight until he found a mangled bicycle with one good wheel and lugged it back home. He managed to lift a bolt cutter from the factory while no one was looking, and late one night broke into a diner that had gone out of business, tearing out a single panel of acoustical tile that, as far as he could tell, no longer belonged to anyone. By eight the next morning, the bolt cutter was back where it belonged, the acoustical tile was under his bed, and no one was the wiser.

Over the next few nights, he pulled the boats apart without damaging anything. He cut the spokes out of the bicycle wheel and glued the motors into place on the inner rim, creating a ring of little propellers, all wired together and linked to a nine-volt battery he had boosted from the local hardware store along with the glue pot. He shredded the acoustical tile with a meat grinder through which his mother often put small amounts of stew beef and too many slices of day-old bread when trying to make enough meatloaf to go around. Then he cleaned out the grinder and mixed the shreds of tile in a bucket with enough carpenter's glue to make a malleable slop, which he carefully built into little mounds around the toy motors, leaving a small air space around each one. When he was done, each motor lived in a little igloo made of shredded acoustical tile and glue. Breathless, he started them going; there was breeze, and virtual silence. The motors generated some heat on their own, but it was neatly dispersed through the wad of soundproofing.

Finally, he sliced open the rubber tire and moved it to the inside of the wheel rim, cutting holes so the propellers could protrude and spin, while the motors and their padding were concealed behind the rubber tubing. Then he taped the whole thing together and took it to his father. Four weeks had gone by since he'd had the idea.

Big Vin looked at it for a long time, watching the little propellers spin. He put a thick arm through the center of the wheel and saw the graying hair on his forearm dance. He became quietly pensive, not a usual mood for a man who was given to a steady diet of Irish whiskey and amateur boxing on Sundays. Finally, he spoke.

"Keep the damn thing out of sight while I think, will, ya?"

Vincent took this to be a good sign, though he was never sure with Big Vin. At least his father hadn't clouted him across the ear and called him a bloody dreamer, which was the alternative response. Big Vin never said much, and never explained anything he said, so his son had grown used to living in suspense, in a world that was sometimes hard to decipher.

Two days after Vincent had shown it to Big Vin, on a Sunday, the old man dragged his son out of bed and had him pack up his bicycle wheel cooling system. The two of them rode the subway to the Bowery office of a lawyer named Francis Rafferty.

FRANCIS RAFFERTY was not a man to come in on Sunday. He was pushing sixty-five, and had, at one time, been a figure of some consequence at Tammany Hall. But that had all gone out the window when Fiorello LaGuardia had been elected mayor of New York and meted out appropriate punishment to those who had spent years as part of the Tammany political machine. Rafferty was no exception. He managed to avoid prosecution in a number of Democratic scandals that LaGuardia made sure were laid bare but lost everything he had except his law license and a house in Florida that no one but he knew existed. He decamped from Tammany Hall and moved his office to a small set of rooms above his brother-in-law's saloon. His wife was gone. Cancer. His dreams were gone. His children had long since moved to Chicago and California and were almost never in touch. His memories—of power and patronage, of evenings of poker, of brothels, of champagne dinners at the Central Park Casino—were vivid; they tortured his restless sleep. Now he subsisted, a gaunt, looming, hollow-chested figure, on dribs and drabs of business from Irish immigrants like Big Vin—men with petty disputes and grievances, who had never known the ample pleasures of the American Dream and never would.

Yet Big Vin, who had once had him write a threatening letter to a life insurance salesman who wouldn't leave him alone, had convinced him that it would be worth his while to meet after church on a day when neither Donnelly needed to be at work. Father and son climbed the stairs adjacent to the barroom, and Rafferty met them at the door to his office. The place was sweltering.

He greeted young Vincent with a weak-willed handshake from an oversized, bony, moist hand. Vincent felt as if he had been touched by the devil himself, but his father displayed nothing but enthusiastic gratitude for the learned man's attention. The office was sparsely furnished with the items Rafferty had been able to rescue from Tammany Hall—a bookshelf, two cracked leather chairs, and a desk, on which were piled books and papers that looked like no one had touched them since before the Great Depression. There was a window that faced the Bowery, so soot stained as to be relatively useless as either a lookout or a source of light. The lawyer sat behind his desk with his hands steepled as Big Vin explained the challenge of cooling a theatrical lighting instrument, while Vincent unwrapped his invention, set it on Rafferty's desk, and connected the battery. The propellers spun in silence. A couple of sheets of paper lifted weakly from the piles on the desk and, eventually, glided off to the floor. Rafferty nodded at Big Vin, who reached across the desk and disconnected the battery. The three of them sat for a long moment.

"A patent," Rafferty said finally. "What you need here is a patent, because for all I know about it, maybe you've got a fortune in your hands, and you don't want it stolen out from under you. I need to get you a patent."

Big Vin shifted uncomfortably in his chair.

"A patent," Rafferty continued, "is a registration with the U.S. government that protects an invention and asserts that you own it and no one else does. Anyone who wants to make one or use one would have to pay you a license fee for your ingenuity. So, naturally, I need to get you one."

"What would such a thing cost?" Big Vin asked.

Vincent's eyes shifted between the two older men. He was hungry but suspicious. He had never heard of a patent.

"You can't pay me anyhow," Rafferty responded, "so what's the point of the question?"

"Well, maybe," Big Vin began, but Rafferty held up his bearlike paw to stop the conversation.

"I'll cover the costs," Rafferty said, "and we'll split the profits. Half for you and the boy, half for me. You'll incur no expense, and if money comes in, you'll get your fair share."

"Half?" young Vincent interjected, suddenly agitated. He, after all, was the one with the ingenuity. "You want half?"

Big Vin put a hand firmly on the boy's thigh and squeezed it until Vincent felt a nerve pain running all the way into his foot.

"We're most grateful, Mr. Rafferty," said Big Vin. "You'll

let us know when there's papers to sign or . . . whatever the hell there is."

WHEN RAFFERTY WAS alone again, he went to the window, through which he could barely make out the figures of Big Vin and his son disappearing down the stairs of the subway with their treasure wrapped in brown paper. Then he walked down the stairs himself and let himself into the shuttered saloon. Going to the bar, he poured himself a half a tumbler of Jameson and carried it back up to his office. He sat for a long time staring at the wall opposite his desk, on which his law license hung in a battered frame. That and a ream of stationery declaring him to be Francis Rafferty, Esq., Attorney at Law, were most of what was left of the practice.

Everything he knew about patents he had now said aloud. He had no idea how to get one or whether the United States government would take any interest in a rescued bicycle wheel with some toy motors glued to it. And he wasn't sure whom to ask. All he had was a hastily drawn agreement sitting in front of him signed by himself and Big Vin, agreeing to split any profits that emerged from the thing fifty-fifty.

Have I got to the point, he wondered, *where this constitutes a good day's work?* Apparently, the answer was affirmative, because he tipped the whiskey glass to his lips and savored the familiar taste of the old country, of the dinners with former mayor Jimmy Walker's minions, with the girls who leaned over his shoulder, their hair coming undone, as if both he and they were in an illustrated magazine caricature portraying the decadent pleasures of lust in the big city. This, this half glass of Irish whiskey and this half interest in a gizmo—this was all he could pin his hopes on.

3

JUNGLE GARDENIA

LONG BEFORE SHE adopted her mother's maiden name and became Aurora Shelton, years before she had ever encountered either Ike Harris or Vincent Donnelly, back when she was five-year-old Aurora Feik in Oceanside, California, her mother, Beatrice, had lifted her up from the floor and sat her atop the Magnavox console record player in the living room, just as music was beginning to play. Her legs dangled down over the speaker, and she held a doll that she was rarely without, a little blond doll with hard plaster arms and legs. The sound that emerged from the speaker was Ethel Waters singing "Taking a Chance on Love," and Aurora, lacking any other way to express the almost hysterical level of excitement she felt, began to laugh and threw her doll as far across the room as she could. When she told the story later, she always swore she could feel the vibrations of Waters's voice come right up through her thighs and backside, right into her spinal cord, although she was never sure that this was entirely true. True or not, the experience, she used to say, had ruined her life. From that day on, she had to have music. And that never changed.

She was an army brat; her father, Staff Sergeant Michael Feik, trained recruits in one outpost after another, and within a year he'd be overwhelmed with draftees headed for Europe and the Pacific. He barked orders and meted out punishment and expressed disgust with the results of the young soldiers' pathetic efforts twelve or fourteen hours a day, and it never occurred to him to change his attitude when he came home at night. The world was there to be disciplined, to be found wanting and to be punished, to be tyrannized if necessary. His anger felt satisfying to him, like biting down on a piece of rare roast beef and feeling it tear under the incisors. He allowed himself to believe that it produced results, and that, perhaps, he was so good at his job that the army felt he was irreplaceable. This, despite the reality that he never advanced at all but was simply shifted from base to base on a never-ending journey that seemed to have no destination. This, no doubt, was as much a source of his rage as anything else, and it clung to him in all weathers.

The family moved around a lot during the war years. It was a faceless expedition. The bases were all but bereft of character or individuality. Row upon row of barracks housing, and the officer's quarters varied only in their construction materials: brick in the Midwest, clapboard in the East, timbers in the West. Yet once indoors, the houses were of a depressing uniformity—two stories, with a small kitchen, a living room and dinette, a central stairway that led up to two bedrooms. The wallpaper, when there was wallpaper, tended to the generic: tendrils of some unidentifiable creeping vine climbing a silver-gray latticework from coast to coast.

For Beatrice, it was hard to know where she was, exactly. And sometimes she wondered whether her daughter even knew how far they had moved. But Aurora always knew. From the time she was old enough to ride a school bus, first in Oceanside, later in military towns from Pensacola to Colorado Springs, she became an immediate outcast. She was pretty. Too pretty, which would have made her a target anyhow. But she insisted on singing like Ethel Waters—or she believed she was singing like Ethel Waters—at the top of her lungs as the bus hummed along. The swing music that her mother played at home was forever in her head. The rhythm of the bus wheels caused it to thrum through her—and out it came. This made her a target of almost anything sadistic her schoolmates could imagine doing to her, which was not an unfamiliar state of affairs, given her home life and the way she saw her father treat her mother, and sometimes even her. The one thing her schoolmates couldn't do, however, was to get her to stop singing.

She had no idea who Ethel Waters was, really. She didn't know that Waters, after beginning her career in Black vaudeville in the twenties, had achieved stardom of a sort in Hollywood and, within a few years, would be taking care of a little girl, on Broadway, a million miles from any place Aurora Feik could imagine. That little girl would be played by a twenty-five-year-old actress in a play called *The Member of the Wedding*. Julie Harris, who still seemed like a child, would portray a fictional little girl named Frankie, while Aurora was a real little girl, and Ethel Waters was only taking care of her by proxy, and had no way of even knowing she was alive, much less in need. But in Aurora's imagination, Waters had somehow replaced the little blond plaster doll. In some ways she had even begun to replace Beatrice.

It was beginning to dawn on Aurora's mother that her dream-soaked view of the world was increasingly at odds with her actual existence. Playing the dutiful wife of a professionally and perpetually bellicose career army man was beginning to tell. Beatrice cooked and vacuumed and changed the sheets in one faceless home after another and began to watch the clock at around eleven in the morning, waiting for the cocktail hour to roll around. The other army wives seemed grateful for stability after the decade of the Great Depression. But Aurora's mother wasn't well liked by them, really. When the radio wasn't on she played records for herself and Aurora. She smoked, and hummed, and made herself Manhattans with two cherries. She carried on an undisguised love affair with a product called Jungle Gardenia, an atomized toilet water that caused her to dream of the big city, and that she was in it. It was her opium and took her out of herself. She never seemed really to be listening to anything anyone had to say, as if whatever it was wasn't worth the time it took to hear it. The wives thought she was stuck-up, though, largely, she was only adrift. Her blond hair always seemed to be straying out of the pins she had put it up with, and sometimes her eye makeup ran. She had been a pretty girl, tall and angular but graceful. That was all beginning to change a little too soon. She was getting soft. And she wasn't much motivated to do anything about it. She thought of Aurora as her best friend, maybe her only friend.

Had Aurora chanced to meet Ethel Waters, she would have come to understand that they actually did have some things in common, including the instability of their earliest years. On that front, at least, Aurora couldn't really compete in the misery department. She was a little white girl and Waters was Black. Aurora was born into a fractious family, but Waters's birth was the product of the rape of a thirteen-year-old girl by a disreputable jazz pianist with a heroin habit. Like Aurora, Waters grew up moving from place to place, never staying in one location for much more than a year, never knowing what a home was or how to live in one. For Aurora it was not quite that bad, and she didn't claim otherwise. But later in life, when she told the story of being sat on the Magnavox, she always suggested that something in Waters's voice must have insisted that they were soulmates because of their rough crossings from birth to the day someone encouraged them to sing in public. She also, once she had read Waters's autobiography and knew the truth, spent hours pondering how the rape that had resulted in Ethel Waters being born could be, on the one hand, such an unspeakable act of cruelty and madness, and, on the other, have had the blessed result of importing the piano man's DNA into such an innocent vessel, the girl who carried Ethel Waters to term and delivered a baby who would bring joy to millions of people. Decades of suffering lay ahead, but great art happened too. What was that about? She would wonder about it until the day she died.

There were some days when she wondered whether she was the only person in the world who had fallen in love with that song—"Taking a Chance on Love"—but then she would remember, or she thought she remembered, being a very small child on one of the army outposts and hearing it played on a trumpet. Just a solo trumpet working over the unmistakable melody. She had been walking with her father past the entertainment tent on the way to or from some meeting he had to be at when she heard it, and she tore her hand from his to follow it. Inside the entertainment tent, where the USO shows used to come once a month, a small, sandy-haired man, in uniform, was standing alone with a trumpet, playing for himself, as she so often sang for herself, and he was playing that song. She stood transfixed, and he stopped to notice her. She didn't want him to speak—she wanted him to play. She held an imaginary trumpet to her lips, and he understood. He put the horn back up and began again.

In a moment her father came up behind her and scooped her up in his arms, turned, and carried her out to wherever it was they were going. She kicked at him a little, but even though she was very small, she had learned that his authority was absolute, and she listened as they moved farther from the sound, until it couldn't really be heard. As she grew older, she sometimes began to doubt that this had happened. But in other moments she was quite sure of it. The problem was that she dreamed about it so vividly that there were days when she concluded it was only a dream after all, not a memory.

It was not until she was thirteen years old that she met the first sympathetic man she had ever been aware of. By this time, the records that she had listened to as a little girl in Oceanside had been replaced by others: Bing Crosby, Tommy Dorsey and his brother Jimmy, Benny Goodman—who had a hit record with a cover of "Taking a Chance on Love"—Dinah Shore, and the Andrews Sisters. But overall, she could never warm up to these newer recordings by white bandleaders and singers. Something always drew her back to the colored singers, as they were known then, and her mother agreed. They preferred Ella Fitzgerald with Chick Webb and His Orchestra, and Aurora remained loyal to Ethel Waters.

On the day that Aurora realized she had become attached to Marius Huwiler, she was barely a teenager. Marius Huwiler was a music teacher at the middle school in Junction City, Kansas, where Aurora's father had landed after the war, at Fort Riley. Huwiler was a reticent man. Only in his early thirties, he had a pronounced widow's peak; his dark hair had been receding since he'd graduated from college. His skin was pale and his expression perpetually fretful. His brow, amplified by the receding hairline, was most often furrowed, perhaps because his eyebrows seemed perpetually raised, as if in anticipation of something unexpected and potentially alarming. He was not a comfortable man.

Aurora was in the school chorus, singing the alto part in a vocal arrangement of "America the Beautiful" that Mr. Huwiler had created for a school assembly. She never listened to the words of the song, really; she was simply fascinated by the way the harmonies fit together. She thought it possible that Mr. Huwiler was a genius. He seemed remote and diffident except when conducting his chorus of middle-schoolers. In those moments, raising his right forefinger to forcibly pull sound out of a class full of reluctant and largely embarrassed students, he became another man, animated, and filled with a kind of pathetic passion. Music class was the last class of the day.

"Aurora," he said to her as she was gathering books and heading to the torture chamber of the bus one afternoon. She looked up from her book bag.

"You have a voice, my dear," he said. "But you make no effort to blend. It's like you only want to hear yourself."

It stung, and he saw it.

"I'm only telling you this because you can actually sing," he said. "Don't be hurt by it. Just think about it."

Then he turned away and hurried out of the room, a man who, having said what was on his mind, was too shy, or frightened, or some combination of the two, to stick around and hear a response, even from a middle-school girl.

Aurora was not hurt; she was crushed. She had no idea what he meant. His beautiful arrangement was the only thing she was concentrating on. Had she ruined it? Did he not know how magnificent it was? She huddled in her seat in the back row of the bus, and something emanating from her must have served as a warning. No one spoke to her, much less taunted or teased her. She got off the bus in silence and walked up the path to her house, cradling her books in front of her.

The door was open. Aurora paused reflexively. Her mother never left the door open. Then she swung the book bag onto her shoulder, opened the screen door, and walked in. Something smelled terrible, acrid and sour.

She ran to the kitchen, where whatever had been planned for dinner was burning on the stove, the inside of the pot blackening into a dangerous molten mass that looked alive. It had not caught fire yet. Aurora grabbed a pair of pot holders out of a kitchen drawer and rushed the pot to the sink. She turned on the water, which steamed in protest as it hit the pot, the smell of fish flooding the air. Then she saw her mother.

Beatrice was on the floor of the living room. Aurora could see only the top part of her torso through the kitchen door. It was on the carpet, moving up and down in even, peaceful breaths. Aurora moved to her, her own heart thumping in her breast. Beatrice was not pale or troubled looking; she was not dead or ill, only unconscious. The mother looked as peaceful as the daughter was agitated.

There was a rocks glass on the end table by the sofa, empty except for six maraschino cherries. An empty bottle of Four Roses stood next to it, cap unscrewed and lying in an ashtray full of cigarette butts. The living room was rank with stale cigarette smoke, bourbon, and the artificial scent of gardenias, fighting off the smell of burned haddock. Aurora surveyed it, suddenly calmer.

"Mama?" she said. But Beatrice was dead to the world. Some part of Aurora understood that her mother had finally, after many tipsy evenings, had the bravery to achieve a state of complete oblivion, and damn the consequences. She was out.

Her daughter was one of the consequences. It wasn't until later, when she occasionally flirted with unconsciousness herself, that she came to understand something about the cost. Now, she was concerned only with her mother's welfare.

She got down on her knees and put her ear to Beatrice's chest. The heartbeat was steady and calming. *Nothing is wrong*, Aurora told herself. *My mother is asleep. It's all going to be fine. Tomorrow, if not tonight*. She went upstairs to her parents' bedroom and turned down Beatrice's twin bed. She got out a nightie and a bathrobe, and then sat on the bed for a moment, wondering what else might be needed, but she could think of nothing. Beatrice was in no condition to brush her teeth or wash her face before bed. She went back down to begin the process of getting her mother upstairs. It took some doing.

"Come on, Mama," she said. She raised her mother to a sitting position and draped Beatrice's arm around her own neck as she had seen Henry Fonda do for a wounded Union soldier in a movie she had shared with her mother the previous Saturday. Beatrice stirred and snorted slightly, opened her eyes, and looked at her daughter with unfocused pupils.

"How dare you wake the dead?" she asked. Then she laughed. Then she said, "Oh, God," and tried to go out again. Somehow Aurora got her onto her feet. Beatrice said various angry and affectionate things in no particular order, but never spoke her daughter's name or acknowledged that that's who Aurora was.

"Let's go to sleep upstairs," Aurora said, coaxing her mother toward the staircase.

I have no idea what I'm doing, she thought. *What if I drop her? Or lose her?*

Maybe she was supposed to call an ambulance. Or call her father, though that seemed like a particularly unwise idea. She kept going. The only way to control the situation was to follow the path she'd chosen. So, she hiked Beatrice up first one stair riser, then another. Eventually, she knew they would arrive at the top. And that conviction, somehow, kept her calm, and in command.

In the bedroom, Beatrice momentarily saw herself in the floor-length mirror beside the dresser. She seemed to recognize that she was drunk, that her pale green print dress was askew, that her hair had come completely undone and was falling in her face. She blew it out of the way with a sharp, acrid exhale of breath.

"Jesus," she said. "I didn't think you'd see me like this."

"It's okay," Aurora said.

"Goddamn right it's okay," Beatrice told her, abruptly in no mood for sympathy. "Just something that happens. A tragedy behind every window. None of your goddamn business in the first place, as a matter of fact."

"It's okay, Mama," Aurora repeated. "We're here now. Let me help you get ready for bed."

Beatrice was asleep again as soon as her head met the pillow. Aurora pulled a cover up around her and turned out the light. Then she retreated to the living room to empty the ashtray, put the Four Roses bottle in the trash, and tidy up. There was not much to do about the stench of burned food coming from the kitchen. But Aurora opened all the downstairs windows and waited.

At six, when her father returned, she had done all her homework. She had eaten a little cheese that was in the Kelvinator and gone up to her room. But her hard-earned sense of calm deserted her when she heard him open the door.

"Bea?" he called. "What the hell caught fire?"

Michael Feik had dreaded this day that he knew would come. He knew his wife had long since become a drinker. He had no patience for that. Life was hard, and people had to have the stamina, the discipline, the fire to conquer it. Beatrice had begun to be a disappointment a long time ago, and some part of him, a part he kept hiding from, knew that this moment—the moment when she simply gave in and ran into the arms of her own weakness, her own shame—was inevitable. It infuriated him.

"Goddammit, Bea!" he barked. "Goddammit to hell, where are you? Aurora, get yourself down here, double time!"

Aurora was on the stairs, gray with fear.

"Mom's . . . sick," she said. "She's asleep."

"She's drunk, Aurora," he said. "Time to call things by their right name. You're a big girl."

Aurora nodded, unable to call her mother that word. Drunk.

Michael Feik took a couple of steps toward the stairwell, then stopped, turned, and walked to the Magnavox, which had moved with them from one outpost to another. He had hefted it himself on more than one occasion, never willingly. He stared at the blond wood console with its speaker covered in a brown mesh cloth made bright with a diagonal pattern of shiny golden thread.

"It's all the same," he said to no one in particular, though Aurora was the only one there to hear him. "It's all the same. The goddamn cigarettes and the Jungle Gardenia and movies and the goddamn records!"

This last word he spat out as if it were a name for the ultimate human poison. He lifted the lid on the record player and picked up one of the 78 rpm shellac records and cracked it across the corner of the console. It shattered, black shards scattering across the floor.

"Daddy!" Aurora shrieked.

He turned, and she saw the hatred on his face, the helpless anger and the disgust. He turned back and took a second record, smashing it against the wooden cabinet. One after another he smashed them, each crack against the wood driving Aurora's impulse to back up the stairs as if she were being physically assaulted. But she could not turn away. She had to stand and see what her father was doing, to witness each betrayal of her inner life. The floor was littered with the wreckage, torn labels, and black sharp-edged asymmetrical triangles and trapezoids with curved edges and grooves visible, reflecting in the lamplight.

He worked silently, breathing hard. In a final gesture of triumph, he tipped the Magnavox console onto its front, and Aurora could hear the tubes shattering within.

Her father stood staring at the mess around him, a man alone with his masterpiece of resentment. There was silence. Finally, Aurora turned to go back up the stairs.

Her mother was standing immediately behind her. Beatrice was a ghost in a nightgown, her face gray and wet with tears, surveying the damage from the second-floor landing. Their eyes met, but Aurora could not read Beatrice's expression. There was nothing there to read—or too much.

AURORA DID NOT SLEEP, did not even try. At four *A.M.*, she got out of bed and went downstairs. Her ears echoed with the tirade her father had directed at her mother behind closed doors, which she had not been able to avoid hearing. But she set to work as diligently as she could. She found an empty cardboard box in the garage and began depositing all of the shards and fragments of the broken records in it. They looked pathetically sparse in the bottom of the box—there would have been room for many more—but Aurora kept at it until they were all picked up from the living room rug. She put the box back in the garage and was about to leave it there when she had a thought about commemorating—what?—the evening's destruction? The music that had been silenced? She wasn't sure. But she reached down into the box and extracted a shard that still had most of a familiar label glued to it. The song title had been torn off and was somewhere else in the box. This, the remaining jagged piece of black shellac disc and the semblance of the label, could stand for them all. *This*, she thought, *I shall always keep.*

She placed the jagged fragment in her bathrobe pocket, went into the kitchen, and found the carpet sweeper in the utility closet. In a quarter of an hour the rug was clean. Aurora had cut her fingers in a few places digging black flecks of the broken records out of the nap, but with the Magnavox tipped back into position, it was possible to believe that nothing had happened here—that all was as it had been on the previous morning. Even the stench of burned fish was beginning to abate. Aurora wondered if the world could ever actually be put back together in that way. She had her doubts. Upstairs, she put the broken record in her top dresser drawer and dressed for school.

She got through the first half of the day without incident. But when she carried her lunch tray from the cafeteria line to a nearby table, Marius Huwiler was waiting for her.

"Are you hungry?" he asked.

"I don't think so," Aurora said. "I don't feel very well today."

"Bring your lunch," the teacher said. "And let's go to the music room."

Curious, Aurora followed him. Once there, she set her tray on the piano. Mr. Huwiler sat at the piano bench.

"What I meant yesterday," he said, "is that you can almost really sing, and I never hear anyone who's a student at this school who can."

Aurora nodded blankly. She had no idea where this was leading.

"Do you want to sing?" He asked.

Again, she nodded.

"All right," he said. "Sing."

He waited. She waited. He looked at her and raised his eyebrows as if waiting for something to happen. She wasn't sure what. Finally, he lifted his right hand, stuck out his index finger, and began to conduct her. When he pointed at her mouth, a kind of gestural command, she opened it, and the words, Ethel Waters's words, came out, from an old record she hadn't heard in years, and that was now shattered beyond redemption.

Am I blue?
Am I blue?
Ain't these tears in my eyes
Telling you?

Mister Huwiler stopped conducting and found her key on the piano. He knew the chord pattern and filled in each break in the lyric with a familiar figure.

Am I blue?
You'd be too . . .

And with that, he stopped her.

"Do you know what you're singing about?" he asked.

"She's blue," Aurora said. "She's sad."

"About what?"

"I don't know."

"First," Mr. Huwiler said, "let's do this."

He came closer to her and reached out a hand. For a moment she was afraid he meant to strangle her, but he put his thumb and pinky finger on either side of her throat with the softest touch that she had ever felt. His fingers deftly found her voice box on either side, and he rocked it back and forth, massaging her neck. She could feel it move inside of her.

"These are the vocal cords in there," he said. "These you must relax. Singing is relaxation and vitality. These muscles are the little ones, all around your voice box. They're not strong; you don't want to ask them to do too much work."

She nodded, though she had only the vaguest of ideas what he was talking about.

Without letting go of her throat, he took his other hand and gently pressed at her upper abdomen. She tensed, feeling vulnerable, and then his hand retreated.

"You needn't worry about me, if that's what's happening," he said. "Can you imagine the place I just touched you? Can you find it in your mind?"

She tried, and sort of felt she did. She nodded again, suspended between understanding and confusion.

"Focus your brain on those two places," he said. "Your abdomen, below your stomach, that's where the big muscle is—surrounding the diaphragm—that's the one that needs to push the air through the vocal cords. Don't let the little muscles do the work—they weren't made for heavy work. Give them light work. Now sing."

She tried. It felt odd, like a science experiment not a song. He let her finish a line and held up his hand.

"Now," he said, "I see I've made a mistake. I want you to forget everything I've just said. Ignore it. All of it. And tell me this: Have you ever been sad?"

It took Aurora a moment to realize he was going back to her last statement.

"Yes, sir. Of course I have. Everyone gets sad—that's why it's a good song."

"Exactly. But you don't sound sad. You sound like you're imitating someone's style. Like you're telling me about someone else, not Aurora."

Aurora looked at him. What did that mean?

"Singing is only partly about making a sound. If you can't tell the person who's listening to the story about the *feeling* of the song, the sound is meaningless. You might as well be a trumpet played by a machine. A machine doesn't know whether it's sad or happy—it's just a machine."

Aurora thought about this for a moment before she spoke.

"Are you saying . . . that I sing like a machine?"

"Right now, that's what you're singing like. And I imagine that when I tell you that, because I'm a music teacher and you're just a girl, that it makes you sad, and maybe even angry."

Aurora was silent.

"When a teacher tells you that you're not doing a good job, usually that makes you feel bad. When he tells it to you because he thinks you can do better and should do better, that usually makes you feel scared. So now maybe you have three feelings at once—scared, angry, blue. Does that make sense?"

Aurora couldn't speak. She nodded.

"A song that's sung can say all that, and I can tell you that it can, but I can't tell you how to find that inside yourself. That part you have to figure out on your own. Either you can or you can't. Now sing."

He began to play the piano, and then he raised his right hand from the keys while his left continued to play chords. And he cued her in.

Am I blue?
Am I blue?
Ain't these tears
In my eyes . . .

And at that moment the tears came, and something inside of Aurora let go. The big muscle and the little muscles and the voice box linked up, and she thought she could feel it all—everything he had told her to forget. It was like a spring that had held her insides together for sixteen hours—and maybe for thirteen years—snapped. She couldn't sing any more. She began to wail. Loud, keening sobs came from her, and her body shook like an electric current was running through it. Marius Huwiler stopped playing and watched her. He didn't comfort her or ask her what was wrong. He just waited. She cried and cried. She lifted her skirt to her face and wailed into it like an animal in a trap, knowing only pain. She would cry until she died. The music teacher watched. Minutes passed. And then she felt herself on the other side of the hill, and she knew that soon she'd be able to stop.

He waited until she had composed herself and her breath had stopped catching and came normally again.

"I'm sorry," she said. They were the first words she'd spoken since she had stopped singing.

"You can sing," he told her. "But you look like you need something to eat. It's lunchtime."

WHEN SHE REACHED HOME, her father was waiting for her. Beatrice was gone. The smell of burned fish had all but gone too.

"Six weeks," her father said. "I had no choice, Aurora, you have to see that. She's in a place that can help her, and then everything will go back to being exactly the way it was."

"Can I see her?"

Her father shook his head. Nor, he explained, could they speak on the phone.

"It's best for everyone," he said. "She has to learn that things have a price. Behavior has a price. She wants to be a good woman; I know that. But there's a price."

"Do I have to pay a price?" Aurora asked. Something had to explain the smashed music collection, the dark silence that was descending on the house, and the sudden departure of her only real connection to life. *It's love*, she thought. She loved her mother and missed her already, and for that, she had to pay a price. Her father had not answered the question, and suddenly she needed no answer.

Michael Feik's mother emerged from the kitchen, wearing an apron. Aurora was more than surprised to see the grandmother she had barely come to know since they'd arrived in Kansas. Elsie Feik, who spoke with the remains of a Scottish accent after thirty-five years in the Midwest, stood in the kitchen doorway, still as a corpse and looking not unlike a ghost—pale, gray-haired, lean and wispy, with rimless spectacles.

"Hello, Aurora," she said in a tone that suggested Aurora had just returned from a burial, not a day at school.

"Ma's come to help us," her father said. "She can be here when you get home from school, make dinner, help you get ready for bed, all of those things. Like Mama used to."

Aurora nodded again. Her eyes moved from her grandmother to her father and to the now defunct Magnavox against the wall, its power cord lying curled across the rug like a dead snake.

I have to get away, she thought.

It took her four years.

4

A Young Man of Culture

IKE HARRIS HATED Michael Feik the minute he saw him. Hated his pink and white face, his swept-back hair, his ramrod posture, and his awkward, barking voice. Not Jewish, Ike thought, by which he meant that Staff Sergeant Feik was surely an anti-Semite, possibly a disciple of Charles Lindbergh or George Lincoln Rockwell, who was also a military man. In moments like these, Ike enjoyed the flashes of paranoia that lamped around his brain and gave him something to chew over as he was put through his paces in the broiling sun at the Camp Bullis Military Training Reservation just north of San Antonio. Ike was just tall enough to be eligible and just angry enough to have joined up. Now he had Sergeant Feik to deal with.

He was not used to being bullied. His upbringing had been unusual—unique as far as he knew—but while sometimes bewildering, it had been a largely pleasurable adventure that had left him feeling autonomous.

Albert Horowitz, an exceptionally successful Austrian surgeon in the teens and twenties, had crossed the ocean with his wife and two-year-old Itzhak in 1926 after becoming Jazz Age wealthy in Europe. However, seeing the rise of unbridled stock speculation in New York as a new and peculiarly American form of madness, he cashed out of the market in 1927 and bought gold. When the market crashed two years later, he bought art and real estate at dramatically discounted prices. He offered his wife the opportunity to become the art buyer, and within a year she had amassed a collection and established long and lasting relationships with a number of New York dealers hungry for clients with ready money. She had taste, a patrician bearing, and splendid clothes, and had it not been for her pronounced nose and her last name, they might have mistaken her for old money. By the winter of 1933, when many men were stuffing old newspapers in their clothes to keep warm, her husband was preparing to sit back and enjoy life—especially an Adirondack lodge he had just purchased on Tupper Lake. But while crossing Fifth Avenue one blustery afternoon, he became disoriented, turned to go back, and collapsed in the center of the roadway. By the time an ambulance had gotten him to Mount Sinai Hospital he was gone, dead of a stroke at forty-seven.

The widow Lenore, who was called Ollie for some reason that no one could remember but that dated back to childhood, was inconsolable for a year, at the end of which she decided that her behavior and mood were ridiculous and beneath her dignity. Her husband was gone, and nothing she felt or did was going to bring him back. She got out of bed, dressed to go out, walked from the museum-like apartment on Park Avenue and 73rd Street to the Cunard Lines office near Grand Central Station, and booked passage to Le Havre for herself and Ike, who was just turning ten. She called her lawyer and arranged to change their names from Horowitz to Harris, making "Ollie" a legal name and transforming "Itzhak" to "Zachary." She told herself it was time to stop being so damn sad and so damn

Jewish, though she would never deny her heritage directly; she was seeking, she told friends, nothing more or less than a clean slate. She had passports made for the two of them and prepared a trunk that would serve them in France and beyond. She had no thoughts about where they would go from Paris or when they might return. Her hair, once flaming red, had gone gray during her year of mourning, and she now transformed it into a silvery blue helmet, courtesy of the latest dyes and frosting techniques available in beauty technology at that time. She discarded her old wardrobe, and spent several weeks purchasing a new one, more up to date. The new decade—the thirties—was almost half over, the national mood had flattened into a trudging slog through a swamp of bad news, and she felt that although the Great Depression had left her largely unscathed, it was important to acknowledge its existence. Her new clothes were somber and modest, though frightfully expensive. A year earlier, she had been the youngish, irrepressible red-haired wife of a leading European doctor in Manhattan society. Now she was reborn as an elegant middle-aged widow of means, committed to playing her proper role without having much of an idea of how to do so.

Ollie Harris, as she was forever thereafter known, had worked hard to rid herself of her Austro-Hungarian accent, and, by the time she returned to Europe, seemed like a native-born American with a fine ability in languages. She spoke French and German fluently. She could get by in Italian and Spanish. And her son, similarly multilingual little Zachary, was beginning to show signs of being a piano prodigy, though he regularly begged his mother for something he could carry with him—a trumpet.

Hitler's ascendency in Germany had not yet made much of a dent in France, where mother and son landed in the late spring of 1934, at least not in society. The battles between the

French fascists and the popular front raged, with general strikes and calls to action, but for Ollie and Zachary, none of it was much of a presence. They were involved in a series of soirees and dinners, nights at the opera and the ballet, and days of visiting galleries and museums, little Zachary tagging along on his mother's arm as if he were a Lilliputian version of a slightly bored American husband, dragged away from the office for the grand tour. She took him to every dinner and every evening's entertainment. He went to sleep late and awoke after ten to a cup of good French coffee and a croissant. He considered himself an adult in every way except size, though much of what he encountered was incomprehensible to him, for all the excitement and pleasure of it. Standing in front of the *Mona Lisa* one afternoon Ollie turned to him in a sudden moment of compassion.

"Do you know what you're looking at?" she asked.

"No," her son replied, "but I know I'm seeing it."

They had adjoining rooms, complete with gilt-edged piano, at the Ritz while his mother looked for a suitable apartment. One night, as Ollie put down her bedside copy of Andre Gide's *Les Faux-monnayeurs*, she heard muffled sobs from the next room. It was not like little Zachary to cry—he fancied himself above that kind of thing. A *bad dream*, she thought. But when she arrived at his bedside, she found him fully awake, sitting up and using his bedclothes as an extended handkerchief to sob into.

"What is it?" She asked.

"I don't want to pretend to be Zachary," he said piteously. "I miss Daddy. I miss home. What happened?"

Between wails he listed his school friends, all of whom he would never see again. His favorite restaurants, the movie theater on Lexington and 86th where he and his father had passed happy Saturday afternoons at double features, the ice cream man in Central Park, the stamp collectors store on Madison, the German appetizing store in Yorkville, the Brooklyn Dodgers. He mourned each player individually: Cuccinello, Koenecke, Lefty O'Doul. Through tears he enumerated an ever-growing inventory that measured his loss and gave definition and dimension to it. Somehow it had all caught up with him at once.

Ollie comforted him in her arms and let him cry. He wore himself out and eventually fell into a deep sleep against her breasts. When she was sure he wouldn't reawaken, she carefully slid him down into his bed and returned to her own, where she stayed awake trying to find something that would make things better.

The next morning, they sat drinking coffee. "Would you like to be Ike again?" She asked him. "There's no reason really that we have to call you Zachary. You could be Ike, just like you always were."

He toyed with his croissant and considered the matter seriously, as he did most things. She waited, feeling some sense of hope mixed with guilt. This wasn't really a solution to anything, but she wasn't sure that a solution was needed in the end, other than time. He was homesick. Still, a gesture was required, and now she'd made one. Finally, he spoke.

"I'd like to be Ike," he told her. "I am Ike, and I'd like to be Ike."

"Very well, Ike," she said. "That's done."

"And I'd like a trumpet," he added sheepishly.

FOR IKE, this had been a long time coming. The loss of his father had driven a massive hole into his heart, and his mother's yearlong retreat into the bedroom had been a bewildering betrayal. He didn't know why she had done it. He felt that he had been abandoned twice. The live-in maid, a Black woman named Estelle Dunmore, whom his parents had brought north from the backwater Mississippi town of Rolling Fork, had raised him for the better part of the year now. Estelle saw to his everyday needs but provided little in the way of emotional support or amusement. He was curious about her life, but she didn't seem inclined to be forthcoming, and didn't seem interested in his. So, the European trip had begun as a great relief. Suddenly, after a long absence, his mother hung on his every word, answered questions, listened to him play the piano, and treated him like the grand and sophisticated adult that he hoped he was becoming.

The trumpet, truth to tell, was her own damn fault and she knew it. She had been unable to resist an invitation to a jam session featuring the trumpet player Tommy Ladnier, who was touring Europe. He was playing after midnight with a group of French jazzmen who were eager to sit at his feet. Ladnier was a Louisiana native who spent his career in the shadow of Louis Armstrong, but like his sometime partner, the soprano sax virtuoso Sidney Bechet, he felt most at home in France, where the people accorded him at least a modicum of respect. Ike had never heard anyone like him—had never heard jazz, had never really known what a trumpet was. But moments after climbing down a winding flight of stairs and pushing along behind his mother as she swept into the confines of Le Cave de la Heure d'Or, he was changed.

The place itself was a dark substratum stone cellar, long and narrow, with a vaulted cobblestone ceiling like a catacomb or an ancient tomb. The room was filled with smoke. Ill-matched chairs and tables—card tables, end tables, enamel kitchen tables—lined the walls. At one end was a raised platform on which five musicians crowded one another. Black-skirted waitresses, some young and some old, shimmied through the crowd carrying cocktail trays above their heads and setting drinks in front of the customers, who were hushed and in the thrall of the music.

Ike and Ollie settled down among a throng of her Parisian acquaintances. He craned his neck to see the musicians, and at the center of the stage he saw Ladnier, small, wiry, and lean, draped in a loose-fitting suit that he seemed to have inherited from some larger person. His brown skin shone, and his horn was tilted upward at the ceiling; the notes he played ricocheted off the hard, curved stones and landed with the precision of gunshots. The other musicians followed his lead as he worked his way through a solo in what Ike would later know was a tune called "Dyin' by the Hour."

Ike had never heard anything like this, and yet he knew its gentle swing and wide, comforting melodic turns were purely American. He felt at home. And he felt that if he could play music like that too, he could make the sounds of home any time he needed them. The piano—Czerny exercises and Chopin—was all well and good, but it didn't sound the way he wanted to sound. Tommy Ladnier did.

Ike sat transfixed watching Ladnier sway on the bandstand as if he were a part of the music, not simply the man playing it. He didn't even notice when a beautifully dressed man with thinning hair and a pencil mustache settled in the seat next to Ollie and offered her a cigarette. Ollie smiled at the man and took one, let him light it, and turned her attention back to the stage. She put an arm around Ike and whispered to him, "Isn't he marvelous?" Ike didn't react. Even her whisper was an intrusion. He barely noticed when the well-dressed man took Ollie in his arms and led her onto the crowded parquet floor in front of the bandstand to dance. He kept her there for most of the night. Ike sat alone, happy to be in an inviolable private world.

Ladnier played until almost five A.M. When the audience

finally let the band quit, Ladnier waved his trumpet at them and disappeared behind the stage through a black drape. Ike and Ollie were driven home by the man with the pencil mustache, who introduced himself as Count Willie Palaffi, from Budapest. He was very gallant and left them at the door of their apartment house with a full bow, after which he swept himself, his cape, and his walking stick back into the cab and drove off. The sun was just beginning to rise, lending a slightly surreal quality to the street. Streaks of yellow and pale red fell in irregular patches across the buildings, and, in the sky, the clouds appeared an angry ashen gray as the light began to fight its way into Paris. Ollie stopped to admire it all.

"We'll sleep all day," she told him. "No school for you."

Ike thought that sleep would never come; he was too stirred up inside from his visit to Le Cave de la Heure d'Or. But within moments of feeling the cool purity of the pillow against his cheek, he was gone, and wouldn't stir until late afternoon, when he found Ollie sitting in her room with a split of champagne and a small tin of caviar, ready to begin again.

IKE GOT HIS TRUMPET, and was determined to take lessons from Tommy Ladnier himself, but Ladnier had returned to New York. Ike had to settle for a tea dance French trumpeter named Jacques Suvet, who was more of a schoolmaster than a jazzman. Nonetheless, he applied himself, and, within six months he could trill his way through the scale in all twelve keys and confidently play the melody of "Dyin' by the Hour," if not his idol's spectacular improvised solo flights around it.

Meanwhile, Count Willie Palaffi had become a fixture in the apartment that Ollie had found on the Île de la Cité. He didn't live with them at first, but eventually he and Ollie gave up any pretense of simply keeping company, and he installed himself in her bedroom. The Count—though his title was an obvious pretense and Ollie referred to him as "my no-account Count"—might have presented a serious threat to Ike's happiness, but he turned out to be a mixed blessing for the boy. True, he made Ike jealous of the relationship he and Ollie had previously and suddenly enjoyed as an exclusive club for two. But, on the other hand, he gave Ike some relief from the endless round of parties and dinners and club engagements, and the increasingly unsettling sense that he was being made to act as both Ollie's son and her husband. Ollie made sure that Ike was included whenever he wanted to be. They made an odd trio, out clubbing until all hours, occupying a box at the opera, or dining in formal splendor at Tour d'Argent, but Ollie insisted, and Count Willie was most accommodating. He also taught the boy to fly a kite.

They remained in France until March 1938, when Hitler moved into Austria, and then they quietly picked up and took themselves to Zurich, where Count Willie introduced the now fourteen-year-old Ike to the world's most elaborate electric train set at the toy store known as Franz Carl Weber. The trains were spectacular, but Count Willie quickly realized that Ike was now too old to be seduced by such things. And Ike, who felt neither more nor less misunderstood than most fourteen-year-olds, was quick to express his disdain though he came to regret it in later years. From Zurich they moved by private car, and in a state of some confusion, back through France to Amsterdam. There they eventually boarded a boat for Denmark. Ike was now glued to the newspapers, which he could read in almost any language. And in every language, the news was progressively dire.

Copenhagen was magnificent, but Ollie knew by now that the only safe course of action was to get back to America. They moved quickly to Helsinki and from there boarded the SS Korsholm in January 1939. There were icebreakers in the harbor to keep the ocean lanes open during the bleak winter months, and a glacial gale blew across the decks day and night. Ike, Ollie, and Count Willie, who was traveling on a hastily arranged but reasonably convincing Norwegian passport, mainly stayed indoors and played whist. It had been almost six years since mother and son had seen American soil. Ike turned fifteen on the boat—a teenage American boy with a most peculiar education. When he finally returned to school in New York, he was an outcast among his contemporaries. He had no real friend back home now save the trumpet he brought with him.

OLLIE LOCATED TOMMY LADNIER in a Lenox Avenue walk-up and arranged for Ike to meet him and have a lesson. Although Ike had not seen Ladnier since the jam session at Le Cave de la Heure d'Or half a decade earlier, he was wildly eager. This was a moment he had dreamed about and never believed would occur.

He arrived for the lesson by himself by subway, a half hour early on a rainy June afternoon. The vestibule of the old tenement was clean but worn, the floor tiles crazed with cracks and chips. The stairway was narrow, and the treads tilted away from the wall, as if they might pull apart from it if a big enough man tried to climb them. Ike, slight and barely five feet tall, ascended lightly and quickly and rang the bell. There was no answer. He knocked two or three times, and then, with no great confidence, let himself in.

What he found inside made him inhale sharply, and then regret it. There was an acrid smell in the darkened flat—a mix of illness and old, unrefrigerated food. It was sweltering. The shades were drawn. A single light was burning on the bed table and a gray-skinned man was sitting on the bed, his elbows on his knees, propping up his chin. He wore a sleeveless undershirt and tattered silk pajama bottoms; a lit cigarette poked from between his index and middle fingers. Ike stared. It was Tommy Ladnier, though he was all but unrecognizable—shrunken, gray-haired and dead-eyed. Something in his face had sunk backward.

The two looked at each other for a long moment, Ike trying to find the once ebullient bandleader in Ladnier's vacant face. Finally, giving up, he spoke.

"Mr. Ladnier," he said. "I've come for a lesson."

Lanier nodded and drew on the cigarette. He gestured to Ike's trumpet case but didn't speak. As Ike placed the case on the deeply grooved floor and got out his horn, Ladnier reached for a Dixie cup on the bed table and spit into it. Then he replaced it and reached for another, which was half full of some kind of brown liquor. He took a short sip and replaced the second cup next to the first. He lifted his head as Ike put the trumpet to his lips.

Ike's heart was racing. He inhaled and exhaled several times without being able to bring himself to begin. Ladnier observed him, impassive, with a reptilian stare.

Finally, Ike realized that if he didn't begin immediately, he never would, and he lurched into the first notes of "Royal Garden Blues," one of Ladnier's mainstays. But as he mangled the first attack of the intro, a figure he hadn't seen lurched up behind Ladnier in the bed. It was a woman, very dark skinned with twisted lips and wild hair, her bloodshot eyes fixed on him in terror. Her nightgown was a thin white ticking that twisted around her emaciated body. She had been fast asleep, and the first note of "Royal Garden Blues" had jolted her. Ladnier swept one of his hands behind himself and placed it on her shoulder to keep her silent and low in the bed. The two of them stared at Ike, who had no idea what to do next. Inhaling, he attacked the first chorus of the piece, tried to improvise around another, and then concluded with a short tag. The horn got him through. He dared not let go of it.

Ladnier watched him for another long moment, then took another slug of whiskey.

"How I'm gonna teach you?" he asked, finally. It was the first time he had spoken.

Ike contemplated the possible meanings of this statement. The old trumpet player turned to his companion in bed.

"I can't teach this boy," he said to her. She moaned lightly, as if in pain, but said nothing. Ladnier turned his attention back to Ike.

"What I'm goin' teach you?" he asked.

Ike shrugged, now beginning to wonder if he had played so brilliantly there was nothing left to learn.

"You can't even play the music you already know," Ladnier said.

Ike's heart fell into his feet, and his feet could not move.

"And I can't teach you," Ladnier said. He sucked in his lips, and Ike suddenly saw that this assertion had nothing to do with Ike's playing at all.

"No teeth," Ladnier said. "I got to get me a set of teeth or I can't play nothing. Ain't worked in most half a year. Your mama sounded like she got some money. You get me a set of teeth and I'll teach you."

"She gave me five dollars," Ike said. "For one lesson."

Ladnier stubbed out his cigarette and put out his hand for the money. Ike thought for a moment about holding it back under the circumstances, but it seemed unrealistic, not to mention uncharitable. Ladnier took it and put it on the crowded, filthy night table.

"What you say, boy? A set of teeth."

Involuntarily, Ike put the horn to his mouth and felt his

teeth, upper and lower, backstopping his lips against the pressure of the mouthpiece. Ladnier was right. There was no way to play without teeth. Slowly, he lowered the horn, having already learned something he never would have thought about otherwise.

"Teeth," Ike said.

Ladnier rose, stooped, took a step toward Ike. He reached out to touch Ike's jaw and mouth but began to cough. Ike took a step backward. His heart jumped as he saw Ladnier stumble, unable to keep his balance; the man pitched forward, his hand missing Ike's face by an inch, as he toppled onto the floor.

Ike backed farther away, as the woman in the bed began to whoop like a fire horn.

"Don't touch him!" she wailed. "He just gonna lay there. I can't get him up. He be there till he come to. Then he get up and get back in bed. Now scat!"

Ike stared at Ladnier's body on the floor and reached down for him.

"Don't touch him!" the woman repeated. "Let him be!"

Ike saw the terror in her eyes and imagined what his own must look like. For a moment he stood frozen, then, still clutching the horn, he turned and ran out of the apartment and down the four flights of stairs to the street.

There was a phone booth on the corner. Ike called Ollie, who, thankfully, picked up. She told him to wait. A misty rain had begun to fall. A half hour passed. Ike thought of Ladnier on that magic night at Le Cave de la Heure d'Or, where that very same body had conjured the spirit of eternal life and joy and wondered where that all could have gone. In later years, Ike's sometimes melancholy demeanor would be a source of amusement to his fellow musicians up and down Broadway, but as he stood here in the rain, at fifteen, on Lenox Avenue, all the elements of his personality seemed to have fallen into place.

At last, with Ollie's touring car nowhere in sight, the door of the apartment building opened and Ladnier's wraithlike companion emerged in her nightgown, limping toward Ike in the rain.

"He can't play no more," she said to Ike. "No teeth."

"I'm sorry," Ike said. She nodded at him and handed him the pasteboard trumpet case he had left on the floor of Ladnier's flat. He took it and nodded. Then she took his hand. In her palm was the five-dollar bill that Ladnier had taken from him.

"You didn't get no lesson," she said. "He ain't had no teeth. He knew he ain't had no teeth."

Ike closed her fingers around the bill, declining to take it. He turned away and walked down Lenox Avenue as the wind kicked up, heedlessly carrying the trumpet in one hand and the case in the other. Within moments he was overtaken by his mother's Packard town car, with Count Willie at the wheel. The rear door opened, and Ollie reached out a hand to gather him in. Once settled in the back seat, he turned to see that she was pouring gin from a flask into a silver picnic cup. She expertly added tonic from a bottle that was hidden in a neat compartment between the seats. She handed it to him, and, with her other hand, deposited a sedative into his open palm. When they got back to 73rd Street he slept for fourteen hours.

FOR TWO YEARS Ike took lessons from a Julliard piano teacher named Henry Vesey, who forced him to alternate between Hayden's piano sonatas and Gershwin's Three Preludes, with occasional forays into the works of Scriabin and Fats Waller. Vesey also introduced Ike to a new kind of music—Broadway theater songs—the backbone of what would come to be called the Great American Songbook.

Ollie had never trusted the Broadway musical; she was an opera buff and a symphony-goer, and certainly not above "slumming" at jazz clubs where she felt "authentic" American music originated. Vesey, however, had a nighttime job holding down the piano chair at Rodgers and Hart's new show *Pal Joey*. And while the teacher didn't take any of these show tunes too seriously, he professed to be grateful for the gig, and for the sense of camaraderie that could be found in an orchestra pit. It was only a matter of time before Ike wangled an invitation to sit in. The occasion was his seventeenth birthday, and Vesey presented the opportunity as a gift.

Ike emerged from the subway at the Times Square station, surrounded by a crowd of people moving more quickly than he was, many of them rushing, he would later learn, to Leblang's Ticket Agency where discount tickets for Broadway shows could be had at the last minute. For decades, the agency had occupied the basement of Gray's Drugstore, and people assumed that the drug company was also in the ticket business. But the building had met the wrecking ball in 1938, and by the time Ike arrived, Leblang's was operating out of a storefront on 44th Street. There were couples arm in arm, single women racing from their work as secretaries and stenographers, and single men, immaculately dressed and seeking a cheap ticket to a Broadway show—any Broadway show that had tickets at risk of going dead. Ike was in no such hurry.

As he climbed the stairway at the southeast corner of 42nd and Broadway, the glow and gleam of light pierced the blackness. Ollie had taken him to Carnegie Hall and the Met many times, but that was sedate. He'd been to darkened clubs to hear jazz more than once, but though his mother was an eager consumer of high and low art, she had no tolerance for, and didn't believe in, what she called "the commercial roar"—Broadway. It stood in the middle, and she had no interest in the middle. Ike immediately understood that this pretense had caused a significant lapse in his upbringing. A half a block from the subway station, he realized that he was home.

The place was in transition, an untamed jungle of contradiction and cohabitation. The low stone and green wooden structure of the out-of-town newspaper stand left a trace of the nineteenth century, while the gleaming neon signs above Woolworth's and Whelan's dime stores fought for dominance with the more familiar lighted bulb signs that flashed from the Loew's State and Astor theaters. On one side of the street was a gleaming poster for a disreputable-looking film called *Honky Tonk*; Clark Gable, larger than life, clutched an equally outsize Lana Turner, his intentions less than honorable. Immediately adjacent, the Astor marquee advertised Walt Disney's *Dumbo*. Ike passed Childs Restaurant, above which was a large painted sign declaring, "All New York's Talking About the Childs 60-cent Dinner!" Immediately adjacent, another sign proclaimed that one would certainly have "A Happier Morning After With Bromo Seltzer Tonight." Ike couldn't help but wonder about cause and effect.

At the corner of 47th, he encountered blinking neon advertising Papena, the Wonder Drink. Ike barely had time for a large one, which proved to be a delicious combination of orange, pineapple, a raw egg, and something else unidentifiable, a raw papaya, he later learned, mixed in a machine he had never seen before. He felt deeply nourished by it, whatever it was.

At ten past eight, he entered the stage door of the Ethel Barrymore Theatre and asked to see his teacher.

Ike climbed down the stairs to the basement and looked up in wonder at the heavy wooden beams undergirding the stage floor above him. He had never been in such a place. He entered the pit through a black drape and gazed out over the rail at a well-dressed audience beginning to fill up the auditorium. The place looked to Ike like a wedding cake full of people—the raised plasterwork was as white as icing, lacing itself over a mocha surface that defined the shape of the balcony and the boxes. The ceiling shone with metallic paint that had been glazed in pale beige reflecting the shadows thrown by elegant chandeliers. The theater—this theater—was a place of indescribable romance and glamour, even before the play had begun. It promised every known human experience. Even the splendid concert halls of Europe had never struck him in this manner, perhaps because he had never seen them from this perspective. Now, from the sunken and black-carpeted confines of the pit, he felt like a groundhog surfacing unexpectedly into a garden of such magnificent grandeur that he felt unworthy. Yet he wanted to spend all the remaining days of his life in this very spot. He had arrived at the epicenter—the center of the center.

The band was conducted by Harry Levant, whom Ike would later come to know as the brother of Oscar Levant, a Gershwin acolyte, piano virtuoso, and depressive wit who became something of a movie star. Harry, less of a personality and more of a workhorse, tore into the overture with tremendous gusto, and soon Ike was watching the musicians intently, while listening to the vocals and dialogue peeling off the stage above him. The tap dance penetrated him like volleys of gunfire. He was captivated not just by the songs, with their light, jazzy beat and harmonies, their tricky and literate lyrics, but as much by the story, by the implications of sex and betrayal, of blackmail and hard-edged negotiation over business and love. How, he wondered, could Ollie have kept him from this while instead subjecting him to the trials of almost five hours of *Die*

Meistersinger von Nürnberg, which she then dismissed with the wave of a hand as nonsensical Nazi propaganda? Where had this been all his life?

Ike became a fixture in the pit at the Barrymore, a kind of mascot, welcome at all eight performances a week, and missed when he did not appear. So it was hardly surprising that, after a few weeks, Henry Vesey offered to let him take over the keyboard here and there, and, after a few weeks of watching Ike settle into the role of guest artist, insisted that the two of them go out for a drink after the second show on an early spring Saturday.

They left the Barrymore at a little after eleven P.M. and hopped on the independent subway downtown to a place that Henry Vesey liked called Mon Plaisir. He told Ike that they might even have the honor of running into Lorenz Hart, who had written the lyrics for *Pal Joey.* He had been seen there many times, and certainly liked his whiskey. The bar was down a flight of stairs on MacDougal Street, and it was not lost on Ike that when they entered, there was not a single woman in the place except for the bartender, who wore a tuxedo and the bloodiest shade of lipstick Ike had ever encountered. The walls were padded with Kelly green Austrian drapes, and the low ceiling was painted black. Art Nouveau sconces provided what little light there was. Lorenz Hart was nowhere to be seen. But Vesey, it seemed, was a regular, well-known, and much liked. There was a table in the back waiting for him, and although he waved to the bartender without placing an order, two martinis swiftly arrived and were placed on the table with a fresh ashtray. Vesey downed half his drink in one long slug and took a cigarette from a silver case that he explained casually had been a gift from Cole Porter, "an old pal." Ike declined the offer of same. He had no idea how to smoke.

"What is this place?" Ike asked.

"My second home," Vesey said, slipping an arm around Ike's waist. "Back in the twenties it was called Eve's Hangout, and there were no men allowed. Then it got raided and poor Eve was deported back to Poland, but the place's heart is as gay as a goose. So now it's for us. Or didn't you know?" He finished his drink in a second swig, as if he needed strength.

"Didn't I know what?" Ike asked, progressively uncertain about what was happening to him, but certain that it was not what he intended.

"That I love you," Vesey said. "I didn't mean for it to happen this way. I know you're barely more than a child, and I'm not like that. But I've fallen hopelessly in love with you. You're all I think about."

Ike backed away, knocking over his drink in the process. Icy gin poured across his suit pants, turning his knees and thighs clammy and damp.

"Another!" Vesey shouted, suddenly performing for the crowd. He held the empty glass to Ike's lips.

"You need to catch up," he said. "I've gotten ahead."

"Way ahead," Ike said, now standing.

"I've shocked you," Vesey said. "I've messed it all up. Don't be angry. Just have a sip. I won't touch you again. Scout's honor."

Ike was silent. He looked at Vesey, suddenly a frightened lank-haired man who had made an egregious error. He had shown his heart to one who didn't love him. Ike had heard about men like Vesey, had hardened his heart to them in the abstract, had heeded warnings from other boys, and even from his mother and Count Willie, who had let him know that the music world seemed to have more than a fair share of such dangerous and immoral people. But seeing his mentor, sitting with an empty martini glass on a wet table, a lit cigarette burning in an ashtray in front of him, his long, graceful fingers opening and closing involuntarily as if there was a keyboard under them, Ike's heart broke for the first time. The man was like a ladybug lying on its back, trying to find a way to get its spindly legs back on the ground, helpless and lost, facing the possibility that the world had come to an end. Ike sat back down.

"Mr. Vesey," he said. Then, "Henry."

Vesey looked at him and his fingers stopped moving. He waited, his eyes wet in anticipation and fear.

"I can't," Ike said. "I just can't."

The silence that passed between them contained a world of loss for Henry Vesey; Ike could feel it. Finally, Vesey spoke.

"Kiss me once," he said. "I'll make do with that."

Ike looked at the face in front of him, quite a beautiful face. Pale, with sharp, chiseled features and dark brows. It was a face anyone could find attractive, but it was a man's face. Ike didn't think. He leaned in and his mouth met Vesey's. Vesey's tongue, just the tip of it, parted Ike's lips and met the tip of Ike's. That's all it was. Ike backed up and stood.

"Good night," he said. He turned and made his way swiftly through the crowd of men smoking and gesturing, joining hands and touching each other in a simple, social way. He had left his coat over the seat by the table in the back but dared not turn around. He stumbled up the stairs and into the cool air of MacDougal Street, where he took several sharp breaths. He could still feel Vesey's tongue on his own, and he was overwhelmed with sadness. In the chill of the early spring air, he began to walk north toward the apartment on 73rd Street, convinced that he would never see the pit of the Ethel Barrymore Theatre again, and that he would never see Henry Vesey again. He was crushed with sadness for them both.

—

"*SO THAT BIG FAIRY* made a pass at you," Ollie said when Ike emerged the next morning after another night in which sleep had given him some distance from events he had no intention of facing. As he sat at breakfast, he looked through the open pocket doors to the dining room and noticed that a Matisse canvas was missing from above the mantelpiece.

"Piano players are the worst," Ollie continued, without apparent concern for Ike's condition. "They have those long fingers, and they never want to use them on the keyboard. Or on me."

Count Willie looked up from his newspaper. "This one," he said, gesturing at Ike, "is no fairy. A little short perhaps. But the women will fall at his feet."

"Where's the painting?" Ike asked.

"Sold," said Ollie. "Count Willie is gradually driving us into the poor house, but I'm regulating it carefully."

The Count disappeared behind his paper again with an impertinent grunt. He and Ollie had married almost immediately after arriving in New York, and she was, according to the documents, now Countess Palaffi, though what a legal investigation of this matter would have discovered no one knew, and no one asked. The Count was likely not a count, not a Norwegian certainly, and probably not named Palaffi. Ollie suspected he was a Hungarian Jewish peddler who had somehow found his way to Paris in search of fortune, if not fame. This she was happy to provide. He was a skilled and accommodating lover and happy to stay otherwise in the background and follow her cultural lead. In the fictional world they inhabited, she supposed, perhaps she was actually now a countess, but the thought of calling herself one seemed too preposterous to take seriously. She was content to let the Count spend her money and keep her happy and amused. As far as finances were concerned, she had him on a leash; some nights he also had her on one. The entire situation was more than satisfactory.

"The thing is," Ollie went on, "I won't suffer from his excesses at the card table or the racetrack. But it's time that you knew that you're going to have to work for a living. I love this man, and I'm going to let him spend all our money. Gradually."

Ike didn't respond. He was thinking about the view from the pit at the Barrymore that he would never see again, and the likelihood that Henry Vesey had suffered through a sleepless night. As he was contemplating this, the doorbell rang. In a moment, Estelle Dunmore, who had gone to answer it, entered the dining room. She was carrying Ike's overcoat, and a small envelope. Ike took the coat sheepishly and put it on the empty chair next to him. The envelope contained no note, but inside it was a single ticket to the Monday night performance of *Pal Joey*. With some surprise, Ike realized that he had never actually seen it.

5

Sticking to the Union

T*HE LIGHTING EQUIPMENT* at the Ethel Barrymore Theatre, which was illuminating *Pal Joey* on the night Ike Harris attended, was supplied by the factory in Maspeth where both Vincent Donnelly and his father, Big Vin, were employed. Recently, Vincent's little brother Pat had signed on as an apprentice. None of them had ever visited so glamorous a place as the theater that Ike had come to think of as a second home.

Vincent had waited two months to hear from the attorney Francis Rafferty, pestering Big Vin weekly, but Big Vin counseled patience. These things took time. Patents. Paperwork. Bureaucracy. It was all very complicated. Finally, when the first frost came, Vincent remembered how insufferably hot it had been on the day he and Big Vin had ventured down to Rafferty's office, and he decided that a change in the weather meant he had waited long enough. He left work at lunchtime with the excuse that he had developed a raging fever and took the subway back to the Bowery.

The door to the stairway that led to Rafferty's law office was locked. There was no sign of life. Vincent's heart raced and he could feel the adrenaline beginning to pump his body into a rage. He pounded at the door for a couple of minutes, but he knew, as surely as he'd ever known anything, that Francis Rafferty was gone. Finally, in the full sway of his anger and sense of betrayal, he turned and strode into the deserted saloon on the ground floor, a sixteen-year-old on a mission.

"Where is he?" he demanded of the bartender, little realizing that he was addressing Rafferty's brother-in-law.

"The attorney?" the man asked, looking back at Vincent over half spectacles. He was a round man with a long fringe of hair around the sides of his head, but only a speckled, wrinkled, baldpate on top. He wore a green cardigan with just the bottom button closed, and it framed his belly in a graceful curtain of tatty wool.

"Rafferty," shot back Vincent. "My lawyer."

"You're too young to have a lawyer, boy," said the barman, "but not too young to have a whiskey. It'll calm you."

"Got no money," Vincent spat out. He was in no mood to be distracted.

"Pfft," said the barman and poured a Jim Beam, indicating that Vincent should at least take a sip, which the boy did. It was hot.

"Name's Hynes," the barman said. "Arthur Hynes. Rafferty is my wife's brother, and it's far too late to find him here. He's gone south with the birds, though where he goes to is anybody's guess. You won't see him again until the springtime."

"He's supposed to be getting me a patent," said Vincent, now nursing the whiskey more comfortably and beginning to feel the good effect of it.

"Is he now?" Hynes raised his eyebrows. "Well, I'm sure I've no idea what a patent is or why you'd want one, but if he's getting it for you he must be fetching it from the land of the coconut palm to bring back with him. He never said a word about it to me."

"Is he a good lawyer?"

"Well, I wouldn't say that," Arthur Hynes opined carefully. "He's a lovely fella. But as far as I know he never did any actual lawyering so's anyone would notice. My wife, Madge, says he has a natural ability to make friends of enemies."

"When does a lawyer do that?" Vincent asked. It occurred to him that the barman was sort of doing the same thing, but somehow it seemed appropriate to a barman, not a lawyer.

"Well," said Arthur, "for instance, when I wanted to open this place and needed to get the liquor license sorted, he represented me. That meant he brought the man from the liquor board and me up to the flat for a plate of cold cuts and a whiskey or two. He explained what a swell and reliable fella I was, which was just what I wanted to hear. Then he explained to me what a strict and aboveboard and unyielding fella the liquor board man was, and that was exactly what he wanted to hear. Then he handed the liquor board fella an envelope with five one-hundred-dollar bills in it, which he called the "application," and two weeks later I had a saloon. That's what kind of a lawyer he was. But I don't think he has much trade now."

By this point, Vincent had polished off the Beam, and Arthur Hynes had poured him a second. "I'm a Jameson man myself," he said. "Irish whiskey. But what I've learned in the saloon business, is that here in America, you drink gin in the summer and bourbon in the winter."

"I didn't know," Vincent said. "I never had a drink of anything. It doesn't seem life should be this way, where your lawyer says he'll do something and then he runs off for the whole winter and doesn't even tell you."

"Business life is however it is," said Arthur. "The trick of it is understanding how it is and figuring it out from there. If you think you're going to make it be some other way, you'll likely spend your whole life digging a ditch. And you'll die broke."

Vincent thought about this silently for a while, as he sipped his second-ever drink more slowly than the first. He was now dizzy and a little confused by how he had gotten to this point when he had only come to see about his patent.

"You owe me for two drinks," Arthur said, "and I don't expect to see the money for a few years. But I get the sense you're the kind of fella that'll come around and pay me one day. And when Francis returns—when the trees begin to flower in the springtime—I'll let him know you were looking for him."

THE NEXT MORNING, Vincent took his bicycle wheel fan system to work with him. Ignoring his father's firm command, he marched up to the offices of Charles Conley, who owned the plant. Mr. Conley's secretary was surprised to see him, a very young man with a circular package wrapped in brown paper and tied with binder twine, asking to see the boss. But she took the request into the inner sanctum, with the understanding that Vincent had only a half hour lunch in which to be interviewed.

Conley gave him fifteen minutes. The man sat behind his desk smoking and looked at Vincent with apparent eagerness.

"So whaddaya got?" he asked. "Neither one of us has all day." He was bright-eyed and apparently friendly, not at all the patrician scold that Vincent had been fearing in his mind. It occurred to him that, after working in the factory for two years, he had seen the owner only from a distance, and then only once or twice. That they occupied two different worlds was not lost on him but seeing Conley close up and hearing his common New York accent, seeing his mop of unruly red hair, noticing that his shoes, which he had swung up onto his desk, were scuffed and run over, he was surprised at how close he felt to the man. Conley was just another guy whose nose hairs needed clipping, with a lot more money and power than Vincent or his father had. The question was how he'd gotten there.

Vincent untied and unwrapped the package and placed the wheel on Conley's desk. He explained what he'd done and why. He set up the battery and the little propellers spun, just as they had for Rafferty. Conley looked it over carefully in silence while Vincent waited, thinking that certainly this would be the moment when his fortunes changed.

Finally, Conley looked up at him.

"I only know how to do this straight up, kid," he said. "I cut straight to the truth because none of us is going to be on this planet very long, so there's no time for bullshit, you know what I mean?"

Vincent nodded dumbly. He was admiring his newly affable relationship with the powerful Mr. Conley and waiting for the punch line.

"It's a toy, kid. That's all it is."

Vincent wanted to cry but didn't. A toy? Why? Couldn't Conley see the possibilities of turning it into something more?

"I appreciate that you brought it to me to look over, but it can't work, not for anything we need here. It's clever—you're a clever boy. But what you got here is a toy."

Vincent left the office deflated, determined not to even tell Big Vin what he'd done. And, in fact, he kept silent for as long as he could.

Seven months later Conley proudly sent a letter to his various customers among the lighting designers and general managers along Broadway introducing a new lighting instrument called the Conley Autoflow, which used a series of insulated mini fans to fend off the heat of its bulb, thus increasing the life of both the bulb and the instrument itself and presenting a significant cost savings in the long run, not to mention a boon to public safety. He'd had the first model fabricated outside the factory at a metal shop in Ozone Park. The day he introduced the plans on the floor of the plant, the workers applauded loudly, and Vincent felt his first impulse to murder. It would not be the last.

As the new Conley Autoflow took off in the marketplace and orders piled up, Vincent didn't have to wait for his father to come after him—the two of them were spending time on the line each day manufacturing the damn things. Conley's office was closed to them now, although both had tried to see him. Still, they needed their jobs more than they could afford to seek justice.

"You're a feckin' fool," Big Vin told his son as they walked home after work. Vincent didn't have the ammunition to disagree. "If you'd a waited for Rafferty to come back from his vacation like I told you, we'd be living in a mansion in Long Island on the feckin' beach! We'd own Breezy Point outright!"

This at least gave Vincent an opening, though he spoke softly and without a lot of conviction.

"That lawyer was never going to help us," he said. "We needed a real lawyer."

"So now it's my fault?!" Big Vin lifted a giant paw against his son but didn't bring it down. "It's all my feckin' fault I suppose."

They trudged home in silence after that.

"*JUSTICE*," *ARTHUR HYNES* said to Vincent, "is not a business term."

Vincent was at the bar after work on a Saturday, but before the place got busy, which, perhaps, it never did. He had explained to the old man what his invention was, how he had come to think it up, how it had been stolen from him by Conley, and the appalling humiliation of having to spend ten grueling hours a day manufacturing the lighting instruments that were making Conley get richer and richer. Hynes was impressed, but not excited.

"Justice," he reiterated, "is for those who can afford to sue for it, and for those who stick a shiv in somebody on the street and get sent to the hoosegow. The rest of us are merely spectators."

"So what do I do?" Vincent was sipping his second Jim Beam of the evening and feeling sorry for himself, though his murderous rage had again passed.

"Well, there's revenge," Arthur said to him. "You can kill the little redheaded snot and get sent to the electric chair. How does that appeal?"

Vincent didn't bother to answer.

"I thought not. So what's left to you? Let me ask you a question. I'm a barman, I don't know fuck-all about anything. But in your world, where you don't have a really good job, a high-up-the-ladder kind of a job, what would a job like that look like?"

This was a question Vincent had never really considered. He was just a kid who felt lucky to have work on the line. But the lucky part had evaporated, along with his adolescence. He was now a man, he felt: a wronged man, nursing a drink in a bar. Things could go any one of a number of ways. He gave the matter some thought as Hynes attended to a couple of other early drinkers. When the barman circled back to him the second glass was empty.

"You'll not get more than two drinks from me—you're still a boy. And besides, I can't afford to have you running up too big a bill. But get yourself back here tomorrow after church, and we'll go to work on this. The lord only knows how."

"Why are you helping me? Trying to help me, at least?"

"To tell the truth," Arthur said, "I get a little bored running this place. Especially in the winter, with Rafferty nowhere in sight. I hardly have a damn thing to do. Then there's the fact I don't have a lad of my own. Only a daughter, and I lost her. And besides, you're the best story that's walked in here in a while."

That night, Vincent felt a vague sense of guilt as he tried, without much success, to sleep. He was concerned that he was turning to this near stranger rather than his own father for help, but he knew, somehow, that Big Vin's advice would simply never get him anywhere in life. His father was a hardworking man, but he was bereft of imagination, and he was, for a big man, frightened of everything. Fear seemed to drive his every decision and be the source of what little wisdom he had to offer. Who knew what Arthur Hynes could provide instead, but the man seemed content to think things through in a way that was unfamiliar to Vincent, who, at the moment, needed some way of seeing beyond the horizon of endless work for not enough money. He didn't want to live and die on a sooty side street somewhere between Long Island City and Maspeth. He didn't even know which township he lived in, and it didn't seem to matter. The next morning at eleven, he was back at the bar.

"Follow me," said Hynes, taking a key from a drawer beneath the cash register. He unlocked the door to the stairway and led Vincent up into Rafferty's abandoned office. The two of them entered; Hynes lifted the window shade and took a seat at Rafferty's battered desk.

"Now," he said, "what the hell is this thing you sent Rafferty off to get? A patent."

"It's protection," said Vincent. "It's something—a piece of paper—that you get from the government that says an invention you invented belongs to you and no one else can use it without paying you for it. That's how he explained it."

Hynes sat at the desk for a while, thinking. Vincent watched him closely, waiting for a lightbulb to go on inside his head, but nothing seemed to be happening. Once or twice the old man inhaled sharply as if something was stirring in there, but then he settled back. Finally, though, he put both his palms down on the desk and leaned forward toward Vincent with a vaguely conspiratorial air.

"What if you already had one of these things? A patent. It's a piece of paper, you say?"

"But I don't."

"Who knows that you don't? Does Conley know that you don't?"

Vincent shrugged.

"If a lawyer wrote a letter to this Mr. Conley explaining that you had a whaddaya call it—a patent—on this thingamajig. And that Conley might end up owing you a fortune for it, or going to jail, and that you were going to prosecute him to the fullest extent of the law, and all of that kind of thing, maybe he'd see some reason."

"Do you think?"

"How would I know, I'm a bartender," said Hynes. "But I think he might do you a favor to get rid of you. What kind of a favor could he do you?"

"I don't know," Vincent said. "But we don't have any such letter from a lawyer. The lawyer's gone."

"But," said Arthur Hynes, "he's left behind one of the key tools of his trade." He opened the top drawer of Rafferty's desk and pulled out half a dozen sheets of paper. "His stationery."

MADGE HYNES LOOKED over her husband's crudely typed letter and sighed.

"It's a good thing you've got more than one sheet of this foolscap," she said. "This will simply never do."

The three of them were sitting around the Hynes family dining table, a heavy-legged dark brown circular thing much battered by age. Also at the table was a girl of two or three in a high chair—Arthur and Madge's granddaughter, whom they were trying to raise after the catastrophic loss of their daughter. She had died in childbirth after delivering the baby out of wedlock. The father, Vincent learned, had fled back to Ireland. Little Maggie Hynes was adorable even to Vincent, who didn't have much time for kids, generally speaking. She was all smiles and the occasional giggle, and content to play with her food and a small doll shaped out of a squashed-up bar towel that her grandfather had mocked up for her. She let the others talk, more or less without interruption.

Madge Hynes, who spent her day typing correspondence for a druggist and sundry dealer in the East Twenties, had seen a lot of letters come and go, and had no scruples whatsoever. She was as round as her husband, and as gray haired, but much better dressed, given that she spent her days in a respectable place of business rather than a bowery saloon. Respectable as it appeared, however, it seemed to her to be largely a place where drug users could readily get a morphine prescription filled with no questions asked. It was a good business, and she was quite happy to be working for a concern that was so good at satisfying the needs of the customers. Who they were and where they went when they closed the door behind them, she had no idea. It didn't concern her. She was content to live and let live.

"For one thing," she said, "a patent is likely to be a thing that has a number to it, probably a long number. We'll need to give it a number. And then you'll have to assume an appropriately threatening tone; that's what the lawyers do—they make it sound like they're about to have a stroke any minute over whatever the matter is. We get lots of letters from lawyers down at the store. And you'll need to have a deadline for a response as well, such as 'by the end of business Friday' or some such. I've seen that in letters many times."

Together the three of them worked until late, as Maggie slept in a crib in the corner, and by the end of the evening they had concocted what sounded to them like a reasonable demand for one hundred percent of the profits from the new Conley Autoflow lighting instrument; it was expressed in high dudgeon, to the degree that they were able to fabricate such a tone, and left open the possibility of a meeting "of all parties, to effect an acceptable reconciliation."

"I can be Rafferty as good as he can," Arthur Hynes explained.

"Better," said Madge. "I grew up with the old fribble."

Hynes took the subway uptown the next morning and mailed the letter from the post office adjacent to Grand Central, assuming that the more respectable postmark might have a salient effect.

"AS SHAKEDOWNS GO," said Charles Conley, "this is the first one that's ever made me laugh out loud."

He was sitting behind his desk, facing Vincent, Arthur, and Madge, who had come along for the ride with a steno pad to take down the conversation in shorthand, which she had no idea how to do.

"Do you have any idea how long it takes to get a patent?"

"Nonetheless," Arthur began.

But Conley cut him off with a raised hand. "Let's not even talk about my threatening your legal license, Mr. Rafferty. The facts are these: Your 'client,' this boy, came in here and showed me a toy he'd built. Afterwards I got to thinking about it. He had a basic notion that made some sense, but he'd built a toy. I'm not in the toy business. I took the thought—it was only a thought—to a certified licensed engineer and developed it at great personal cost. I paid the cost. Me. You didn't pay the cost because you don't have the wherewithal to pay it. That's how it goes in America. Any questions so far?"

"How can it be that I get nothing?" Vincent asked, his dander up.

"Have you earned anything?" Conley asked.

There was a moment of silence. Vincent looked at the older couple who had unaccountably waded into this mess on his behalf. He felt the tightening clamp of his own adrenaline, and his first impulse was to stand up and demand his rights, trying to turn Conley's obviously spurious explanation of how the Autoflow had come into being on its head. The man had fallen into a pot of gold, and the fact that he'd had to invest a little money to do so was beside the point. He had the money to invest. He hadn't had the idea. He was, in that sense, a complete fraud.

But before Vincent could open his mouth to say any of this, it occurred to him that Arthur Hynes was no less of one, for all the twinkle in his eye. And Madge, with her steno pad covered with meaningless loopy pencil markings, was not exactly who she was representing either. And even he, Vincent, was uncertain that anything he had done was worthy of a patent. A patent was an idea that had been put into his head by a largely disgraced old man with a law license who, when not pretending to be an actual lawyer, was escaping to Florida. In a sense, Vincent thought, what we have here is a room full of actors, playing out a small farce, though without an audience to appreciate it. And then he realized that wasn't quite true; there was an audience of one. This sudden revelation caused him to remember Madge Hynes's description of a lawyer as someone who could make friends out of enemies. And without thinking further he said something that he hadn't expected to say at all and didn't even know he was thinking.

"The important thing," he said to Conley, "is that we made you laugh."

Conley stared at him for a moment, utterly caught off guard. Then he laughed again.

"You find this amusing?" Hynes asked, looking at Vincent with a wounded, bruised stare. "After all I've done for you?"

But Vincent had somehow changed. He felt the power in the room swing toward him; he wasn't sure why. His adrenaline went back to wherever it had come from. But he also knew surely that he had not yet entered a world where he could win in the way Conley had won. That would have to wait until later. For now, he would have to settle for incremental victories based on unexpected perceptions.

"When was the last time you laughed?" he asked. "I mean really laughed. Laughter, as we know from the people who make film comedies, has a value. Charlie Chaplin is a rich man."

Conley looked vaguely baffled, but not unpleased. It seemed, perhaps, he was beginning to take a liking to this crazy young man. Vincent sensed his opportunity.

"Let's get one thing straight," he said to Conley. "You can't take this man's law license away because he's a bartender."

Conley was looking more and more incredulous but seemed to be trying to hold it in, aware that this might be the most memorable meeting he would have for some time.

"This is his wife, Madge," Vincent said, turning to her and

taking the steno pad from her hand. "This is not shorthand," he said, "as you can easily tell by calling your secretary in to look at it. And I'm not eighteen, which is the age I'm supposed to be before you can employ me. I turned sixteen last August. And you didn't invent the Conley Autoflow, while we're on the subject of what's what and what's not. But it'll be the best thing that ever happened to you anyhow. I invented it, and we all know that. But the main and most important thing by far is that we made you laugh."

"Jesus Christ, kid," Conley responded. "What the hell do you want from me?"

Vincent breathed a great sigh of relief. This was exactly what he had hoped Conley would ask him, because he'd been thinking about it ever since Arthur Hynes had put the question to him in the bar a couple of days earlier: a really good job, a high-up-the-ladder kind of a job.

"The union," Vincent said. "The guys who make a good living don't work for you in the factory—they run the lighting and the electrics in the theaters, but I can't get that job because it's a union job. That's what I want—a union job. And, Mr. Conley, that's what I just earned."

Two weeks later, months before his actual seventeenth birthday had passed, he held a union apprentice card in his hand. In addition, he had five dollars in his pocket, a gift from Big Vin. On the Saturday before he was expected to show up to start work at the bottom, he took the subway back to the Bowery and walked into Arthur Hynes's bar. Hynes was jiggering a keg of ale into place under the counter and screwing in the line that led to the tap.

Vincent sat himself down at the bar and placed the union card in front of him where Hynes could see it. Next to it, he lay the five-dollar bill.

"For the four drinks," he said, when Hynes looked up. "And

for everything. And to Madge. And send my love to Maggie. Thank you. And if there is ever anything—anything—I can do to return the favor . . ."

"That was quick work," Hynes said as he looked over Vincent's union card and held it up to the light. Then he poured Vincent a Jim Beam.

"On the house," he said. "The one and only time."

Vincent took the drink in two quick swings.

"So," Hynes asked him, "what do you think of all this?"

"I think," Vincent said, "that if there's a fish, I can catch it."

6

COUPLES

IN THE SPRING OF 1954, Aurora Feik applied for and was offered a job at a Christian summer camp outside of Randolph, Kansas on Turtle Creek Lake. She showed her father the letter from the camp, and he assented to her going off to work for the summer. She told him she would write back immediately and accept the position, which she did not do. She was seventeen and had no actual intention of working at a summer camp, Christian or otherwise.

The plan she had made instead was not entirely thought out, but it seemed to her that she needed to take one step at a time. In the four years since she had rescued her mother from the living room floor, the family had moved three times, and Beatrice had been sent off to two different private hospitals to try to "get her feet back on the ground and begin life anew," as one of the local ministers who had come to visit had said. The problem, Aurora could see, was that Beatrice had no interest in beginning life anew. She liked alcohol far better than she liked life, and Aurora thought her mother was not to blame for this. Beatrice didn't have much of a life—no one did who lived around Michael Feik. He had not had much difficulty shipping his wife off to one sanatorium or another, especially as the army paid for it. By now he had landed for what seemed likely to be an extended stay in his undistinguished career at Fort Campbell, on the Kentucky-Tennessee border, training future paratroopers who would go to Korea; it was destined to be his last commission.

Whatever the disastrous consequences of growing up as Beatrice Shelton Feik's daughter may have been, there were compensating assets to be measured. Aurora had developed an independent streak and the certainty that she could take care of herself and figure things out, because she knew she would have to. She had tried to be a good girl, on the one hand, but, on the other, she didn't feel that either of her parents needed to know what she was up to. She didn't feel she owed an explanation to anyone. She boarded a St. Louis–bound train in Clarksville, Tennessee, with a trunk checked through to Lawrence, Kansas.

Her mother, sober and somber, drove her down from the base and kissed her goodbye with only a bare hint of emotion. Aurora returned the favor. For a long time, there had been a kind of conspiracy of silence between them. Aurora never mentioned Beatrice's drinking, never acknowledged that it happened at all, never felt in any way empowered to talk to her mother about anything that mattered except, sometimes, music. And Beatrice never let on that she had even a clue about the many ways in which she had utterly failed her child, the only real object of her passion. It was too painful even to contemplate. Each of them silently carried the knowledge that, in some different world, they might have been each other's one and only lifeline and protection against the man in the family. But that world never seemed to emerge. If Beatrice felt that Aurora's departure was in some ways the final catastrophe in her life, she didn't let on. She had already done enough damage. Aurora got on the train.

She sat for a long time watching the pale green world of early June out the window. The leaves were not yet thick or saturated in color with the heavier look of midsummer; it was a promising but unfulfilled landscape, an adolescent world. After a couple of hours Aurora took out the bologna sandwich that Beatrice had packed and ate it silently. No one sat next to her on the train, and she didn't seek company. She was more than satisfied to ride away from home, farther and farther, leaving things behind. She could feel it in her diaphragm—a letting go of all that. In St. Louis she changed trains and fell asleep with her head against the window of the passenger car as the train chuffed west and the world darkened around her. She was contemplating the venture that lay ahead with equal amounts of anxiety and excitement, but eventually it sapped all her energy and simply knocked her out.

Fort Riley had not changed much since she had last seen it four years earlier. The barracks were there, as was the two-story house she had lived in on that awful night. From memory, she retraced the path that used to be her bus ride to school. It took almost an hour to walk it, but she had wanted to see the house first. When she got to the school the place was all but deserted. Summer vacation had begun. Still, the office was open, and she let herself in. The secretary was new.

Aurora explained that she had been a student there four years earlier, and that she was trying to locate a teacher named Marius Huwiler. The secretary looked in a small wooden box full of file cards, pulled one of them, and copied Huwiler's address and phone number onto a blank card, which she handed to Aurora.

"He doesn't work here anymore," she said. "But here's the last address we have. He might still be there."

"Do you mind if I look around?" Aurora asked.

"It's pretty much locked up," the secretary replied. "But

you're welcome to walk through. Did you have a good time here?"

Aurora paused before answering.

"I don't know," she said finally. "I think I learned something."

The music room door was locked, but Aurora looked through the small square glass and saw the place where Mr. Huwiler had put his fingers on her throat and massaged her vocal cords into relaxation. It was a characterless room with a couple of bulletin boards, shelves of sheet music, and a utilitarian upright piano as its only distinguishing features. The piano was pushed up against the wall now and had a canvas cover over it.

It was a confusing emotion that welled up in her as she looked through the window. She had long since considered and discarded the idea that Mr. Huwiler had designs on taking advantage of their physical encounter. He was trying to show her certain things about the technical aspects of singing by touching her neck and abdomen. And yet, it had been an intimate touch, a private touch, and she had come undone emotionally moments later, and couldn't say which events had been determinative in that happening. In the years since, she'd been kissed at a few high school dances, and once a boy had pushed her against a lamp post in the dark on the way home from a movie and tried to touch her. But none of it had any effect on her, while the events in the music room still stirred her in some way. Was she walking into some kind of trouble now? She wondered, but she was undeterred. She stared briefly through the little window in the door and turned to go back out into the sun. She asked the secretary to call her a taxi and spent two of the twenty dollars her father had given her getting to the address that she'd been given.

It was a split-level ranch house in a subdivision that had

been built immediately after the war to capture the market of returning young soldiers and their young wives, who had been blessed, in return for their service, with government mortgage help. But when she rang the doorbell, a different man came to the door. He was short, and had a military-style buzz cut, but his eyes were soft and gray. He was wearing an open-necked white shirt and khaki slacks and could have been one of her father's recruits on a day off, only a few years older. He looked at her quizzically, but sweetly, as if he was anticipating some mildly pleasant news.

Aurora asked if this was the place that Marius Huwiler had lived.

"He still lives here," the man said. "He's in the garden."

"He was my teacher," Aurora said.

"And you've dropped in?" the man said. Aurora couldn't tell if his tone was welcoming or ironic. She was silent.

He swung back the door and gestured her in. The house was nondescript and spare, but she could see a baby grand piano in a living room down a half a flight of stairs from the entrance hallway. Behind it was a row of framed sheet music covers featuring Art Nouveau and Art Deco portraits of women in exotic poses—one a pirate girl, another a carelessly clad beauty in the arms of a mounted policeman on a steed, a third gazing into the eyes of an Arabian sheikh. She had never seen anything quite like them.

"Whom shall I say is calling?" asked the man who had let her in, again with a vague overlay of ironic formality. But he needn't have asked. Mr. Huwiler was approaching from the kitchen, removing a pair of gardening gloves. He stopped and looked at her for a moment, registering confusion, then recognition.

"Aurora Feik," he said. "My singer. Jonah, this is my singer."

The man called Jonah raised his eyebrows. "You're joking," he said.

Aurora, startled to be recognized in this manner, was invited into the living room and Jonah, now identified as Jonah Kingston, was sent to the kitchen for iced tea; he reappeared with a tray moments later.

"Let's not mince words," Huwiler said. "I'm glad to see you but what in the world are you doing here? No one comes back to Junction City intentionally."

Aurora took a deep breath and made the speech she had been rehearsing, in one way or another, for four years. She had left home on the pretext of taking a summer job. She had picked a location near Fort Riley, because in actuality she wanted to take singing lessons from Mr. Huwiler, which her father would never condone. She wanted to be a singer, and she was quite sure she didn't want anything else. He was the only person she could think of who might be able to help. From here she could send regular postcards home, and keep her parents' suspicions at bay, at least for a summer. After that, she'd have to figure out what to do next. She would be eighteen in October, and at that point it would be her life to live.

The two men listened in silence, Marius Huwiler growing ever more restive. Perhaps this plan wasn't as convincing as she had thought. Perhaps it was childish or ill-conceived, or perhaps Mr. Huwiler didn't want any part of her or didn't like her—that was her greatest fear. From time to time Huwiler looked at Jonah, whose face was impassive as he nursed his iced tea. But Aurora didn't know what else to do. She had no backup plan. This had to work, somehow. She tumbled on.

But as she spoke, something else was happening. As she watched the two men, she saw eye contact pass between them, and in a flash, she understood—these were the glances of men bonded by some understanding that went beyond friendship and convenience. It was the silent language of partners. She was watching the two men silently signaling understanding and risk assessment and she knew, though she didn't yet know that she knew, that they were a couple. She remembered how it felt when Mr. Huwiler had touched her abdomen, but her fear that he was interested in her as anything other than a singer had been entirely mistaken, or a fantasy, or both. He was not interested in women at all. Certainly not in that way she had feared.

She had heard of such things, but only vaguely. Now, as the reality began to crystalize, she understood that the thing they were communicating was the palpable sense of exposure. They couldn't possibly take her in, make her any part of their lives, or let her see whatever it was that they were to each other. It was none of her business. But she understood that, much more important, it was not, under any circumstances, to become public.

When she had finished her speech there was a long silence that she didn't know how to break. But she sensed what was coming. Her plan was impossible, a child's fantasy, not a workable design. How could any grown person sympathize with it, much less accept it? She sat waiting for the inevitable, for the proposal to send her back, to call her parents, to call the police, to call someone and bring the entire enterprise crashing down on her.

Finally, Mr. Huwiler spoke. "I ran away from home at fifteen," he said, looking at no one. "I had no choice."

Jonah held up his hand to stop whatever might come next. "How would you live?" he asked. "And where? And what would you do for money? Marius can give you singing lessons but . . ."

It took her a moment to realize what was being offered.

"I can't stay here," Aurora said. "I understand that."

"You do?" asked Jonah Kingston.

"I think I do," Aurora said, and left it alone. "I thought I could get a job, and that there would be a place I could board. That you might know of someplace, and then I could sing, and work as a waitress, or in a five-and-dime or something like that, and pay for lessons until the fall, when school starts up again. I didn't want anything from you but lessons."

"I'm not teaching at the school," Mr. Huwiler said. "That's over."

Aurora nodded, not letting on that she already knew, and not speculating, except in her mind, about what the reasons might be.

"Can you type?" Jonah asked her.

She nodded. "I took typing this year. I'm good at it."

Jonah nodded curtly. "It's a lot to think about," he said.

"I shouldn't have come," she said. "Only I didn't know what else to do."

"Call, write, ask how he might feel about it? Before getting on a train?" Jonah said, growing irritated.

"But," Aurora said, "how could I have explained it if you had written back? My parents would have seen the envelope. Besides, you would only have said no."

Jonah nodded in agreement. "That is no doubt true," he said. "What you need to do now is take a walk. I know every house in this development looks the same as every other one and it's not exactly a scenic route. But you took us by surprise, and now you need to give us an hour. There's not a damn thing to see out there, but that's what you have to do. Come back in an hour."

Aurora nodded.

"Don't get upset, and don't assume anything, because I don't have the slightest idea what we're going to say to you, but give us that hour, will you?"

When Aurora had left the house, Jonah moved over next to Marius on the sofa and took his hand.

"I know it's crazy," he said. "But that's the girl you wanted. I get that, believe me."

"You bit her head off," Marius said. "And she can sing. Or she could. But I don't know. We could be inviting a catastrophe. She's basically a runaway. But so was I, back then. Can't you go to jail for that? She's run away cleverly, at least."

"And maybe she'll get away with it," Jonah said.

"But she's a fugitive, for god's sake," Marius countered. "We can't make it our problem, can we?"

Marius sighed.

"She's your singer," Jonah repeated. "I know."

Jonah Kingston had come back from the war and mustered out at Fort Riley. On the night of his discharge, he met Marius Huwiler in a roadhouse he had heard about in nearby Leonardville. Marius was playing the piano. Within six months Jonah's mission had been transformed from managing a battalion of infantrymen in the Pacific to managing the emotional life of the high-strung music teacher he had fallen in love with, who was, as far as he could tell, the only artist he had ever known. Marius was like an exotic flowering plant to Jonah—mercurial, his health subject to changes with the weather, not always willing to display himself, but beautiful to watch and exhilarating to care for.

Jonah was not prepared to feel this way about anyone—he had lettered in boxing in high school and had thought of becoming a professional bantamweight after the war. Aesthetics were foreign to him, as was tenderness. His father was a policeman. Still, he had settled down with this man, who liked to reminisce from time to time, especially after a few drinks, about the mysterious afternoon when he encountered the only real singer ever to come through Junction City's public school system. And about how she had disappeared at the end of the school year, never to return or be replaced. Jonah knew that there was now some potential danger ahead—he'd fought in a war, after all. But he also knew that Marius might not survive the second disappearance of Aurora Feik. And Marius's survival had become his lifelong mission.

"Maybe you can teach her," Jonah continued, "if the rest is up to her. What if you had no idea of how she got here or whether her parents know or anything else. If you were ignorant of all that."

"But she can't stay here," Marius said, starting to bend. "Not even for a night."

He also was thinking about danger, about the rumors that had gotten him dismissed from the school without any proof of anything, and about the prospect of sinking further into an unnamed disgrace that goes hand in hand with taking risks when your whole life needs to be defined by not taking them. But she could sing. And what the hell was he doing in Kansas anyhow, now working in Ogleby's Music Store in downtown Junction City, if he couldn't at least teach the one pupil he'd ever met who night amount to something? He sat silently for a long time while Jonah looked at him. Finally, Jonah leaned over and kissed him, but Marius was largely unresponsive.

"I have a thought," said Jonah.

WHEN AURORA RETURNED from a long walk down seemingly endless identical streets named after various lesser U.S. presidents, she found Marius Huwiler gone. Instead, when Jonah greeted her and led her into the music room, she found two women sitting in stiff back chairs near the piano.

Angela Bartlett and Toni Landry had already been spoken to by Jonah. Toni, who was younger, thinner, and more delicate, with dark eyes and hair, was familiar to Aurora. She was a history teacher at school, though Aurora had never been in her class. The other one was called Barty; Jonah introduced her as Toni's good friend. She was, he explained, the chairwoman of the Kansas League of Women Voters, an organization Aurora had never heard of. Her hair was gray, and she wore slacks. She had large, owlish eyeglasses and wide cheekbones that gave her an almost Native American look, and she displayed a quizzical half smile. She looked like someone who would be easy to interest in almost anything anyone had to say. Jonah explained that Barty and Toni shared a house in the same development and that the four of them had become acquainted through the school, where Marius and Toni had first met while he was still teaching.

"We've been talking," Jonah said to Aurora. "Frankly, I asked Marius to step out—these things make him very uncomfortable. I think he needed a walk more than you did. But I asked Barty and Toni if they would take you in for a few days to give you a chance to find a place, to look for a summer job, just a place to perch."

"We'd be happy to do that," said Toni. "You're a former student, after all," Barty remained silent but nodded, the inscrutable near smile seemingly frozen in place. It seemed to Aurora that they were acknowledging that all of them, including she, were, somehow, outlaws, escapees, citizens of some shadow country.

So it came to be that Aurora Feik went to live with the first lesbian couple she had ever met, to avoid moving in with the first gay male couple she had ever met. The men, particularly Marius, felt that having a seventeen-year-old girl in their house might arouse suspicion, while the women believed that they could easily pass her off should anyone ask. No one talked about returning her to her parents or getting her a room in a boardinghouse. Each couple had a spare bedroom, because neither could afford not to—the idea that they shared a bed was simply not something that anyone ever could know. The two bedrooms in both houses were furnished with equal care, but only one was ever used until Aurora moved in.

She took up residence a half mile from where she would study singing and stayed there all summer. They said she was welcome, and, for a while, she was. Jonah Kingston got her a job as a summer typist at the local liquor wholesaler where he worked as a regional salesman, and she saved her money, except for the five dollars that she paid to Marius Huwiler every week for two singing lessons, one on Saturday and one every Tuesday evening, and the twenty dollars she paid every two weeks to Barty for board. Nothing was ever said about the strangeness of the living arrangements, which was not hard for Aurora to understand; she had grown up in a house in which nothing was ever said. Being left to figure things out for herself was a familiar situation for her. And every other day, during the lunch hour at work, she wrote a postcard or a letter to her parents, inventing stories of the doings at Camp Mount Olive, stories just dull and unremarkable enough to seem real. Sometimes she professed homesickness. Her father wrote her back—she had set up a postal box in Randolph—instructing her to be strong. Her mother sent love and, once, a dozen cookies packed in a shoebox with tissue paper. Years later Aurora would reflect that the two homes in which she passed the summer of 1954 were the first two she had ever spent time in where life seemed normal.

Barty was a political firebrand with a maternal instinct. She was bent on educating Aurora about the state of women in America; it was, after all, less than four decades since they had won the right to vote. Toni was just as passionate, perpetually trying to reshape Barty's pronouncements with some historical perspective. Women, she never tired of pointing out, had been voting in some of the western territories since the 1880s. Dinner table conversations, which had been sullen and formal in the Feik household, were lively almost to the point of being explosive. Barty was only interested in what the future held and how to get there. Toni preferred the past and what it meant as a foundation. Aurora listened with fascination to the two women dissect the morning's liberal paper, and the more conservative one—"that fascist rag," Barty called it—that came in the afternoon. Occasionally Aurora would offer a bit of a thought that had occurred to her from hearing all of these conversations, or report an encounter among the stenographers and secretaries at the liquor warehouse downtown, who claimed to be severely strapped by their low pay and sick of the disrespect that was their daily diet, dished out to them by the men who ran things, or their husbands. At these moments Barty would stop everything to question Aurora closely about what had happened and what she thought about it.

"How are these women going to change things?" she asked Aurora one night when Aurora had detailed a conversation between two women, one of whose husbands had stayed out drinking and playing cards until three and then awakened her to demand a plate of bacon, eggs, toast, and a fresh pot of coffee. Aurora thought for a moment and then told Barty that change was never discussed at the factory. The daily gossip was merely a statement of how things were.

"What do you think about that?" Barty asked.

"It should change, I guess," Aurora said, "but that's not going to be my life anyhow. I'm going to be a singer."

"You think a singer's lover can't wake her up in the middle of the night and demand eggs and coffee?"

"I won't have a lover," Aurora said.

"You're pretty enough to have two," Barty said. "So be careful."

Aurora did not think of herself as pretty. But that night, stripped and looking in the mirror, she tried to look at herself scientifically, or at least objectively. Was she scrawny, angular, and bland? Or tall, willowy, and graceful? Not graceful. Definitely tall. Her figure was appealing, she decided, or would be. Her ankles were satisfactory. She had no waist, however, and her rib cage was too wide. Her face was round and inquisitive, but was it pretty? Her teeth were too big. Her skin was pale and looked to her as if no blood ran through her body at all. Her wrists were too narrow. Finally, she gave up in frustration—how does one ever know what one looks like? Hair: blond. Eyes: green. Feet: too large. She brushed her teeth and got into bed. As she drifted off to sleep, she thought about those few minutes in front of the mirror, and hoped she'd never have to do that again. She vowed to pay closer attention to politics. But it was difficult, because, no matter what, no matter where, there was always music going on in her head. She couldn't stop it. And the women had no record player.

For that, she would walk down to the Huwiler house, where Marius, even when he wasn't formally teaching her, encouraged her to spend time flipping through the record collection and putting on whatever looked intriguing, which was everything. The records themselves had changed completely from what she remembered. They were now twelve-inch plastic discs, each marked by the word "unbreakable" on the label, and each holding six songs on a side, rather than the single song that the hard, shellac discs she remembered all too well had contained. She marveled at them, though that word—unbreakable—caused her to wince. If only it had been that way.

She listened to one after another of the long-playing record albums, and heard, for the first time, Mozart, and Brahms, and, most startlingly, Mildred Bailey and Dinah Washington.

She played them by the hour and wondered what had become of Ethel Waters.

The record cabinet ran along the wall behind the piano, built low to the floor. Marius had dozens of albums and, at each end, scrapbooks, travel folders, maps and other paraphernalia had been stuffed in and forgotten over time. It was while rifling through the record cabinet one day that she put her hand on a small yellow magazine that had, no doubt, been there for years. Its cover featured a striking Art Deco design and in bold, block type were the words *SEX PSYCHOLOGY*. She stopped cold.

She was alone in the room, waiting for Marius to return from the music store after closing time. Jonah was on the road selling. Aurora looked at the magazine, which bore the date March 1941. On the cover, promoted in serious-looking type, were articles called "Sex in the Modern Prison," "Phallic Cults in Harlem," and, underlined crudely in ink, "Homosexuality: The Problem and the Cure." The price was twenty-five cents.

More fascinated than stirred, she turned the pages to learn what she could, but the magazine was unrevealing. The prose was wooden and largely incomprehensible to her. An author named Karl Lund began his treatise by writing, "The problem of homosexuality suffers at present from the emotional horror with which the general public regards both the topic and the patient." The author went on to describe any interaction between two men as homosexual, but not "perniciously homosexual." Aurora was lost.

She continued to read, but the entire magazine was without useful information, as far as she could tell. Its only purpose, she surmised, was the collection of the twenty-five cents that anxious individuals had at one time shelled out to learn something that was never revealed in these pages. She paged through the entire thing, quickly becoming bored and distracted. The only advertisements in the magazine were for other publications of a similar nature, promising further revelation and wisdom. She knew they would deliver nothing of the kind. And then, on the last page, there was one ad that was different. "The Theatre" it said in bold type across a full page of listings for Broadway plays and musicals, with titles like *Crazy with the Heat*, *There Shall Be No Night*, *My Sister Eileen*, *Panama Hattie*, *Two for the Show*, *Pal Joey*. And then, there she was: Ethel Waters starring in *Cabin in the Sky*. At the Martin Beck Theatre. That must be the place where the Martin Beck Theatre Orchestra made the record that had started everything. Her heart lifted, as if a mystery she had never tried to confront was suddenly solved.

What these theater listings had to do with sex psychology she couldn't imagine, though she constructed a scenario in her head in which Marius Huwiler, fourteen years younger, had traveled to the great city of New York, to the Martin Beck Theater, wherever it was, to see this show, furtively buying a copy of the magazine from a newsstand, to try to learn, really learn, about the challenge of being himself, to understand the problem of homosexuality, whatever it really was—and the cure. But as she turned the idea over in her mind, the door handle turned, and there Marius was in the hallway. She stuffed the yellow magazine back where it had been and stood up, smoothing out her skirt. Marius came down the stairs with a record album in his hand.

"You're here early," he said.

She nodded.

"We're not going to sing today. We're going to listen."

He slipped the record album out of the white paper bag marked with the name of the music store. The record sleeve was bright red and featured a cartoon: Five male heads across the top were leering at a young woman wearing only a pair of pajama tops. The cartoon did more for Aurora than all of the pages of *Sex Psychology*. It was dark and alluring, and somehow funny. She liked the combination.

"A new Broadway show," said Marius. "*The Pajama Game*. A hit show. Shall we see what it sounds like?"

Aurora had never listened to an original cast album all the way through. She had only a vague idea of what a Broadway musical was. She'd seen some movie musicals and always found them puzzling, though she admired Gene Kelly's dancing and his easy way with a song. Still, how such a thing could be put onstage live was a mystery to her. But Marius helped her through. By listening and simultaneously reading the story synopsis from the back of the album sleeve, he conjured the whole thing for her and for himself as well. He painted a grand picture of romance and comedy, and, in this case, even politics. The show was about a union and a strike at a factory. Even Barty would have approved. The album ran just under forty-five minutes, but it took them twice that long to make their way through it, and when they were done, they sat in silence for a while, glowing in the happy ending and the journey they'd taken, thanks to modern technology.

"Will you teach me to sing that song?" Aurora asked.

"'Hey There,' he said. It was already climbing the hit parade.

"No," she said. "The other one. The one about coming to a new town and how everyone might hate you."

It took him a moment to figure out that she meant "A New Town Is a Blue Town," which was, in his mind, an odd song to focus on. It was harmonically complex, melancholy, and defiant at the same time, and the least like a show tune of any on the record. It was really a kind of art song. Then he got it.

"Is this a blue town for you?" he asked.

"Not anymore," she said. "But until now, every town has been. Every one I've ever lived in. I think there have been seven of them. That song . . . I didn't think that was a feeling anyone else ever had."

In early August, Barty and Toni began to feel hemmed in by Aurora's presence. She was not a nuisance in any particular way—she was just always there. Marius had been teaching her as much of the American songbook as she could digest and seemed to be making progress. But Barty and Toni couldn't really get interested in any of that, and Aurora practiced incessantly, a cappella, since the piano was in Marius and Jonah's house. They were pleased that Marius seemed hopeful that Aurora could be a real singer, but the more vocally confident she became, the more emotionally on edge she seemed, and this had begun to wear on them too. It was as if the songs had become a part of her—full of expectation and heartbreak and loneliness and fulfillment—but none of it was real. They were only songs.

On Saturday afternoon of the second week of August, Marius returned from the record store for Aurora's lesson in a state of anxiety and expectation. After Jonah had gotten a glass of beer in him, he explained that he'd had a visit that morning from Otts Oscard. The name meant nothing to either Jonah or Aurora, but Marius was besotted.

"Otts Oscard and His Debutantes," Marius explained. "God, I first heard them when I was a kid—they were Otts Oscard and His Society Syncopators. Then Syncopators became Swingers about ten years ago, and now they're just Debutantes. Three girl singers. But one of them is suddenly pregnant, and she's gone home to mother."

Otts Oscard had been running a territory band since the late 1920s and was now well into his sixties. These bands in their heyday had crisscrossed the Midwest and the South, playing for dancers in hotel ballrooms and restaurants, on live radio broadcasts and recording sessions, accompanying popular second-tier singers. By the 1950s they were in pitiful decline. The big band sound was fading. Jazz fans had discovered bebop, and pop fans had moved on to Perry Como. In any case, the entire world would soon be done in completely by the electric guitar. But Otts Oscard knew no other life and was continuing to pick up bookings when and where he could. It was a rickety existence, and now he was a Debutante short in Junction City, Kansas; Marius had already put a bug in his ear about Aurora.

"It's a job you can get, because it's not a job anyone wants," Marius told her, honest to a fault. She didn't know whether to be pleased or to cry. But it was—perhaps—a job.

She would audition at the music store downtown on the following Monday night. Marius told her she was about half prepared. She had taken rudimentary piano lessons at a couple of the schools she had attended and came to Marius able to read music passably, but not well. He had spent the summer alternating between the technical—on Saturdays—and the interpretive—on Tuesday evenings. He had spent some time teaching her rudimentary harmony, and they could sing duets with some fluency, though he was inevitably forced into uncomfortable keys because his voice was low. She had never sung in a trio, but they spent a little time in the next several hours listening to the Andrews Sisters and the Boswell Sisters on the record player. Both sets of siblings sounded alarmingly virtuosic to Aurora, though she found the singing completely without feeling.

"That's what he's going to ask you to do though," said Marius. "Trios are all about sound, about sound making people feel happy. Never mind what the lyric is saying. Stay upbeat and on the beat. You'll get it figured out."

They worked for four hours on Sunday. For the first two, all they did was listen.

"Harmony is about your ears," Marius explained. "You can make your voice do what your ear can hear."

And so, Aurora got her fill of the more famous trios. Then Marius played the parts on the piano and Aurora picked out the middle, the bottom, the top, and sang it as if it were a game. By the end of the day, she felt that she would never hate a song as much as she now hated "Bei Mir Bist Du Schon."

On Monday, Aurora went to work in a state of panic. Somehow the day passed—she did no work, and the other stenographers and secretaries concluded that she was in the first day of a painful menstrual cycle but afraid to say so. They covered for her silently and knowingly. That night, as Aurora prepared to set off for downtown, Marius had one other piece of advice.

"Otts Oscard chases women like a dog chases cars," he said. "Like a dog. Stay alert. Don't go places with him alone; don't linger after a performance. He's sixty if he's a day, but in his own mind he's a romantic idol like Rudy Vallée. Irresistible."

"I'm seventeen," Aurora said, quite appalled. "And I don't have the job."

"Tell him you're eighteen," Marius cautioned. "Otherwise, he can't hire you."

In truth, she was three weeks short of the day, and, with luck, no one would ever know the difference. She tried to shake it all off.

Aurora had spent some time at Ogleby's on Saturday afternoons after her lesson. She loved the overstuffed little shop, which featured musical instruments—chiefly pianos, guitars, and mandolins—sheet music, and, best of all, recordings, separated into bins by category in the middle of the store. The light was dim, the walls dark and long unscrubbed, and the place smelled of cardboard and dust. In the back was a small room, barely bigger than a phone booth, in which one could don a set of earphones and hear the latest numbers, played on a record player by Cyrus Ogleby. Cyrus, who seemed moderately beleaguered by having to play these recordings, which she never bought, was a stout little man with a handlebar mustache; his wife, Lottie, who was perpetually perched on a stool at the corner of the glass-topped counter reading the newspaper, was his virtual double, except for the facial hair. She disapproved of Aurora, who never spent any money. The two of them were indifferent shopkeepers, and they knew almost nothing of music, having inherited the place from Cyrus's bachelor uncle in the 1920s, when every reputable family in the area still required a piano in the parlor and a steady supply of sheet music. For expertise, they had come recently to rely on Marius Huwiler, who was neither a great salesman nor a particularly energetic employee. But he knew his stuff.

In the evening, Jonah drove Aurora and Marius to the store. Marius almost didn't come at the last minute, but a stern look from Jonah righted him and he got in the passenger seat. The Oglebys had opened the place up, and Otts Oscard, in a shiny suit and wearing a silk scarf, had brought his two remaining Debutantes with him. He was a theatrical sort, with a voice that he could not adjust to circumstances, so that it always sounded like he was broadcasting to an audience, even in the confines of the music store. His bald head was combed over with a few strands of artificially jet-black hair, and his cheeks sagged sadly. Aurora could hardly imagine how Mr. Huwiler's characterization of him could be true, but she couldn't help noticing that he touched each of the Debutantes whenever possible as he placed them along the back wall. They seemed bored and a little irritated to be working on their night off, not that there would have been much to do in Junction City on a Monday evening. They were well into their thirties, dressed in rayon sundresses, and seemed no more like debutantes than the women in the steno pool at the warehouse. They shook hands with Aurora, and one, who chewed gum while the other smoked Old Golds, raised her eyebrows at her as if to express some utter disbelief at the circumstances. Aurora was unable to interpret the gesture. She didn't know if she was the cause of some irritation or being welcomed into a world of permanent bewilderment.

Otts Oscard handed Aurora a tattered binder of sheet music and then sat at an upright piano along the wall.

"Find one you know," he said, and she settled on "Mr. Sandman," which was on the radio every day that summer.

She took her place between the other two women, and listened to the chord that he played, note by note.

"You're the middle, honey," he said. Aurora looked down at the page and began to sing.

She was far from sure she was on the right notes. She tried to stay a third above the low voice, correcting the sound when the idea of a third seemed like it might make a mess. But as she sang, she realized that she was trying to read the notes from the page—using her eyes—when Marius had so clearly instructed her that trio singing was all about using your ears. As she reached the second chorus of the song—"Mr. Sandman, I'm so alone . . ."—she took a big breath, folded the book shut, and dropped it on the floor. The song, she realized, as the words were slipping out of her mouth, was idiotic. What had happened, she wondered, to popular music? Somehow the question was completely liberating. The song itself became nothing, merely a springboard for whatever sounds she could hear in her head. Listening to the other two Debutantes, she began to sing by instinct, believing that the harmonic world of the moment would suffice if she could just trust it. The three of them made it through the second chorus and a third, one that had the temerity to rhyme Pagliacci with Liberace—God, she hated it—but she sang anyhow: meaningless words that somehow added up to a splendid sound. What it meant she couldn't exactly guess; but the sound created emotion, a simple satisfaction at what harmony was.

She was as relaxed at that moment as she had been anxious all day and all the previous sleepless night. She was, she realized, doing something she knew how to do, perhaps for the very first time in her life. For a moment she believed that it didn't matter what Otts Oscard thought of her, nor even what Marius Huwiler thought. She was flying free in a way that she hadn't since the days of the school bus. The feeling lasted until the number was finished, at which point she looked up at Otts Oscard and discovered that she was suddenly in quite a panic.

Oscard showed her nothing.

"Pick up the book," he said, "And pick another. And this time, read it."

They sang three more terrible songs. Aurora kept the book in her hand and stayed on the right page, but she was faking. The notes swum in front of her eyes, and she sang whatever she sang. At some point she began to believe that Oscard couldn't tell the difference. She made sure never to meet Marius's eyes—a sign of fear or disapproval from him would have finished her, and he had no poker face at all. At the end of the fourth number, the smoking Debutante put down the book.

"Make up your mind, Otts," she said. "I need a drink."

Oscard pulled himself up from the piano and looked hurt.

"I was just beginning to have fun," he said. Then, turning to Aurora, he added, with a casualness that suggested he was enjoying torturing her, "Sing something by yourself."

Aurora froze. Marius walked to the piano.

"May I?" he asked. He sat and played the intro to "A New Town Is a Blue Town." Aurora wanted, at that moment, to marry him and have his children. And she started to sing. She remained completely unaware that this was a man's song—defiant and brash, for all its minor key beauty and pulsing intensity. Perhaps no woman had ever sung it before or would ever sing it again. But she was singing it now, and it was hers.

SHE WAS PAID forty dollars a week and swore that she was eighteen years old. Otts was not fussy about paperwork, and handed it off to the band's road manager, booker, and bookkeeper, a gaunt little man called Monkey Monkton who chewed toothpicks incessantly to keep from smoking. He had a hacking cough and was always stepping out of performances when it overtook him. Besides, he'd been hearing the band's repertoire for years, and wasn't interested in anything but collecting the nightly take and making sure the bus was in working order. He made it clear that he couldn't have cared less if Aurora was eighteen or eighty.

Aurora left Junction City on a Wednesday, after a tearful farewell cookout at Barty and Toni's place. Marius seemed remote for most of the evening but stopped the proceedings as they were about to get up to clear the table.

"I've been thinking of one thing all day," he said. "You can't be Feik."

Aurora looked up at him, confused but expectant.

"No one named Feik can get famous. That just stands to reason."

A silence hung in the air as Aurora considered this. Finally, she spoke. "Shelton," she said. "My name is Aurora Shelton."

All four of the adults turned to her for an explanation.

"My mother's maiden name," she said. "Sometimes I wish she'd been smart enough to keep it."

"You'd never have been born," said Barty.

Aurora had no response to that. "The least I can do is give her back her name," she said. "It's a lot better than having my father's name, that's for sure."

Jonah offered a fulsome toast to the future of Aurora Shelton; he felt he was doing what his partner simply couldn't do, but that was what he had signed on for. Marius all but broke down when he hugged her goodbye. He couldn't speak at all, and Aurora knew enough not to make him try. She remained silent as well and they held each other until Jonah honked the horn—he had to get her to the bus, which pulled out at ten.

On the bus, she realized, for the first time, really, that she would be traveling with a bunch of men—the two remaining Debutantes were the only other women on board. The men came in all ages, all shapes and sizes. They smoked, they drank from flasks, and they played poker incessantly, a flattened cardboard box placed across their laps for a table. But Aurora immediately noticed one who sat alone, a small man looking out the window pensively. She knew him, she thought. She was almost sure he was the man whom she had stopped to listen to all those years earlier, when she was a little girl and the war was on. He had played "Taking a Chance on Love" on the trumpet.

7

THE TRUMPET AND THE WAR

IKE HARRIS HAD taken over the first trumpet chair for Otts Oscard and His Debutantes by a circuitous route, which had begun with his unexpected escape from Michael Feik.

In the summer of 1942, as the brutal torture that was officially known as basic training was beginning to take a significant toll on his weight and health, not to mention his darkening mood, Ike entered the mess hall one evening as the blistering sun was beginning to fade and discovered a sign tacked on the wall.

> Military Band Required
>
> For the celebration of the arrival of General Arthur Klein and his staff at a dinner dance to be held in the USO Tent, building #404.
>
> Any recruit expert at performing music please report to your Staff Sergeant that you are to be excused from afternoon drills August 9 and report to Building 404 with your instrument prepared to rehearse.
>
> Signed,
>
> Alan Alwine, Camp Commander

Ike had no idea who else had seen the sign, but he knew enough to put a stop to the spread of such information. With an unconvincing cough to cover the sound, he tore it from the wall and crumpled it into his pocket. He knew exactly one other trainee at Camp Bullis who played music, piano as it happened, a stooped young Chicago boy named Sid Lupowitz who fancied himself a composer. In the hours before taps (Ike was the bugler), he raced to Lupowitz's tent and dragged him out of a poker game and showed him the sign, and the two of them made the rounds of the camp, scaring up a band. Lupowitz knew musicians because he was always asking them about the nature of their instruments so that he could learn more about how to compose and arrange for an orchestra. He was an annoying character, unwilling to drop any conversation that he could figure out how to prolong, and flush with a confidence in his own genius that bordered on the pathological. He disagreed with anything anyone said, purely for the purpose of trying to advance a more convincing argument from the opposite point of view. He could not be shut up. Ike liked him. He was crazy.

By nine P.M. they had found ten players including a trombonist, a drummer, four sax players—one of them also proficient on clarinet—two violinists, another trumpeter, and a flautist who could double on piccolo. With Ike on lead trumpet and Sid Lupowitz conducting from the piano, they were now a band.

Others had perhaps seen the notice as well, but Ike and Sid were able to actually rehearse for two days after training hours in an abandoned barn on the outer edges of the camp's property. Passion for escape from the sun drove them all with equal intensity. Sid wrote out lead sheets and primitive arrangements for three Sousa marches, and Ike was able to notate "I Could Write a Book," which he remembered from *Pal Joey*, for dancing. For good measure they threw in "Deep in the Heart of

Texas," which they thought would get a laugh, since that's where they were, and they couldn't imagine that General Arthur Klein, whoever he might be, would be any happier about being there than they were.

They won the job without serious competition. A week after the dinner dance, the entire band received orders that they were being transferred to Newport News, Virginia, General Klein's home base, to be, in effect, the house band for the local USO and the entertainers for whatever social events General Klein could think up. Ike Harris never saw Michael Feik again, and never marched in formation again, either.

The band in Newport News developed into a crack aggregation, especially as the players seemed to have relatively few other duties. General Klein became their protector. He was a corpulent man given to shorts, socks, and sandals, who seemed to have somehow worked his way through the ranks to the point where he functioned independently as social director for a camp whose only purpose was to house prisoners of war, of which there were but few, all of them Italians. They were headquartered a half mile away, and one of the few things that the band members had to do besides rehearse and play was to guard the prison barracks in shifts. Ike enjoyed this more than the others because he still had a little Italian from his European youth, and with practice, more of it came back to him. He was grateful that the German murderers who were captured and sent to the States were so far being quartered somewhere else, where he didn't have to think about what he would do to them if he ever got his hands on them. He was aware that the Italians were also the enemy. But they were different somehow, just Italian kids—many barely twenty. It was hard to hate them.

General Klein, who took a liking to Ike Harris, was in business for himself where music was concerned, and he loaned the band out to other gigs, sending them by rickety bus to play for dances, most of them not even on army bases. Ike and Sid quickly understood that the general was being paid cash money for their services, none of which ever found its way into their hands, but it was a hell of a lot better than marching. Guilt nagged at Ike that there were soldiers—hundreds of thousands of American boys—who were being sent overseas to fight and die, but what could he do? For all intents and purposes, he belonged to General Klein.

After a couple of months of playing weekend gigs at country clubs and Masonic halls, Ike approached the general and asked to speak with him privately. Klein smiled tersely, not sure what was coming, or whether to be annoyed by it.

"This is an excellent arrangement," Ike said to him. "The boys all want you to know how appreciative they are."

Klein nodded, silent.

"We're not asking for anything," he assured the general. "You've given us more than enough already."

"I appreciate that," said Klein, still not sure what was coming.

"The thing is," Ike said, "one day the war will be over. All I've ever wanted to be is a musician. I understand musicians. But I can see that for a man like you, there are certain other activities that you're an expert at. These activities could be useful to a musician like me. Booking a band, understanding how to do business with people who want to hire musicians. If a player understood the listener, the customer—which is the dance hall or the ballroom—and also understood the point of view of the band members, well, that could be a useful pair of skills. I would like to learn from you."

The general looked at Ike for a long time.

"You want to be my partner?" he asked.

"Your apprentice, sir," Ike said. "Just your apprentice. Your unpaid apprentice. That's all I ask."

From that point on, the general hid nothing from Ike in terms of how the business was conducted and was soon letting Ike negotiate deals with surrounding bookers and managers. Nothing was ever said about the band's status as a military outfit. No one asked, and everyone seemed to understand that in hard times, times of war you might say, people did what they had to do. The band, which changed its name for every gig, played dance music and hot jazz, using stock arrangements that Ike and Sid would request from the general, who would order them from a music store in Baltimore. Sid goosed them up with a few tricks of the imagination, and soon the band had a kind of sound of its own. General Klein was happy.

Within a couple of months, it seemed to all of them that, in an unpredictable time and place, they had arrived at a relatively permanent sense of security within the military establishment. General Klein was gradually earning enough money to buy himself a decent-sized house when the war was over, and Ike Harris was gaining expertise that would serve him as a contractor for the rest of his days, while perfecting a hot trumpet style that no one, at least no one in the vicinity of Newport News, Virginia, could compete with. Sid Lupowitz introduced a few original compositions into the repertoire, and the band played on.

It was an Atlanta saxophone player named Poke Belmore who first brought some reefer into the band's barracks, which also changed the mood in a pleasant way. Shortly after this, Ike reported to General Klein with a requisition request for two dozen blue lightbulbs, which the band members hoped would create a more suitable atmosphere after hours. Klein looked at him skeptically.

"Blue lightbulbs?" He asked. "For what use—blue lightbulbs?"

"For the purpose of inspiring better and more music," Ike said. "What do you care for what use blue lightbulbs?"

The lightbulbs were delivered the next day.

It was under these bulbs that Sid Lupowitz, the most compulsive of the band members, began to sort through each new bag of marijuana that Poke Belmore delivered, separating the seeds from the leaves and stems. Sid was concerned that the meager legitimate money they were all being paid to help win the war was being pooled and squandered on reefer when it should be perfectly easy to grow the stuff in the dirt behind the barracks for free. Within a month, some sorry-looking plants were lined up like a dying army out back. But nothing could be harvested, and nothing survived for long.

One night while staring, quite stoned, at the pathetic rows of plants behind their home, one of the more sentimental soldiers—the violinist with bad teeth and skin—declared that their labor had produced what looked like a crop of dehydrated prisoners of war, waiting to die or be sent home.

"I ache for them," he said. "May the Lord have mercy on their narcotic souls."

The band members sat in baleful resignation, gazing at the row of dying plants like a proper bunch of mourners.

"The Italians," Ike said suddenly, not necessarily meaning to say it aloud.

The band members turned to him.

"The Italians," he repeated, now warming to the idea. "The Italian prisoners of war know how to grow things. The Jews are chicken farmers, but the Italians grow vegetables, don't they? Tomatoes? They're Italians."

The next day, on guard duty, he put his language skills to the test and rounded up a trio of young Italian prisoners of war who had grown up on dirt farms in Calabria. He handed them an envelope of seeds. He explained that the plants, once harvested, would belong to the band, but that the all the prisoners would receive extra rations of food—good food from the outside world, with special treatment for the three farmers, including red wine, if the harvest was good. The food and wine could, with a little pre-negotiation, be brought back from the various bars and dance halls the band would be visiting on a regular basis, and while the plants remained unnamed, the Italians knew enough not to ask.

It was an excellent arrangement. The Calabrians proved extraordinarily green-thumbed, and, Ike suspected, were somehow grinding up the base's kitchen waste to make a fertilizer—an idea that would never have occurred to him. By the end of Ike's first nine months in Newport News there was a thriving marijuana farm growing in enriched government soil. The Italians were reasonably well fed, and the band, after much discussion and dispute, was known as Ike Harris's Kings of Rhythm. Sid Lupowitz was not happy but understood that his name was too Jewish to be heading up a jazz band in the American South.

FROM THE BEGINNING of this adventure, it was, of course, doomed. As the war ground on, General Klein's ambition began to grow into a kind of alarming hubris. He arrived one night and entered a haze-drenched barracks lit only in dim blue bulbs. The place had begun to resemble an opium den in a B movie about the Tong wars. He had the good graces to ignore the obvious and announced, "Men! You've been entered into the military band competition in Washington, D.C. You will report to rehearsal tomorrow at 0800 hours in Building 118 and depart for Washington by rail at noon. You will be in uniform, right and proper, with your eyes focused, your instruments polished, and your knapsacks packed for a five-day furlough to our nation's capital. You will win the competition, or each and every one of you will find yourself on the front lines trying to remember how to use a rifle before someone uses one on you. Do I make myself clear?"

He didn't wait for a reply, and none was forthcoming. Ike Harris and his Kings of Rhythm were left stunned and at a loss as to how to respond. They were not a military band. They were a dance band, a jazz band, a big band. It had been a long time since any of them had looked at a Sousa march or "Off We Go, Into the Wild Blue Yonder." They were used to having the wild blue yonder come to them.

Washington, however, proved a fitting adventure, and, for Ike, a golden opportunity to hear better bands. They were quartered in a salesman's hotel near the Pentagon. At night, they were bused to a large auditorium, where they tried, pathetically, to compete with large aggregations of brilliantly trained musicians who played everything from classical music to marches to popular songs of the day. Half the bands were Black and half were white; the color line was never crossed. The integrated army was still five years away.

The ragtag Kings of Rhythm were seated at one side of the stage while a large and brilliantly precise band of Black musicians ran through the usual repertoire. The crowd assembled for the contest wouldn't let them go. They were just too good. Clearly, Ike could see, as the bandleader looked around at the men behind him, they had not planned for an encore, and had nothing prepared. After a moment of confusion, the leader called over his shoulder, "Royal Garden Blues," and began to stomp off a tempo with his left foot. He sat at the piano and banged out a four-bar intro, after which the band launched into a performance that Ike knew at once was entirely improvised. It was glorious to hear—a band of forty creating a polyphonic masterpiece out of thin air. The crowd began to whoop and shout. At a certain point, Ike was overcome with desire. He would never forgive himself, he knew, if he let the moment pass. As the band came to the end of a chorus, he shot out of his seat, put his trumpet to his lips and began to do his best Tommy Ladnier imitation.

The leader looked at him, flummoxed, and then turned to the band to hush them down to a simple, rhythmic background beat and let them comp along, so that the soloist could shine. For the audience, the sight was startling—a little white man standing in front of an all-Black band shooting notes skyward. In Ike's mind, the notes were bouncing off the barrel-vaulted ceiling of Le Cave de la Heure d'Or. He played a chorus and didn't know how he had played it. He saw Ladnier on the bed, old before his time and toothless, reaching for a cup and spitting into it. The notes he played bent and danced and wailed and mourned as he replayed Ladnier's sad decline. He did his best to tell the story that might need no words, and send a greeting up to heaven, where Ladnier no doubt now resided. As he drew to a close, the bandleader was ready, cueing the band into the shout chorus—all men at full volume—that landed the number on the moon. There was nothing else anyone could have played after that.

As the bands were packing up behind the auditorium, the Black bandleader approached Ike, who was now thinking that he had overstepped himself; no Black player would have done that to a white band or bandleader. He didn't know quite what had gotten into him. He was on point of apologizing when the leader spoke first.

"I been telling everybody for two years now," he said, "that the only good thing in the world about a segregated army is that I get all the best players."

"It's true," Ike said.

"Now, we're not gonna win this contest. No Negro band is gonna win this contest. But it doesn't matter—we still got all the best players. Till you come along." He stuck his hand out. "Charlie Vodery," he said.

Ike introduced himself, still not sure if Charlie Vodery was pleased or annoyed.

"You've got a hell of a band," he said.

"Yes, I do," Vodery said. "The best. But you—you play Tommy Ladnier better than Tommy Ladnier ever played himself."

"Thank you," Ike said, feeling slightly better.

"That's what you're supposed to do, one generation down," Vodery said, giving away nothing. "If you hadn't played it as well as you did, I'd have to kill you. But now I don't have to do that. Maybe I'll see you on the other side of the war."

He turned on his heels and walked off. Ike watched him go, not at all reassured.

BACK IN NEWPORT NEWS, things had undergone a complete transformation in five days. General Klein was nowhere to be found. The marijuana farm had been scorched into nonexistence as if General Sherman had marched through on his way to the sea. The Italians were nowhere in sight either, and an entire battalion of German prisoners had replaced them. The blue lightbulbs were all that remained in the empty barracks.

A General William Knudsen was occupying General Klein's quarters. He had neither a sense of music nor a sense of humor. Ike found himself standing in front of the general's desk at 0800 the morning after the band's return from D.C.

"As far as I can tell," the general said, "you organized this so-called band. Did you benefit financially from it?"

"No, sir," said Ike.

"Did you consider that you were following orders when you went and played where General Klein told you to?"

"Yes, sir."

Knudsen looked at him hard. Ike stood at attention. Half a minute went by, as Knudsen waited to see if Ike would volunteer anything. Ike was not about to do so.

"The members of your so-called band," Knudsen said, "are being reassigned as I speak. You won't see them again."

"Yes, sir," Ike said. "May I ask?"

"What is it?"

"Where am I being reassigned?"

Knudsen sighed unhappily, as if he'd lost an argument and hadn't yet gotten over it.

"Some damn fool heard you play at that contest in D.C.," he said. "You're being assigned to Pershing's Own. That is all."

Ike saluted, turned, and took a deep breath. Pershing's Own. That was the official United States Army Band. The band. They'd been making records since the 1920s. They also spent considerable time overseas, sometimes in the line of fire, which was a concern. But for now, the palmy days were done. He was really in the army. But in a band—the official band.

The rest of his friends from the Kings of Rhythm were nowhere to be found, and he knew enough not to ask after them. He got his kit together and reported to a transport that took him from Newport News to Hampton Roads, where Pershing's Own boarded the SS *Mariposa*. A week later, Ike found himself in Casablanca.

For the next two years, until the war ended, he played concerts in North Africa, entertained the troops during the Rhineland campaign, and performed in hastily constructed entertainment tents in England as troops were gathering for the Normandy invasion. He played in hospitals and in opera houses. He was strafed in Antwerp and accompanied Lily Pons in Paris. Later on, when he tried to add it up, he calculated that he had played the trumpet for between eight hundred and nine hundred hours over a two-year period without ever playing a piece he really gave a damn about. He was proud to have raised some spirits though.

In 1945, he left Europe, sadly having neglected several opportunities to lose his virginity. He was back in New York for Thanksgiving, age twenty-one, honorably discharged, eating turkey and stuffing prepared by Estelle Dunmore with his mother, who was becoming a genuinely old woman, and Count Palaffi, who had by now run through more than half of her money.

IKE TOOK UP virtual residence at the union hall, showing up daily and playing pinochle with a raft of unemployed musicians, many of them recently returned veterans. A measle of a man named Isaiah Monkton came by once a week looking for small bands for weddings, Bar Mitzvahs, christening parties, high school reunions, and other marginalia. Ike wasn't proud. He took fifty dollars from Ollie and let Monkton beat him out of every penny over three weeks of pinochle. That, apparently, was enough to get him hired.

"You can't be that bad a card player," Monkton said to him as he handed him a slip of paper with the address where his first postwar gig would take place. "But I appreciate the commission. They call me Monkey," he said.

Within weeks, Ike found himself playing an unending string of weddings in an unmemorable series of hotel ballrooms. On nights when he didn't work, he was able, occasionally, to take in a show, which is how he found himself standing in line at the box office of the Martin Beck waiting to buy a ticket for a Harold Arlen vehicle called *St. Louis Woman* behind a pretty, originally dressed young woman in a red felt hat cocked at a slightly sinister angle, and brown corduroy slacks. She was engaged in a heated discussion with the box office treasurer, who was refusing to take a personal check for a ticket. The performance was about to begin, and Ike hated the idea of missing a downbeat, still stirred by memories of the *Pal Joey* overture all those years later.

"Excuse me," he said, "let me pay for a pair of tickets; you can write me a personal check and we won't be late. I want to see the house lights dim."

The woman turned and looked at him. She smiled. "What if the check bounces?" she asked, indicating the man in the box office. "That's what this guy thinks will happen."

"Then I will have taken you to the theater," Ike said. "But it won't bounce."

As it turned out, the overture was thrilling, and Arlen had penned a couple of tunes that Ike wanted to put to use immediately, especially one called "Come Rain or Come Shine" that cried out for a trumpet solo. But the rest of the show was a shambles. Ike realized for the first time that it was possible to have a disappointing night at the theater. But he had met Missy Cozzens, whose check proved good. They spent a couple of weeks going to the movies and dancing and necking at Coney Island, but no more than that. She wasn't free with her body or her favors. It was not for her. She seemed to Ike a little sad, a little lost, a little angry, but good-hearted and smart. She wasn't the kind of woman you would meet on the road with a band. She worked in an advertising agency—a business she hated with a viciousness that seemed unnecessarily harsh to Ike—and wanted to be a news writer for a radio station, though no one was eager to let a woman have such a job in 1946. Ike felt for her, which didn't stop him from kissing her goodbye each night they met and leaving it at that.

Gradually his fortunes shifted, no thanks to Monkey Monkton. It was Poke Belmore, the sax player who had introduced Ike to both marijuana and blue lightbulbs, who provided the opportunity with a phone call. After the war, Belmore had returned home and found himself holding down the first saxophone chair with the Bobby Sherwood Orchestra, which traipsed through the South on a specially outfitted bus. The band had landed in Memphis for an extended engagement on the rooftop terrace of the Peabody Hotel, and one night the lead trumpet player ran off with the daughter of the hotel's general manager. Neither could be found, and twenty-four hours later Ike Harris found himself in Memphis playing society band arrangements with a not-bad band for decent money. He promised Missy Cozzens he would keep in touch, and it nagged at him that he only rarely did.

In the morning after his first performance in Memphis, he walked down to a one-arm joint on Beale Street, which was only a couple of blocks away, for breakfast. Seated at the counter he was attended to by a blond waitress who looked, for all the world, like she had stepped out of a Norman Rockwell illustration in *The Saturday Evening Post*. Her blouse was starched and featured an aqua and yellow checked trimmed collar and breast pocket. A matching plaid cloche covered her hairnet. A name tag pinned through the plaid patch at the top half of her pocket identified her as Laine. Ike found her adorably southern, a curiosity from a faraway land.

On his second morning back at the diner he worked up the courage to speak to her.

"How'd you get that name?" he asked her as she was refilling her coffee cup. "That's an unusual name."

"My mother's maiden name," she said. "She was a Laine and my daddy's a Canby."

"So, you're Laine Canby," Ike said. Good detective work there.

"Yes, I am," she said. "And you're a good trumpet player."

It developed that Laine Canby had two jobs. She was a waitress in the morning and the hat-check girl at the Peabody rooftop at night. Sometimes they let her sell cigarettes and take pictures of the customers, which paid a little better. And she liked music.

After a week of breakfasts, accompanied by a mild amount of chitchat, Ike was surprised when, as he slipped fifty cents under the coffee saucer for a tip, Laine Canby swept it up and replaced it with a small brown envelope.

"I had this made for you," she said. "Don't open it here."

Ike was puzzled but flattered. He returned to the hotel and went up to his room, which he shared with two reed players; it was empty at the moment. Lying back on the bed, he opened the seal on the little envelope. Inside was a small black-and-white photograph of Laine Canby, naked. Ike's heart jumped in surprise. She was posed on a settee, not in any kind of professional cheesecake pose, but sitting primly, as she might in a formal portrait. Ike looked away, and then decided it was her intention that he be invited to stare. She had beautiful shoulders and breasts, her nipples small and erect. A wild thatch of thick pubic hair suggested to him a wildness of spirit, though he realized that there could be no causal connection. And yet, there must have been a wildness of spirit that inspired this unusual courting technique. He wondered if she had ever done this before for anyone else and decided that it made no difference. His eyes worked their way down the photo to her ankles, slender and primly crossed. It was an altogether paradoxical piece of work—a picture of a debutante who had forgotten to dress before posing, as in a dream that he might have had.

That night he stepped off the bandstand between sets and moved to the hat-check booth, and there she was. He had puzzled over what to say to her besides "Thank you," but had come up with nothing satisfactory. Everything that passed through his mind was either too wolfish or too timid. He was at a loss.

"Hello," she said, an opening bid.

"I wanted to thank you for the picture," he said. "You are a beautiful sight."

"Thank you," she said, "I had it made only for you."

This was an invitation to an invitation, and this was where the conversation, in Ike's mind, had always stalled. Now he was on the spot and said the only thing that came into his mind.

"Would you like to go to the movies sometime?"

She looked at him for a moment in shock, and then burst out laughing. "The movies?" she said.

Having begun down the path, he had nowhere to turn. "Tomorrow," he said. "After you get off at the diner. We could . . . get to know each other."

"Now that sounds like fun," she said.

But there were customers behind Ike, and she signaled to him with her eyes that he'd better step away.

THEY DID NOT go to the movies. She had a little apartment on the second floor of a building on Gayoso Avenue that she shared with two roommates who worked until six. When she got off at the diner after the lunch rush, they had exactly four and a half hours before he would leave her alone to dress for the evening hat-check gig while he went back to the hotel room to get into his tux and grab his horn. It was during these few hours a day, every day for almost a month, that Ike Harris learned whatever he could about satisfying an eager lover.

He was awkward, and then, after a few days, he was not, and yet he was never sure that he was really pleasing her or getting things right. He had no idea if she was having orgasms or not; she didn't complain or communicate on the subject. But it was not until the second week of their regular encounters that she uttered the phrase that would change his entire way of thinking about women and sex. They were tangled in a top sheet on the bed kissing when he worked up the courage to pull away and asked her if his touch was too rough or not vigorous enough or somehow off-base. Something was not quite right, and he thought he might as well confront it.

"What do you really like best?" he asked, made confident enough to ask it by a week of compliant sighs and moans, but still unconvinced.

"When you play me like a trumpet solo," she said. "Just play me."

Just play me like a trumpet solo. From that moment on, every encounter provided the potential for inspired improvisation. There were no good or bad notes in the scale, only the right or wrong notes, which he had the joy and the privilege of trying to differentiate. It was the music of the body set free from whatever notes might have been on the page.

Truth to tell, he had, in the past, sometimes thought of the idea of a woman as the trumpet in his hands, but never once considered the idea that she was, instead, the music it might play. The world opened to him, and he improved. He and Laine Canby became virtuosic lovers, and yet, somehow, never fell in love. Perhaps it had all happened just too easily. Perhaps there was something about the slightly sordid reality of the stolen hours that bothered them both. Sometimes he wondered if the photo was a first for her; she swore it was, but who knew what she had done in the past? Perhaps it was something about her provincial life that he hated himself for not being able to forgive. She was a poor girl with a spotty education, no knowledge of the world and not much curiosity about it. Nothing wrong in that, he told himself—she was young, lovely, of an endlessly positive turn of mind, and a generous spirit. What more could he ask? Why was it important to him that she read books or newspapers?

There was something else, something she had said casually, that, in the end, made it impossible.

Drowsing in bed one afternoon, dreading the moment to come when they'd both rise and head for work, she asked him, "Does this place bother you? Kind of run down."

"Not at all," he responded, for the place itself didn't.

"If I had the money," she said, "I'd have my own restaurant—a café, more like. I'd treat the customers nice, treat the help nice, make up the recipes, make the pies myself. I can bake a mean pie. And I'd want a nice little house somewhere, farther out to the east, you know? Not so close to niggertown."

He remained silent. He had no idea how to react. This was her city, her culture, her heritage. He only knew that he couldn't ever be a part of it.

They parted friends when the band hit the road. She wasn't really in love with him either. The idea of a final time, one last farewell fuck, seemed somehow ridiculous to them both, hefting a meaning onto their relationship that simply wasn't there; it had never arrived. They went to the movies.

THE BAND MOVED ON, and Ike moved on. From Poke, he learned where all the other army musicians had gotten to, and reestablished contact with them all. They introduced him to others. At noon each day he made phone calls from wherever he was—as expensive as long distance was—and hunted for bands with suddenly missing trumpet players, or players whose behavior, drug and alcohol consumption, or all-consuming need to indulge in romantic chaos was, or would soon, create a vacancy. Better bands wanted him. Art Mooney took him on. Then Tony Pastor. He crisscrossed the country a dozen times, playing in clubs, ballrooms, and movie theaters, where, in major cities like Chicago and Kansas City, the big bands played a short set between features. The work was good, but never secure, and less than a career. Ike began to place other musicians in other bands, and when bands needed players, the leaders would call him for suggestions. He was contracting without really knowing it. When Pastor's band was laid off in Syracuse, Ike got his piano chops back in order by taking a job at the best local brothel in town, where he was paid in trade, and given a place to sleep during the day.

It was an instructive time. Women who had sex for money, he discovered, couldn't be played like music, and couldn't play, not really. Everything he did seemed to thrill them beyond any reasonable expectation. Some were better actors than others, but it was impossible to divine, even as he became friendly with them, what might actually please them, or where their minds wandered when they thought of love. Wherever that may have been, they had lost hold of it, or were saving it for someone else. He became sad for them, and unsure about himself. There was no real pleasure, he feared, on either side. And everywhere was the whiff of the transactional that seemed inimical to intimacy. As Ike continued to make calls, he wondered if the same thing might happen with music. That was the risk he feared most of all. He saw the women at their nightly work, and he knew, empathically, that the indifference and bravura fakery must never happen between him and his trumpet.

By this point he had shared himself with many women—singers, fans, hotel workers, a small army of band followers who turned up in every city. There had been a dental hygienist and a bookkeeper, and more than one housewife. The pleasure of it was transient but lovely, and often sweet. The partings were sad, but never tragic. This was the world he was in; the trumpet played twelve notes, with bends and smears in between. And yet, anything magnificent, blistering, bluesy, even funny, could be made from those simple tools—placed in the right hands. The physical act of love was no different. The tools were simple, yet the promise of invention was infinite. But in Syracuse, it all died somehow, for him and for the women. It was like being back in Pershing's Own, playing military marches. He packed up and went home.

IN 1953, he got a call from Tommy Dorsey's manager. He was playing in a television band in Detroit at the time, for a variety show called *Goin' Steady*, hosted by Betty Clooney, who was trying to build a career that could match her sister Rosemary. It was not to happen. Betty was watched over by her uncle Henry Guilfoyle, who was charged by the family with keeping her on the straight and narrow path, like the good Kentucky Baptist that she was. He had been thoroughly failing at this job for some time by the time Ike arrived and joined the band, but Betty Clooney never showed the slightest interest in him. She preferred what she called "the Latin type."

Dorsey, it turned out, spread a wide net, especially when in search of a key player. Where his first trumpet man had gone Ike had no idea, but the job was open. He flew to New York and auditioned for Dorsey and a couple of other key players. Notably absent was Tommy's older brother Jimmy, who had rejoined the band after swearing he would never do so. He and his brother didn't like each other, and Jimmy had gone off on his own for a few years, but the era was ending, and there wasn't room for two Dorsey bands anymore. Tommy was the bigger star, and Jimmy came home with his tail between his legs, though he would never admit it, and took a gig in his younger brother's band.

The music was glorious, but the situation was unendingly stressful for Ike, and for everyone. As they toured the bigger venues around the country, neither brother called the other by name, and they barely spoke. When one referred to the other he would simply call him "the brother." They sat down to break bread together only when their mother came to visit, during which time both brothers were full of bonhomie, which vanished as soon as she was safely out of earshot.

Playing Tommy's tricky, balls-out arrangements did something to Ike's heartbeat. He could feel it in his chest cavity, which seemed to expand to its limits with a strange combination of satisfaction and fear—on one hand, it was almost competitive to run riot with these other players. On the other hand, it was close to pure glory—pure perfection, which arrived and fled with each number they played. Tommy liked tension, and not only in his personal life. There was no set program for the band. He would call titles out and then immediately count them off as the musicians scrambled madly through their books to find sheet music. If somebody in the band clammed a note, Tommy would rehearse the entire band after the nightly gig was over, keeping them playing at full gallop until three or four in the morning, at which point he would turn and say, "Goodnight, shit-heels." He was always the first man out of the room. One night, during a four-bar trumpet rest, Ike pulled the horn away and said to his boss, half-joking, "How long do I have to be in this fucking band before I can relax?"

"When you're fired, you'll relax," Dorsey replied, as the

music swung on and Ike got the trumpet back to his lips, barely in time.

It all came crashing down in New York, at the Café Rouge in the Hotel Pennsylvania. The hotel paid New York scale, but the Dorsey band worked for double scale, and the musicians were told that they would be paid half of what they were used to. For Ike, it was too big an insult. He demanded a meeting with Dorsey and the band's manager, a heavyset, largely silent goon named Carmine Segretto. Segretto loomed over Ike, his heavy eyebrows hooding his half-closed eyes. Dorsey sat behind him in an expensive suit, gazing out the window.

"Ever since I joined this band," Ike said, "Everyone tells me we're the New York Yankees of Swing."

"We are," said Dorsey, now looking Ike in the eyes.

"So, you're gonna pay us like we're the Brooklyn Dodgers?" Ike asked.

"That's right," said Segretto. "It's New York scale."

Ike thought about his months with General Klein, and everything he had learned about negotiation and keeping the conversation going, playing for what you can get, keeping it all within the realistic bounds of the possible. Today, it just didn't resonate.

"Fuck it, I quit," said Ike. And he turned to go.

"So long, shit-heel," Dorsey said quietly. "Now you can relax."

Quite quickly, Ike realized that he was not simply out of work—he was blackballed. Dorsey had waning power as the big bands faded out, but he remained a giant in the music business and was not to be crossed. When he said "relax," he apparently meant that Ike would have no choice. Suddenly no one would hire him. His calls about other players went unreturned. Just shy of his thirtieth birthday, with nothing but time on his hands and not much to show for the preceding years, he moved back in with Ollie and the Count. He had been on the road since he left the army and had never needed a place of his own.

This gave him an opportunity, however, to return to the place he had once felt was his natural habitat, and to turn back, if not with a full heart, to Missy Cozzens, whom he now knew had shed the ad agency and was working as a press agent's assistant for the New York branch of the Socialist Party of America.

It was in the spring of 1953 that he escorted Missy to the 46th Street Theatre for one of the last performances of *Guys and Dolls*. Things in the district had not changed so very much. The Camel cigarette sign had moved to the east side of Seventh Avenue and now featured a smiling man who blew real smoke rings. Pepsi had replaced Coke above the neon-lit island that formed Duffy Square above the Latin Quarter, and a new, giant lighted sign advertised Admiral televisions, a product that hadn't even existed when Ike had been a regular guest in the pit of the Ethel Barrymore. Lorenz Hart had died, and Richard Rodgers was now writing with Oscar Hammerstein, but their new show, *Me and Juliet*, was a disappointment, or so it was said.

As for Missy Cozzens, she was still unstylishly original in her clothes, still sad, still spending too much time typing. Ike was in his fourth month of unemployment, with a dwindling supply of money and no real prospects. For a brief moment it seemed they might be soulmates. They shared a room at the Hotel Astor, a room that overlooked Broadway and all of that lit-up, commercial splendor. There were too many cocktails. It was a bluesy, slightly bewildered kind of night, by the end of which he had realized that Missy Cozzens had a knack for feeling mistreated—by her employer, her parents, her roommates, and even, on the night they had met years earlier, the treasurer of the Martin Beck Theatre.

"I still don't understand why he wouldn't take a check," she said, putting her head on his shoulder.

"Company policy," Ike said. "It wasn't about you, I promise."

"I know," she said, "and then sometimes it feels like it was about me. I was good for the money."

Ike was silent, and a little bored. They made plans for the weekend, and he returned home to his mother's place after buying Missy an early breakfast at Childs. She had to be at work at nine.

There was a phone message for him in Estelle Dunmore's large, loopy hand. He was to call a Mr. Monkton, long-distance in Omaha, Nebraska.

Monkey Monkton had fallen as far as Ike, though perhaps from a lower perch. For reasons he had no desire to go into, he was persona non grata with Local 802 in New York, and had found himself adrift in the Midwest, finally hooking up with one of the last of a dying breed: Otts Oscard. The band was finishing an engagement in Omaha with a local trumpet player who wasn't willing to leave home. Things were tough, as always.

"What makes you think you're allowed to hire me?" Ike asked. "Dorsey saw to it that no one would ever hire me again."

"Fuck that," said Monkey. "You should have lost a couple of pinochle hands to him. You think he's checking up on who plays trumpet for Otts Oscard and His Debutantes?"

"Well," Ike said, "when you put it that way . . ."

"Get your ass out here. At least you won't starve."

Gratefully, Ike broke his date with Missy Cozzens; he was

glad to have the excuse. She took it reasonably well, though not without mentioning that he, at least, now had the kind of job he wanted, while she still yearned for a similar fate.

A month later, Ike was sitting on Otts Oscard's bus, staring out the window and thinking about all the women he had known, all the time he had spent, joyfully, sweetly, gratefully, all of that pleasure and all of those faces, arms, breasts, and thighs, the voices, the accents, and the ideas he had heard from then and thought about and rejected and accepted. Women had taught him what the world was, more than the army, more than his mother, more than music. Women had taught him everything, even, with Missy, about disappointment. At the same time, he conceded there was always a price to pay for happiness.

A young lady, surely no more than eighteen, took a seat next to him. She was, he surmised, the replacement debutante, her young, open face free from makeup, her hair in a simple ponytail. He was drawn inexorably and without explanation to a feature he had never before paid much attention to in any woman: her wrists and forearms, as slender and sculpted as a doe's forelegs when it is just beginning to walk. His heart nearly broke at the beauty and vulnerability of them. Was it simply that she represented a challenge to all the jaded, disappointed, exhausted men on that bus, he wondered, or was there more to it than that? As he tried to look away from her and back at the view out the window, she settled one of her arms down on the armrest between them, and he swiftly removed his own forearm and let it rest in his lap. He did his best not to stare at the narrow expanse of pale skin, because he was thinking about the price. Of all those women in all those cities all over America: Why was Missy Cozzens the one who was pregnant?

8

DEPARTURE

I*T WAS HARDLY* surprising that in the six years Ike Harris and Vincent Donnelly had both worked at the Winter Garden Theatre they had never actually met. Ike worked virtually underground, in the orchestra pit, while Vincent spent his working hours in midair, training a follow spot on the actors from the lighting grid. Within the building, they were in different universes. They were also, among other things, in different unions.

But Vincent was nothing if not a union man, and his arrival at the Winter Garden had been paid for in time and sweat. After his encounter back in the Maspeth factory with Conley, with his union card in hand, he was sent to a warehouse, which everyone called "the shop," to rack and rerack various lighting instruments and pull them for productions that needed them. His hours were better, and the pay was, for the first time, respectable, but it was backbreaking work, no different than loading bricks or cinder blocks. The fact that a lot of the lights he was hauling were of his own invention didn't help.

But Vincent had long since learned that opportunity, when it came, would be the serendipitous confluence of hard work, good luck, and an idea. Who knew where ideas came from? A rusty bent nail in an old fishing pier could be the beginning of an idea. So, he worked. Although the union, Local One of the International Alliance of Theatrical Stage Employees, encouraged no such pace, within a couple of months, Vincent Donnelly could load a show into a truck faster and more accurately than anyone else, and he just as quickly learned the equipment needs of shows that were sending out multiple touring companies, so that when a tour manager showed up to supervise the load for a production of *Annie Get Your Gun*, *Carousel*, *Wish You Were Here*, or *The Pajama Game*, Vincent didn't even need to look at the lighting plot. He made sure that the operator, whomever it might be, was aware that he didn't need to—he had it memorized. He was ahead of the game. He was, in the words of Antoine Berget, a "bright boy."

Antoine Berget was a bottom-of-the-barrel presenter. He took out the cheapest, fastest-moving tours of aging hit shows that he could manage, which perhaps explained his name and the obsessive care he took with his person. He was, as the shop foreman Tim Donovan described him, "gay as a daisy in May," and there's no doubt that neither of his names were real. Behind his back, Antoine Berget was known as Iggy Bronkowitz, though no one knew where that name came from either. Some wag in the shop had made it up years earlier. No matter. The billing was "Antoine Berget Presents," and what it meant was that there would be no stars and not much scenery, a cut-down orchestra, rented costumes from some previous tour—and "popular prices" for tickets. Mostly his productions played split weeks—the front half in Omaha, the weekend in Wichita, followed by Des Moines and Iowa City, and on around the country for the thirty-six good touring weeks, traveling by bus and truck, laying off in the summer, and then beginning again.

Berget never spent a dime he didn't have to on his shows,

which allowed for his magnificent Hong Kong suits; he maintained an immaculate Van Dyke beard, which gave him a vaguely Mephistophelean look, and in addition to his cheapskate budgets, it was assumed that he was stealing from the take as well, though no one had ever proved it. He was a striking presence on a shop floor filled with men in blue jeans and T-shirts scuttling around with equipment over their shoulders or on rolling pallets. Vincent caught his eye almost at once, because a bright boy was someone who wanted to get somewhere, and Antoine Berget knew, from experience, that those kinds were useful. He couldn't keep them long, by and large, but while he had them, they made his life easier. After observing Vincent's unflagging energy and dedication, he stopped him in the middle of a workday on the shop loading dock.

"Kid," he said.

Vincent looked up, as if the moment he had been waiting on for almost two years had taken him by surprise.

"This plot doesn't quite fill a truck, and I've been thinking. Might it be carried in half a truck?" Berget spoke slowly, as if contemplating the exact nature of the universe, though the question was simple enough.

"Half a truck," Vincent replied. "You want me to reorganize it?

"If I could get it in half a truck, you see, I could use the other half for costumes and props, and if I could organize those a little bit better, I might save a whole truck." His speech slowed even further, as if he were communicating some great and ancient wisdom that might take time for the young man to absorb, but Vincent knew better than to finish his sentences for him. The man whom so many referred to as a pompous crook was Vincent's ramp to the highway of life. He was to be taken utterly seriously.

"If I save myself a truck," Berget explained, "it would be

profitable. Can you calculate what it costs to run a truck around this great country of ours for a year? It costs money."

Vincent thought about the way the lights were rigged and loaded, and the racks that held them. He realized he could easily pack them more tightly and accomplish Berget's goal, but it seemed to him that there was a better way to prove his utility.

"I could design and build a rack," he said. "A tighter rack. I don't know if I could save you half a truck."

"Save me half a truck," Berget said, "and you can ride in the truck. See the USA. Supervise the load-ins and load-outs. Have you ever witnessed a magnificent spectacle like Rodgers and Hammerstein's *Carousel*?"

The truth was that Vincent had not. He had never seen a show of any kind. Antoine Berget, the butt of many a theatrical joke, and possibly the most pretentious bottom-feeder in the business, had become his new hero. But he didn't say yes. The debacle of the bicycle wheel remained very much in his mind. He walked away from Berget, toward the door to the loading dock, signaling that Berget should follow. There was no reason to do this—they were alone out there—but he felt that a sense of conspiracy might interest the man. Berget did follow, and, standing on the wide metal platform to which the trucks backed up to be packed, lit a cigar and looked at Vincent expectantly.

"A new rack," Vincent said, "could be a new idea. A new kind of product. It would save you half a truck, which would give you an advantage over your competitors."

Berget nodded and spoke a single word.

"But . . ." he said. He knew something was coming.

"But," Vincent answered him, "how long would it take for all of those competitors to simply come to the shop and demand a similar rack? Once one of your employees goes to work for someone else, he'll talk about how you travel your shows, and the jig will be up. You will have had an advantage for a season, maybe two."

"And . . ." said Antoine Berget.

"And if you owned," and here Vincent paused for dramatic effect. "Or *co-owned* the company that made these racks, you could share the profits with your co-owner, and you wouldn't have to lift a finger."

Berget smoked. Vincent waited.

"Why?" Berget asked finally. "Why wouldn't I have to lift a finger?"

"Because," Vincent said, "your co-owner would build the racks during the summer when the tours are laid off anyhow. You could revolutionize the business."

"You know some fancy words," Berget said finally, but Vincent could see by the man's far-off look that he was pleased by the idea of revolutionizing the business. Even though they were talking about trucking lighting equipment around the country for bargain-basement Broadway show tours, pioneering something new, especially something that would improve profit margins, appealed simultaneously to his sense of self-importance and his penurious nature.

"I put up the money," Berget said. "You build the things, but not for half. I take 60 percent, you take 40 percent. After all, you can't get into the business without my money. But I'm already in the business. You need me more than I need you. Therefore . . ."

Vincent considered a negotiation but demurred. Instead, he said, "There's only one thing, and, believe me, Mr. Berget, I trust you as much as I trust anyone in the business. But I won't show you the design until the contract is done and signed. It will work," Vincent said. "I already have it in my head. But I've been careless in the past. Entirely my fault, but still." He was flying blind. He had no idea how to build what he had just proposed. But opportunity was opportunity. Berget held out his hand and Vincent took it.

"In the meantime," Berget said, "Knock 30 percent of the equipment off the *Carousel* order and fit it in half a truck. You figure out what we can live without. I want to put the costumes in there with it. The show takes place mostly in the dark anyhow."

"I can do that," Vincent said, "but the rest of the deal also holds. I ride in the truck, I'll supervise the loads, and even with 30 percent less light, I'll find a way for the show to look good enough."

Berget nodded and walked to his car, a black Cadillac. He saluted Vincent with two fingers and drove away. Vincent walked from the loading dock to a nearby oil drum that served as an outdoor trash can and vomited into it violently.

IT WAS IN St. Paul, Minnesota, that Vincent got his first chance to operate a follow spot.

By this point he had loaded and unloaded *Carousel* in more than two dozen cities, working through the night to get the trucks rolling before two A.M. in order to arrive at the next stop on the tour by noon, to be loaded into a new auditorium and checked out by a half hour before curtain. He had also seen *Carousel* nineteen times, and it never failed to make him cry. He'd had sex with six members of the female ensemble, was working on a seventh, and was so sleep deprived that he sometimes found himself napping through the "*Carousel* Waltz" backstage on the bench that served as the only piece of scenery in act one, scene two, until he was unceremoniously upended by the stagehands who had to move it on immediately after the waltz was done. And he was getting paid. Life seemed full of promise.

In St. Paul, at the half hour call on a Saturday night, the stage manager came to Vincent and announced that the spotlight operator, who had done the matinee, had, in the intervening two hours, gotten drunk and beaten up a cop who had tried to arrest him for shouting at women on the street. He was now cuffed and in the drunk tank.

"We'll do the show with one spot," he told Vincent.

"It's *Carousel*," Vincent said. "There's two lovers, there's two follow spots. I'll handle it."

Any respectable tour would have had three follow spots, but this was an Antoine Berget Production.

"I don't call the spot cues," the stage manager said. "You're on your own."

"I know the show," Vincent said. "And I know how to turn the lamp on and off, and it'll be better than nothing. With any luck, maybe it'll be better than that."

He clambered up to a booth above the balcony and got himself in position. He manned the lamp, put on a set of headphones through which he could hear the stage manager calling all the fixed-instrument light cues, the cues for scenery, and the cues for the curtain to go up and down, and realized that, among all stagehands, he and the other spot operator were the only ones who were truly a part of the drama, part of the story. Everyone else was doing what they were told when they were told to do it. But he followed the actors assigned to him in a kind of partnered ballet of light, crisscrossing the stage as the actors moved, staying with them, escorting them to their exits and awaiting their next entrances like a respectful, even adoring, footman. The blocking, with which he was reasonably familiar, stayed the same each night, and although he'd never specifically taken note of it, he fell into a rhythm, a kind of automatic brainwork; it was almost like driving a car. He was there when needed, the lamp went on and off and moved with—it seemed to him—a poetic grace. The music played, the story engulfed and eventually tore up the audience, and he, Vincent Donnelly, self-made factory boy now grown to a man, realized that he was no longer watching *Carousel*; he was in *Carousel*. It was the greatest night of his life.

By the next morning, he felt deeply uncomfortable about the whole experience. In truth, the show's ability to reach his emotional core was a kind of unknown territory for him. He was a blue-collar kid from Queens and felt somehow threatened by the hints of what might be inside of him. He was a regular man, not an artist, not an aesthete, a word he had heard used only by Antoine Berget. He had no desire to embrace the idea of sensitivity—that was for the actors, the artists. He was much more comfortable at the poker table, and, thankfully, on the *Carousel* tour there was a game that never ended. In every city, on nights when the show did not have to travel, the game would pick up right after the exit music had been played. If Vincent wasn't dating up a company member, he would happily join the table, grateful for the wisecracks, the beer, and the sense that his normal body had returned to him—not the one that was subject to tears and heartbreak. He was a crew guy, not a poet or a fairy.

When the show hit Cincinnati, a character none of them had met before arrived backstage and sat in as if he had always been there. His name was Cappy Casparian, and he announced himself as Antoine Berget's business partner—his money partner. Vincent, who was also Berget's partner in a business, was curious.

Cappy Casparian had found himself rich when his father sold the family plumbing fixtures company and had a fascination for show business. He had dabbled in traveling circuses and invested in a couple of bad movie deals before he somehow found Antoine Berget, or, more likely, Berget had found him. What he loved about Berget's shows was that they always made money, and they always played Cincinnati, where he lived. And he always got to bring his friends to the theater to genially show off, while also getting in a couple of nights of poker. He seemed about forty, but was almost completely bald, with a nose that suggested an earlier life as an unsuccessful boxer, though the truth was he had broken it by walking into a glass door in a hurry. He'd never bothered to get it fixed. He drank only Coca-Cola without ice, and generally comported himself as the biggest idiot in the room. He behaved like an Irish setter, and Vincent took him for a patsy, a kid who had grown up rich and never needed to learn anything. And yet, somehow, despite his erratic unnecessarily ebullient behavior, all three nights that *Carousel* spent in Cincinnati he left a winner. The other crew members attributed this to dumb luck, but Vincent didn't think so. He didn't think that Cappy Casparian was cheating, merely that he was—somehow—always winning. He vowed to get back to Cincinnati on the next tour and watch more carefully. Although he had lost a little money, the game with Casparian in it was much better than the game without him. Casparian made up words, he handed out cigars, and he gave back money when a crew member seemed particularly forlorn about losing it.

Vincent broke two dates with two different chorus members to play and observe, but he couldn't crack Casparian's system. He put it on his list of things yet to be learned.

IN THE MID-1950s, Vincent sold half his interest in the successful light-rack business to Antoine Berget, for the price of a down payment on a house in Hoboken, just across the Lincoln Tunnel from the West Side of Manhattan, a twenty-minute train ride from Times Square. There was enough left over for him to buy a piece of a theatrical concession business that sold orange drink at intermission in the Broadway theaters. He would continue this pattern, selling a half interest for a profit, buying into another ancillary theater business, and then selling half, for the rest of his working life. It was a successful path to wealth, and he did it with an almost supernatural instinct for success. He knew when to buy and when to sell. At times he owned pieces of costume shops, prop businesses, a ticket broker, and the company that made uniforms for the doormen and ushers. He told no one.

For additional security, he embedded himself within powerful families of the union, whose Byzantine structure he had studied diligently. Local One was largely in the hands of a small group of "original families"—direct descendants of the union's New York founders before there was a national union. When IATSE came into existence, Local One joined up and took first position among the locals. New York meant Broadway, after all. The original families remained in a position to make things happen, and Vincent did enough research to discover one of the families had hailed from Galway, as his father did, and still had retired members receiving pensions.

Using all the charm he had, he introduced his father, whose brogue had never thinned out, to the two elderly Ennis brothers who had retired to South Ozone Park with their wives. He joined them in a weekly dinner that—accompanied by a couple of Jamesons each—devolved into a sentimental celebration of the old country, to which the Ennis brothers still sent monthly checks in support of the less fortunate members of the family back home. Soon the invitations came; his brother Pat to be an apprentice, and Big Vin to join the concessionaires union Local 32BJ, so that he might remain a useful member of society and work close to his son, who was soon elected to the business council at his own union. Soon enough, Pat was working as a prop man with Berget, and his father, who was now sixty, was selling orange drink at the Mark Hellinger Theatre.

Vincent, no doubt, no longer needed to run follow spots and could have become a head electrician at any one of several Broadway theaters, but his heart was in the spotlight balcony. He loved the work. He was twenty-nine now, owner of a house with a mortgage, and had moved his mother and father to more comfortable quarters nearer to the Ennis brothers, to whom they had now become attached. He lacked only a suitable lifetime mate, though it was hard to picture giving up his unending opportunities for pleasant—and often sudden—encounters with the many talented women who passed in and out of his place of business. Each was part of the world of a show, a single story that told itself eight times a week, for some unspecified period of time. The population of these worlds came and went, ripe with possibilities. The theater, he had discovered, was a world of short-term affection that declared its passion loudly and with complete sincerity, and then moved on, like any other performance, to the next world, the next town, the next season.

Sometimes, as he sat at McHale's bar on Eighth Avenue nursing a single Miller High Life after a performance of *West Side Story*, which was enjoying a return engagement at the Winter Garden, his mind would drift back to Arthur Hynes's tavern and to Rafferty's law office above, and he would vow to get himself down there—it was only a twenty-minute ride on the BMT—and see what was left, and who was left. It had been a world ago, it seemed to him. But he never managed to make the trip.

When Aurora Shelton's letters home from summer camp stopped arriving, Michael and Beatrice Feik became concerned. Michael's long-distance call to Camp Mount Olive quickly established that Aurora had never been there, and, now in a frantic state of panic, her parents set off for Leonardville, Kansas, using the postmark from her biweekly letters as the only clue they had. At ten past three in the morning, somewhere west of Sedalia, Missouri, they were engaged in a fierce argument over the music on the radio. Beatrice wanted some old-fashioned dance music to keep her awake as she drove, and Michael was hunting for a country-western station, holding a lit cigarette as he went for the dial with his two free fingers. As Beatrice reached out to stop him, the car veered off of Route 50. It flipped over a boulder, ripping the gas tank open. The cigarette flew. The resulting brush fire took until well after sunrise to contain, and the bodies were not identified for several days. When they were, authorities had no idea that there was a child somewhere out there in the world who had just become an orphan, the day after her eighteenth birthday.

Aurora, who had intended to call her parents after she'd been on the road for two weeks and attained her majority, might never have known what happened to them if it hadn't been for the U.S. Military Death Gratuity Program. The police had no particular interest in understanding what Michael Feik's family situation was, but the army owed money to his surviving offspring, and the army took such things seriously.

Aurora had been trying, without success, to reach her parents by long distance, and, finally bewildered by the endlessly ringing phone, wrote them a letter telling them the truth about where she was and what she was doing and declaring her independence. It was a letter they would never read. Michael Feik's camp commander had it unsealed after obtaining proper permission through channels and discovered that Aurora Feik was on tour with a dance band under another name. He wired the camp commander at Fort Riley, who had his secretary do some research, and the tour route was discovered. The band was on a swing through the South and West, playing one-night stands in Oklahoma on its way to Arkansas and Louisiana. A young sergeant caught up with them a week later in Pine Bluff, where they were scheduled to play a Friars Club dance that night. It had been over a month since the accident. The young sergeant delivered the speech he'd been rehearsing for two days, wished Aurora his sincerest condolences, which were somewhat compromised by his obvious relief at having done his duty and gotten it over with, and left her the paperwork that would, when properly filled out and returned to the authorities, result in a check for seven thousand dollars being delivered to her.

Aurora was speechless, bereft, lost—and free. She watched the young sergeant's car disappear down the road back toward Kansas and realized that for the first time in her life, she was truly, and in every sense, alone. The only person left on earth that she owed anything to was Marius Huwiler.

By this point in the tour, Ike Harris had begun to look after Aurora as a kind of guardian, or so he convinced himself. His first gesture, after the two had confirmed their meeting in the USO tent ten years before, had been to tell Otts Oscard that she was, in fact, a minor, and that he would certainly land in jail if he laid a hand on her. He failed to mention that she would turn eighteen the week after he made this speech, and it had its desired effect. Otts reluctantly kept his distance.

On the night of her eighteenth birthday, Ike took her for her first legal drink. This was not a date. Her birthday needed to be kept secret because to be legally hired she was already supposed to have had it, and to keep Otts at bay she was not. But she felt she needed to celebrate it even so. They spent an hour in a local tavern. Under the influence of a single sloe gin fizz, she told him of the strange and quite unexpected summer she had spent with Toni and Barty, Marius Huwiler and Jonah

Kingston. He was nonplussed, more at the matter-of-fact way in which she related it than in the situation itself. He had by now come to realize that the world he had joined was, among its other virtues, a refuge for a hidden population.

Having been thus confided in, his impulse was to tell her about Missy Cozzens, and his impending fatherhood, but he demurred. What kept him from speaking he couldn't quite say, but it seemed better left alone. It was her birthday, after all. Shouldn't she be the center of attention? Besides, he himself was not sure what he thought about it all. The one thing he did think about was that, day by day, in ways he could not calculate, but could no longer deny, he had gotten to the point where he was thinking about Aurora Shelton at least twenty times an hour. She had settled in his unconscious mind and would not leave. Nor did he want her to.

Missy Cozzens was a free thinker. She did not insist on marriage. She understood that she might be something of an outcast as a single mother in New York, but she rather enjoyed the defiance. Her parents were left-leaning storekeepers in Brooklyn who had been swept into the Communist Party during the Great Depression and had neither disavowed it nor been particularly rewarded for their loyalty. Missy, who now fancied herself a novelist, never actually produced anything that could be published, but she had left the ad agency and was currently pecking away at a typewriter for two hours every day, after which she found marches and protests to attend. She certainly wasn't prepared to marry Ike Harris on such slight acquaintance, nor was she prepared to give up her child or the experience of being a mother. Marriage, in any case, was a form of legalized prostitution, she said. She would be perfectly happy outside of conventional morality—as long as Ike supported the child and allowed her to continue her writing career, which he was currently financing with half his paycheck.

Ollie had advised him to do nothing of the kind—she knew a perfectly good and discreet abortionist who had once been a partner of Ike's father. And shouldn't Ike have as much say in the matter as this kook he had managed to knock up? Ike did not think so. He felt responsible, and entirely at the mercy of Missy's point of view on the matter. He would stay on the road until the baby came, and then return to New York to look for work.

It was not an altogether pleasant prospect, but in the meantime, he found that he was enjoying his role as the unofficial protector of Aurora Shelton. He liked being in her presence and liked hearing her voice ringing just slightly above the volume of the other two debutantes, who were making only minimal effort on the bandstand each evening. She had never really learned to blend. He most especially liked to hear her doing her one solo number, which was called "It Might as Well Be Spring." The band laid out on this number, which featured Aurora backed by only piano, bass and drums, with a brief flute solo before she returned to the bridge. Ike never tired of listening to it, in part because he believed every word she was singing. It was a song of hope and confusion–a girl just reaching womanhood, bewildered by feelings she was just beginning to encounter more restless than unhappy. At least that's what Ike took from it, and he hoped she was not unhappy.

But then one evening, he found her in the back of the bus, with the death gratuity paperwork lying in her lap like a lifeless dove. He wanted to hold her, to see if her troubles, her bewilderment, could be physically transferred from her frail body to his sturdier one, to see if he could somehow take charge of her grief so that she would be relieved of it all at once. But the idea of an embrace seemed somehow hopelessly inappropriate, and the notion that her agitation could or should belong to anyone but herself was equally misplaced.

Instead, he touched her shoulder lightly, and she looked up at him and began to cry.

"I know," he said, "that you wanted to speak to them, eventually, when the time was right."

She shook her head and tried to collect herself.

"I killed them," she said. "I told myself I would write by my birthday. I told myself I would only have this little bit of freedom. A little time to myself. That's all I wanted. And now I've killed them."

He took a seat next to her.

"You did not kill them," he said, though he wasn't sure what else to say on the matter, for in some sense, he understood that her decision to duck into the shadows of anonymity had been the cause of their attempt to find her, which had, in turn, killed them. There was no way around that part.

"Accidents happen," he said. It sounded hollow and ridiculous even before she turned to him, her eyes accusatory in having caught him in such a fatuous cliché. She did not speak.

Finally, he said, not knowing quite why, "my father died in the middle of the street."

"In a car?"

"No. He was enormously smart. His brain was his best asset. But one day he was walking across Fifth Avenue in New York and an artery in that brilliant brain just gave up. Burst open. His brain killed him. The best thing he had. You never know what will kill you. And you—you—are not allowed to take responsibility for the death of your parents any more than I am for mine. I won't allow it."

Assertion, perhaps, was better than logic. She sat very still. In the silence, he became aware of the familiarity of her scent, something he didn't realize he had become increasingly taken with over the weeks they had spent in close quarters. Cedar and something of the ocean's salt but overlaid with a faint floral presence. Gardenia. She used something with gardenia.

He knew better than to speak of it but could find nothing else. He would sit there all day and into the night in silence if necessary.

She suddenly spoke.

"My mother," she said. "My mother deserved better. From me. From life."

"Maybe," Ike said. "Maybe she did."

In reality, Aurora was not absorbing the news at all. She was thinking about her father's immeasurable rage, which had driven everything, and now even himself, into oblivion. What she couldn't know and would never learn is that it was not she who was responsible for her parents' death at all. It was music—an argument over music—that had killed them.

Ike was lost in an entirely different world. In another four months, he would become a father. Now Aurora was suddenly an orphan. And Ike, who wanted only to comfort her, was thinking about himself—about whether he would or could be a better father than Beatrice had been a mother to Aurora. Or would he die in the middle of the road, leaving behind a lost child with a crazy mother? Parenthood, he thought, was the most unsolvable of all riddles.

"Aurora," he said finally, "is there something I can do?"

"I don't know," she said thrusting the paperwork at him. "I have to fill this out, I don't know if I can."

Ike looked at the death gratuity form and his heart seized. He tapped his thumb against it in an involuntary tic, and took a quick, shallow breath.

"Michael Feik," he said. "Your father is—was—Staff Sergeant Michael Feik?"

"That's right," she said.

"I thought your name was Shelton,"

"My mother's name," she said. "Yes. I'm Aurora Feik."

"Jesus," Ike said. "I'm sorry. I mean . . . it can't have been easy. He put me through basic. At least as much of it as I got through. I apologize. I shouldn't have said that—you must have loved him very much."

"I hated him," Aurora wailed suddenly, turning to Ike and then just as quickly back toward the front of the bus. She collected herself immediately. "The only thing I have from him is a fragment of an old 78 that he broke when he turned over our Magnavox instead of beating up my poor drunken mother That's what he really wanted to do. My favorite song. I have a shard of an old broken record. That's all he left me and he didn't even mean to. I hated him; I hate him. Even dead I hate him."

It was too much. Ike put her hands on her shoulders, but she bucked him off with a violent lurch.

"Leave me alone," she cried. "Get off the bus! Just get off the bus! Get off the bus!"

"I'm sorry," Ike said, withdrawing his hands and retreating down the aisle. "I'm so sorry."

FROM PINE BLUFF the bus moved on to Monroe and crossed the state line into Vicksburg.

Ike kept his distance. When the band finished its nightly gig, he stepped quickly into the bus and waited for the night driver to climb on board and take them to the next. But in Vicksburg there was a layover, which meant a hotel. He and Aurora had not spoken for almost a week when she approached him in the lobby as they were waiting to check in.

"I owe you a drink and an apology," she said. "But I don't think I can apologize without the drink."

Mississippi, alas, was the last remaining dry state in America, and the bar at the hotel was featuring coffee and ice cream sodas. Only the passing of a ten dollar bill to the barman produced the hoped for result, from an unmarked bottle stashed behind a mirror that swing open like the front of a medicine cabinet.

The place was all but empty—it was midafternoon.

"What do you drink?" the barman asked them in a languid drawl.

"I don't know," Aurora said, turning to Ike. "What do I drink?"

"Bourbon and soda," Ike said. "Make it two, please."

The apology was brief, and Ike had the good graces to reject it.

"No apology is acceptable," he said, "because none is necessary."

"My father," she started, but couldn't continue.

"I can tell you what little I know," Ike said. "He was a disciplinary terror to his men, which was his job. But I don't know anything about his home life—or yours. Except that you ran away from it. And maybe that's all I need to know."

"What happened in the bus . . ." she trailed off again.

"Never happened," Ike said. "You dreamed it or made it up. A terrible, unavoidable fantasy. But I never witnessed it."

"I love you," she said simply. What she meant by it he had no idea. Then she took a sip of her drink and lowered her head sideways onto his shoulder.

"That you mustn't do," Ike said. "There are good and present reasons."

They headed west again to Alexandria and Lake Charles, where there was a letter waiting at the local VFW hall for Aurora. As the band set up, she opened it, standing off in a corner. Ike glanced at her from time to time as she read through some paperwork. After his instrument and music were in place on the bandstand, he walked over to her, and she showed him the contents. Along with some forms to be filled out and signed was the death gratuity check.

That night, after the concert, Aurora sought him out; he was having a beer in the local tavern, where cut after cut of Ernest Tubb and Hank Snow were pealing from the jukebox. She sat next to him at the bar and ordered one herself, though she discovered quickly that she didn't like the taste.

"It was a good show," he said, though the place had been scantly attended by dancers who seemed only to know how to two-step.

"I need to talk to you," she said. "I need your help."

"Anything," he replied.

"Can you keep it quiet for a little while?"

He turned to her. *Confidences*, he thought.

"I sent the check to a bank in New York," she said. "Monkey helped me."

His heart sank, unaccountably.

"I didn't want to bother you," she said. "You told me there were good and present reasons."

Ike nodded. If she registered the distress on his face, she didn't comment.

"The thing is this," she said. "Monkey will lend me bus fare once the check clears. He trusts me."

"I trust you," Ike said.

She let this pass in silence for a moment, as the song on the jukebox faded out, and was replaced by Kitty Wells singing "Cheatin's a Sin." What passed between them was unspoken, and neither of them could have described it with any certainty. Ike was wondering if Aurora could possibly have fallen for Monkey Monkton, a grim little man of fifty or so. It seemed impossible. Still, he hoped she'd speak, which she did not. Aurora's face betrayed something, regret perhaps, or resignation.

The moment between them lingered, disrupted only by the sounds a tavern makes, a low rumble of conversation, a woman's heartbroken voice on the jukebox, the tonk-tonk of billiard balls colliding. Finally, Ike could stand it no longer.

"How can I help?" he asked.

"I need a song," she said. It sounded selfish, even to her, but it was true. Where matters of musical taste were concerned, in the absence of Marius Huwiler, there was no one else to turn to. She pressed on, joyless, but determined. "Monkey gave me some agents who will see me in New York, but I need a more grown-up song. A real love song. That's what he says. You'll know the right one for me. It's a big favor, I know. But if I have a song, I can get off the road, quit the band, and head for New York."

Ike sat for a moment as Kitty Wells continued to pour out her heart. A song, the thought, feeling unentitled to his disappointment. He asked the bartender for a piece of paper and a pencil. Using a square cardboard coaster as a ruler, he quickly drew the lines of a musical staff on the page, drew some bar lines, marked it in her key and wrote out the notes.

"It's only a lead sheet," he said.

"You can write out the notes even while other music is playing," she mused. "How can you keep one tune in your head while another one is on the jukebox?"

He shrugged. "I'll write out the words," he said. And we can rehearse tomorrow."

"I love you," she said. It was even more baffling the second time.

Ike looked down at the blank, impromptu piece of sheet music and began to write. The song was "I Could Write a

Book" from *Pal Joey*, and it brought back memories of Henry Vesey, the orchestra pit at the Barrymore Theatre and his first unwanted kiss, but the song itself was easy to write down, and it was a song for a grown woman, a polite but seductive expression of passion. It took only five minutes to write out the whole song. As he was finishing, the jukebox faded again, and a new number came on. Homer and Jethro, a novelty duo out of Knoxville, were covering "Hernando's Hideaway" from *The Pajama Game*. Aurora began to laugh, the first time Ike had heard her laugh at all since the accident.

"Listen to that!" She said. "That's hilarious."

He pushed the piece of paper across the bar to her.

"This is better," he said. "At least it's true."

She read through it, though whether she made a connection to their present moment he could not tell.

"Thank you," she said.

"You're welcome," he replied. "And I would have given you bus fare too, by the way."

"Oh, God," She said, "Monkey is such a miserable little man. But you told me there were circumstances," she said. "So, I thought . . . there are circumstances."

Another moment passed before she asked, "What are the circumstances?"

Ike exhaled and drained his beer.

"I'm about to become a father," he said.

She looked struck and stared straight ahead into the mirror above the bar.

"You're married," she said. She sounded dead or angry or both.

"I'm not," he said. "But you've had enough messes for a lifetime, and you're only a kid. You don't need any new messes. And you can't be fretting about mine."

IKE HARRIS STAYED on with Otts Oscard for another two months. He had agreed with Missy that he would remain on the road, sending some money every month, until the baby was due, but he was now suddenly restless. He missed Aurora, missed her singing, and wondered what would happen to her. Otts Oscard never bothered to replace Aurora, and the two remaining debutantes had begun singing duet arrangements that were neither as satisfying as their imitations of the Andrews Sisters nor as popular with the dwindling crowds. Ike could feel with cold certainty the band crumbling as the world turned. In Tallahassee they opened the bill for Carl Perkins, whose "Blue Suede Shoes" drove the crowd mad, and Fess Parker, who only really knew one song—"The Ballad of Davy Crockett." It was hard to miss the handwriting on the wall. Ike put in his notice. When the band hit Miami, he boarded the Orange Blossom Special and headed home to Manhattan.

9

ARRIVAL

AURORA SHELTON got to New York with a legacy of $7,000 in the bank, which seemed to her like a limitless supply of money, and not a soul in the world to whom she had to answer. She was, however, determined to be frugal, while at the same time educating herself about art and culture, and, especially, music. She took a room at the Hotel Pennsylvania across from the massive, gloomy pile of Penn Station, now less than decade away from its disastrous demolition, and then went to the bank where her money was resting comfortably. She withdrew enough for what she imagined a week's expenses would be and sent a money order to Monkey Monkton for the bus ticket he had bought her. She wrote to Toni and Barty, and then to Marius Huwiler, asking for recommendations of plays and musicals on Broadway and explaining all that had happened. His response was long, sympathetic, and detailed. He went through the Sunday theater section of *The New York Times*—he only bought the Sunday Times once a month, and looked forward to it keenly, fifty-five cents well spent—and sent her the ABC theatrical ads, circling the ones he thought she might find interesting, though he had seen none of them.

Going to the theater once a week—a balcony seat could be had for two dollars and thirty cents—she finally actually saw *The Pajama Game*, which thrilled her, and *The Teahouse of the August Moon*, which surprised her because there was no music. But it was *Wonderful Town*, a tale of two young sisters arriving from Ohio with nothing but ambition—they barely mentioned who their parents were—that gave her courage and enchanted her. She left the theater with her mind spinning, knowing that, for her, band singing was a thing of the past. She wanted to be in one of those shows. She wanted to be in all of them. She wanted someone to write a part for her, to write a song for her, and she wanted to believe that these ambitions were anything but ridiculous. She would insist on success; she would do what she had to do to make them not ridiculous. After all, she had no one to answer to but herself.

She went to the Metropolitan Museum of Art but had to leave because she found it overwhelming and too hard to comprehend. She had better luck with the Museum of Modern Art, where she could at least wander from room to room without encountering so many different cultures and millennia.

What she did encounter were young men, many of them eager to buy her a drink or take her to a movie. For a couple of weeks she resisted, but then she began to say yes, with dismal results. They were bank clerks and office boys trolling the museums on their lunch hours, not looking for art but for the likes of her: a lonely girl in the big city. This was not a role she was willing to play for them. She could not become interested in a man who worked as a bank teller and aspired to be a manager. She preferred her solitude, and her primary companions remained Marius and Jonah, and Barty and Toni; she called both couples on the phone downstairs on Sundays.

She moved from the hotel to the Brandon Residence for Women on 85th Street near Riverside Drive and stopped wasting time on young men. She used $250 to enroll in an acting class for a semester and began to study voice with a teacher Marius found for her. All she really wanted now was to be some combination of the two sisters—Ruth and Eileen, the smart one and the pretty one—in *Wonderful Town*. And she wanted to find someplace where she could stand up and sing Eileen's charming "A Little Bit in Love," her new favorite song. She had, after all, spent time as a professional, as she explained to her teacher, with Otts Oscard and his Debutantes.

No one in New York had ever heard of the band, including her teacher, a facile piano player and sometime cabaret singer named Danny Walton. He was a juvenile in personality and style, and even name, who wore shirts with cuff links and argyle sweater vests. But he was no longer actually young, his hair was dyed, and while Aurora appreciated everything he taught her and all of his suggestions and criticisms, and felt herself improving, she knew that he was, at bottom, the exact thing she must avoid ever becoming. Whatever his dream had been, it had never become acquainted with reality. He didn't try to touch her physically. She understood immediately upon meeting him that he, like Marius, had no interest in women.

He did, however, teach her how to audition, and went with her as her accompanist on the rare occasions when one of Monkey Monkton's agent friends could get her seen for something. Finally, after a year of nothing but lessons, cheap food, and extravagant dreams of glory, during which her fortune dwindled by almost half, she landed an ensemble berth in a bus-and-truck production of *Miss Liberty*. It was a split-week tour that would take her around the country, including a stop in Topeka, where, she fervently hoped, Marius and Jonah would come to see her, even as invisible as she would be among a dozen female singers.

With *Miss Liberty*, she learned what it really meant to take the raw materials of a show out of a box and turn them into a living, if sometimes limping, thing. The show rehearsed in the barn-like Anderson Yiddish Theatre on lower Second Avenue, where a fitful attempt to reignite the glory days of Thomashefsky and Maurice Schwartz was faltering and between bookings. On the first day of rehearsal, as the management tried with scant success to get the heat working, the production's producer, Antoine Berget, made a rousing speech to the company, his fine clothing and overgroomed appearance standing in stark contrast to the surrounding tatters. As the pipes banged and steam hissed, a piano tuner worked at an infuriatingly methodical pace to get ready for the music director to begin teaching Irving Berlin's score to this group of young, largely untried actors who were about to embark on a thirty-six-week journey into the unknown for almost no money a week. Berget exhorted them to hold up the grand tradition of the American musical comedy so that the whole country—the little people—could see its greatness, neglecting to mention that *Miss Liberty* had flopped on Broadway, and only Berlin's name—and certainly not this particular score—made it worthy of showing to the great unwashed. Aurora didn't care. She had been raised among those provincials and had been one of them. Now she was something different—an actress. It was more than enough. Surely, she would make friends. Surely, she would have a real romance. Surely, she would return to New York a changed woman. When the tour was due to lay off the following June, she would be almost twenty and a thoroughgoing professional.

Back in New York, as the decade turned, she booked a replacement job as Polly Peachum downtown in *The Threepenny Opera* and lost out on the role of The Girl in an oddball little musical called *The Fantasticks* that would open in 1960 to disappointing reviews and run for forty-two years. She played the role in summer stock instead.

IKE HARRIS and Vincent Donnelly would finally get to know each other as a result of the unexpected Actors' Equity strike of 1960. It was the picket line that brought them together.

The actors union, wanting for the first time to set up a pension plan for its members, decided, for reasons that are lost in time, that rather than strike across the board, they would shut down a single show. And on June 1 they walked off a hit production of *The Best Man*. The League of New York Theaters and Producers responded by locking out everybody—they were not about to contribute to a pension plan for actors; theater tickets were already too expensive at a $9.60 top. The audience was dwindling and the cost of production was soaring. It now cost more than $350,000 to produce a decent-sized musical. Within a day both the stagehands and musicians joined the actors on the line.

It was while crossing behind the Winter Garden on Seventh Avenue three hours into a four-hour shift that Ike Harris found himself asking Vincent Donnelly, whom he certainly recognized and had been exchanging nods with, to hold his sign so that he could fish a turkey sandwich out of his pocket.

"You're the trumpet player," said Vincent, handing the sign back to Ike, who was now chewing. "Vincent Donnelly," Vincent said. "Follow spot two. Fucking hot day to be walking a line. Fucking hot all week. You'd think they could strike in October—this is killing me."

"And it's not even my union," Ike said as they turned west on Fifty-First and began the circle again. "Or yours."

Vincent laughed. "Musicians scare me. They're too powerful." He scratched his head, growing serious. "I don't think light has that kind of power. Music makes a feeling inside you.

Light doesn't do that. When I was first starting out, *Carousel* almost killed me. Every night. It was the music."

"*Carousel* could kill anyone," Ike said. "Try playing it sometime."

"That's the point," Vincent said. "I could barely operate my lamp. I don't know how you do it. How do you play and not cry?"

"You're supposed to make other people cry," Ike said. "You're supposed to make the audience cry. That's the nature of the job. That's what they pay for."

After their required hours of parading while exchanging war stories—Broadway war stories—the two men repaired to McHale's for beer and cheeseburgers. The air conditioning in the place hit them as they crossed the threshold the way a heroin injection hits a needy addict. McHale's, with its gummy floor, its broken jukebox, and its permanently disarrayed restrooms, was a kind of low-rent heaven. This pattern repeated itself for three days—four hours of walking and talking, followed by cool air, cheeseburgers, and beer.

In their seemingly endless revolutions around the theater, Vincent had told Ike about his misadventures with the barman Arthur Hynes and the disappearing lawyer named Rafferty, and Ike had shared his alternately cheerful and harrowing run from the fascists before the war and his war years—joining up and forming a band—so that by the time they finished their third round on their third day, a certain kinship had formed, though they could hardly call each other friends. Paying for the drinks, both Ike and Vincent reached into their pockets, coming up with a couple of soggy bills, some Kleenex, a pocketknife (Vincent), and an unused and useless theater ticket (Ike). They spread their collected fortune and assembled detritus on the bar and separated the money from the rest. Staring down at the mess, Ike was struck by the ticket. He had purchased it for Missy who could not attend, of course, because there were no performances. He flipped it around on the inevitable oak bar that seemed to grace all fake Irish pubs—McHale's was one of dozens but favored by stagehands—and the two of them stared at it. The ticket, a green piece of pasteboard printed by the Globe Ticket Company, listed the theater with its address, the name of the attraction, the seat location, the date of performance, and broke down the cost into its three components: The established price was $8.25. The federal tax was 77 cents, and there was an additional city excise tax of 58 cents. Total cost: $9.60.

"Innovation," Ike said, slurring audibly, and slapping the bar. "You had the bicycle wheel, and the lighting rack. I created a marijuana plantation with Italian slave labor. Clearly there's nothing we cannot do. Let's solve the strike."

Vincent laughed, but Ike was serious. Every time he marched around in circles at the theater he cursed Staff Sergeant Michael Feik, who had taught him to march, and then pushed away thoughts of Aurora Shelton tearing into him in the back of Otts Oscard's bus, with the death gratuity paperwork lying in her lap. It was all very disturbing; he didn't want to think about anything that marching made him think of. He missed playing the trumpet licks in *West Side Story,* and he didn't want to be haunted by dark thoughts. There was only one way out—get everyone back to work.

"Look at this," Ike said. "Why can't the city pay for the pension plan? Give the excise tax money to the producers, let them pay for the actors' retirement, and then steal an equivalent amount of money from some other budget, and no one will be any the wiser. Let the subway pay for it. Or the fire department, or the cops."

"Ike," said Vincent, "you're a dreamer."

"I am a dreamer," Ike said. "You're the pragmatic one. I'm just a schmuck who plays the trumpet. No one in the city is going to listen to me. I'd be thrown out of Gracie Mansion quicker than a kazoo player. You solve it, Mr. Pragmatist."

They had drunk enough to display some struggle as they moved slowly down Eighth Avenue toward their respective apartments, but when Ike let himself in, the phone was ringing. It was Vincent.

"Come out for one more round," he said. "Now *I* got an idea."

Vincent contacted Tommy Ennis the next day, and it was the Ennis brothers who pulled together Mayor Robert Wagner, the city comptroller, Ike, and Vincent at an Italian place up on Arthur Avenue in the Bronx, where no one would find them. The mayor was horrified at the thought, but, as Vincent knew, he could not turn down a request for a meeting from one of the Ennises. There were simply too many related entrenched unions: the docks, the Fulton fish market, and the construction industry that was at that very moment remaking Sixth Avenue into a glass and steel corridor of faceless, interchangeable skyscrapers soon to rob the place of whatever scattershot character it had once possessed. This was not just about Actors' Equity, or the stagehands or the producers, or, for God's sake, the trumpet players in the pit. It was a union situation in New York City.

Tommy Ennis, his gray comb-over beginning to fall into a slack rag mop over his forehead and across his watery green eyes, looked at the mayor with a deeply sympathetic frown, and drummed his fingers on the white tablecloth now stained with a fine spattering of red sauce—it had been a generous lunch, for which no check would be delivered—and spoke in a voice that suggested he might break into a soft, seductive chorus of "Killarney, My Old Home O'er the Sea" at any moment.

"And you can't fail to see," he crooned, "that this is about more than all of these fine drivers of employment and civic harmony put together, important as each and every one of them is and may be. It's also about the thing your very great city is most famous for: Not the New York Yankees, nor Wall Street, not the Empire State Building, the construction of which led to the death of more than one member of my family. It's about Broadway, Mr. Mayor. Broadway. The place to which the entire world wishes to give its regards, as my fellow countryman Mr. Cohan once duly noted. Broadway. We don't want a mess on Broadway. Do we now?"

In the end, the agreement contained one unwritten codicil, which was that no one—no one—must ever know that the solution was not the blind inspiration of Mayor Wagner himself. No one was to breathe a word—not to Equity, not to the union bosses of Local One or Local 802, not to whomever either Ike Harris or Vincent Donnelly happened to be sleeping with and sharing delicious secrets with.

"Loose lips sink ships," said Wagner. "Believe me you don't want to be one of the ships that sinks. There are never any survivors."

"Listen to the man," said Tommy Ennis with a nod. "A word to the wise."

Less than two weeks after the lockout was called, Vincent was back in his spot tower and Ike was in the pit, and Chita Rivera was belting out "America" to a satisfied audience. The mayor of the greatest city in the world had come up with the inspiration that had saved everyone from a fate worse than death: no Broadway. Ike Harris and Vincent Donnelly should have remained fast friends from that day on, but by the time the weather turned cold, everything had changed.

—

ON A MONDAY MORNING in late August 1960, the phone rang at nine A.M. and awakened Ike Harris from a perfectly decent sleep.

"Wake up, you little bastard," said a vaguely familiar voice on the other end. "We're coming to the Winter Garden! You'll be playing my music again."

Ike's brain racked back through the past, back through countless dance band gigs and a handful of Broadway shows, all the way back to the war. It was Sid Lupowitz.

Lupowitz, after becoming the resident composer at an adult Jewish summer camp in the Catskills, had written the music for something called *Nowhere to Go But Up,* a sort of send-up of Prohibition-era Warner Bros. movies, and he'd found a producer. The show was slated to go into the Winter Garden because *West Side Story* had finally given up the ghost, a victim of summer doldrums. For Sid Lupowitz, this was the opportunity of a lifetime, which he thought was well deserved and long overdue.

By this point, Ike had been the house trumpet player for almost five years. His return from Florida and the Otts Oscard aggregation had been a return to unemployment, and he was about to become a father. After consulting with Missy and with his mother about his best prospects, he made the phone call he was hoping never to have to make. Through the union, he'd obtained a number for Henry Vesey, the only man who had ever kissed him. They had not spoken since that night. Ike had never thanked him for the ticket to *Pal Joey*. Henry had never gotten in touch. Fifteen years had gone by.

Vesey met him for coffee at Schrafft's on Fifth Avenue and 13th Street. It was midafternoon and the place, with its aqua vinyl booths and stools, was almost empty. When Vesey walked in, Ike saw at once, and with shock, an old man. His hair was gray and plastered across his forehead. His suit was too large, his eyes dimmed and rheumy. Vesey settled into a chair delicately, as if something—a knee, a hip—was giving him trouble. He smiled at Ike and spoke without a hint of self-consciousness.

"You're still devastating," he said.

"You look good too," Ike said haplessly.

"Lung cancer," Vesey said without emotion. "They keep telling me it's a kind of pneumonia that's hard to cure, but I know what I've got. Not much longer is what I've got. To tell the truth, I'm just glad I can clap eyes on you one more time. I didn't think that would happen."

"I'm sorry," Ike said, beginning to tear up. "Oh my God, I'm so sorry."

"Sorry about what? That you're not a fag like me? That's not your fault. That I'm gonna die? Not your fault either. I drew the short straw, that's all." He began to cough, and then reached into his inner breast pocket for a pack of cigarettes.

Ike turned one down and pointed to the one that Vesey had just placed between his lips.

"Are you sure?" he asked.

"Only pleasure I've got left," said Vesey. "I can't really taste food anymore, or keep much of it down, I can't get a hard-on, I can't concentrate on a book. Martinis nearly kill me with stomach pain. There's cigarettes and there's music. Everything else has run out on me. And pleasure was all I ever had, so I'm riding these two to the end of the line. Don't feel bad. I've lost lots of friends. You will too."

Ike tried to drink his coffee. Something in Henry Vesey's attitude seemed profoundly brave and, at the same time, profoundly phony. It was almost a great performance.

"I had no idea," Ike said. "I should have kept in touch. I should have been better. I should have at least written you a thank-you note for the theater ticket."

"Not so," Vesey said. "That ticket meant 'Good-bye, don't grieve for me, and don't make it worse by staying in my life.' You did good on every count."

Ike nodded. Henry coughed. Ike felt terrible about what he needed to ask; it seemed trivial and self-serving under the circumstances. But he didn't have to ask.

"Trumpet players are a dime a dozen," Vesey said to him, unprompted. "But I think I could get you on as a sub at *Plain and Fancy*. I've got friends there and they feel sorry for me."

"God," said Ike. "I would be so grateful. I've got a baby coming, and I just left a band on the road, where there's about to be no bands."

"It's a different world," Vesey said. "Rock and roll is going to kill all of us, but not me. I won't be here when it happens."

"Anything I can do," Ike said. "Anything."

Vesey sat quietly for a moment. Finally, he took as deep a breath as he could and spoke.

"Two things. Visit me in the hospital—once—whenever that is. And come play "Danny Boy" on the trumpet at my funeral. I don't know why," he said, and, completely without warning, the mask fell away, and he began to weep, holding his Schrafft's monogrammed napkin over his face. Ike waited. The waitress heading for their table made a quick U-turn and doubled back into the kitchen. They sat alone. Finally, Henry lowered the napkin and spoke through his tears.

"I don't know why," he said, nearly choking on each word, "why I've always loved 'Danny Boy' so much. I'm not even Irish."

IKE PLAYED HIS first performance of *Plain and Fancy* a month later subbing for the second trumpet player, who was taking his daughter off to college. A month after that, he took over the part, and was subbing for the first trumpet as well. Two months later Henry Vesey called him to come to the hospital, and ten days later, at eleven in the morning, Ike was playing "Danny Boy" at a downtown funeral home attended by a handful of other musicians, and the few men with whom Henry Vesey had remained friends. After the service a middle-aged woman approached him with her husband in tow. She was Henry's sister, she said, and she wanted to thank him for his performance. She had come in from Cleveland on the train and was on her way back. She shook Ike's hand and departed quickly, uncomfortably, as if she had just seen something that she didn't want to know was true and needed to get away and be alone.

Ike watched her go, wanting to say more, to tell her the story of Henry Vesey's kindness, to ask if she knew why "Danny Boy" was his favorite song, to explain that his relationship with Vesey had been central to his love of Broadway music, but she was gone, and there was a lot he'd simply never learn. And besides, he had a matinee of *Plain and Fancy* to get to.

The birth of his daughter, named Lil in honor of Louis Armstrong's piano-playing wife, had gone smoothly. They were home within a week, and Ike and Missy decided it was time to figure out exactly who they needed to be to each other. Marriage was not in the air, and they had never even really lived together. But now they had a child.

Missy Cozzens had, it seemed to Ike, become a different person since the days of their fitful courtship. While he was out on the road, she had quit her job to spend the entire summer of 1954 glued to the Army-McCarthy hearings on the little TV in her studio apartment. She had survived on rage and the small amounts of money that Ike had been sending her, which were supposed to be building a nest egg for the baby's arrival. His return had not rekindled their romantic relationship; she was eight and a half months pregnant, and he wouldn't have dared ask, even if he had desired her, which he did not.

Missy had decided her future lay not in literature, after all, but in advocacy and politics, and Ike ought to get involved.

"I just want to say," Ike told her when she brought up the point, "that at least there has been no blacklist on Broadway—and I now work on Broadway."

"Broadway is fluff," she replied. "Except for the occasional Arthur Miller play. It's not a place that a responsible grown man should be wasting his life."

"Music is my life," Ike said.

His political leanings were her own, but his passion was not. And he didn't like being insulted. He left the apartment and told her to call him when she had calmed down. He went back to his mother's place and reclaimed his old bedroom, at least for the moment.

They lived apart from that time on. Ike didn't know whether to be loyal or not, loving or not, supportive or not. He was not entirely faithful but had lost some part of his taste for romantic adventure, and felt in a perpetual state of compromise. Some nights he sat alone in the dark in his studio apartment in Hell's Kitchen and felt like crying. Was it Missy he felt for, or himself? His inability to come to any definite conclusion about love, sex, loving anyone in particular, kept him isolated from the one question he refused to ask himself: What had become of Aurora Shelton?

The only constant in his life was that he loved his baby girl, even as he had lost all tolerance for her mother. His own mother seemed unsurprised when he consulted her.

"Some people are born angry," she said to him one morning when they met for breakfast at Childs. Ike had sworn off Schrafft's. "Some, like Count Willie, are born reckless and charming. Some, like you, are born with talent without madness. That's rare. You have to take what you can get. You're not Mozart, but you're still alive at thirty-six, and he wasn't."

"What does that have to do with me and Missy?" He asked.

"She's a pretty smart biscuit," said Ollie, "but lost and angry, and it's too unsettling for you. You'll work something out. Just don't let go of that baby girl. I love that baby girl."

"Oh, God," Ike said. "Me too."

"It will all work out," Ollie said, though the likelihood that she believed it was only fair. But she did love the baby, her only grandchild, and if it came to her intervening at some point to keep Lil Armstrong Cozzens Harris in her life, she knew she would.

IKE TOOK HIS daughter for her first look at Times Square when she was five, hoisting her onto his shoulders and parading up the sidewalk from the *New York Times* building, which was about to be sold to Allied Chemical, past Bond Clothing Store and the Camel cigarette man, still blowing smoke rings as big as truck tires, and up toward the Winter Garden, where he worked. He wanted her to see the glamour and the excitement of the center of the earth, but, seeing it through her eyes, eyes that had never encountered it before, he realized that something sad and distressing had begun to happen to the place. Like a pair of shoes that one simply assumes is forever new, the theater district had begun to get scuffed and bruised. Everywhere Ike looked he encountered signs of decay, barely visible, but enough to leave him depressed. What, exactly, had happened to the place while he was not paying attention? Even the Camel man himself was a study in peeling paint across a scarred surface. A couple of marquees, once grand rococo creations, had been replaced by cheap, squared-off metal rectangles, with no decorative elements at all, and no lights. The

Hotel Astor still showed off its finery as it dominated the block between 44th and 45th on the west side of Broadway, but, looking up at its fine mansard roof, he could see that its once-rich green patina was largely overlaid with soot that marked it as a dowager, doing her best in a world that had moved on. He felt sick at the apparent inexorability of these changes, and sicker at how it could have been that he had never noticed them.

Lil, however, seemed indifferent to the entire spectacle. He had hoped to see her enchanted. Instead, she was bored and wanted ice cream, and he couldn't really blame her. He bought her a drink at Orange Julius, now occupying the stand where once, on his first night in the pit at *Pal Joey*, he had enjoyed a cup of "Papena, the Wonder Drink," which he noted, taking a sip of Lil's beverage, was the same damn drink. That, at least, had not changed.

He wanted to take her into the Winter Garden and show her the pit, the auditorium, the dressing rooms, and the stage, but she was becoming restive and wanted to get back to her mother; it was time for her nap. He realized with distress that his dreams might not be hers, his pleasures might not be hers, and that she was far too strong willed to argue with about it. He dropped her at home, kissing her and Missy goodbye for what would be the next month. The following day, he left for Philadelphia for the tryout of Sid Lupowitz's show. As the lead trumpet player, he, the concertmaster, and the drummer were the only members of the New York band traveling. They would pick up local musicians in Philly.

Sid Lupowitz, whose ebullience was really on display only when he talked about himself, had played through the entire score on the piano for Ike before they left, the two of them hunkering down in the Winter Garden pit. Ike was sentimentally inclined to Sid, who had made a band out of nothing during the war years, but he was not impressed with the music.

After a couple of years of playing *West Side Story* every night, Sid's work seemed to him clubfooted, a little simplistic, a little vulgar. He had no trouble hiding his reaction from Sid, however, because Sid asked for no reaction and instead provided Ike with one before he could speak.

"Dynamite, right?" He asked. It was not even a rhetorical question. It wasn't a question at all.

"Here's the hit," Sid said, launching into the title song, which wasn't bad. Ike shook his head, tapped his feet, and smiled.

"The syncopation!" Sid shouted over the piano, continually impressed with what he had done.

Ike gave him thumbs-up. That was good enough for Sid, who took it to be a cry of sheer joy.

At the end of the demonstration the composer rose from the piano, turned his ass toward Ike, and pointed to one of his buttocks.

"I've got it right here," he said. "The formula for a hit show. In my back pocket."

We'll see, Ike thought, but he didn't speak. There were no pockets on the back of Sid Lupowitz's trousers.

He didn't see Sid again until the orchestra rehearsals in Philly, which were presided over by the show's music director, a wiry and exacting individual named Herbert Greene, who was coming off two years conducting *The Music Man,* and Red Ginzler, the orchestrator who spoke softly with a slight stammer and mostly kept to himself as Sid and Herb Greene argued about every tempo, every shift in dynamics—everything. Ike bore it with as much patience as he could muster. Ginzler corrected wrong notes and introduced an occasional new idea. Ike was immediately impressed that the orchestration, which featured wild flights of fancy in the woodwinds and brass, was dramatically superior to the music itself, and this gave him faint hope. Ginzler, virtually silent, had topped Lupowitz, who was a volcano of complaint. Though the atmosphere in the room was poisonous, the score, played by a brassy band in sophisticated pastiche-like twenties arrangements, sounded sort of okay to Ike.

While the band rehearsed in a drafty studio on the fifth floor of the Forrest Theatre, the cast was downstairs with a rehearsal pianist and the director and choreographer, running tech rehearsals, setting lighting and set move cues, seeing how quickly costume changes would need to be made and setting up the sound effects—mostly, it turned out, machine gun noises. It wasn't until two days before the first performance that the cast trooped up to the fifth floor to sing through the score with the band for the first time.

Ike looked up and watched them file in; they seemed eager and happy to greet the band that would support their efforts. For the first time, they would sing the show and hear it the way it was intended to sound. Ike recognized a couple of actors from TV, and one who had been in the chorus of *West Side*.

And then, nearly in the back, he spotted Aurora Shelton. His heart jumped when he saw her, with pixie short hair, dressed in a turtleneck sweater and jeans. She did not notice him, for which he was grateful. It gave him time to gaze at her unobserved. She had grown up. She was a young woman with a ready smile and pale, perfect skin. She wore no makeup. Her clothes were unremarkable. His head swam a little at the sight of her bantering with the young man who, he would soon learn, was playing her opposite number. She was the ingénue, the nice girl, the center of innocent sanity in a world of gangsters and bootleggers. She had words to say and a rather bland, uninteresting song to sing. When she stood to sing it, the company applauded politely, but Ike could barely play. He watched her as though she was a star—the only star—as she found her way through the musical mediocrity that Sid Lupowitz had provided. And then she sat down.

Halfway through the rehearsal day she noticed him. He saw it happen. She looked over at him and her head snapped back in surprise. He lifted his trumpet in a little wave and she blew him a kiss from across the room. At the next break he worked his way through the crowded rehearsal room to where she was standing. He was about to speak when she threw her arms around him in a guileless gesture of affection.

"My God," he said, trying hard to breathe, "it is so good to see you."

They had drinks after rehearsal, and she was giddy about the prospects of finally being noticed on Broadway. Ike listened, letting her go on, watching her mouth move, which was pleasure enough. She asked him about himself, about the baby and Missy, but his responses were brief and general. They recapped the previous years and how they had come to be reunited in Philadelphia of all places. Ike, who had rarely been so happy to be anywhere, tried to keep things professional, but he didn't want them to end. Finally, walking her back to the hotel, he asked her, "how do you like your song?"

She winced a little and took his hand unexpectedly.

"It's not 'I Could Write a Book.'"

"Not many songs are," Ike said. "We'll see."

The first performance was not a triumph. The show was tedious and short on laughter, and only the title song landed. When the curtain finally descended at 11:15 in the evening, Ike threw caution to the wind and went immediately to Aurora's dressing room. He had to see her. Her song, no more of a problem than many other elements of the show, had landed with a thud.

She was in shock, almost in tears. She had never been this

exposed onstage before; in a chorus you could hide. In an off-Broadway theater you could pretend you were in a living room. But to be out there alone in front of 1,200 bored theatergoers and to be let down by herself and them—it was unbearable. Her dresser picked up her wig and departed, leaving them alone without a hint of interest as to why the first trumpet player had come rushing up to see her—this was show business, after all. The room was suffused with the scent of stage makeup and gardenia, cedar and something new—Aurora's perspiration, a hint of crushed wet desiccated leaves, which Ike suspected she would take pains to hide. She reminded him of a good Burgundy. He sunk into a chair across from her as she cleaned her face in the mirror and pulled her robe carelessly around her.

"It's awful," she said. "God-awful. I hate it and I don't know if I can go on singing it."

Ike, who had climbed the stairs wondering what he would say to bring comfort, put his hand on her shoulder and took command.

"I have one piece of advice. I've seen a lot of shows in trouble. Some pull it off, some don't. You never know. But please, do not—please, please do not—be the one to complain to anyone about your song. Everyone meeting downstairs in the house right now is ready to kill either himself or every other person in the room. They're only one step away from wanting to kill you too. In every show, there's a victim. Your job is not to become the victim. Don't become a part of the problem. Leave that to me."

And with that, he turned and left the dressing room.

They played through the weekend—a Saturday matinee and evening, making cuts and rearranging things. After the Saturday night performance, Ike buttonholed Sid in the hotel lobby.

"That ballad for the ingénue," he said. "Sid, you of all people, can do better. It should break your heart, that song."

Sid looked at him imperiously. "You too?" he asked. "How come every guy in the building is in love with Aurora Shelton?"

Ike was silent. Was this true?

"The song is fine," Sid said, "if she could just fucking sing it. We've got bigger fish to fry."

Before Sid could move, Ike turned tail on him and pointed to the back pocket of his slacks. Thankfully there now was one there.

"Look in your pocket," he said over his shoulder. "There's a new ballad in there somewhere."

He walked to the elevator and got in, leaving Sid Lupowitz in the lobby.

On the following Friday, after Ike had nursed Aurora through nightly bouts of insecurity over brandy, he was called to a hastily scheduled ten *A.M.* orchestra rehearsal. There was a new song. Herb Greene handed out parts, but Red Ginzler was nowhere to be found. He had, Greene explained, gone back to New York answering a call from Frank Loesser. Sid raised his eyebrows. Abandoned for *that little pisher.* It was too much to bear.

"But I think you'll like this," said Greene. "It's like a jazz tune—like Lupowitz plays Ellington. For the ingénue."

The song was beautiful. Ike had no idea what it was about—without Aurora in the room to sing it there was only the music, no lyric. The title was "Out of Sight, Out of Mind." The band made its way through the tune once, and then there was what looked like a musical interlude. Ike, sight-reading his part for the first time, saw the notation that he was to insert a Harmon mute, stem in, in the trumpet. As he began to play, he realized it was a solo, his solo, with only the stand-up bass and a few piano fills behind him. It was gorgeous, a sweet, heartbreaking variation on the tune, the trumpet notes slipping from one to another in an unpunctuated series of slurs that rose and fell like hope itself. He suddenly sounded like Miles Davis, and he didn't even know how he was doing it. It elided into a final chorus of the main part of the song, which, presumably would be sung. At the end, there was silence.

Herb Greene started to give notes, but Ike was paging back through his part on the music stand to look at that solo. There were some words, in a tiny, fine handwriting beneath the Harmon mute cue. Now that he wasn't playing, he could read them. They said, "Ike Harris solo—play better than Ladnier would."

Ike raised his hand and Greene turned to him.

"Who the hell wrote this arrangement?" Ike asked.

"Whoever it is, you should send over a bottle of gin," said the trombone player sitting in front of Ike. "That's a hell of a solo."

"Charlie Vodery," said Greene. "Ace Negro arranger. Did us a favor with Ginzler gone."

Sid looked over at Ike. "You remember Charlie Vodery," Sid said innocently. "You fucked up his whole encore when we were in the army. So I called him."

Ike smiled, remembering his encounter with Vodery after the army band contest in D.C.

"We're even," he said to Sid.

"Even my ass," Sid replied. "You owe me more than you can ever pay."

Aurora learned the song that afternoon. She was sort of stunned by how beautiful and telling it was compared to the rest of the score, not to mention the bland and turgid ballad it replaced, but she kept the thought to herself. It went into the show that night.

She began it with some uncertainty, but by the time she got to the bridge, she was really singing. She looked out into the dark, blinded by the follow spot, and something happened. It was like a tripwire. Facing an audience she couldn't see, launching into the body of the tune once more, the back of her thighs and her calves began to vibrate, or tingle. Or so it seemed. She felt it creeping up her spine, and for a moment, thought something awful was happening to her body. The beginning of some kind of nerve degeneration or circulatory failure. But what was she to do? As the tune went into the trumpet solo she turned, as directed, away from the audience, and began to pack prop clothing into a suitcase. But in her mind, she was trying to cope with the fear. Three bars before the solo ended it hit her. She was sitting on the Magnavox, with Ethel Waters's voice shooting up through her legs to her spine. She was that voice. No, not that voice, but that power, that certainty that control, and that perfectly assured musical sound. Wherever the arrow had been aiming all this time, here was its destination. Bathed in a cold sweat of joy, she turned back to the audience and sang the final chorus, her voice ringing above the orchestra with heartbreak; determination and bewilderment fought each other off as they did in the lyric. She sustained the last note, watching the tip of Herb Greene's baton for the cutoff, and hit it perfectly. The audience, lethargic until that moment, erupted.

I'm here, she thought.

Over the course of the next two weeks, Aurora's curtain call began to get a few whistles and bravos. And every night, though he could not see her from his position in the pit, Ike tried to touch her with the Harmon mute, the Miles Davis slurs, and the most heartbreaking siren song he could create. It rose up out of his soul and moved through his lips to the horn and out into the world where everyone could hear it. A declaration of love unguarded. He could hear in her voice that she must love him too, or at least the him that was present in the sound he was making.

They met in the bar every night now, and after she'd been singing the song for a week, she finally told him.

"You got me that song," she said. "I know you did. Thank you. It could change everything."

All he said was, "I'm glad you got it."

"That solo," she said, "that's you."

"In every sense of the word," Ike said. "I didn't write it, but I'm playing it like I did. Can I ask you . . . what are you doing while I'm playing it? What's it doing there? I can't see you from the pit."

"I'm packing," she said, "I'm packing to go back to the Midwest after the big city has done me wrong. I turn upstage, put a pair of stockings and a dress in a suitcase, close it, and turn around to the audience to sing the final chorus. And every night I think while I'm doing it, why is that girl going back to the Midwest? This girl surely isn't."

Ike nodded. He was disappointed that his playing was covering such a mundane act. He was hoping it was about a kiss. Or something that meant something. Or that she heard it that way.

He took her hand; she had taken his on various occasions so easily, yet this somehow cost him in a way he did not believe it had ever cost her.

"I can't help it," he said to her. "When I play it . . . I don't know how else to say it—it's like we're wrapped in each other's arms for sixteen bars. The loveliest sixteen bars."

She let go of his hand, perhaps shocked, or just thinking about his boldness in saying it. He put his elbows on the table and his chin in his hands, just to look at her. Neither of them had touched their drinks. She took his forearms in her hands, just above his wrists, returning his look earnestly.

"Ike," she said. "You've got a little girl and a kind of a wife, and you're thirty-five years old."

"Thirty-six," he corrected. There was no point in painting it any other way, he thought.

"All my life I've been running towards freedom," she said. "I escaped from an impossible house, from a father that I don't want to be reminded of, you know, from a two-bit trio, from the road, from the chorus, and now I'm free. I can't give that up. I just can't. Do you understand that?"

Ike looked at her for a long time. Her loveliness was impossible to turn away from, but her eyes didn't change, didn't soften, didn't glance away, just held him there. For a moment he wondered what he could say to change her mind. But the moment passed. What kind of a man would try to change such a mind?

"I understand you perfectly," he said.

"I love you," she said in that affectless tone in which it always came out. It was enough to drive a man insane.

NOWHERE TO GO BUT UP loaded out of the Forrest in Philadelphia and trucked north to Manhattan on a Sunday. By Tuesday afternoon it was loaded into the Winter Garden, ready for a week of previews before opening on the following Thursday. The tryout had not instilled confidence. Two actors and four songs had been replaced. The choreographer had been sent packing. A joke writer had been hanging around. And Ike Harris and Aurora Shelton had carefully avoided each other for the last week of performances and on the train ride north. There was not much of an advance sale waiting for them in New York, and previews would be papered with college students and senior citizens, out-of-work actors and members of various unions, all of whom tended to be generous audiences, especially when they didn't have to pay to get in.

On Wednesday night at a little before eight-thirty, Vincent

Donnelly swung onto his perch behind follow spot number two as the audience murmured below him. He checked his cue sheet. He had memorized the moves during two days of tech rehearsals but had paid scant attention to the show itself. It was all but impossible to judge the quality of a production during tech. The actors were standing on their marks and speaking their words, but it could hardly be called acting. There were interminable pauses as pieces of scenery slid into place or descended from the fly gallery—moves that were repeated over and over until the stagehands had mastered the most graceful possible arrivals and departures as the set changed and the story progressed. There appeared to be no story. Vincent had dosed off a couple of times, and the entire atmosphere was somnolent. But now he was alert. There was an audience, and within moments, there was an overture, bright, jazzy, but hard to characterize in terms of quality, not that it was any of Vincent's business, or even that he considered himself a reliable judge. It was noisy enough for all practical purposes.

It started with four gunshots and ran through a bunch of razzmatazz, interrupted by one fetching ballad that Vincent thought might have possibilities. Then the bathtub gin music returned, and the whole thing wrapped up with the drums providing the sound of a Tommy gun, and an actor appearing at the top of a stairway, twisting this way and that until he fell in a choreographed herky-jerky motion, as if each gunshot were hitting a different part of his body. On the final, grim note of the overture he collapsed flat on the stage floor, to a roar of applause from the audience. *Backers,* thought Vincent. Or maybe it was better than he suspected.

Toward the end of act one, the ingénue began to sing that ballad. She moved with a kind of grace that seemed to him completely absent from the rest of the show, and he felt that his light was dancing with her, waltzing against the vulgarity of the surrounding landscape.

At the end of the act, he consulted a Playbill to find out who she was, but her credits were negligible. Some tours. Like every other ingénue in 1960 she had played Sarah Brown in *Guys and Dolls* in summer stock and done some operetta at the Muny in St. Louis. This was her Broadway debut. Through two more previews, he followed her with his spot as if he were a suitor, trying to keep her in the dead center of the beam, making the instrument itself invisible, and merely allowing her to be luminous as if light were actually emanating from her, not from him. It was a game, but a dead serious one. He wanted to be perfect. He wanted her light and his to be joined. And then, at a certain point, he understood that he wasn't simply rooting for her. During the evening show, as she turned to pack her suitcase during that beautiful ballad, accompanied by a sinuous muted trumpet, Vincent Donnelly knew for certain that he was feeling something he had never felt before. Without meeting her or ever having seen her before the middle of that week, without knowing, really, the first thing about her, he had fallen hopelessly, desperately in love with Aurora Shelton.

Part Two

10

TELEVISION

AURORA SHELTON and Vincent Donnelly were married on September 13, 1964, at the New York World's Fair. Mayor Robert Wagner, who had his summer offices at the fair he had sought so tirelessly to promote, performed the ceremony. The stagehands union, which boasted more than three hundred members working the fair, had called in a favor for Vincent and, of course, the mayor remembered him well from the strike, though they both successfully pretended to be strangers to each other. Vincent's mother refused to attend because Wagner was not a priest, and her son was marrying a Protestant. Several of Aurora's friends from the chorus of *Foxy* boycotted the event because of Mayor Wagner's aggressive attempt to close down every gay bar in New York before the fair opened, lest the hordes of tourists arriving from across the world get the impression that New York was some kind of moral cesspool. Though he'd go down in history as the first mayor of New York to hire minority workers in meaningful positions at City Hall, Wagner knew he had to draw the line somewhere; the Stonewall Riot was still five years away.

On the afternoon of the wedding, which was bright and

cool, Ike Harris was in France, where it was already nighttime, sitting at Le Cave de la Heure d'Or waiting for the music to begin. The place hadn't changed. The war had come and gone, as had the 1950s and almost half of the '60s. Even on the streets he could find few overt signs of the invasion and occupation that he and his mother and Count Palaffi had fled in advance back when he was a child. The substratum nightclub, with its vaulted cobblestone ceiling and black-skirted waitresses, appeared virtually undisturbed, though the nature of the clientele had changed with the times. There was not a tuxedo in sight. French jazz lovers, dressed in jeans and print tops, sparsely populated the place, many of them gray haired and lonely, looking for dance partners who could keep up, or were game enough to try. Except for the surrounding ancient stone, they might all as well have been in the rec room of a retirement community. The patrons could really dance, though, and Ike watched couples change partners, as if one woman were as good as another, or might be at least as good a dancer. But Aurora was his only thought. Somewhere, she was marching down an aisle. He was drinking Ancient Age, the only bourbon the bar carried. He felt lucky to get it.

Ike had felt an acute need to return. It was Yom Kippur eve, in fact, and he was planning to atone with jazz. The only woman he had ever loved was being given away to someone else, not by her father, whose life had ended in fiery immolation a decade before, but by a Midwestern ex-music teacher who had come to New York for the honor of seeing to it that the job was done well.

Ike couldn't stand to be where all this was happening—it was too painful for him even to be in the same country. He'd taken a leave from maybe the best theater gig he'd ever had—playing first trumpet for Barbra Streisand in *Funny Girl*—to return to the place where he'd first heard the horn played by

Tommy Ladnier, the place that had sealed his fate as a trumpet player, that had led eventually to his delusional belief that he could bring Aurora Shelton into his life permanently merely by playing well enough. It had all started here, in these remains of an ancient catacomb. It occurred to him that romantic calamity no doubt predated even the era when such catacombs were constructed. Ike was one in a long line that began at the beginning. He half remembered an old blues that Ladnier had recorded:

Adam and Eve in the Garden of Eden
Certainly must have shook that thing.

This early in the evening, the place was half empty. Ike sipped his drink gloomily. He had booked a room at the Ritz, where he vowed to spend the night alone. He was going to spend it as Zachary Harris, the disconsolate boy who wanted only to keep the name he was born with. It was a foolish notion—the jeans and cheap flowered blouses all around him told him what he had so often read: You can't go home again.

It had been four years since *Nowhere to Go But Up* had spent its dismal week of life on Broadway, a disaster from any number of points of view, but a nearly mortal calamity for Ike, though he'd hardly realized it at the time. At the final curtain on that Saturday night, he—like everyone associated with the show or the theater—had been put out of work. He had only the vaguest idea that Vincent Donnelly had fallen through the beam of his own follow spot and landed against Aurora's heart. The lighting grid and the orchestra pit were about as far from each other as you could get in a Broadway theater, and despite their marriage of convenience during the Actors' Equity strike, Ike and Vincent had not remained close.

On the final night of the show, feeling beaten by its failure, Ike had let himself into Missy's apartment shortly after midnight, when the sad farewells had been said at the theater. He poured himself a half tumbler of I. W. Harper and looked in on his beautiful Lil, who had recently moved from a crib to a bed. He did not awaken Missy but made up the sofa in the living room. He had his own apartment, of course, but simply couldn't face it. He needed to be somewhere populated. And the sight of Lil, at peace and asleep in the pathetic maid's room that had become her nursery, was enough to get him through the night. She might have no interest in Times Square, or the theater, or art of any kind, but she was his, as no one else was.

In the morning, Ike, Missy, and Lil breakfasted together on French toast and coffee. Ike was grateful for the company and helped Lil bite off pieces of her toast as she tried, without much success, to make animal shapes out of them. Missy was not amused—she believed in cutlery, and, newly, vegetarianism. But before breakfast was done, they'd agreed to meet up for dinner at an Italian joint in the Village that had become Lil's favorite spot for spaghetti and tomato sauce, the only dish she could be counted upon to consume on a regular basis. Ike left the house after breakfast and walked up to the Winter Garden, which was deserted. Stagehands would begin to load out the set on Monday, but on Sunday the place was like an empty synagogue, darkened and locked down except for the stage door. An ancient stage doorman named Clodfelter—no one seemed to know his first name—greeted Ike as he entered, a fedora pushed back on his head.

"You missed most everyone," Clodfelter said to him. "They've been coming in to clean out their dressing rooms. Sad fucking thing."

Ike nodded.

"You know how it is with a musical," he said to Ike. "Sometimes you drive right off the bridge." He took a slug of coffee from a stained cup.

Ike nodded again. "I just wanted to take one more look," he said.

"This one meant something to you?" Clodfelter asked, squinting in disbelief.

"Damned if I know why," Ike said. It was no business of Clodfelter's. The doorman adjusted his hat.

Ike wandered out into the auditorium and looked up at the set for the finale, which was still as it had been when the curtain fell for the last time, but unlit and dismal, except for the spectral shafts of yellow given off by the inevitable ghost light that was burning center stage. There was always a ghost light, a single bulb surrounded by a metal cage on a five-foot pole, at the center of every unoccupied stage on Broadway. He had never understood its purpose—though he supposed it kept people from tripping over cables and other pieces of scenery that might be lying around. Older folks believed it kept the ghosts of past performances at bay—God forbid that Hamlet or Captain Hook should suddenly reappear, much less the long dead actors who had played them. The people of the theater, he thought to himself, are really a primitive tribe. On the other hand, was he not a part of the tribe? Who was he kidding?

He looked down into the pit, but it was simply a black hole of felt baffling and cheap carpet. The elaborately carved wooden rail surrounding it was showing its age—split and chipped and needing varnish. The auditorium wanted paint. The felt fabric on the seats was threadbare and torn in spots. Ike stood and bowed his head for a moment. He offered a silent prayer, though to whom or what he couldn't have said, for the restoration of his only place of worship.

Down the block, at the Criterion, the marquee was advertising a double feature of *The Rise and Fall of Legs Diamond* and *Why Must I Die?* Ike watched them each twice without seeing them at all.

When he emerged, it was dark—daylight saving time had ended a couple of hours after the show had closed. Depressingly, all matinees would conclude in darkness for the next six months. He began the walk back from the movie theater to the subway stop on the corner of 50th Street when he saw Aurora. She was walking along Broadway, head down and determined, toward the theater from the corner of 51st. He watched her head under the marquee and turn east toward Seventh Avenue on 50th. She was practically marching. Something stopped him from signaling to her, but he didn't descend into the subway, as he had planned, either. He was supposed to be in the Village for Italian food in less than an hour, but he just stood there. Minutes passed.

He moved to the front of the theater, where photos of the shuttered production still hung in the display cases. He looked at Aurora, pictured with her suitcase, ready to return home to the Midwest, her mouth open in song. The photographer had snapped the shutter right after Ike's trumpet solo. He shook his head and turned, just in time to see her passing the front of the theater for what must have been at least the second time—or maybe the fiftieth. His eyes followed her as, once again, she turned east on 50th. Ike couldn't help but wonder how long this had been going on. He waited.

In less than five minutes, she reappeared, rounding the corner of 51st street and crossing under the marquee again. She was circling the theater like an animal trying to find the hole in the barbed wire fence of a corral that would let her back in. Ike saw at once that they were prisoners of their own inertia, the ones who had found it impossible to run when someone shouted fire in an underpopulated theater. It could not be allowed to continue—not for either of them, but only one of them had the power, perhaps, to put an end to the suffering. Ike fell in beside her.

"You too," he said.

She looked up, startled.

The two of them turned east. But rather than head up Seventh at the corner, where the back of the theater was dark and deserted, Ike took her arm and squired her across the avenue, eastward, away from the district. They walked in silence. Across Sixth, then Fifth. As they crossed Madison, she finally spoke.

"At some point," she said, "we have to decide where we're walking to."

"Wait here," Ike said as they stepped up onto the sidewalk, and he moved to a phone booth. He called Missy and explained that something had come up at the theater, and that she would have to take Lil to the Italian joint without him.

"She'll be disappointed," Missy said, the exasperation in her voice showing her own annoyance, not Lil's. "She doesn't get many evenings with her papa."

The words cut through Ike in ways he would never be able to tell her.

"There will be lots of evenings from now on," he said. "I'm out of work."

"You won't be spending them with us," Missy said.

"I will," Ike said, having no idea if what he said was true. "Please," he added, "I'm not at my best just now."

He emerged from the phone booth and, for a panicked moment, thought that Aurora had vanished. But she was standing in a doorway. A light snow had begun to fall; she was protecting her hair. He bought an umbrella from the newsstand on the corner and moved to her side.

On Second Avenue there was a chichi Provençal place called L'Amérique, to which Ike had never been. The stucco walls were salmon colored, the waiters were tuxedoed, and the wine list extensive. Ike pointed, and the sommelier appeared moments later with a bottle of Bordeaux that featured a rendering on its label of a dramatic twelfth-century château. The two of them drank, and Ike pointed to the label.

"Do you know how you can tell the quality of a fine wine?" He asked.

Aurora shrugged.

"You count the windows on the picture of the château. The more windows, the better the wine." Ike counted quickly. "Eighteen windows," he said. "An excellent château. I lived in France, you know."

Aurora laughed. It was the first time Ike had heard her laugh since Homer and Jethro's "Hernando's Hideaway" on the jukebox in Lake Charles.

They dined on escargot and capon, little white potatoes, and wilted spinach.

"How well did you know my father?" Aurora asked as the sommelier uncorked a second bottle of wine. Ike was startled.

"Much better than I knew my own," he said. "I don't think I really remember my own much—he took me to the movies on Saturday afternoons. I remember that. And Ebbets Field."

"My father didn't believe in the movies," Aurora said, "or anything that might set your mind free—music, books, other worlds. I had to run. You see that."

Ike nodded.

"I became very determined," Aurora said. "In some way, I guess I actually have my father to thank."

"He was focused," Ike said. "I'll give him that. No one ever committed to screaming at me the way your father did."

"He was screaming at me years before he met you," Aurora said. She shook her head at the memory. "He broke things, too."

"He tried to break me," Ike said. "That was his job."

"It wasn't his job to break me," Aurora said.

"He didn't," Ike said, raising a glass. "Nothing will stop you."

"Do you think?"

"I knew your father, and if he didn't break you, nothing ever will."

"But my mother . . ." she began, and Ike held up his hand to stop her. He was feeling suddenly expansive and wise. Maybe it really was a very good château.

"I'm going to say something pretentious and philosophical, and I hope you don't take it the wrong way. I never met your mother, and I know you loved her a lot, and that she gave you music in some way or other. But it is only given to some to survive. Some not. That's just the way things are. My father keeled over on Fifth Avenue. My greatest trumpet idol lost his teeth and his career and his ability to stay away from the bottle, and that was the end. Sometimes it's the end. But some survive. You, for instance."

They drank in silence. The check was delivered. Ike suddenly felt that perhaps he had made a mistake, that it would have been better to keep it light for her, that he should have said anything to distract her from her somber recognitions and recollections. He had wanted only to lift her sprits and his own, but had somehow forgotten his mission. He changed directions in a way that he found always easier to do when he was fueled by alcohol.

"Here's one way to look at it. You don't have to go to work tomorrow, and there are better shows out there waiting for you. So, this one went over Niagara in a barrel and broke up on the rocks. Lots of them do. In the end, they're only shows. And there are lots of them."

He paid the check, and the two of them passed out into the street. The night was cold, but the snow had blown through, and the stars were out. They were full of very expensive food and wine.

"Come," he said. "It's early yet."

He hailed a cab and directed the driver to take them to Central Park South, where the horse-and-buggy drivers waited for fares. There wasn't much trade on a chilly November Sunday evening, so he was able to make a quick bargain for a trip through the park that would drop them at the top, at 110th Street. The driver, in a top hat and smelling vaguely of cheap whiskey, bundled the two of them into the buggy with an excess of plaid blankets, and the horse set off through the darkened park.

The lights from the Fifth Avenue apartments made a lovely nightscape. Ike and Aurora sat next to each other but touched only sporadically and seemingly by accident. As they drove, Ike narrated the sights they were passing—an entirely fictional account that included the Eiffel Tower, Montmartre, the Alps shining with snow, and small farms and chalets that were perfect and tidy. They were, in fact, dramatic views that could be glimpsed from the windows of the toy electric train set he remembered from the store the Count had taken him to in Zurich. Imagination and memory swirled inside him as the very fine wine worked its way through his brain.

Evidently pleased by this cockeyed fantasy, Aurora tucked herself into him, and listened. It was her impulse to be charmed, to be grateful that this man, to whom she believed she owed so much, should be making such an effort to make her forget, to look elsewhere instead of behind her, to let her know what she already knew—that he was in love with her, and that the complications of his circumstances were to be forgotten for this night, even if he had no idea what he would do about them. It broke her heart in some way that, fueled by fine wine and passion, he spoke so much and knew so little. Certainly not that the during the last week, she had been visited after each performance in her dressing room by another man, the man who followed her every move on stage with a lamp.

Vincent Donnelly was not a whimsical man, not a man likely to count the number of windows on a wine label or declare that the Swiss Alps were visible from a horse-and-buggy clip-clopping up Park Drive North. He had seemed, in fact, a man of extraordinarily simple gestures and direct speech.

He had appeared for the first time the night before the show opened, after seven sad previews, a dark-haired, black-eyed man with a high forehead and immaculate fingernails, his work clothes belying the trouble he took with his personal care. He had introduced himself as her follow-spot operator. And she expected, given how closely he had been watching her, that he might say something nice about her performance. He did not.

"I've seen each move you've made onstage seven times," he said. "I've heard you talk and sing this role seven times."

She waited. But he was not tongue-tied or poetic.

"Seven times isn't a lot," he explained. "I followed Nanette Fabray with a lamp once for over four hundred shows. I've followed you all around the stage for seven, like a loyal servant, which is what I am, and now I'm in love with you, and I will always be in love with you, and I'm sure you can't even remember my name yet."

"Vincent," she said.

"That's right," he said. "I'm Vincent. I'm not exactly inexperienced with women, but I can't say I've ever courted one—really courted, in the way my father would talk about in the old country. I've never cared enough about any particular one. But here's the thing I need to tell you. I've found what I want. And I don't think it's your job to teach me how to court you, that's my job. I'll learn it. I'll become a virtuoso if you'll let me. I just thought . . . well, since it's what I want, I should let you know. There's no sense in either of us being surprised. Every time you enter, and I get to shine my lamp on you down from above while you're moving across the stage, it's like I'm reaching through the light to touch you. I know what I was put on earth for. That's probably as much as I should say tonight. And besides, my mouth has gone dry just looking at you. I love you very much."

And with that, Vincent Donnelly bowed stiffly and backed out of the room. It was one of the more astonishing performances Aurora had ever witnessed, and it wasn't until late that night, as she tried to drift off to sleep, that it occurred to her that the speech had been memorized. Vincent, she thought, wasn't much of an actor. But obviously, it was important to him to get it right, which touched her.

Each night following, he had appeared. With flowers one night, and with a single rose the next. He didn't stay long. They talked easily once his initial speechmaking had worn off. And on the third night he told her about her performance—a detailed analysis of where she was brilliant, and where her writers had let her down and not allowed her to be brilliant. He complimented the song and the beautiful trumpet solo that was now nightly making her tear up as she turned away from the audience. He told her he loved her most in that moment, "and not only because when I look at your back, I believe I can see into you. Something about the way you carry your shoulders, the sadness and the hope that's gotten dashed, but won't die. I see that. It's very real."

Now, as she sat now in the buggy, in the crisp late autumn weather, beneath a mountain of blankets and next to the first man to whom she had ever said, "I love you," she could only think of one thing. She would need to escape, again. Protection had always come with escape.

Ike brought Aurora home just after two a.m. They had gone from Central Park to Harlem and spent two hours at a club where Teddy Wilson was playing the piano. No longer in his prime, he was still a master of grace, and the keyboard floated beneath his fingers. They had each had a couple of glasses of cognac, and, on top of the wine at L'Amérique, Aurora's head was spinning. The music was lovely; Ike was lovely, a compact man with a kind, round face, sandy hair that was already beginning to thin, and small, delicate fingers that touched her fleetingly, and never without grace. His goal of making her forget the closing, the way she had been ignored in the reviews, the loss of time and passion expended on *Nowhere to Go But Up*, was a noble one, and largely succeeded. She felt unlatched from despair and disappointment at this moment, from the endless hours of work that had led to nothing. But carefree she was not. She knew that she would be hung over and miserable in the morning. Nothing was simple, nothing was pure. No emotion seemed to exist that was not counteracted by its opposite. She felt powerless, seduced, resentful, happy to be free of everything and yet locked down in a different way. She dared not ask him to take her home now, but when Teddy Wilson finished his second set, Ike stood and fetched her coat from the cloakroom.

At her front door he did not hesitate, but leaned into her and kissed her, tentatively at first and then with such hunger that she could not help but respond. They held each other in the vestibule of the brownstone on West 67th where she lived on the second floor. She felt his body pressing against her, and hers responding, even through two heavy overcoats. She wanted to take him upstairs but could not bring herself to say the words. There was simply too much confusion in her life. She held her mouth against his and waited, her body alive and her head swimming. Finally, he pulled away and took her face in his hands.

"We've had quite a lot to drink," he said. "And as Jimmy Stewart once pointed out, there are rules about such things." The quote was lost on her, but it didn't matter.

He made sure she got safely past the inner glass door with her key and stood watching until she had disappeared up the stairs.

WHEN THE PHONE RANG, Monkey Monkton was trying without success to win a stubborn solitaire game for the third time, which he did not consider cheating. To reverse his progress and begin again, was, he felt, a part of his education though what exactly he was learning he couldn't have said. It did not seem to be making him a better card player. His office was small and bare, as befitted a man whose new career as a talent manager consisted of handling three relatively unrecognized clients, one of whom was Aurora Shelton. A Playbill for *Nowhere to Go But Up* sat on his desk, along with a copy of Aurora's contract, which he had never had the energy to file. He had managed to get her taken on by the William Morris Agency, which he considered a managerial triumph, and he knew some bright young fellow in business affairs over there would have the contract properly catalogued in case anyone needed to look at it. He stabbed out his cigarette, pushed his hat back on his head, and picked up the phone. Aurora was in Utica, New York, having stepped off the 20th Century Limited to make the call.

"I'll be in Chicago tomorrow morning and switch to the Chief. That means I'll be in Los Angeles in three days. And I'm going to need to find work. A club, auditions at a movie studio, something. I only have a minute, the train's leaving. Find me some work, Monkey, please."

Monkey Monkton stared at the mouthpiece as the phone went dead. Los Angeles. He had never been west of the Rockies. He tapped the buttons on the phone to get a dial tone and called Aurora's agent at William Morris in New York to see who he knew in the L.A. office—the big office.

IT WAS LIKE AURORA to travel by train, or by bus, along roads. All of her touring had been done that way, not to mention the many moves between army bases when she was a child, which had been accomplished in station wagons. The thought of flying to Los Angeles never crossed her mind. It had been only a year since the first commercial jets had begun coast-to-coast operations, she would have been terrified to get in one, and, besides, she needed to feel the distance, feel the miles receding behind her. It had been that way ever since her escape to Junction City at seventeen. Airline travel would not seem real to her for years to come.

She had the porter make up her bunk and slept most of the day as the train rocked westward. A little after five P.M., as the Limited pushed through Sandusky, she awakened and went looking for something to eat. Her head had stopped hurting, and the queasy feeling in her stomach was almost gone. The dining car was just opening, and the staff was kind. The cook provided tomato soup and a grilled cheese sandwich, even though these were technically lunch menu items. Then she returned to her bunk and was almost immediately asleep again. Whether exhausted or simply in needy pursuit of unconsciousness to avoid the tangle of the last week was not a question she asked herself. She closed her eyes and let dreams take her. She could always dream on trains.

What she could not have dreamed of was the diametrically opposing reactions of her two suitors when they discovered that she was gone. Ike Harris, sensing her need to sort things out, kept his word to Missy, spending evenings with her and

Lil, and making sure that his daughter had her fill of spaghetti. He began composing a letter—a love letter, he supposed—to Aurora, but never got very far. He and Missy reached a truce, and some nights he slept over. Some nights they even shared a bed.

Vincent Donnelly consulted the contact sheet from *Nowhere to Go But Up* and called Aurora's agent, who was listed there. He was informed that Aurora was in Los Angeles for some appointments with movie agents, and was hoping to get a guest shot singing on *The Steve Allen Show.* Vincent couldn't imagine an agency as big as William Morris lifting a finger for a client as insignificant as Aurora Shelton, so he informed the crew chief at the Winter Garden that he'd be taking a leave from the next show, *The Unsinkable Molly Brown,* because of pressing family business. Most stagehands lucky enough to be employed by a Broadway theater could not have gotten away with this cavalier coming and going, but Vincent was now protected; thanks to the Ennis brothers and their continuing friendship with his parents, he was family. He went from the Winter Garden to the nearest BOAC office and bought a ticket on a jetliner to Los Angeles. He called his father, his brother, and a few of his poker regulars from the airport and let them know he wasn't going to be around for a while. When his flight was called, he thought about the possibility that he might die—he had never flown before. But the risk seemed worth it. What was life without her?

Pete Byron met him at Norms on Sunset Boulevard for breakfast two o'clock the next morning. Known to his colleagues as Lord Byron for obvious reasons he, like Vincent, had begun life as a spot operator, in his case for the Civic Light Opera in L.A. But he had long since moved on to the more lucrative work of crewing on movies, where lighting technicians were called gaffers. He was a hulking figure, a tangle of jet-black chest hair seemingly trying to escape from the open collar of a Hawaiian shirt. His bushy black mustache looked vaguely nineteenth century. Hair protruded from his ears, from the back of his fingers, his forearms, and every other visible part of his body, except his head, which had been shaved clean, though Vincent suspected that, had it grown in, there would have been no more than a light fringe around his ears. Poor bastard. Hair everywhere except where it belongs.

He wore a gold Saint Christopher medallion around his neck, and something that looked gaudier than a World Series ring on the fourth finger of his right hand. He ordered six over easy eggs, extra bacon, toast, and grits. Vincent was impressed and vaguely nauseated. Lord Byron could eat, could drink coffee like a fiend, and had power. Just now he was heading up the electrics department on a Fred MacMurray vehicle called *The Absent-Minded Professor* at Disney. An outdoor night shoot had ended at midnight, and breakfast at two was nothing new to him. Norms was open twenty-four hours. This was Hollywood.

"Tommy Ennis said you needed a favor," he said, wiping egg yolk from his mustache. "When Tommy calls . . . you know."

Vincent explained that Aurora Shelton needed to audition for Steve Allen, and that her agent was no doubt too distracted by more important clients to attend to this fact. Was there any way to make it happen?

"There's always a way," Lord Byron said. "It might take some doing. I know a guy who's on the crew at *The Tonight Show,* and I bet he knows a guy at *Steve Allen,* so let me do a little work on it. I will say one thing for Steve Allen—he has some pretty broads sing on that show. Lotsa nights I turn it on to look at Jenny Smith and them. I don't know if any of 'em are going anywhere, but he seems to like to have pretty girls around. He and I got that in common. This Aurora girl, what do you think?"

"I think she's the most beautiful woman in the world," said Vincent. "I've got to find a way to make her want to marry me."

"Ah," said Byron. He paused. "This is a hell of a funny way to do it," he concluded. "But that makes it into a mission. Let me see what I can do."

Lord Byron was as good as his word—he believed himself as much of a romantic poet in his heart as his namesake, though he had never figured out how to make a relationship last more than a couple of months and could never remember who the original Lord Byron was, exactly. But he did believe that life was ruled by passions uncontained, and that was how he lived his own life, always on location finding someone new to fuck, while the women he left behind in L.A. were either furious or otherwise occupied by the time he got home. He had no desire for anything else in the foreseeable future, and generally thought that the most reliable pleasure in his life, other than the unending hunt for pretty women who wanted to be in the movies, could be found at the blackjack table, especially on out-of-town shoots, where there was company per diem involved. But the opportunity to act as Cupid had never been handed to him before; he took the assignment as seriously as he could. Besides, he didn't want any trouble from the Ennis brothers.

Vincent, meanwhile, did his research on Allen's late-night TV show. He learned from a newspaper interview he found at the library downtown on 5th Street that Allen was an inveterate searcher for new singers with new songs—he rarely hired a vocalist to sing a standard. A pianist and composer himself, he had established a pattern of recording these new singers and their new songs, putting one of his own compositions on the B side of the record, and thereby assuring himself some royalties if the A side was a hit. Aurora, of course, had a great song that almost no one had ever heard, and Vincent considered calling Sid Lupowitz and having him special-delivery a copy of the "Out of Sight, Out of Mind" to him at the Chateau Marmont, where he had installed himself. But then he thought better of it. He suspected that if Aurora heard that a new song was required for the audition, she'd get hold of a copy herself.

This was nothing more than a hunch, but sometimes you have to play a hunch. Watching her in the reflection of his light for those few performances he had intuited that, even in repose, even playing the innocent young woman in a world of mayhem, she moved toward the audience, she won them by controlling them with the sheer force of her will. She was likely, he believed, to want to do things with as little help from the outside as possible. He had developed a theory over the years, which he had yet to see proven false: Some performers were hot—they pursued the audience and took them. Others were cool and waited for the audience to come courting. The hot ones didn't want help from anyone, the cool ones needed it to survive. It was, he supposed, like any seduction. Aurora ran hot. She'd want to have the idea herself and accomplish it on her own. She wouldn't appreciate being helped. Though he had no clue about her history and didn't know why, he intuited that she believed in self-reliance. In fact, Vincent concluded, the less she understood about his manipulations in this case the better.

He refined his thinking on this point until it clarified as he sat by the somewhat shabby pool at the Marmont, which was in a state of deterioration prior to its spectacular rebirth some fifteen years hence. What would be best, he decided, was that she might wonder if he had a hand in it, but never want to confirm it. That he was looking out for her without trying to control her destiny.

The audition took place a week later. Lord Byron had gone through the crew of *The Tonight Show* to the crew of *The Steve Allen Show* where the head carpenter was sleeping with a reed player in the *Steve Allen* band. The reed player talked to the musical director, Donn Trenner, who talked to Allen, whose assistant then called the agent at William Morris, who was quite startled to get an inquiry about a client he had never, to the best of his memory, heard of. He rifled through the files on his desk until he found the telex from his East Coast counterpart, read it quickly for the first time, and got on the phone to Aurora, who had been in town for less than a week, the train having taken its own sweet time. In fact, Vincent's BOAC jet had flown over her head before she reached New Mexico.

As it happened, she did not need to call Sid Lupowitz or anyone else. On the night that *Nowhere to Go But Up* closed, she had brought a large cloth satchel with her to the final performance. At the end of the show, she had snuck into the pit, paged through each player's book, and stolen all the pit parts for "Out of Sight, Out of Mind"; she now had the entire orchestration, as well as the piano/conductor score, which she'd removed from Herb Greene's conducting stand. She had all of it with her in Los Angeles when she stepped off the train at Union Station.

For two days she tried, unsuccessfully, to reach her contact at William Morris from her room downtown at the Biltmore. She was on the point of placing a person-to-person call to her New York agent or getting in touch with Monkey Monkton when the West Coast office called her. The voice on the other end of the line sounded like that of a high school boy, but he was calling with apologies and startling news. Steve Allen wanted to see her. It had all happened so quickly.

"We have very good connections here at William Morris,"

the voice on the other end of the line said. "We look out for the clients. We put them first."

AURORA EXPECTED TO be met by some kind of casting director or talent scout when she arrived at Steve Allen's theater on the corner of Vine and La Mirada, but when she pushed open the stage door there was Allen himself, his horn-rimmed glasses and swept-back black hair instantly recognizable. He was a tall, imposing figure, but surprisingly soft-spoken and friendly, which was a welcome shock, especially as Aurora was a stranger and quite terrified, as she always was at auditions. She suspected that Steve Allen knew all of that. He also knew something about her—that she had been in this one flop and was an army brat, and that she had a new song—the only really good song in the show, he had been told. How he had found this out she did not know, but she was impressed.

"I'm writing a show myself," he said. "About Sophie Tucker—the last of the red-hot mamas. Does that phrase mean anything to you?"

Aurora looked puzzled.

"That's what I was afraid of," Allen said. "Well, thank God most of the Broadway audience is older than you are. What do you have for me?"

Aurora reached into her bag and produced the piano-conductor score of "Out of Sight," which Allen propped in front of him. He looked at it for a moment, and then began to sight-read it. He was good. He played it through once, ignoring the trumpet solo, and then played it a second time, improvising around the melody like a real jazz pianist. Then he stopped and read through it without playing it, just looking at the pages of sheet music.

"This looks like the original piano conductor score from the show," he said.

Aurora thought for a split second, and then decided to risk it.

"I stole it," she said. "On closing night."

Allen cackled a falsetto laugh that was familiar to late-night TV viewers everywhere. "Good girl," he said. "You rescued a treasure. It's a really good song, you're a beautiful young woman, and let's do it on the show."

"But," Aurora said, "you haven't heard me sing yet."

Allen cackled again.

"Well," he said, "you've got me there. I'm an idiot. Sing!"

NEWLY MARRIED TO one of the dancers from his show—the courtship had lasted all of two weeks—Sid Lupowitz was in the midst of a poker game with Ike Harris and three other pit musicians when his wife called in from the bedroom, "Holy shit, Sid, they're playing your goddamn ballad!"

Sid dropped his hand and rushed into the bedroom, followed by the others. There on a black-and-white TV set that was drawing reception from a pair of rabbit ears, was Aurora Shelton singing "Out of Sight, Out of Mind," with what sounded like the original orchestration. Ike stood transfixed as Sid cried out in pain, "They better pay me some fucking royalties!"

Ike had never seen Aurora like this. She had been fitted with a floor-length off-the-shoulder dress in black, with trim that ran down the full length of her body. Her hair was up in an elegant chignon that made her seem like a blond cousin of Audrey Hepburn. She was breathtaking and singing perfectly. It was almost too much to bear. He wondered idly if someone would attempt the trumpet solo. Indeed, someone did, a Hollywood studio musician, proficient and soulless, who launched into it and tossed it off accurately but heedlessly. Ike didn't care. Aurora was on TV. On *The Steve Allen Show.* Sounding and looking, for all the world, like a star. His heart swelled and broke.

He threw in his cards and went back to Missy's, awakening her from a sound sleep. She was groggy, but not annoyed. This had been coming for a couple of weeks.

"What's up?" she asked, turning on the lamp on the bed table.

"We're not actually a happy couple," Ike said, stating the obvious.

Missy looked at him blankly for a moment.

"It's hard to be happy when you're in love with someone else," she said. "In case you think it's fun for me to watch you killing your own soul, it's not. I'm not enjoying it a single bit. It's insulting and it's actually killing me along with you. So why don't you go back to your place, come over here tomorrow and get your stuff, and leave us alone."

"Because I am in love," Ike said.

"With Lil," Missy said. "But she's mine, and, actually, she's all I have because I sure don't have you. Every time you fuck me you get farther away."

"But," Ike began, drawing Missy up to a sitting position.

"Ike," she said, sounding for all the world like she was talking to a six-year-old, "I'm not prepared to have a custody battle at one in the morning. Get out of the apartment. You could have waited until tomorrow, but you didn't—so no more sleep for me tonight, and I won't be of any use tomorrow. Maybe the weekend. But for right now, please, I'm asking you nicely, just get the hell out and leave us alone."

With that, she turned out the light, plunging the room back into darkness, and slipped back down in the bed, turning away from him on her side in a mockery of sleep. Ike had nothing to say. He stood for a moment as if the interview might not be over. Then he turned and left the apartment.

He thought of Lil as he descended the staircase of the brownstone, but he thought of Aurora, too, dressed to kill and singing that song that he had nurtured into existence. What was she doing in Los Angeles? How had that all happened? What was she thinking would happen to her next? And what would happen to him? The New York night that greeted him on the street, cold and moonlit and empty. There was nothing to do but walk. *It's a hell of a big city,* he thought as he crossed into the Sixties and headed west toward the river. How does one ever become worthy of loving that woman? A single trumpet solo, no matter how well you played it, was never going to be enough.

HE WAS QUITE surprised when he turned up two days later at his mother's place to find Missy sitting at the kitchen table poring over a ledger that he had never seen before.

"Meet my new collections manager," his mother said to him dryly. Missy looked up and gave him a noncommittal wave.

Ollie took Ike to lunch at the Madison, a tony deli in the Eighties, and tried to explain the situation as clearly as she could. The Count's health was beginning to fail, although no one knew what exactly was wrong with him. No one really knew how old he was, either. But Ollie had just celebrated her seventieth birthday and was beginning to get her affairs in order. Despite her second husband's tendency to amass debt in various ways, Ollie had kept a weather eye on her assets, selling an occasional painting to subsidize her charming ne'er-do-well's habits. But the last one was a mistake. She had sold a small Arthur Dove painting for six thousand dollars in 1956, which had just been resold for $150,000.

"Shame on me," she said. "That won't happen again. I've hired Missy to catalogue everything, check on current prices, watch for trends, and use the collection to make money, not lose money."

"What does she know about art?" Ike asked. He was peeved that his exodus was about to be complicated in some unpredictable way that had, as was so often the case, his mother at the center of it.

"She'll learn," Ollie said. "And frankly, I don't care. It's an insurance policy."

Ike looked up from his very expensive borscht, mystified.

"Lil," Ollie said. "I'm not losing Lil. I never had a little girl around the house, and I'm quite mad about her, though she never does anything she's told. Maybe that's why."

"Are you going to take her to nightclubs at three in the morning when she's ten?" Ike asked, remembering his own upbringing, about which he had mixed feelings.

"Depends who's on the bill," said Ollie. "Besides, she is only six. I have time to think about it. It will be good for you too. You love her as much as I do. You don't want to lose her. And I'll be paying Missy, so that will relieve you of another responsibility. The thing you have to understand is, I like Missy. She's a pain in the neck, and contrary as hell, and angry all the time and often irrational, and you don't love her and never did. But I like her. So that's what I've done. Finish your soup."

ABOUT A MONTH after he had first seen Missy at his mother's apartment, a month after Aurora's appearance on *The Steve Allen Show,* Ike descended the stairs of his Hell's Kitchen apartment and opened the little door of his metal mailbox on the ground floor to find a letter from California. The envelope was thick, containing several pages that were covered with a looping, large cursive script. Midwestern handwriting, he thought to himself as he sat at the small glass table in the kitchenette and began to read.

Dear Ike,

I have been trying to write this letter for a week or more, to explain why I have disappeared from your life without warning—unless you considered our kiss at the door a warning. I didn't mean it to be one, or perhaps I did. I don't know what I meant. It was the loveliest evening of my life in some ways, and the most tragic, and I think it let me know what I had to do.

As you may know, I am in Los Angeles, trying my luck in a different world. New York became just too complicated. I hope you can understand. I knew I couldn't wake up on Monday morning and try to find a show to audition for or spend the day waiting for a call from you, or—well, other things that might happen. I bought a train ticket instead. I guess I do that sometimes. Get on a train. At the moment I hate Broadway and everything it stands for and how I tried to pretend I belonged there, the way you so clearly do.

In a way it has been good. I've sung on Steve Allen, and he wants me back. I might be booking a role on a new sitcom, which I know is sort of stupid—no singing and I'm not really a funny person—but I need something that isn't a matter of life and death: I've never had that. Am I a coward? Do you hate me for not wanting to be on your street anymore, doing the thing I believed I could do? Maybe you should.

I do know that I must ask you to let me go. I can't be yours. So often I thought that maybe I could, or maybe I should, or maybe we could work it out somehow. But I shouldn't have even considered it. I don't know why I spend so much of my life craving simplicity and clarity and a way forward and then being drawn to what is confusing and so hard to sort out. But I'm not young anymore, not really. I can't let myself be pulled into things, even when I seem to need them. I know that you love me, but your life doesn't really change, and I can't share you with a daughter and her mother and your mother and, well, I know that something would happen, and I would just run away again. It's what I do, and I'm not proud of it. I know that the song that got me hired by Steve Allen only came about because of you. But gratitude isn't the same thing as "I can be with you forever." Yet even as I write that phrase, or sentence, or whatever it is, I know that a part of it is true. I hope you can be happy with that part, or at least live with it—perhaps not today, or next month, but some day. It is what I have to give you, and it is all I have to give you.

I hope one day we'll see each other, and we'll be able to just say hello and talk over old things and not be angry or sad or insane with the sense of what is lost and missed. I hope that is true. It is all I want. For the moment, 3,000 miles of distance will have to be enough. I wish for you to find someone to love, to find happiness and satisfaction and peace. And I wait for the day when the name of that damn song will be true: out of sight, out of mind. For now, I will have to settle for the first part—out of sight. And I ask you with a free heart to do the same.

Aurora

Ike folded the letter and put it in his desk. He had known, or had feared, that something like it was on the way, yet he felt as if he had been run down by a city bus and was dying on the street, like his father before him. He paced the apartment. He contemplated a trip to Los Angeles. He contemplated suicide, but only for a moment. He contemplated sleep, alcohol, playing his horn in a long, self-indulgent paean to the blues, but none of it seemed sufficient, and all of it seemed somehow ridiculous. In the end, he took no action at all. He sat back down at the table and wept.

11

Feet of Clay

VINCENT DONNELLY HAD, in fact, managed to get himself into the audience on the night Aurora sang "Out of Sight, Out of Mind" on *The Steve Allen Show.* She looked spectacular, and the song went over big. At the show's conclusion Vincent went backstage to greet her, knowing that she would be surprised, hoping that she would be happy. Largely, she was confused. It was overwhelming to have done this on national television, and Randy Wood, who ran Dot Records, for which Allen recorded, had beaten Vincent to the dressing room and was deep in conversation with Aurora, Allen, and Donn Trenner about making a recording. There were no other well-wishers. Vincent barged in, saw the look of utter bewilderment on Aurora's face, lifted a hand in apology and backed out. He waited in the hall for a half hour, while the conversation concluded.

"My friend Lord Byron," he said, giving her a hug when his turn finally came, "he's an electrics guy out here—he tipped me off you were gonna be on. I caught a plane. I'm sorry I didn't warn you, but I hoped it would be a good kind of surprise."

"I don't know what it is," Aurora said breathlessly. "It's a surprise—all of it. I can't breathe. I don't even own this dress. They want to make a record. Buy me a brandy?"

Vincent stayed in L.A. through the entire New York run of *The Unsinkable Molly Brown*—over a year. At first, he calibrated his time with Aurora carefully from a two-bedroom stucco house that he sublet in Santa Monica. He kept tabs on her as she made the rounds and auditioned for TV shows and the occasional movie, but he took her out only once every couple of weeks. They saw *Splendor in the Grass* and *The Guns of Navarone*. They went to the Hollywood Bowl. When he could get a follow-spot gig, he took it, working the rock shows at the Santa Monica Civic Auditorium. He covered Chuck Berry. He covered Sam Cooke. He covered Rosemary Clooney, with Aurora in the audience, but the place was half-empty.

"Out of Sight, Out of Mind" debuted on the Billboard chart at number 104 and rose to number 48 over the course of three weeks. It got some airplay but couldn't compete with "Will You Still Love Me Tomorrow" and "Love Potion No. 9." It was getting to be a tough time for show tunes.

As the song began to fade. Aurora got a second date on *Steve Allen,* singing a mediocre cha-cha that was clearly going to go nowhere. She was bitter and mad at herself for agreeing to sing a bad song on national TV. She wasn't sure how it had happened. There were a lot of powerful people who were suddenly advising her. A William Morris client had written the song, and Monkey told her it couldn't hurt to improve her standing with the agency. It hurt. It was an obvious mistake, and she prided herself on not making them. Vincent took her to dinner afterward at Musso and Frank, which, like her only recorded single, was also beginning to fade. Afterward they had chocolate sundaes at C. C. Brown's on Hollywood Boulevard. After a couple of bites, Aurora looked up at him and said, "When you first met me, you said it wasn't my job to tell you how to court me, but I'm going to tell you anyhow."

Vincent froze, not sure what was coming next.

"Ethel Waters lives in Los Angeles," she said. "I've wanted to meet her since I was a very small girl, but I never thought I'd be in the same place she was at the same time. She lives here, somewhere. I read it in the *Herald Examiner.* I've never really cared about meeting most celebrities, but I have something to say to her, and who knows how long she'll live? I don't know how to find her. But maybe you have some connections or something. I could ask William Morris, but I don't really want to talk to them after tonight. Maybe you can find her?"

"A quest," Vincent said. "Ethel . . . ?"

"You've never even heard of her?" Aurora asked. "But you should have."

Vincent's immediate thought was that Steve Allen, Donn Trenner, or the folks at Dot Records would probably have an easier time finding Ethel Waters than he would, but he was honored to be asked. Quests that ladies were forever sending knights out on, hoping they would prove their worth or die trying—he was fine with the concept. And besides, the name did ring a bell, at least. Ethel Waters. Colored. An old-time sort-of movie star or something. Maybe a singer.

Ethel Waters was living in Pasadena, and she was easy to find: She was working part-time for Billy Graham's crusades, singing, and lending her name to what she saw as God's work, which was the first thing Vincent learned when he asked around. She still had an agent, who connected her to Vincent. Vincent made the arrangements and dropped Aurora off at the front door of a modest bungalow with a well-kept flower garden out front. The agent had informed his client that she would be having a visitor, a young admiring singer looking for advice.

Aurora could barely walk the cement path to the front door. It was almost too difficult a reality to confront. Ethel Waters was not the distant memory of a recording star on a 78 rpm disc; she was an actual woman, of no great means, just as Aurora was. When she first heard "Taking a Chance on Love" she'd been little more than a toddler. Her mother had been young, about the age Aurora was now. And Ethel Waters had been famous. Now here was this little bungalow banded by geraniums on a nondescript street; the air was scented with eucalyptus, and the sun was beating down mercilessly, leaving no place to hide. Aurora stepped forward and rang the bell.

She was greeted by a large, elderly Black woman with a shock of white hair, dressed to the nines. Ethel Waters had taken care with her appearance, and was perfumed with some indefinable floral scent, as if waiting for a date on a Saturday night. But Aurora could immediately see that, beneath the old, beaded skirt of her dress, which must have dated from the forties, her ankles were swollen. There was a gap between two of her front teeth that had widened during the years, and Ethel Waters revealed it without embarrassment as she broke into a broad smile. Aurora extended a hand.

"Honey, give Mama a hug," Waters said, her voice delicate and flutey. "I haven't been hugged by a young girl in so long I can't even remember it. They didn't tell me a white girl was coming to see me. What are you doing being a white girl?"

Waters held out her large sagging arms and clutched Aurora, who wrapped hers around Waters as best she could. Was this happening? Was she locked in an embrace with this woman, this voice, this creature whose power had been, for all these years, absolute? Aurora felt her throat catch, but then she and Waters let go of each other, and Aurora took a step back.

"It's very simple," Aurora said, composing herself by falling into a formal cadence. "You've been the most important woman in the world to me since I was five years old. And I never was sure that I'd get the chance to tell you."

"Well, I'm still living, if that's what you mean," Waters said, gesturing Aurora into the room. "You might have come too late. But thank the Lord you got here in due time. You met Ethel Waters." She spread her arms as she said her own name and bowed slightly from the waist. "And now, Ethel Waters is gonna sit."

She lowered herself painfully into a wide upholstered armchair many times recovered, currently boasting a floral print.

"Praise Jesus," she said, presumably grateful for the chair and her ability to get into it. After that, she was silent. She waited. Aurora took a breath and reached into her handbag. She extracted the jagged remains of the only Ethel Waters record she had—the torn label, the fragment of black shellac, a relic. She handed it to Waters, who examined it quizzically and then looked up at her.

"And a story goes with it," Waters said. Aurora didn't know if she was impatient or annoyed, but she didn't seem happy to see this talisman that Aurora had kept with her now for more than a decade.

Aurora told it as quickly as she could—her parents, the music, her mother losing her grip, her father's tantrums, her escape by train to Marius Huwiler and the car accident that had brought it all to an end, at least for the family. Waters listened in silence. Then she handed the shard back to Aurora and looked skyward for a moment, as if searching for some divine inspiration. Finally, she spoke.

"Miss," she said, "I just shot a TV show, did you know that?"

Aurora shook her head.

"Route 66," she said. "I'm so big now I couldn't move fast enough for the camera, so they just set me down in a few places—in a car, in a bed—and let the camera roll and let me speak my words. I didn't move because I can't move anymore, not like they need you to move. I got some kind of congested heart failure, and I spend every day regretting that I can't open up a bottle of whiskey and have at least a little nip. I go to pray instead. Mr. Billy Graham wants me to help him build his crusades and he lets me do as little or as much as I can. If my name helps, that's good. If my voice helps, that's better. But that's all I can do. I paid my bill to the government taxes, I stopped fooling with the bottle, and I'm dying anyhow. I had two cars once, and two men to drive them. I used to could go into one of those fancy movie executive's office and have a fit. Oh, I always know how to have a fit. It's something you don't really have to learn if you grew up the way I did. But I had a gift for it, I'll say that. I could really have a fit. I'm about to have one now.

"You come here to meet me because the way I could sing thirty years ago has given you something you need, well, I'm grateful for that. But are you asking me to solve this mess you're in? Your mama and papa and all these people screaming and drinking and breaking things and leaving you to figure it out all by yourself, well, I had to figure that out my whole life. I'm talking about my life. I don't have time for your life—I got almost no time left at all. I was put on earth to do the Lord's work, it's true; that's why I stopped acting in all those foolish movies and things. I'm here to do the Lord's work, Miss, and I only got one thing to say to you: The Lord helps those who help themselves, didn't you ever hear that?"

Aurora was speechless. She just stared at the old woman in the chair, who, suddenly, could have been anyone. They stayed that way, in silence, for what seemed like a very long time. Finally, Waters shifted her weight and spoke again.

"Go on into the kitchen and get us some iced tea, will you? I'm parched after all that. I saw you on *Steve Allen,* you know. We're not strangers. I just didn't know you were the one who was coming here."

Aurora did as she was told. When she returned with a tray, Waters was dozing in the chair. Aurora set a glass of iced tea beside her and sat, waiting. In a moment, Waters snorted and awakened, looking around as if reorienting herself. Then she fixed her gaze on Aurora.

"That song you sang, that cha-cha song. That wasn't anything. Why'd you do that if you can sing? You're pretty enough to go places, what you want to sing a song like that for?"

"I don't know," Aurora said. "There was a lot of pressure."

"You should have pitched a fit, you'd have gotten a better song. Give me back that thing," Waters said. "That broken record."

Aurora fished it quickly from her bag and handed it to Waters, who looked at it more carefully this time.

"That's not a Decca record," she said. "I made some good, good songs for Decca Records, and every time I recorded some piece of shit for them, God forgive me for using the word, I felt bad for a month, like I had killed someone or run over a dog or something. Sometimes it still comes and grabs me in the night, how could you have done that? How could you have given them what they wanted when you knew it was trash? You're not a trashman, you're a star!"

Aurora wasn't sure which one of the two of them Waters was talking about.

"You're a white girl," Waters said. "You don't have to give them a single thing on God's green earth that they're looking for. What are you looking for? That's the only thing that matters. Now, isn't that what you came all the way to Pasadena to hear me say? You knew I was supposed to say it, and I knew it too. It's like you handed me a script and I said the words, like on *Route 66*. And I don't even know if it's the truth. We're in a business. I did good in this business for a while, but life is long if you're lucky. Then sometimes I think it's not so lucky. You could die young, and they'd remember you more. Is anyone gonna remember you, Miss? I bet you wonder about that."

Aurora nodded. She did wonder about it, in fact, all the time, and felt ashamed that she did.

"Everybody wonders that. You gotta cut a big road through the field if you think anyone is gonna remember you. They remember Shakespeare. They remember Mozart. I don't know, maybe they'll even remember Duke Ellington. But are they gonna remember Ethel Waters? Hell, I can't even get my agent to call me back. I'm gonna die singing in the choir for Billy Graham. Another white man. And I'm supposed to feel lucky about that?"

Aurora went to her side and gave her the glass of iced tea. Waters took a long pull at it through the straw that Aurora had found in a kitchen drawer.

"I would like to kiss you," Waters said to her after Aurora had taken the glass from her. "I would like to be thirty-five and dress up in a tuxedo and take you out to a club and kiss you. Back in my day they would've burned the place down. Black woman in a tuxedo kissing a fine young white girl like you. And I wouldn't have done it—I don't want to start that kind of trouble. But I would have dreamed about it. There is so much you just never get to do. And then Old Man Mose comes to get you. Look at me, honey; I don't mean Miss; I mean honey. Look at me. The flesh is weak, and I know there's too much of it; I don't try to pretend. Your body isn't gonna be kind to you, it doesn't care about you, and the things it wants, it doesn't care what you think about that either. And there comes a time . . . there comes a time when there's nothing left to do but to praise the Lord, because that's the last chance you got. You can't see that now. Your body's taking care of you, bringing everything to you, whether it's your titties or your vocal cords. Make sure you don't blink. Because when you open your eyes again, it's all gonna be different. Don't sing those bad songs. Don't do what they want you to do. Learn how to throw a fit. And thank the Lord every day that he made you white. You'll never sing like me, but you'll live like I never could. You're a white girl. What I care about your story? You're white, you're young, you're a sight to behold, and all that just makes me mad. It's not your fault. But it does make me want to go hurt someone. Now give me another sip of tea and take back this old broken record. I don't need no broken record—I am one."

Aurora had time for a walk around a nondescript block in Pasadena before Vincent Donnelly pulled up in his used Ford Fairlane. He stepped out of the driver's door and walked gallantly around the car to open the passenger door for Aurora to get in. When they were both seated, he gunned the car toward the freeway and asked, "How did it go?"

"Take me home," Aurora said, "and take me to bed."

AS A LOVER, Vincent was a taker. Had he given it any thought, which he never did, he might have promoted the idea that sex was really about abandon, and that by taking without self-consciously giving, he was freeing his lovers to do the same. If there was a place to meet in the middle, so much the better.

Inside the front door of the stucco house in Santa Monica, which she had never seen before, he kissed her fervently, backing her gently against the living room wall, and she pushed back not with her body, but only with her tongue. She wanted all of him that she could have. Aurora had been with men before, including a couple whom she suspected were unsuccessfully trying to prove their interest in her, or in women at all, but she had never encountered a force like Vincent Donnelly. He lifted her gently by her waist. His hands were enormous. He carried her into a back room, his bedroom, which was unadorned and lonely looking—a bed, a night table, and a wooden chair. Nothing on the walls, and only chipped green paint on the trim of the one window to give a hint of color. It was negative space, anti-romantic. There was nothing there but their two bodies. And she knew, the moment she saw this monk-like cell, that he had come out here, had crossed the country on an airplane, only for her. He had no other life here.

Vincent laid her on the bed with surprising delicacy and balance and stepped back to look at her. She looked up at him and thought only for a moment about the decision she had made. She wanted it to be the last decision, the last one she would make that day, or maybe forever. She wanted his hands on her, and his mouth and tongue, and she wanted him to lead her somewhere she hadn't been, to a place where she could let go, just for those moments—completely let go of the world, all its disappointments, the humiliations, the false hopes, the confusions, all the things her mother had described all those years ago so succinctly: a tragedy behind every window.

He reached down and undid her blouse. He lifted her into a sitting position and unsnapped her bra. She felt her power slipping away. As she arched her back so that he could remove her skirt and panties, something very strange happened. He moved to the chair and carefully laid her clothes over the back of it. Then he turned to look at her. He was fully dressed, she completely naked. But when she looked up into the eyes that were staring helplessly down at her body, she realized that, by doing nothing, by simply being there, as unguarded and available as she had ever been to any man, she had taken over. She hadn't asked for this to happen.

He stayed dressed. He just looked at her, his breath coming fast. And then finally, after what seemed like an eternity, during which she could feel herself growing warmer and her body loosening, he moved to the bed, and began to kiss her, his lips, his mouth everywhere—on her face, her neck, her shoulders, and breasts. She cupped the back of his head like a baby's and let him have at her nipples, and she thought, *yes, I will give him this, I will give him my body, my rib cage, my belly and the small of my back. Whatever this is that I have, this instrument that I have never trusted and can never trust, I will give it, right now, to let him make something of it.* Vincent devoured her gently at first, then with more force and urgency. Covered her with his mouth and hands, tracing the contours of every curve, her calves, her thighs, her ears—there was no place he didn't touch because he wanted it all, or so she told herself. He placed his hands on her hips and pulled her toward him, getting to his knees and moving his face between her legs. This had never happened to her before, but she didn't care and didn't judge; she just wanted to give. Not to let him, but to give to him, so that he could take all of her, or try. As his tongue began to trace itself around her, she gave him what she had never discovered before. She wailed, her first real orgasm taking her by surprise, her hands grabbing at the sheets, waiting to come back down, and yet wanting for it never to end. In truth, they had barely begun.

YEARS LATER, Ike Harris would say that he remembered the exact moment it happened—that the afternoon when Vincent Donnelly first took Aurora Shelton was something that jolted him from three thousand miles away. The very instant—it was evening in New York by then—shook his own body, a sudden, inexplicable intake of breath and then a sickening feeling, as though his bones were melting inside of him. He feared he might have to play the second act of *Molly Brown* as an invertebrate, a slug, a caterpillar, a jellyfish on the black carpet of the orchestra pit. How had he let it happen?

He stopped the new number two spot operator after the performance that night and asked him where Vincent Donnelly had gotten to for all this time, and the man, whose name he did not know, answered him in one fatal word: California.

Ike stopped at a bar on the way home and downed three quick bourbons; he did not return to the theater for three days. He booked a flight to L.A. and then canceled it. He tried to find a home number for Aurora in L.A. but there was no listing. He called William Morris in New York and California and got the same response: Confidential numbers were not released to strangers. He read and reread Aurora's farewell letter to him—it could hardly be clearer that she had declared her freedom from him, and there was nothing to be done about that. But Vincent Donnelly? Really? The man with whom he had solved the strike? It was a betrayal—if betrayal it was—worthy of Stalin, of Hitler, of Torquemada.

Then he tried to calm himself down. Maybe he was imagining it. But not likely. He considered burning Aurora's letter in the garbage can on the corner of 50th and Broadway but decided that he would be arrested for starting a fire in a public place. Too melodramatic anyhow. There was no point in carrying the folded paper over to his mother's place, where there was a fireplace—she would just ask a lot of questions he couldn't answer.

And then he just stopped. Either he was laboring under some paranoid delusion about Vincent's reasons for being in California, or he was right, and it was too late. Either way, he needed a shower. He was a professional. He put the letter back in his top desk drawer, put on his tux, and went back to work, arriving shortly before half hour.

"I was surprised you didn't show up at Brixton's retirement party," one of the viola players said to him as he entered the pit. "You been sick?"

It was the remaining lousy viola player who had so irritated Leonard Bernstein back in '56, when *West Side Story* was being written. The other one had died. Ike ignored him; he had no time for fifth-rate players whose jobs were protected by the union, and this one had managed to work his way up to house contractor. A decent politician, but a terrible string player. And who the hell was Brixton? The name was familiar.

It was somewhere during the second act, as he listened to the poor bastard violist grind his way through the show's weakest ballad, that it occurred to him that Albert Brixton, who had apparently had a retirement party while Ike was storming around his apartment unbathed for three days, was the drummer at the Imperial. He was also the contractor at the Imperial. Interesting, Ike thought, bringing the trumpet to his lips on cue, how despair was sometimes the mother of invention.

IKE DIDN'T OFTEN meet with the head of Local 802, a heavyset mediocre ex-reed player named Alphonso diComo with a shocking head of blue-black hair that looked like it had been colored with the kind of ink used in comic books. He was an imposing figure, complete with shiny suit and diamond necktie stud. But he was not a hard man to see if you needed him.

"You know how the strike got solved?" Ike asked him, settling into a chair across from diComo's massive desk, which needed dusting.

DiComo tapped his index finger against the side of his nose but did not speak.

"I kept a lot of your men employed instead of marching around in circles," Ike said. "And now I need a favor."

DiComo nodded. "Coffee?" He asked absently. "Bernice, honey, two black coffees, all right, sweetheart?"

The secretary provided them silently, left the room, and closed the door behind her.

"She knows when I ask for coffee . . ." diComo said, raising his eyebrows slightly. "We're alone."

Ike nodded in response.

"Make me the contractor at the Winter Garden. We got a terrible viola player," he said, "but he's the contractor. Also we got a good drummer, who's dumb as a post. Al Brixton just retired—move the viola player to the Imperial and make him the contractor. Let 'em have my very good drummer. I'll hire a new drummer and a good young viola player, the band will get better, and the Winter Garden is a flagship. The Imperial is just a theater."

"You a contractor?" diComo asked dubiously.

"Let me tell you about my days in the army," Ike said. "Good coffee."

I*T WAS THE BEGINNING* of a streak of bad luck at the Winter Garden, flagship or not. This was good for Ike in a way. He got to hire a lot of different players for a lot of different flops, including, most humiliatingly, an eight-performance run of Steve Allen's Sophie Tucker musical. Ike found himself, playing Allen's score—neither better nor worse than the one Sid Lupowitz had composed for *Nowhere to Go But Up*—but hiding from the composer who had once featured the love of his life on his late-night TV show. He couldn't face meeting the man. He did his best to put Aurora from his mind, and Vincent Donnelly too. He didn't expect it to work, but at least there was a new business to build.

He hired an assistant, an out-of-work chorus dancer named

Cee-Cee Austin, who was known on the street as the most astoundingly athletic chorus girl on Broadway who never worked; she was Black. Integrated choruses were still some years away, and Cee-Cee Austin, strikingly statuesque if not exactly beautiful, able to leap great distances and tumble and partner and toe dance and tap, took class and waited for a revival of *Porgy and Bess* or *Carmen Jones* to come along. Just entering her prime as a dancer, she spent her days sitting in a straight-back chair in Ike Harris's cramped office making phone calls to musicians and managers and keeping Ike's files in order. Over sandwiches, they exchanged pleasantries, and bits and pieces of their lives crept out, but each remained suitably guarded. Ike pondered the rage that must have been simmering inside of her but didn't ask. She, in turn, could see his focus drift more often than it should, though if she had a clue as to what or who was on his mind, she did not say.

He was aware, peripherally at least, that Aurora was turning up in a series of guest roles on various TV shows in Hollywood, each one wasting her in a different way: wronged wife, stenographer, nurse, high school teacher. He waited for a sighting of Vincent Donnelly but knew that his erstwhile drinking companion would not return anytime soon. And in any case, Ike asked himself, had he not been told to move on? He moved on.

Missy Cozzens, it turned out, was born for the job Ike's mother had given her. Having rattled around as an angry ad agency assistant, failed novelist, distracted political agitator, and careless mother, she found herself devoting hundreds of hours to understanding Ollie Harris's collection of paintings, prints, lithographs, and sculpture and then tackling the entire New York art market. She was reborn. It was a thicket of snobbery, competitive class-consciousness, envy and greed, all of it disguised as aesthetic appreciation. Missy was completely enraptured by its very lack of soul or sincerity. It seemed to her to be incontrovertible evidence that the worldview she had seemingly been born with was the correct one. It was like living inside a nasty satire that she found deliciously amoral. She became the devil's disciple. With Ollie's permission she began to make small purchases and sales, and, over the succeeding years, larger ones. As artists' reputations rose and fell, the collection grew in volume and value.

As for Lil, when she wasn't in school, she could be found wandering the halls of Ollie's commodious apartment, watching Ollie's new color TV or sprawling on the living room floor reading books. She rarely spoke unless questioned about something; she seemed perpetually preoccupied. She had few friends. But neither Ollie nor Missy seemed to notice.

Missy gave up her apartment and moved in with Ollie a couple of years after she went to work there. The two were inseparable, especially as Count Palaffi's hospital stays became more frequent. He was dying of colon cancer by this point, and it was eating the inside of his body piece by piece as he fretted and smoked incessantly.

For Ike, there really was joy only in the time he could spend with Lil, who had no interest at all in the theater, but had fallen in love instead with baseball. There were a reliable number of day games at Yankee Stadium, and, when it was unveiled, at Shea. Ike willed himself to become a baseball fan, learning the names, strengths and weaknesses, and personal quirks of the players the way he had for years come to know each member of each ensemble he had led or played in. The game began to fascinate him because of its natural kinship with music, the nine-man ensemble pulsing toward and away from home plate with every pitch, each of them sent spinning into action when the ball was hit, moving with a practiced virtuosity no different from a brass section handing off a melody to the strings as a song moved from section to section. Lil kept score and rooted hard for the Mets, but to Ike, it was just a new kind of music, and, when played well, a beautiful thing to watch. Perhaps it could even fill a void.

12

Lord Byron, Romantic Poet

LORD BYRON HAD arrived in New York two weeks before the wedding with the expressed intent of fucking the bride before she had time to become one. He had no desire to disrupt Vincent Donnelly's plan to take a wife—all he wanted was his just reward. It only seemed fair, given the part he had played in it all, and how little she knew about it.

He knew this much: He had really started something. Vincent and Aurora were in L.A. for good, it seemed. And after their first real encounter, after Ethel Waters, they were seldom apart. Byron didn't really believe in these kinds of long-term love affairs, but he watched with interest, mostly from a distance. When he was not on location, he would meet them for a movie or Italian food, usually with a new or untried woman on his arm. It soothed these companions, he believed, that he had friends who seemed to be committed to each other.

Aurora, picking up what work she could, loved to tear apart movies in minute detail—story points, character development, and even the ways in which the camera often became the storyteller. It was the way Marius Huwiler took apart a song and put it back together. Vincent, more pragmatic and mostly focused on lighting effects, was content to marvel at her natural dramaturgical bent, which made him love her more deeply than ever. She was, he felt, both more instinctive than he was, and just plain smarter. She knew why a scene worked, and why, when she was on the set of some episodic TV drama, a scene couldn't work. More than once she inhaled and opened her mouth in preparation to object about such moments, but then she would remember Ike Harris's advice in the dressing room in Philly: Don't be the problem. People don't hire actors who are known for being a problem. And she would tell herself, *It's only a TV show. An hour on a Thursday night, including commercials. People watch it for free. Just do your blocking and say your lines.* And what was Ike Harris doing in her brain anyhow?

As the months passed, however, one negligible gig after another began to create a kind of nagging fear that there was too much waste going on. She was not singing—that career had died away without explanation. Steve Allen's people never called. She was going where her agents sent her. She was not really acting but posing and speaking. It was easy work, but mind-numbing. And the thing she had escaped from, the terror of failure in a theater where a live audience could love or hate her, the rush of adrenaline as her vocal cords opened and an orchestra swelled, began to seem the very definition of life. Los Angeles was easy. She and Vincent could play tennis on Saturday mornings and then go out to brunch with Bloody Marys and huevos rancheros. They could return home, go to bed, and go to the movies again.

One such afternoon she turned to him as he awakened from his postcoital doze. The sun was beginning to set as the fog rolled in.

"Vincent," she said, "this doesn't feel like a love affair anymore. It feels like we quit work and retired to Santa Monica."

He laughed. "Maybe we should just sit on a bench on the pier with some day-old bread and feed the pigeons," he said.

"I don't think so."

"Maybe we should get married. I can't think of a time when I won't want to be here in bed with you next to me. Forever."

She took his hand. It was not the most romantic of proposals, but it was what she wanted to hear. She had come to feel the same way—that while her work might be unfulfilling or ridiculous or demeaning out here, she always felt—what?—at home with Vincent? Did she even know what a home was? She wasn't sure, but this felt like a safe haven, a bond, something that could sustain her. It felt, more than anything, like the answer to some question she had never quite formulated. She turned and kissed him, but before they could lose themselves in each other again she stopped and pulled her head away from his, looking at him earnestly.

"Not in Los Angeles," she said.

They returned to New York City in late 1963, but Vincent's job at the Winter Garden was long gone. He got hooked up at the Mark Hellinger, less than a block away, waiting for the arrival of something called *Rugantino,* an Italian musical with a primitive system of what would later come to be called supertitles. It had never been tried before. The producer, coming up in the world—or not—was Antoine Berget, who had seen the thing in Rome during a two-year escape from the IRS. Vincent was not hopeful, but he was employed.

Aurora, after almost three years in television, had gotten herself a small foothold again, almost on Broadway. As her wedding to Vincent rushed toward her, she was cast as Julie, the doomed mixed-race torch singer in a brief revival of *Show Boat* at the cavernous New York City Center, where they were bringing back two-week runs of popular shows at popular prices on a subscription series. The shows were like an urban extension of summer stock. The straw-hat season ended on Labor Day, which meant that there were plenty of sets and costumes and props that were headed for winter storage, and they could all be rented for a song. *Show Boat* was cheaply mounted and under-rehearsed, but from Aurora's point of view, as an overall reentry enterprise, it was certainly better than nothing, even if the timing was inconvenient. Between rehearsals she shopped for a dress and looked at apartments with Vincent. They had blood tests and filled out a license application, almost as if it were an afterthought. The show and her impending wedding twined around each other in ways that threatened to shatter her concentration completely.

She noted that she was playing a character who was not white, but who had always been cast with someone white (the ability to pass was a key plot point) but she didn't complain—she got to sing some first-rate music. And she was surprised and secretly more nourished than she thought she should be by her first set of rave reviews, which buoyed her up even though almost no one would get to see her; the run was only two weeks. But the good reviews were achieved at a cost. The plain fact was that *Show Boat* gave her nightmares.

She'd had the first one during the second rehearsal week after a day of blocking out the scene in the second act where Julie, a once-beautiful, once-promising young torch singer who had descended into middle-age, alcohol-soaked despair, sat on a piano and sang an old chestnut of a ballad called "Bill." Something about the lyric touched her, though she couldn't say exactly what.

He isn't tall or straight or slim
And he dresses far worse than Ted or Jim
And I can't explain why he should be
Just the one, one man in the world for me.

She paused each time she got there, and the third time they ran it, just before the end of the day, she had to stop. She just sat in silence on the piano and stared. *Just the one, one man in the world for me,* she repeated in her mind. Would she ever sing it right? Would it ever even be right?

That night she had the dream for the first time. It recurred again, irregularly, over the brief rehearsal period, and then, like an unwanted debt collector, was on the doorstep of her subconscious every night during the run. She found herself chasing after a train, running down dirt paths, down abandoned tracks along the river. The feeling of abandonment, of death, of the failure of love followed her. She was always alone and running, and the trains, when she glimpsed them, were putting an ever-increasing distance between her and them. She would never catch them. Someone, or something, was on board and racing away, but each time she awakened she could not discern who or what it was. It would have been comforting to know, and in the dream she knew. But once awake, it became a mystery once again. And that banished sleep for the night.

It did not take her long to realize that *Show Boat* was the culprit, and that "Bill" with its modest certainty and simple declarations, was dogging her steps.

She confessed none of this to Vincent, who was cheerfully looking forward to what he called "the big day," but as the run went on, she became increasingly agitated and confused, afraid to go to sleep and unable to stay awake. Short as the engagement was, she found herself counting the days until it was done—the show, the wedding, the shuddering uncertainty that dogged her steps to and from the theater. And that song. Every night, it tore the place apart, and left her exhausted. Thankfully, she did not need to reappear until the curtain call.

It was on the Thursday afternoon of the second week, four performances from the closing, that she entered her dressing room one afternoon to find a note in an unsealed envelope. It was from Lord Byron. The wedding was to be a private one; neither Aurora nor Vincent could see the upside of publicizing a marriage between an aspiring actress and a stagehand. No one from California had been invited. But here was Byron, bunking at the Warwick Hotel, a couple of blocks down from City Center. Would Aurora join him for a drink after a performance and keep it between them? It was hard for her to think of a reason to say no. She had begun to need a couple of drinks after each performance anyhow.

In the time they had spent on the West Coast, her main impression of him, besides the wide variety, shapes, and sizes of the many women he had introduced, was of the gradually accruing collection of showy metal jewelry that he seemed to favor—a ring made of wrapped wire, a leather bracelet featuring a metal plate bearing his name, and one time a pirate skull-and-crossbones necklace made of twisted silver tubing. Aurora thought of him as a kind of coarse, friendly monster, his body powerful but unshaped, his shaved head more like a weapon than something to think with. She really didn't know how to feel about him but was fond of knowing someone who seemed to come from the other side of the Hollywood underworld. No one was yet talking about cocaine or poppers or group sex in swimming pools—the orgiastic explosion of American values that accompanied Woodstock and the Nixon years was still a few years away. But there was something about Lord Byron that was already headed there, to some reckless destination, and Aurora knew it. He remained on the edge of her life with Vincent, but an intriguing presence, nonetheless. He was not sensible. But he did seem to be getting a tremendous bang out of life. And now here he was at the bar at the Warwick, which was all but deserted at eleven P.M., alone at a back table. He stood to greet her.

"Are you happy?" he asked. He gave her a kiss on the cheek and held her by both wrists. "They love you."

"I guess I am," she said, giving away nothing.

"I was there tonight. In the mezzanine—I think I got the last single ticket they had. That ballad in the second act—it felt like you were singing to me directly. In the last row of the mezz in a twenty-five-hundred-seat house. What the hell—who can do that?"

"Thank you," she said. She had no interest in describing the cost.

"Can I tell you why I'm here?"

"I was hoping to learn."

The waiter brought a glass of champagne and a bottle of beer. Aurora smiled. She never drank champagne, but tonight she thought she would. Byron was not who she thought she needed, but somehow his presence brought a breeze from California, and her present anxiety could hide in the novelty of it.

"That," said Lord Byron, "is the exact set of words I was hoping to hear and in that order. 'I was hoping to learn.'"

She looked at him quizzically, then smiled, but he refused to enlighten her about the phrase itself.

"I wanted to hear you sing live on a real stage," he said, "and I wanted to know what all the fuss was about. My good friend Vincent, he told me that he fell in love with you because you sang a certain way when he was your spot operator and he felt that the two of you were joined by the light. I didn't know what the hell he was talking about, until tonight. I'm not a poet, no pun intended. But tonight I wanted to go upstairs to the balcony, stick a shiv in the spot operator, and take over his lamp. I got jealous." He laughed at the idea, pleased with his declaration of passion.

"I'm glad you came," said Aurora, "but let's not get out of control. Jimmy's a good operator."

"Maybe I'm not jealous of Jimmy," said Byron, taking a long pull on the bottle of beer.

Aurora looked at him. A big, bear-like man with a child's eyes and a half smile that seemed calculated to seduce. Whatever sincerity there was in it was a passing thing, and she knew it.

"Jealous of Vincent?" she asked. "I thought you and Vincent were great friends," she said. The waiter brought a second champagne. Where had the first one gone?

"That's what I meant," Lord Byron said, "about 'I was hoping to learn.' I was hoping you'd say those words. Because I feel like you've got some things to learn. After all, you're about to marry this guy, and he's a great guy. But he was no friend of mine."

A darkening feeling settled into the pit of Aurora's stomach, and she knew she was about to discover something she didn't want to know. But it was too late. Pete Byron had ambushed her. If there was something to know about the man she loved, she probably needed to know it—in case it was true. Here she was again, chasing after the train. She drank.

Lord Byron pushed back in his chair and launched into the story—the call he'd received from one of the Ennis brothers, the fraternity of stagehands across the country, his meeting with Vincent, his manipulation of the various crew members at *The Tonight Show* and *The Steve Allen Show,* and all that followed. He overplayed his role a bit, but what he said was largely true. It was he, and not Vincent, who had gotten her on *The Steve Allen Show,* and it certainly had nothing to do with the William Morris Agency, nor with Aurora herself. True, Vincent had requested Byron's help, in the not-so-vain hope that it would pay off romantically. But it was he, Lord Byron, who had had the power and the connections to get the favor done.

"What I did," he said, "I'd happily do it again, but I just want you to understand I'm the one who did it. I'm the reason you're with Vincent Donnelly, and the minute I saw you I regretted it, because I wanted you for myself. If only I'd known you existed."

Aurora cocked her head to one side and looked at Lord Byron steadily. He seemed willing to be the object of her gaze. Turning things over in her mind, she understood that what he had told her made good sense. She had long pushed away the thought that Vincent had played some unspoken part in the television appearance that had, in effect, launched her still modest career. But what was he doing there, standing in the door of her dressing room afterward, while she was talking to Donn Trenner and Steve Allen about making a record? Why had he lied to her about it, or at least not told her the truth? There had been, in effect, a conspiracy, albeit a private one between these two men, in which she was both victim and heroine. It unsettled her, in part because she had almost knowingly allowed it to remain undiscovered. She was complicit in a way. Still, was her future husband planning to go to his grave holding this secret to himself? It was done out of love for her. It was, in effect, a gift. Shouldn't that be enough? Wasn't the secret a measure of devotion?

The entire matter raised an unanswerable question: What else was he capable of keeping from her so easily? What else would he do that she would have no clue about? What kind of a man is able to manipulate things with so little care for whether his soon-to-be wife knows the first thing about it, even when it's all about her? A manipulator. She felt more undone by it than she meant to. Or was she simply playing a mad scene in her head, Lady Macbeth approaching the altar? Such scenes, she knew, were hardly uncommon: brides going into a panic. A certain reckless chaos had taken over inside her, and she looked

Byron in the eye. Was she flirting? Or pleading for something? She really couldn't tell.

"Did you know?" Byron said when the silence had become uncomfortable. "Did you suspect?"

"Get me another champagne," Aurora said. He signaled the waiter, who quickly appeared with a fresh round, her third, his second.

"Just tell me one thing," Aurora said after taking too big a gulp of the champagne, almost choking. Her head was beginning to spin a little.

"Anything," said Byron, settling back in his seat, suddenly her best friend.

In repose, there was something creature-like about him, and very West Coast. Jeans, a work shirt with the sleeves rolled up, a pack of Lark cigarettes protruding from one of the rolls at the elbow. The shades perched on the dome of his shaved head were an entirely unnecessary touch, part of a costume really, but one he wore every day. He did not belong in New York. He would go back to L.A. and slip back into the world he knew—a world she would never know. She stared at him a beat too long.

"I lost you," he said, jolting her out of the reverie of appraising his appearance and demeanor. He smelled of some woodsy cologne that she quite liked. "You wanted to ask me a question."

Aurora took another slug of the champagne, and the glass was almost empty.

"Did you find Ethel Waters too?"

"Ethel Waters," Byron mused. "Who is Ethel Waters?" His eyebrows went up. It was an innocent face. He really didn't know.

Aurora nodded. Not Ethel Waters. Good. Only Steve Allen. Still, Vincent had a secret. It wasn't a bad secret. But he was planning to keep it—she could see that. Maybe it was the two and a half glasses of champagne on an empty stomach. Maybe it was the train she could never catch. Maybe it was as simple as the fact that she would, in a few days, be a married woman, and that another man had traveled three thousand miles to try his luck with her. Maybe it was just that she was feeling the intoxicating power of being, however briefly, the toast of the town in a brief run of *Show Boat* that was completely sold out and driving her insane. Maybe, she thought, maybe she should have a secret too. Or not.

"Pete," she said. She refused to call him by his ridiculous nickname. "You have a very long and illustrious history with the ladies. You love women, but you can't hold on to them for more than a minute. They wind up wanting to tear each other's eyes out—or yours. I don't think that's ever going to change—you collect them like baseball cards, and no woman really wants to be a baseball card. Not even a rare, autographed one."

"It could be different for us," Byron said.

He looked down, a little shamed by his extravagantly false claim about their potential romantic future, as if he had been caught by a teacher in a lie about losing his homework. She smiled. He really was a boy. He would live and die a libidinous boy.

"I'm flattered," she said. "You came a long way just to see if you could one-up your friend Vincent and maybe have a memorable night with me. You made a lot of effort. I admire that. I'd be flattered even if I thought it was more about screwing me than it was about screwing Vincent." She really had had a little too much champagne. "But no," she concluded.

"No?" he asked, now the little boy who's ice cream cone had hit the pavement and who wasn't going to get a replacement.

"No," she repeated. "I'll tell you one thing about me, and it's this. I learned early to be very careful about my life, and that to get anything I wanted, I would have to become unnaturally determined, and not make mistakes. Especially when they were going to be more useful to somebody else than they would be harmful to me."

"Doesn't it make you hard?" Byron asked.

"I fear that," said Aurora. She swallowed the last of the champagne, and only a hallmark of her determination prevented her from saying the next thing that came into her head. She had wanted to say, *Whether I'm hard or not isn't the point. The point is, it's not my job to make you hard.*

Instead, she stood, pitching a little bit as if on a skiff in the tide, kissed his cheek, and departed, looking for handrails to steady herself.

The next day she and Vincent marched into Mayor Wagner's office and promised to love, honor and obey. Whatever secrets there were or might have been were now officially erased.

IN THE LATE SIXTIES, to avoid a lockout, the union finally gave up on the idea of insisting on four house musicians and a house contractor in each theater, and Ike Harris's job security disappeared. He moved out of the Winter Garden, which took some doing. He was once again a freelance player, often employed, but with no guarantees, which is how he found himself in Toronto in the middle of winter with a train wreck called *Pousse-Café*. He had Charlie Vodery to thank. Vodery had been the first man to get him a job as a freelance contractor, largely because no one wanted to go anywhere near the ill-fated *Pousse-Café,* which ostensibly featured a score by Duke Ellington, who was rarely on the scene. The music director was a genial and talented lifer named Sherman Frank who had conducted Lena Horne in *Jamaica* and shuttled between Broadway shows and the opera house, national tours, and pops concerts. He seemed a logical choice for an Ellington show—he was just an overall music guy. And Ike was eager to go, because Cee-Cee Austin had gotten the job as the lead ensemble dancer—her first in an upcoming Broadway show. She had resigned as Ike's assistant on the day she was cast, a week before Ike had gotten the call from Vodery. When Ike arrived in Toronto, Cee-Cee met him in the aisle and threw her arms around him in a tight, almost intimate embrace. As she pulled back, she said to him, "You've been looking at me for months across a desk. Now you're really gonna see me." Then she turned on her stiletto heels and climbed the rickety plywood staircase that the stagehands had put at the foot of the aisle so that the company could get from the auditorium to the stage.

New scriptwriters arrived daily and shook their heads in despair. The producers, who had never produced anything, had been comfortable with a Black composer and a Black orchestrator—these were the artists—but they wanted a white contractor to take care of business. That's just the way it was, even in 1970. Vodery, who negotiated his own contracts and had run several bands since the war days, was fond of citing Louis Armstrong's relationship with his manager, the Jewish gangster Joe Glaser. Armstrong had been raised by Jews and was drawn to Glaser as a man who could take care of his business. He had even advised a young Vodery, "Get yourself a Jew to look after you," and although mistrust was an inevitable feature of Black life in America, Vodery liked the sound of the words and often quoted them, smiling, though he never took Armstrong's advice. He never needed anyone to look after his business. But Vodery knew that Ike could really play Ellington.

Midway through the Toronto run, one of the producers took over as director, which, in theory, made him an artist too, though there was no more evidence of his artistry than of his producing ability. Audiences flowed through the exit doors at intermission, and some departed long before. Ike, at least, felt a kinship with Vodery and liked what little he saw of Ellington. He liked playing Ellington's music in Vodery's crack arrangements no matter how mediocre some of the songs were. He also liked watching the lithe, dark dancer Cee-Cee Austin.

He had come to regard her as an office assistant, despite her reputation, and was startled watching her doing a remarkable leap during early tech rehearsals when the band was not required. He watched, slumped in an orchestra seat, while eight girls, playing inhabitants of a Storyville brothel, vaulted over the ornate banister of a staircase. All but one of them landed on the floor. Cee-Cee Austin landed on a table and her momentum carried her across it with her arms behind her, flawless legs kicking into the air, until she vaulted again, this time over her own body and on to an ornate divan. It was a move worthy of the Olympics, but Ike never once thought of the Olympics. Once the show was up and running, it earned applause at every performance.

He could not see her from where he sat, but he played the trumpet cue, a burlesque figure that Vodery had fitted out with a shake on the last note, that launched it. Then he waited for the applause. He felt a bit sheepish every time it happened, as if his employment of Cee-Cee had been a kind of imprisonment for which he was responsible. He also knew that however brilliant she was, *Pousse-Café* wouldn't last a weekend in New York. Would she come back to his dingy room and get back in front of the typewriter? It seemed tragic. Over the course of a week in Toronto, his admiration for her expanded as did his sense of doom, and a growing anger that she might never be appreciated for what she really was—a kind of world champion. He thought about her more, in fact, than he meant to.

He was not in love with Cee-Cee Austin. But on the other hand, her short hair was brushed straight up from her forehead in a military buzz cut, and her eyes were piercing and large, as if she saw and recorded everything and forgot nothing. Her breasts were small but prominent in the lavender lace unitard in which she executed her dance solo, lace running along them in a plunging triangle that ended just above her waist. She looked strong and hungry and utterly unafraid. And flops sometimes had a way of bringing people together in the foxhole on the front lines—the cast and the band were dug in, defending themselves from the creative team and the producers, who seemed to be drowning in a sea of ineptitude that was making the performers look bad and the audience hate them. A war was being lost, but the foot soldiers stuck together.

During the third week in Toronto, Ike fell in beside Cee-Cee as she walked back to the hotel after an exhausting two-show Wednesday. A light snow was falling. All rules were made to be broken.

"Are you still dying of a broken heart?" she asked before he could even greet her. "That's what everybody says. You play like it, man. You wail that Ellington stuff. Is it true? Are you dying of a broken heart?"

"I'm just the trumpet player," Ike replied. "We're all dying."

"I'm dying for a bourbon and soda and a bed," she said. "Matinee and evening of this show? It's enough to kill you, broken heart or not."

"How about a bourbon and soda and dinner and bed?" Ike asked.

"Dancers smoke cigarettes for dinner," she said.

He knew it was true. Dancers didn't eat.

"A small salad," he said, "A nice piece of chicken, a bourbon and soda, a cigarette and bed. Listen to the doctor."

"Who are you, Doctor Jazz? That chicken will go right to

my ass," she said. "I have to watch it like a hawk, or it turns into a turkey. Don't tell me you haven't been watching it, too."

He stopped her and took her hand. Their breath mingled visibly in the cold air.

"You have the most beautiful body God ever made," he said, "and I'll eat half the chicken. That's my last and final offer."

"Let's have the bourbon and soda first," she said. She was enjoying herself. "You're Jewish, right? We'll negotiate."

Get yourself a Jew. The bar led to the bed.

THE THIRD TIME they joined together that night he broke through. A lot of dancers, he had learned many years earlier, have trouble letting go of the pose. They want to appear a certain way, even with a man, even when the man is inside them, even when the man is longing only for them to lose control of themselves and lose sight of the outside world completely.

For Ike, it was anti-climactic in a literal sense—there was no chance, at the age of forty-five, he was going to have a third orgasm that night. This one was purely for the transitory pleasure of it, and for her. Her body snapped and rocked, bent and arched itself as if she had let go of it altogether. She let her belly go loose and didn't try to hide it. Creases appeared in her flesh as it bent and torqued—things he suspected she never showed to anyone. Had this ever happened to her before? Ike had no idea, but he wanted her only to dissolve in pleasure to that place where she could forget that she even had a body. A dancer never forgets. But maybe tonight she had.

He fell asleep at about five, feeling that he had played well, a polyphonic duet worthy of the first-rate musicians. They had been like Miles and Bird, the two of them set free in Toronto, in the midst of a theatrical catastrophe that, for all the length of that night, neither of them thought about. The first birds were beginning to sing when they drifted off. *Awake and Sing!* Ike commanded them as he lost consciousness. It was a lovely way to go to sleep.

They were back in rehearsal at one in the afternoon—the choreographer had invented a new, all-singing-all-dancing finale. For the first time, Cee-Cee was not at her best, marking her way through it carefully, but without energy. No one but Ike seemed to notice. Vodery arrived with an orchestration, and the band played through it twice. It was due to go in that night.

Ike tried to take Cee-Cee for an early supper, but she demurred; dancers don't eat before a performance, she reminded him—or ever. And drink? Never. There was something a little distant in her tone, as if suddenly he knew her too well, something he hadn't earned, something she hadn't meant to show him, but now it was too late. He spent the hours between rehearsal and the overture in the robing room, where the band dressed, with a Swiss cheese sandwich and a beer.

The finale was never performed.

The show got off to its usually dreary start. Ike had become accustomed to the indifference, and finally the open hostility, of the audience. Even from the pit he could feel it; it puddled around his shoes as he played, like the seepage from a leaky, disintegrating plaster wall in someone's basement. No matter how hard or well or energetically he blew, he couldn't keep his feet dry with this one.

The exception was that dance number midway through act one; every night he prayed for its arrival. The orchestra went into stop-time at the crucial moments of it, when the girls took flight over the banister. Just after they landed, Sherman Frank drove his baton down with an energetic downbeat like he was beginning Beethoven's Fifth, as Cee-Cee made her way across the table to applause from the—up to that moment—somnolent audience. Four saxophones wailed. Three trumpets traded licks with Ike topped out above them. At least that's how it was supposed to work. But not on this night. In the split-second silence in which the band waited for that stupendous downbeat, a gasp escaped from the audience and Sherman Frank stood frozen, his up-raised baton silhouetted in someone's follow spot. Ike heard the tumble. Cee-Cee had missed the table. There was a thud above Ike's head, and then a deadly silence. Then a rush of feet above him. The band sat frozen. It wasn't a simple fall. A chaotic moment of confusion above, then the stage manager rang down the curtain and Ike knew that something awful, something life-altering and cataclysmic had just happened, not only for her, but for him too.

He paced the hospital corridors until well after sunrise. Cee-Cee had no family in Toronto—no one in the company was within five hundred miles of home. No doctor emerged. Members of the company drifted off, each with an apology to the others, hugs, prayers, curses, but there was simply no news, and they had a show to do, god-awful as it was. Only Ike remained. At seven-thirty, as the sky was turning the fatal purple color of a bruise and a tiny bit of bilious yellow began to creep behind the skyline through the hospital's broad expanse of windows, signaling the beginning of a long day, a doctor emerged from the double doors at the end of a corridor. He was slight, weary, his thinning hair standing in all directions as he removed a paper cap and hairnet from his head. He spoke with an accent, vaguely French Acadian.

"Austin?" he asked Ike. "Cee-Cee Austin?"

Ike nodded. "A friend," he said, so obvious was it that he could be neither her father nor her husband nor her brother. "We're all up here putting on a show."

The doctor nodded. "She's not going to be in any show," he said without irony. "I don't think she'll walk again. I'm sorry."

Ike began to perspire.

"There's a lot of spinal damage," the doctor said. "How much do you know about the human anatomy?"

"Only the heart," Ike said. "I'm a trumpet player."

The doctor didn't question it. He was a dry son of a bitch.

"The spinal cord," he said. "It doesn't regenerate really, not meaningfully. Of course, we don't know for sure. Eleven vertebrae are broken and they, you know, the bones, when they break, they cut into the cord. We don't know yet what we can do. Or what we can expect."

"May I see her?" Ike asked.

"Not yet," the doctor said. "She won't be conscious for most of the day. Normally we only allow next of kin in the ICU. But . . ."

"But we're up here putting on a show," Ike repeated. "I don't even know how to find her next of kin—somewhere in America."

The doctor nodded. "Exceptions can be made," he said. "But someone needs to locate her relatives. Soon."

Ike nodded and stuck out his hand. The doctor took it.

"I'm so sorry," he said. "We try to heal everyone you know, but sometimes . . ."

Ike nodded.

"Thank you for trying," he said. Then he turned and walked away. Where he was going, he hadn't the slightest idea.

The streets were cold. The hotel was lonely and somehow the sight of his bed was simply intolerable. By noon he found himself in the basement of the Royal Alexandra Theatre sitting with the company manager, a short, round young woman named Althea Goldschmidt, trying to locate Cee-Cee's parents. Her agent had no idea; Actors' Equity was no more useful. The two of them made a round of calls to the other ensemble members, but no one knew Cee-Cee very well. She was not from the New York area, nor from the South—there was always an assumption when a Black chorus member made it to Broadway that she had grown up singing in church in Alabama or someplace—and her insurance information had no emergency numbers. Ike tried to recall any trace of an accent in her voice but hadn't been able to detect one. Then he asked to see her résumé. Althea Goldschmidt didn't have one, but *Pousse-Café*'s casting director did, and read it to the two of them over the phone.

"She's been in *The Me Nobody Knows* three times," said the gravel voice on the other end of the phone. "The first time was at Northwestern."

Ike put in a call to the Northwestern University switchboard and discovered that Cee-Cee Austin had never been there. Either she was lying about her past, or she had changed her name. Then it was another call to Equity to see if they had that information. It turned out that Cee-Cee Austin's real name was Cecelia Stokes. And that was a name Northwestern could locate. She hailed from Youngstown, Ohio, and had gotten into Northwestern on a dance scholarship. She had a mother who was no longer listed in Youngstown. Ike called the police there, who put him onto a local Baptist minister, who remembered Cee-Cee's mother well.

"She went back home," the Reverend J. M. Gates told him. "Back to Tutwiler. You know a lot of colored folks came north in the migration," he said. "I remember Bertha Lee Stokes very well. And Cee-Cee too. That's Cecelia I'm talking about. She went off to college, and her mother stayed there until about sixty-five or sixty-six. Then public housing opened up in Tutwiler and she headed home. She said the North didn't do her any good, and she had family back home. I hope that helps you."

Ike inhaled, ashamed that he had to ask the next question.

"I'm sorry, Reverend Gates," he said. "I don't know what state Tutwiler is in."

Reverend Gates laughed a big, dark, laugh that contained a hint of anger. Ike could just see the wheels turning in his mind. *White men. White people.*

"Mississippi," Gates said. "It's right there on the Southern Railroad line. Didn't you say you were a trumpet player? Don't you know W. C. Handy discovered the blues at the Tutwiler railroad station? Everybody knows that story. What kind of trumpet player are you?"

Ike admitted that he no longer knew.

Reverend Gates tried to sound respectful, but "Unh-huh" was all he said.

Ike, now thoroughly humiliated and still panicked about Cee-Cee's condition, thanked the Reverend Gates for his help. Althea Goldschmidt was already on the phone to the Tutwiler police. Bertha Lee Stokes was at the Western Union waiting for funds for a bus ticket to Toronto an hour later. She was not a woman who would get on an airplane.

CEE-CEE AUSTIN awakened the next day and was bewildered to find herself in a body cast in the ICU, somewhere in a country she had never lived in. There was little she remembered, but she did recall who had done this to her. Two days later, when her mother arrived, she had regained her tongue, and was able to use it to devastating effect. With her mother, a long, strikingly lovely, retired cashier from the Youngstown, Ohio, A&P looking on, Cee-Cee focused her piercing gaze on Ike.

"This woman," she said in a drugged and slow drawl, pointing to her mother, "this woman worked a lifetime so that I could do what I fought so hard to do. So that I could be a dancer on Broadway. And now I'm never gonna dance. I'm never gonna send her a wire of money, I'm never gonna send her a picture of me in a line of girls taking a bow on a Broadway stage—all the way back to Tutwiler, Mississippi. I'm not actually gonna get to be on a Broadway stage even for the one night that this show would have put me there for."

"I'm so sorry," Ike said.

"You know who did that to me?" Cee-Cee said. "You did that to me. So you can leave this room, leave this country, leave this business, and find something else to do with your life but destroy people like me who almost got there. And you can carry it on your back until you can cast it off if you live that long. That's your life. I don't want it in my life. Don't say goodbye, don't wave or kiss me or take my hand, I can't feel anything in my hand anyhow. Turn around and go to the door and leave me with my mama. That's what you've got to do. And you've got to do it now."

Ike stood, turned, and walked out of the room as instructed. His heart was black with anger and guilt. Cee-Cee and he had entangled themselves all night in mutual ecstasy, it was true, and he hoped, one day, she would see it that way. But at the same time, he knew, as he walked through the doorway and down the corridor, that he, who was never much of a dancer, who never made human grace seem celestial with the motions of his body, was still walking. He could walk, he told himself, in a rhythm that he heard immediately in a 5/4 time signature with two empty beats at the end. "I can walk, beat, beat. I can walk, beat, beat." The elevator was in front of him, but he took the stairs.

Pousse-Café opened the following Friday at the 46th Street. By Saturday night, it was gone.

13

One More Spring

A*mong the many things* that fourteen-year-old Lil Hardin Armstrong Cozzens hated, the thing she hated most was her first name. She had been told more than once by her father who the original Lil Hardin Armstrong was. She had been, Ike always told his daughter, a pioneer woman, a female jazz player who held her own with the men long before anyone dreamed that such things were proper, or even possible. But the name—Lil—was either a contraction of little or short for Lillian, which was an old lady's name, quite possibly one of the aging yentes one could find on the park benches in the little islands between Broadway and Amsterdam on the Upper West Side when the weather was warm. Lil was not prepared to accept either definition as a description of her own self, present or future.

Next, she hated her mother's work, the soulless, cynical root of its existence, and she certainly had no place in her heart for her father's world—Broadway. The fact that *Hello, Dolly!* had opened and appeared to lift the entire nation up less than three months after its president had been gunned down in Dallas had struck her as obscene, even as a ten-year-old. And a few years later *Hair,* with its extravagant claims of psychedelic authenticity, was in some ways an even bigger betrayal—it was a safe-and-sane tour-bus ride to the deeper and more dangerous culture embodied by the newspaper she devoured every week, *The East Village Other*. Lil had no time for the America she was trapped in. She was precocious, brainy, and a terrible student. She wore one pair of grungy jeans almost exclusively and piled her jet-black hair on top of her head defiantly, rather than run a brush through it. Only in her bed at night, alone and awake more nights than not, did she speak quietly to herself, admitting that if everything was wrong it probably meant that something was wrong inside of her too. She was off in some way, though she had no name for it. But it was hard for her to imagine how she was going to tolerate another fifty or sixty years of this. She had grown accustomed to the humiliation of her semester report card—primarily C minuses with a D in algebra. She hated her algebra teacher almost as much as she hated her first name and her mother's cynical exploitation of the finer classes of the city.

Her father, for whom she couldn't help retaining some affection—he never seemed to want anything from her—told her that he got a report card every week: an envelope with a check in it. If he was out of work, the envelope didn't come at all, which was worse than four C's and a D. When he uttered the phrase to her—"four C's and a D"—he heard the corresponding notes in his head, which he felt was disrespectful of the seriousness of her distress. He brushed the sound away like a gnat flying in and out of his ear and explained that there were bigger humiliations in life. The artists who opened shows on and off-Broadway got their report cards in *The New York Times,* right there in black and white, for all to see. Getting destroyed by the critics caused symptoms that felt like acute food poisoning, symptoms that took weeks, sometimes months, to abate. Lil took little comfort. What he didn't tell her was that, sometimes, if you had been particularly reckless and free of the normal human strictures, you got your report card in a hospital room in a foreign country.

He loved his daughter and wanted only for her to be a happier person than she was, than her mother had ever been, and than he was right at the moment. All he knew was that a certain kind of anger was in her that never seemed to abate. He feared for the outcome. And feared the risk of making it worse. Better they should go to a ball game. After all, he didn't have to go to work.

IN LATE AUGUST 1968, while Aurora Shelton and Vincent Donnelly were trying to tear themselves away from the TV set, where the horrors of the Democratic National Convention and its attendant protests were unfolding, with police in riot gear tear-gassing students in Grant Park and ten thousand National Guardsmen entering the fray, a brown paper package was dropped at the back door of their home in Larchmont. Aurora discovered it when she went out to see if the stars were out.

She had by this time appeared in three Broadway flops since *Nowhere to Go But Up*. She had tried to tell herself that it was just show business, but each one wounded, and each one wounded more than the previous one. The work was staggeringly exhausting. The fear of the mediocre material was paralyzing, and the fact that not once was the miracle of rescue provided, despite her irrational belief that all these shows had been dramatically improved along the way, made her feel stupid. The shows were just as lousy on opening night as they had appeared to be on the first day of rehearsal. Why was she doing this?

There was another result. A promising young performer in supporting roles in four flops in a row stopped being promising. No one blamed her for failures, but no one called with offers either. On her worst days she was convinced that this was her fate: to be a footnote in the world she had fully intended to conquer. She tried not to be devastated when the feeling overcame her. She continued to study voice and acting and keep in shape. She had managed guest shots in twelve television episodes to no particular effect, and was raising two sons in the suburbs. Little Vin had been born eight months and three weeks after the wedding day, and Gareth had followed two years later. For a time she felt split down the middle, motherhood and show business pulling in opposite directions. It was not a good feeling, but the years had sapped her energy and much of her hope. There were a million young women like her lined up to audition, and she certainly wasn't the youngest. Not anymore. She loved her sons, her home, the peace of it compared to the one she had grown up in. But it seemed certain that a part of her had been amputated.

Her life with Vincent fulfilled the one thing she hoped it would. They had built the marriage into an edifice, a monument to stability. She felt as though she had, by unplanned means, arrived at a place where she could at least survive, even if it ran counter to her temperament.

Life could be thrilling, too. In the dark, when Vincent placed his hands on either side of her waist, just above her hips, and lifted her onto the bed, as he did on many nights, she closed her eyes and saw flashes of light in the blackness. She gave herself gratefully, almost always. Vincent didn't talk during these moments. His eyes darkened, and he seemed to travel very far away, and yet, it was those distant, lost and unseeing eyes that penetrated her first, and melted her. He wanted something that he could never articulate with words, but his body took it anyhow, and left her feeling as if her bones had dissolved. He was never gentle until after; he sometimes pinned her shoulders with his open palms or dragged her to the side of the bed while he stood over her and took her that way. And yet she always felt, somehow, that she was in control. That the slightest objection, or suggestion of irritation or boredom, would have brought him to his knees, to tears. Her acquiescence was the source of her power, and she liked that. She held him as she would hold an audience. And afterward he was so grateful that he became a worshipper, holding her carefully in his arms as if she might break in two. Like acting, the rides were wild, and only possible as long as they ended in the calm certainty of home and safety. The savagery of life was to be cherished; so long as it existed within a shell that she could be assured would never crack.

The two boys were a constant mystery to her, but forever intriguing. They were boys. They careened around whatever space they found themselves in, and were forever injured in minor ways, which taught them nothing about caution. If there was a place to fall down or to crash into or to fall out of, they found it. There was a nanny now too, who chased after them enough of the time to make life manageable. She lived in the maid's quarters of the old colonial, just as if the three of them were living in a late-thirties movie directed by George Cukor. Vincent had done very well, and a couple of Aurora's TV episodes had begun to bring in residual payments from overseas exploitation. Some days she thought she was living someone else's life, but it was a pleasant one, she told herself.

The brown paper parcel at the back door contained a script and a reel of audiotape, accompanied by a letter from a producer Aurora had never met named Antoine Berget. Vincent remembered him well. Technically they were still partners, for

Vincent had retained his small ownership share in the lighting rig business. In the letter Berget introduced himself and pointed out that he had given her husband his first job as a spot operator for a tour of *Carousel*. He explained that, while he had been concentrating on touring since the inception of his career, he was now ready to produce his own hit musical. The script was called *One More Spring,* derived from a once popular but now largely forgotten novel by Robert Nathan about three vagabonds during the Great Depression who find love and fulfillment living in a tool shed in Central Park.

"My passionate belief," wrote Berget, who was never at a loss for hyperbole, "is that in this age of terrible disruption and chaos in our country, this uplifting story of people getting through an earlier terrible time in our country with love and generosity will have limitless audience appeal. Also, you would be the star, playing an out-of-work actress in her early thirties possessed of more genius than luck." The point was not lost on Aurora.

"He's a salesman," said Vincent, "and a cheapskate. But not a crook as far as I could ever determine. And without him I would never have met you."

Aurora cocked her head, considering the matter. It was odd, and flattering, that this had not come through her agent, but by messenger under cover of darkness. And somehow it was all vaguely suspicious and dramatic—a brown paper package left at the back door. She liked the eccentricity of it.

"Where's the Wollensak?" she asked.

The songs were good. The script was touching. Aurora had never encountered raw materials for a show that seemed in such good shape. Vincent was amused.

"It's an unpredictable business," he said—something she hardly needed to be told. "How the hell do you know if something's actually good? Remember *Mr. President?* But if Antoine Berget can produce a hit show on Broadway, then absolutely anything can happen."

Aurora was not thinking of Antoine Berget. She was having a moment when she wished Ike Harris were there to give her his assessment of the score. She thought it was good. It had big, fat old-fashioned tunes. She would have liked some reassurance, though she did not mention it to Vincent, who couldn't have given it. And then the moment passed.

FOR VINCENT, one of the side benefits of Aurora being in business with Antoine Berget was that he once again found himself in the company of Cappy Casparian, who was a major investor—and billed as the executive producer—of *One More Spring.*

"I wrote a check," Cappy told Vincent on the first day of rehearsal in an empty ballroom at the derelict Hotel Diplomat on 43rd Street. The entire company was present, and the room was filled with anticipation and excitement. Vincent found himself on the margins and was glad to greet an old acquaintance.

"I wrote a check, and I got my friends to write checks, and that is every single thing I know about executive producing. I don't even know what it means. I'm neither an executive nor a producer, but the Belmont Stakes is this weekend, so I flew in for the first day of rehearsal. Do you play the horses? "

"I don't know," Vincent said, "but Aurora is going to be preoccupied, and if you want some company at Belmont, I'd be honored."

"The chariot awaits for no man," said Casparian. "It awaits on Sunday. I'd be honored too, if you'd be honored. We'll both be honored. That's your wife, the star of the show? That must be nice." Vincent nodded. He had long since given up backstage work for a desk job at Local One, and was by now serving as its president, but with Aurora working again, he knew he'd miss the excitement of an eight show week. The new job was complex in some ways, but dull in most others.

Vincent lost a hundred and fifty dollars at Belmont. Casparian, who was accompanied by an underdressed, unwashed Brooklynite called Mr. Dirt, who was his research expert, blew ten thousand. As his horse made a valiant, failed effort to nose ahead of the favorite at the finish, Mr. Dirt began to bellow fearfully, falling to his knees and flagellating himself with a folded-up racing form. Casparian was impassive.

"I'm depressed now," he said to Vincent. "I may have to kill myself."

"What about him?" Vincent asked.

Cappy glanced down at the disreputable-looking tout, who was still howling at the moon.

"He gets fifteen percent of my winnings," he said. "Which won't help him today. But he's a master statistician. Dropped out of Columbia, and he's a little antisocial. But I like him, and he's gotten me some big wins. Thanks to him I'm almost even."

Vincent and Cappy dropped Mr. Dirt in Brooklyn—he had regained his composure and was busily trying to handicap the Oscars from an article in *People* magazine that he had brought with him. They went to Gallaghers for dinner, after which they proceeded to a running poker game on the fifth floor of a brownstone in Hell's Kitchen. The room was thick with smoke and the smell of stale beer. Vincent was happy. He took a cigar gratefully from Cappy but declined a seat at the table. He just wanted to watch Cappy do whatever it was he did. Three hours of sports talk, dirty jokes, and inspired cursing fits later, they departed, Cappy having recovered 10 percent of his horse racing losses. Vincent still didn't see how he did it.

"We'll play again when the show is in Boston," Cappy said. "I'm off to Cincinnati in the morning. But we'll meet again when we're among the show folk, God bless them."

"I think one of the things I like best," said Vincent, "is when we're not among show folk. Not that I don't love them, but really—give me a cigar and a deck of cards."

"It's an unexamined life," Cappy said, "but it's the only one you've got. Give my love to your wife. I'm counting on her for a hit."

Vincent got home a little after two and fell into bed next to Aurora.

"How's the show?" he asked when she put her head sleepily on his shoulder.

"Confusing," she said. "And I don't know about this director."

"Or the producer," Vincent said. "Or the executive producer." Within an instant they were both asleep.

ON AN AFTERNOON when *One More Spring* was in rehearsal, Vincent's secretary tapped on his office door at the Local One office and entered with a vaguely troubled look on her face. She was a woman of fifty or so with short, steely gray hair and an absolute command of her work and the management of Vincent's. She had been there for decades, far longer than he had. Troubled looks were not an everyday thing with her. Vincent raised his eyebrows.

"There's a young lady here who wants to see you, no appointment, no explanation, wild red hair and a white blouse, gray skirt, sensible shoes, and she says you'll remember her from a high chair. Mean anything to you?"

Vincent was without a clue.

"We better find out," he said.

The young woman entered quietly and stood before Vincent's desk as if she were making an unexpected and unpleasant visit to the principal's office. She was a stranger to Vincent.

"Thank you for seeing me," she said. "I'm Maggie Hynes."

She thrust a letter in front of him, carefully handwritten on paper that Vincent judged to be at least a decade old.

My Darling Maggie,

It does not look so good for me, and by the time you read this I'll be long gone. That's the point of letters like this one I suppose. You will find the will and all of that in good order, and I'm enclosing the key to the safe deposit box where everything is kept. But, of course, there is not much that was actually kept, though I wish it were otherwise. You will have to make your own way, I'm afraid, as the American Dream never really came to visit your grandmother and me, though we did survive the place after all, for a while anyhow.

Should you ever need a favor there is one man who might be able to do it for you. His name is Vincent Donnelly, and he is in the theatrical stagehands union. The truth is that he's no doubt a great man there, but he wouldn't be there at all had he not come into the saloon many years ago, mad as a rabid dog, and ready for a fight. I calmed him down and fed him a drink and together your grandmother and I managed to set him up well, though the method was unusual if I may say so. If you can find him, he can tell you about it. And IF you find him, if you need him, that is, tell him he last saw you in a high chair and hello from his old fairy godfather Arthur

Hynes. If he has the chance to do you a good turn, I'd bet a goodly sum that he will try. If I had a goodly sum.

In the meanwhile, don't fret over me or moon about more than is necessary. I've had a good enough life, the best part of which was raising and loving you. I'm only sorry I can't give you the moon itself because I would, too, and you know it.

Your loving grandpa,

Arthur Hynes

Vincent looked up at her. Indeed, he had seen her in a high chair years before and had never thought of her once since that night. But here she was, needing something. He handed her back the letter. She looked at him with something approaching actual fear.

"Your grandfather," he said, "gave me my first drink, and asked me the most important question I've ever been asked. It took me more than a month to answer it, and everything he says in the letter is true. It brought me to this desk, with a lot of adventures and opportunities beforehand. I'm sorry he's gone, and I'm glad you came to see me, and I wonder what I can do for you."

Maggie Hynes relaxed for the first time. Her shoulders fell a little, and she unclenched her fists.

"I'm very pleased to meet you," she said. "Though I guess we met all those years ago. I don't remember."

"Have you eaten?" Vincent asked. He wanted to take her to lunch.

When they had settled in the dingy comfort of McHale's, a place he continued to patronize with the regular stagehands even though he was now way up in the power structure and the cheeseburgers were nothing special, he asked her about something that had been on his mind on and off for years.

"Whatever happened to the lawyer?"

She looked at him quizzically and then said, "The one who died on the train?"

"The one who had an office upstairs from your grandfather's saloon. Wasn't he related to you somehow?"

"My grandmother's brother," she said. "Francis Rafferty."

"That's right."

"He had a secret house in Florida," she said, "and a secret family there too. No one knew anything about them. He was a secret bigamist."

"You're joking."

"Probably, no one would ever have known, I don't suppose. But he boarded a train at Penn Station with a small suitcase that had nothing in it but a fresh set of underwear and two bottles of Irish whiskey, and when the train got to Tallahassee, he was dead in the sleeper car. His secret wife had come to meet him. When the will was found, he had left everything to this wife and four children we'd never heard of down there. Not that there was much to leave. Nothing for this side of the family, in any event."

Vincent shook his head. There was no way of knowing anything about anything, apparently.

Maggie Hynes, it developed, had been working as a bookkeeper to a man who had just been hauled off to jail in New Jersey. His company—a pipefitting concern that was no doubt nothing more than a front for something else—had gone up in smoke, and she needed work. That was the easy part. There was an opening for a bookkeeper for the Local One pension fund, a backwater that seemed to more or less run itself for decades. The larger concern was finding her a place to live.

"If I give you money, and my wife finds out, what's she likely to say?" he asked. "If I cause the union to give you an advance to rent a place, what's the union likely to say? If I rent an apartment in my own name, then we're back to question one."

He was shocked at himself. Rent her an apartment? He had just met the girl.

"A roommate," she said, shocked that he had wandered into any of this territory at all. "One of the girls who works for you would surely want a roommate."

Vincent installed her at the pension fund, and they sent out a memo in search of roommates. In the meantime, he used petty cash to put her at the Hotel Pennsylvania, and within a week, she had found a friend in the building who was eager to share the rent at her studio uptown. In a surprisingly short time, she had found her own place. Vincent saw her coming in and out of the Local One building and smiled blandly at her, and after a couple of months, she wrote him a note, saying simply, "You have saved my life. Bless you. Maggie Hynes." Unable to decide if he was supposed to answer it or not, he put it in the top drawer of his desk. And he never managed to tell Aurora about its existence—or about Maggie Hynes—at all.

Aurora was in Boston when all this happened, enduring tech rehearsals and getting ready for yet another tortuous opening night out of town. The director of *One More Spring* was a young man named Arthur Bundsman, who had had an off-Broadway hit the previous season that featured a lot of camp humor and tap dancing on a stage about the size of a silver dollar. He was, perhaps, an up-and-comer, or perhaps just a hungry young man with long hair who would work for minimum scale, which was all that Antoine Berget was prepared to pay. He seemed a nice enough fellow to work with in the rehearsal room, but Aurora suspected that, when the surface was scratched, he was clueless and terrified. This much was proven during tech, as his producer and choreographer gradually took the show away from him, making key decisions about lighting and scenery moves, and leaving him to stew, slumped in a fourth-row seat until he finally became so upset that no one was paying the slightest attention to him that he stormed out of the theater one snowy afternoon, only to return with a magnum of champagne, which he sat in the back row consuming from an expensive Baccarat flute he had also purchased for the occasion. He remained quietly drunk on champagne, sneaking out into the alley for a few tokes from a joint from time to time. Then the first preview arrived.

Forgotten and silent for three days, Bundsman lurched to his feet at half hour and demanded that everyone form a circle on the stage and join hands in what turned out to be a slurred prayer to the theater gods. He entreated the company to make magic, to be brilliant, to make him proud, to make the audience roar and weep and bleed, at which point he vomited all over his shoes, and had to be carried out. The performance began forty-five minutes late, after the stage floor had been mopped and dried. As the stagehands were hustling to make things right, Antoine Berget turned to his leading lady, who was as nervous as a cat, and said, simply, "They get paid extra for mopping. It's in their contract."

The performance, as far as Aurora could tell, was neither here nor there. The material was strong, the production dull, but she took a surprising ovation after the one big ballad she had in act one, and a roar went up at the conclusion of a second-act novelty number that she thought had been intended as a throwaway. The audience seemed to be enjoying her. Vincent, who had spent much of the tech period in various poker games with a fretful Cappy Casparian, rushed to her dressing room to congratulate her, though his comments about the show were guarded. As she was changing, uncongratulated by Bundsman, who seemed to have disappeared, possibly forever, she received a note handed to her by her dresser.

> Come to my room at the Ritz Carlton tomorrow at 10 A.M.—#1016. Much to discuss. Berget.

The next morning, she arrived, puzzled but relieved that at least someone was paying attention to her. There was coffee set up, and little cakes. Antoine Berget was dressed in an expensive blue silk robe decorated with an oversize brown paisley pattern that made it look to her like he was covered with giant, curled-up garden slugs. Number 1016 was a suite, complete with fake fireplace, and Berget, who had splashed on too much cologne in anticipation of the visit, led her to the mantelpiece, on which was a small, framed sampler in needlepoint.

"I place it where I can see it every morning whenever I'm doing a show," he said. "Harold Arlen gave it to me the one time we worked together, and I live by its every word of wisdom." The old-fashioned lettering said, "Thou Shalt Not Kid Thyself."

When they had settled down to coffee, Berget waited for a suitably dramatic moment and then launched himself into a speech he had clearly spent time thinking about.

"I'm going to be the most important producer on Broadway," he said, intoning the words with a spectacularly false sense of casualness. "And this is how I'm going to do it."

He had Aurora's attention, but she didn't know whether to laugh or take the performance as a piece of serious drama. She decided to hold her peace and find out if she was in a drama or a farce.

"This show is going to open in Boston to lousy reviews, and I'm going to turn it into a hit. If I can do that, the sky's the limit. I have three secret weapons for doing it, and they had all better be able to deliver, or there will be hell to pay."

Now he had her attention.

"The first secret weapon is Jerry Herman," he said. "He's on a train to Boston as we speak, and he needs to write two songs for this show. I've got him a room in the hotel with a piano, and he's agreed to write me two hit songs, and I already know what they're about. You are going to sing them both, one a solo, one a duet. But they won't go in until after we open here. The second secret weapon is Joe Layton. He's a genius director who blew up his career with bad behavior of every imaginable kind, but he won't blow up with me, or I'll kill him, and he knows it. He's going to restage 90 percent of what's up there during the four weeks we're here and you won't recognize it four weeks from tonight. The final secret weapon is you."

He paused dramatically and then repeated it, unnecessarily, for emphasis. He was a terrible actor.

"The final secret weapon is you. I wouldn't be doing any of this if I didn't have you. The audience loves you, but there's not enough of you. So . . . you're going to end up doing something you didn't expect. You're going to carry this show on your shoulders, it will become a vehicle for you and only you, and in the process both of us will get famous, make money, and win awards. Of course, your leading man will grow to hate you when he sees this happen, but it's a business. Do you understand? The entire plan from beginning to end means nothing without you."

Aurora put down her coffee cup and looked at Antoine Berget. She saw the devil offering her a devil's bargain, though she wasn't sure what was wrong with it exactly. She sat in silence for a moment before it occurred to her that no other devil might ever come along in a moment like this. Finally, she spoke.

"I won't sleep with you," she said, though it was far from

clear to her that Antoine Berget would be interested. Still, you never knew.

"It makes no sense to sleep with your star," Berget responded, as if he had wrestled with this issue before and knew it was coming. "It makes the rest of the negotiations far too complicated. Chorus people of every possible gender are for sleeping with."

Aurora looked at him in shock. Apparently, he had worked out everything in his mind, including his sex life and beyond. And, indeed, it seemed he had. As he led her to the door he said, "I've chartered a boat for the opening night party here—we're going to ride around Boston Harbor for three hours and celebrate. That way no one will be able to read the reviews until we dock. They're not going to be good. Any questions?"

"Only one," Aurora said. "Jerry Herman. Joe Layton. How are you going to deal with the songwriters who thought they wrote this show, and your director? You were so effusive on the first day of rehearsal. You called them geniuses. Do you remember that?"

Berget shrugged and kissed her on the cheek.

"Flowers today," he said. "Lawyers tomorrow."

AURORA WAS FAR from sure that Jerry Herman was going to write her two songs, but that night he came to visit her in her dressing room after the performance, a compact, bright-eyed man with a gentleman's manners.

"You're going to make me look good," he said cheerfully. "And I like looking good. Of course, no one will ever know I wrote these things, but I'll look good to me. And the right people will know because they always find out."

Then he winked at her and backed out of the room gracefully. "You're divine," he said.

Joe Layton had also arrived, sober and thoughtful looking, and within a couple of days there were a series of swift and surprising scenic transitions that hadn't been there before, and a first-rate dance break in the middle of the show's third number. Aurora was impressed, though Layton never spoke to her directly, except to say, after one particularly grueling day of dance drilling, "I'll get to you all in good time. You're not the problem here, you're the opportunity."

"Thank you, I think," Aurora said.

"All I can do is fix three things a day," he said, ignoring her. "And I'm starting with what's most broken."

In fact, Layton never spoke to anyone directly. He barked orders to the company, the stage manager, the music director, and anyone else who had to change anything. His assistant delivered individual notes to the cast.

Late on the third afternoon after the cavalry's arrival, Aurora and Jerry Herman met in the lobby of the Colonial Theatre, where a concert grand piano had been serving as a piece of furniture. Legend had it that Richard Rodgers had written two songs for *South Pacific* on this particular piano when it was trying out in Boston, though some swore that it was The *King and I*. Or the much more inauspicious *Me and Juliet*.

Jerry Herman sat at the legendary keyboard while Aurora sat in an upholstered lobby chair and listened. With the stealth of a spider navigating a piece of drapery, Antoine Berget snuck in behind her and put his hands on the chair back. The song was an irresistible strut that didn't yet have a bridge, but one would soon be composed. Berget shrugged. Aurora liked the tune a lot. By the following day the song was done and an orchestrator was busily writing charts to be copied for the players in the pit.

The ballad, an eleven o'clock number, the final song in the show, would take a little more time. And, besides, it was now opening night. No one could focus, except for Joe Layton, who insisted that the orchestra be called at five P.M. so that the new number could be played down. Aurora stood on the stage with her costar, veteran song-and-dance man Eddie Foy, Jr., and together they sang the lyric over a bouncy orchestration that seemed just fine.

"We'll fix it," cried Jerry Herman from the tenth row, and he marched down to the pit to consult with the orchestrator and the musical director. Aurora retreated to her dressing room.

The first act had continued to be improved by Layton's staging; he had also changed the order of two scenes, which helped with the logic of the story. Just after the first act curtain fell, to modest applause, and Aurora turned to head for her dressing room, she felt a firm hand grabbing her by the shoulder. She looked up to find herself face-to-face with Joe Layton, who had Eddie Foy by the other arm.

"We've got fifteen minutes," Layton said. "Let's do that number."

"What?" said Foy

"I can stage it in ten minutes. You can hold the lyric on a piece of paper. The band has the music. Let's go!"

"Young man," Eddie Foy began in protest, but Layton cut him off.

"Never mind all the histrionics and the bullshit about your long and illustrious career, and what you will and won't do," Layton said. "I'm the best chance you've got for this turkey to become a hit, and if you don't do this for me, I'm getting in a cab before act two begins, and going to Logan Airport and taking the first plane back to Miami. Forever. Now follow me."

Aurora and Eddie Foy entered after the entr'acte, each carrying a piece of paper that Layton had typed up that afternoon containing the lyric. They played a brief dialogue scene and the band, also alerted by Layton, began a gentle vamp. The idea of the number was for Eddie Foy, veteran hoofer, to teach Aurora Shelton, nondancing leading lady, how to be a vaudevillian. The band vamped. Instead of launching into the verse, however, Foy, long experienced and completely familiar with audiences and how they behave, held up the sheet of white paper in his hand for all to see and announced, "Folks, we've never done it before, it's not in your Playbill, but we're going to try it tonight! You'll let us know." And then he began to sing. It was a dirty trick. The number tore the place up.

Aurora arrived back in New York with four big songs in a show that was playing like a house afire—or at least it had been that way on closing night at the Colonial in Boston. Vincent, who had flown up for the closing, accompanied her back home to Larchmont the next day on a privately chartered plane that landed in White Plains. He had a champagne supper waiting when they arrived—scrambled eggs and caviar, toast points and a small green salad. They sent the maid home before they dined, and proceeded directly to the bedroom after, where they celebrated with their bodies the inevitable feeling that Aurora Shelton was about to become a star on Broadway. She sat astride him and did things her way; her sense of power and control was intoxicating, and Vincent seemed to be enjoying it as she moved her body above him to whatever rhythm she chose as he followed, finding himself in a virtually new role. They were forty-five minutes from Broadway, as they often joked, but on this night, all of Broadway seemed to be within reach, the surge of its electric supply driving her higher and higher. Anticipated arrival was an aphrodisiac she had never sampled, and she could only imagine what actual arrival might mean.

Afterward, as she lay happily exhausted beside him, he said, "There's a telegram on your dresser."

A shiver of fear went through her. A telegram? Had someone died? Who sends a telegram anymore, except for dramatic effect? Or was she being congratulated before the fact? The show still had two weeks of previews ahead of it. Silently Aurora went into her dressing room and stared at the yellow envelope for a moment. Then she tore it open, gritting her teeth. Unfolding the paper, she read: *WE HEAR IT'S GREAT. FLYING IN FOR THE OPENING IF YOU CAN SECURE TICKETS. HUWILER.*

MARIUS HUWILER and Jonah Kingston had aged quite differently from each other. Jonah, the military man, had gone to seed like an athlete who has given up running drills for beer and pretzels. Marius, meanwhile, had grown balder and gaunter, but somehow stronger looking than Aurora remembered him. He was still in need of Jonah's calming influence, and seemed to appreciate it more than ever, but he had somehow assumed a leadership role in the relationship that surprised Aurora. Still, the most surprising thing about them as a couple was that they were in late middle age. Pants had been let out. Attempts had been made to hide baldness. They were a fussy older couple.

The two of them arrived on a Tuesday, two days before the opening, and installed themselves at the Hotel Chelsea "because," Marius explained, "Allen Ginsberg is here someplace."

Aurora had relocated from the suburbs to the Americana up on 52nd Street but was dreaming of the Astor, which had met the wrecking ball two years earlier. She couldn't face the commute with the opening staring her in the face. And she wanted to spend time with Marius and Jonah, both of whom, coming from the open flatlands of Junction City, just wanted to stay in town. Vincent accompanied them to the Metropolitan Museaum of Art but demurred when it came to Carnegie Hall. The high-culture scene wasn't for him, and besides, he sensed that Aurora was reliving some part of her youth and didn't need him for that.

Quite quickly it developed that, after a couple of high-spirited postshow dinners at Jim Downey's Steakhouse and Mamma Leone's, which Marius had read about in the food section of *The Kansas City Star,* the trio actually had precious little to talk about. They raised a glass to Barty, who had died of breast cancer the previous August, leaving Toni the house and a small annuity that she expected would last a lifetime. Aurora could see, for the first time, that for all he had done for her, Marius Huwiler really was a lovely, competent, neurotic small-town music teacher, and that Jonah, who loved him and took care of him, was a man of surprisingly few interests. Their lives were circumscribed by routine, by a dedication to the garden, the golf club (Jonah), and church (Marius).

Aurora had assumed that the tectonic shits embodied by Woodstock, by the Vietnam War, by the psychedelic culture that had subsumed much of Greenwich Village, Berkeley, and Boston, and by the dawning of the gay and women's liberation movements would have touched them in some profound way, but quite the opposite was true. They were provincials, living a charmed, if somewhat benighted, existence. They listened to music, went about their routine, and remained undiscovered, which seemed to be their principal shared goal in life.

"I know what we should do," Aurora announced, as a headwaiter at Downey's bowed low to her after taking her Diners Club card on Wednesday night. She was exhausted from the preview performance but knew that sleep was out of the question on the eve of the opening. "There's a place we can go where we'll cause a stir."

By now it was called the Bon Soir, down a flight of stairs on MacDougal Street. As they got out of the cab, Aurora explained to the somewhat bedazzled couple, "This place began life as a lesbian bar called Eve's something-or-other that a Polish woman started, back in the twenties. Then it was a very chi-chi gay club called Mon Plaisir in the forties until somebody figured out that's not actually the way you say "my pleasure" in French, and now it's the Bon Soir, which is correct usage as far as that goes. A lot of the glamour is gone, but they have a piano, and I bet half the chorus from *One More Spring* is already in here. Most of these places are ear-splitting disco and screaming boys doing cocaine in the bathroom, but this one is soft. You'll like it."

Marius said nothing.

She was greeted with scattered applause when she entered. The clientele, mostly young, seemed almost to have been awaiting her arrival—or some of them had. The place was long and narrow, dark and faux-glamorous, with Christmas tree tinsel hanging over black velvet everywhere and a vintage framed female nude over the bar, as if this were the Wild West in the late nineteenth century. Aurora led Marius and Jonah to the back of the room, where a tiny round raised platform served as a stage. An upright piano was pushed against the wall, and a microphone stood on a stand next to it. She moved the mic stand front and center and tapped it until someone somewhere turned it on. After a few amplified taps, the place quieted down.

"Hello, everybody," she said, "I'm Aurora Shelton, and I've brought two very special gentlemen with me. Tommy," she said signaling the bartender, "could you bring each of them a Beefeater martini for me? Come up here, Marius."

As Marius Huwiler shyly stepped up onto the disc-like stage that served as the focal point of the place, she continued. "This man taught me what it means to be a singer," she said, "back in Junction City, Kansas, of all places when I was about fourteen. His name is Marius Huwiler, and I don't think he ever pictured being here tonight. And this is his friend Jonah Kingston, and they share a house in a subdivision in Junction City. No one's ever given them a lick of trouble and they've been together for . . . how long?"

Marius leaned into the microphone.

"Since 1946," he said. "Almost twenty-five years."

The place broke out into a roar of applause.

"Marius doesn't know it," Aurora said, but he's going to sit down at the piano right here and play the song that got me my first job. In B-flat."

Marius looked terrified. Aurora rolled the piano out far enough for him to sit at the keyboard just as their drinks arrived. Marius downed half of his in one gulp and ran his fingers across the keys. The crowd applauded and then settled down.

He played "A New Town Is a Blue Town" for her, and "It Might as Well Be Spring." They had just reached the bridge of "Am I Blue," and Aurora was about to break down in genuine tears, wondering where Ethel Waters was tonight and hoping it was someplace nice, when the front door blew open and a stream of uniformed policemen poured into the place shouting and waving billy clubs above their heads.

"Up against the wall!" one of them shouted. "All you fags up against the wall! Hands over your heads! *Now!*"

The crowd stirred in panic, then raced to comply, but the bartender, grabbing the bottle of Beefeaters from behind him, shouted "Liberation now!" and brought it down on the head of the nearest cop. Aurora backed against the wall of the little stage area and said to no one in particular, "It's Stonewall again. Jesus Christ, it's Stonewall again." She did not move.

As the police and the bargoers quickly meshed into a riot of noise and violence, she saw Marius break for the door. His face was a mask of terror. His brain had clicked into an involuntary impulse toward flight, not fight, but he headed toward the scrum, trying to get around it to the front door. There was no path to be found. Aurora watched in horror as he was sucked from the edge of the crowd toward the center. Jonah, following quickly, wished he had kept his military form and stamina in trim as tried to rescue his lover from disgrace and injury.

The place was coming apart now, and black-and-white police cars were arriving down MacDougal, a swath of swirling red lights appearing through the little window wells up the stairs at the top of the bar's entryway. More cops came streaming down the stairs and into the place, subduing the crowd and cuffing anyone they could grab. Aurora, still frozen against the wall, was ignored for the moment, but she had a bird's-eye view of the event as it was quickly brought into containment. There must have been three cops for every customer. All the young men were led up the stairs in handcuffs, and among them her old music teacher and his partner, now moving in a dutiful shuffle. She had shattered their lives, she thought, and there would be no repair. Idiotically, she kept repeating under her breath, *They're not in Kansas anymore.*

From behind her a cop emerged from the toilet and grabbed her by both arms. As he slipped a pair of handcuffs on her he said, "I don't know what the fuck you're doing here, sister, but you're coming with me. Didn't nobody tell you this place was fairies only?"

VINCENT DID SOMETHING he never liked to do and called Tommy Ennis, Jr., who was now the biggest man at Local One. The elder Ennis brothers had long since passed on, and Junior was running things, which meant he knew Mayor John Lindsay, he knew the Democratic Party bosses in Greenwich Village, the police chief, and the editors of the few local tabloids still in publication. There would be nothing in the papers, and no charges pressed. There would be no bail, and no formal record of any of the three names. It was a lot to get done at four A.M. There were a lot of people who had to wake up in the middle of the night, and there would be a boatload of favors to repay, but what was the alternative? Vincent collected his wife and her two bewildered friends from the local precinct house on Vesey Street at six-fifteen in the morning. Together they all rode back to Larchmont in his Cadillac, no questions asked. He gave each of them a Miltown and put them to bed. *One More Spring* opened on Broadway ten hours later.

AURORA WOULD RETAIN only the faintest memory of the opening performance or how she got through it. She did remember distinctly recognizing the two empty seats she had set aside for Marius and Jonah, who were already at LaGuardia, awaiting a flight to Wichita via Chicago, with a two-hour drive ahead of them after that. She remembered the ovation after her big number that brought down the first act curtain, and she remembered being awakened toward the end of intermission and walked by the stage manager to the spot in the wings from which she and Eddie Foy were scheduled to make their second act entrance. Christ, she thought as she waited and listened to the entr'acte, I'm turning into Judy Garland. The bad part of Judy Garland. Or at least they think I am.

"Jesus, Mary and Joseph," Eddie Foy said to her just before they entered, "I'm looking in your eyes and I can see two orgies, two opium dens, and a boxing ring. Where you been, kid?" And on that note, the curtain went up and they strutted into the light.

One More Spring was an unexpected smash. The morning after the show opened, the line at the Majestic stretched across the entrance to the Broadhurst and the Shubert, turned the corner onto Shubert Alley, and went all the way to 45th Street. The *Daily News* came to take a photograph. Two local TV stations interviewed people who had waited more than two hours to buy tickets. Antoine Berget walked up and down the line himself, pushing a cart with hot coffee and doughnuts, which he gave out freely as he chatted with the customers. He was suddenly the most important producer on Broadway. And Aurora Shelton was a star.

All of this caused a clustered tangle of emotions in the heart of Ike Harris, who was playing a flop called *The Fig Leaves Are Falling* at the Broadhurst next door and got to see Aurora's fans crossing in front of his largely deserted theater entrance each night on their lucky way to catch the newest thing. Thankfully, *Fig Leaves* lasted only a couple of weeks, including previews, and then he was free again. But the feelings—pride, anger, jealousy, vicarious delight, envy, the dumbstruck belief that perhaps there was a God after all, lingered. It didn't help that, when Aurora won the Tony for Best Actress in a Musical, she was serenaded to the stage by an orchestra in which Ike was handling the first trumpet chores. He played that damn song—which everyone knew Jerry Herman had ghosted—six times that night, but only for Aurora did it hurt. She thanked her fellow nominees; her husband, Vincent; the cast and crew, and Marius Huwiler. Then Ike and the band played her off.

Two weeks after the Tonys, Ike, who was contracting five Broadway shows and spending his free evenings holding down the first trumpet chair of the Village Vanguard's big band just for fun, moved his offices to the ground floor of a brownstone next door to Local 802, the musicians' union building on West 48th Street in the heart of Hell's Kitchen. The Vanguard band played only on Monday nights, but there was a faux-Dixieland band that commanded the back room of a place on restaurant row where he could sit in whenever he wanted and riff on Tommy Ladnier's repertoire. A modest fan club began to appear, and soon the club began billing him on a chalkboard outside: "The Dixie Ramblers" it said. Under the name, the proprietor would scrawl "featuring Ike Harris"—on nights when he showed up. That never happened on Broadway, and it was, he realized with amusement, the first time he had been billed by name since he had beaten Sid Lupowitz out of his billing back in the army, in the days of "Ike Harris's Kings of Rhythm." Reluctantly he admitted to himself that he rather enjoyed seeing his name out front.

On his daily walk from his new apartment in the Alwyn Court, on Seventh and 58th, to the office, down 48th and across Broadway, he could watch the district falling apart, piece by piece, right in front of his eyes. The exteriors of the theaters had begun to look like hell. On one occasion he detoured a block south to 47th to look at the Barrymore where he had once played the piano—in direct contradiction to union regulations—in the pit of *Pal Joey.* Nothing had been done to clean or shore up the marquee, which was unchanged but barely recognizable for the soot and the dents left by careless truck drivers and the way it had begun to tilt toward the east. The mighty stone front of the theater had not been power-washed in decades. There was a thirty-foot-long pile of uncollected trash on the curb, and it looked like nothing had played there in months. Ike shook his head and kept walking, vowing to stay on 48th from now on. He didn't need his memories tarnished as if they were a part of the marquee. On Eighth Avenue, on this particular morning, he was propositioned twice. And it wasn't even ten A.M. On the nights when he had to get home from the Broadhurst, down on 44th, he could see exactly what had happened in all the years since his first infatuation. How had it come to this? And would it get worse? Meanwhile, he kept working, and people kept producing shows. He needed a second-in-command to keep track of everything.

The ad he placed in *Variety* was answered by a phone call the next morning.

"Ike Harris?" The voice was vaguely familiar. "This is Cecelia Austin. Can I come see you?"

"Cee-Cee?" he said, the blood jumping in his veins.

"Cecelia now," the voice said. "Cee-Cee was my baby name. Became a stage name. I can't go on the stage anymore, and I'm not a baby."

She walked with two canes, head high, a slight drag in her left leg. And she was quick to tell him that it had taken a lot of physical therapy to get this far. The doctors had warned her she should not expect to get further. But she needed a job; she wanted to work for him again.

"And," she said, "I owe you an apology."

"How can that be?" Ike asked, sitting across from her in the cramped office and looking at her between two piles of contracts on his desk. She remained among the most beautiful human beings he had ever seen. "I personally ruined your life."

"Oh, yes," she said. "I blamed you for all of this. Had to blame somebody. But I had a lot of time to think about it, lying there, wheeling around in a chair, and finally getting up on my own two feet. You think you seduced me? I didn't have to stay up all night fucking you. That was a choice we both made. I made the first part of the choice before we even had that bourbon and soda. That was what I wanted to do, stuck in god-forsaken Canada in a terrible bomb that was never gonna get fixed. It was fun. But it takes two willing participants. You think I wasn't one of them? When a girl walks up to you and says, 'Are you the one with the broken heart?' what the fuck do you think she means?"

"I'm the one who chased after you when you'd done a two-show day and had rehearsal the next afternoon—I've thought about it a lot myself, believe me. I was a shit. I blame myself," said Ike.

"Well," she said, "that's a mistake. And typical male chauvinism—you think you're supposed to make the decision for me. That's just insulting. But as long as you're feeling like a shit, and guilty as sin, you can give me back this job. I gotta eat, even if I can't walk right."

Cecelia Austin proved the most remarkable organizer and problem-solver Ike Harris had ever encountered. Within a week, the office was unrecognizably immaculate.

"You can't be this good at this job," he said to her one evening as he was getting ready to head back to the Alwyn Court, "and be as good a dancer as you are."

"As I was," she corrected him. "Used to be. In another lifetime."

"Fair enough," he said. "But no one is that gifted in two unrelated ways."

Cecelia shrugged. "When you've got two gifts like that—two of them—God reaches down and takes one of them away. You can't have all that. God doesn't like it."

"You're a believer," Ike said.

"After what I've been through?" she asked incredulously. "Don't be foolish. This shit just happens because it happens. That's the god who giveth and taketh away—that's a pagan god. I'm a pagan."

He took her to dinner instead of going home. There was a little French bistro called Chez Napoleon on 50th west of Ninth where he knew he could get a good cassoulet. She had a salad and steak au poivre.

"How's your broken heart?" she asked, taking a sip of a second glass of wine after they got through dissecting the day's business.

"Beyond repair," he said matter-of-factly.

"I always have wondered if I could have fixed it," she said.

"You had as good a chance as anyone. And I wish you could have. But this one was gone for good, even back then."

"Sad," she said. "But there's a part of me that's happy that kind of thing can actually happen in the world. In our business, hearts break every night and put themselves back together again before the matinee."

"Sometimes I wish I had one like that," Ike said. "But you get what you get."

"It's the pagan gods," she said. "Who's the woman?"

"Aurora Shelton."

"You're in love with Aurora Shelton? You and all of Broadway."

"I got there first," he said. "It's a long story."

Cecelia looked at him cross-eyed, and he laughed.

"I didn't touch her then, and I've barely touched her since. One kiss in a stairwell, years ago. By then it was already way too late."

"Poor girl," Cecelia said. "Poor you."

THAT WAS HOW IT BEGAN, but it was never to get much further. Ike went to bed many nights thinking that if he only really loved her the way he so obviously should, they could marry. He'd have real companionship. But he couldn't bring himself to make a move, and anyway, the friendship produced professional results. One afternoon, Cecelia came back from lunch, which she'd shared with two women who manned the phones next door at the union hall.

"Hal Hastings came in," she told Ike. Hastings was Hal Prince's music director. "I'm sitting there eating my club sandwich and he asks me, don't you work for Ike Harris? They know me by the canes. He asked me if you were still playing. They're doing some kind of a show that's got a lot of vintage music pastiche—about old Ziegfeld girls. He's looking for a trumpet that can play that style."

"What did you say?"

"I said you'd play it if you could contract it. You can't go off and compete with yourself playing in bands you don't manage. That would be foolish. You're a unique commodity."

"You told Hal Hastings he had to use me? He's Hal Hastings, for God's sake. He's his own power base. And he uses Morris Stonezek."

"Call him up," Cecelia said. "He wants to meet you."

Cecelia negotiated the deal. Ike looked forward to being back to the Winter Garden, where *Follies* was set to open, but first he had to decamp for the Boston tryout. He was at the Colonial Theatre looking over the orchestra layout in the pit (the percussion would certainly need more room) when he was called to the telephone.

"The Count is slipping away," Cecelia said. "Can you get down here in a hurry?" He was back in New York the next morning.

Count Palaffi went without a fuss. The hospital room was overheated and overcrowded. Ollie sat by his bed holding his hand. Missy, now wearing her steely gray hair cropped short like a retired military man, hovered at the edge of the room and kept going out for smokes. Lil, seventeen, sat in the room's only other chair, completely absorbed by Kurt Vonnegut's *Slaughterhouse Five*. Ike entered and made the rounds, kissing all these women whom he now so rarely saw. They spoke in whispers.

"How long has he been in here?" he asked.

"A week," Ollie replied. "He thinks there's a Filipino conspiracy among the nurses to take over the hospital and kill him with nerve gas. It's the morphine talking."

Ike looked down on the man he had first seen in a dapper moustache and a tuxedo, the man he had met when he was a boy being dragged to Parisian nightclubs before the Second World War. The Count remained a mystery no one had ever tried to solve.

Tommy Ladnier, whom Ike had seen for the first time on the same night he and Ollie had met Count Palaffi, was long gone. And now another part of that vivid picture was about to fade out.

Ike bent down to the pillow listening to the even breathing, and said softly into his stepfather's ear, "Just tell me one thing. Who the hell are you really? It can't hurt to know, especially now."

The Count opened his eyes a slit and stared up at Ike. He spoke in a guttural slur, made worse by the tube down his throat that was draining fluid from his lungs.

"I might ask you the same," the Count said, as if they were conducting a polite philosophical conversation under an umbrella on a terrace over champagne cocktails. "But," he said, and then took a long pause to try to inhale. Slowly he gathered in a breath and reached for Ike's face. "Royalty doesn't ask such questions. And royalty doesn't complain about circumstances, especially now."

And with that, he closed his eyes and his breathing ceased. There was no human sound in the room—only machines. Lil looked up from her book. Ollie closed her eyes. Missy, who had been out smoking, appeared at the door.

"Gone," Ike said. "And now we'll never know."

In truth, Count Willie Palaffi was more or less who he said he was, though no one would ever bother to discover this fact.

He was buried at the Kensico Cemetery in the family plot that had been purchased after Dr. Albert Horowitz's unexpected demise in the middle of Fifth Avenue almost forty years earlier. But Ollie made sure there was an empty plot in the middle, so that she could ultimately rest between her two husbands.

Count Palaffi had been born Wilhelm Palffy, twin brother to Count Fidel Palffy, whose noble brow and unflagging enthusiasm for the rise of the Third Reich had caused the younger twin (by twenty-two minutes) to empty a bank account and flee to Paris, hoping to find passage away from Europe altogether into some other existence. He had been in Paris barely a week when he introduced himself to Ollie. He had never worked a day in his life, and never planned to begin. He was not, in fact, a count on the night he offered Ollie and Ike a ride back to the hotel from at Le Cave de la Heure d'Or, but nonetheless inherited the title in March 1946, when his older twin was hung for treason in Budapest following the armistice, a fact he never learned. By that point both of their parents were dead, millions were missing, murdered, or displaced across the continent, and no one seemed to remember that there had ever been a twin brother who, as it happened, had inherited his brother's title of count and was contentedly playing the horses and betting on baseball games from his Manhattan apartment, wanting for nothing. And that was how it would forever stay. Some mysteries were not meant to be solved.

Six weeks later, Ollie, who was seventy-two, attended the opening night of *Follies* with Lil, who had just turned eighteen. The brooding intermission-less darkness, fitfully interrupted by what seemed like unmotivated blasts of show business, felt interminable to Ollie, who had no interest in watching a show about broken dreams, lost hopes, and wrecked marriages. She could not, for the life of her, figure out who had invented this terrible idea for a Broadway musical. Lil, who sensed her grandmother fidgeting through the final forty-five minutes, was stunned.

"It's the only good thing I've ever seen in the theater," she told Ollie as they filed out and headed for the party afterward. "The only great thing, actually. The death of the American Dream."

Ollie simply shook her head. The world had changed, she supposed. And anyhow, she never liked Broadway, though she had lost her son to its cheap tricks.

"You have to play this eight times a week," she said to Ike when they found each other at the Rainbow Room, relegated, as they were, to an annex adjacent to what she would have considered to be the real opening night party.

"I get to play it eight times a week," Ike corrected her. "For as long as it runs, may it run forever. It's the greatest thing I've gotten to play since *West Side Story*. And always the Winter Garden, why is that?"

"See?" Lil tweaked her grandmother. "Dad understands it."

"I understand it," Ollie replied. "That doesn't mean I have to like it. It just means I missed the exit ramp somehow. I've gone past it. I don't need it."

Within six months, Ollie had moved to Florida, taking Missy and most of the art collection with her. Lil went off to Oberlin and Ike put the Alwyn Court place on the market and moved into his mother's empty apartment—the home he had grown up in, when not touring the Continent. He had decided, in a moment of melancholy fatalism, that this was the place he wanted to die, and he thought he had better grab it while he could. He was only turning forty-eight, but his father, he well remembered, had disappeared at exactly such a moment.

RELUCTANTLY, Aurora Shelton agreed to launch the *One More Spring* first national tour in Chicago and stay with it for twenty weeks. There was money and prestige involved, and she was flattered. She liked the role. But there was more. The tour would spend seven weeks in Los Angeles. Her agents insisted that this was a great opportunity, though in her heart, Aurora knew that she was a stage creature and that the movies would never really come calling. There was something else on her mind, though. She wanted to see if Ethel Waters was still well enough to come see her perform. With the two kids—Little Vin was now nine, Gar was turning seven—and a new nanny, she departed for Chicago on the 20th Century Limited. It was now an arcane way to travel, but she wanted her sons to experience it. She hoped, when they were grown, they'd retain a fondness for the old things. She would send them home by plane with the nanny when school started up again in the fall. Meanwhile, they were on an adventure.

Vincent spent Aurora's first week away wandering the house at night, with a glass of Johnnie Walker Black in his hand. He was bored and too easily successful for his own good. He could hardly think of any more fish to catch. He went to the office every day and moved problems around his desk, but there were no real challenges, nothing worth a good fight. In his darker moments, he had to admit to himself that his wife's newfound celebrity was as much a source of annoyance as of pride. This kind of thing happened, he knew, especially to hardworking but invisible husbands whose wives had become sources of public adulation. It didn't seem fair, but it happened anyhow. The feelings that plagued him were not ones he had anticipated. He thought he was better than that, but what could he do? He drifted off to sleep each night trying to recapture the first moments he had seen her in the light of his follow spot, how his heart had fallen all the way to the stage in adoration and supplication. He took a pill and waited for sleep.

It was one night during the third week of the tour, after the second scotch of the night, after the pill but before sleep overcame him, that the phone rang. The curtain hadn't yet gone down in Chicago, where it was an hour earlier, so he knew it couldn't be Aurora calling. His arm lurched for the phone, knocking over the glass beside his bed. Ice cackled on the wooden floor of the bedroom as the glass broke, and Vincent Donnelly felt a surge of doom in the pit of his stomach.

On the other end of the phone was his kid brother Pat, who was by now the head carpenter at the Lunt-Fontanne.

"Pop's gone," Pat said, a kind of panicked desperation creeping into his voice. "His heart must of gave out."

"What?" Vincent asked, hardly understanding and wishing he had waited an extra hour before taking his medication. Their father had gradually been nudged through channels to the point where he had finished his career as a curtain man, working with Pat at the Lunt, where a musical called *The Rothschilds* was currently playing. He had retired a month earlier but stopped by the theater on occasion for a few hands of late-night poker.

"He came by tonight," said Pat. "Jimmy Deegan let him ring down the curtain for old times' sake, and he collapsed as soon as the exit music began. The poor bastard died listening to all that Jewish music." He began to sob over the phone.

"Jesus," Vincent replied. "Where are you?"

"I'm backstage with a crew of medics, but he's gone!" Pat wailed. "We need a coroner."

"Stay where you are," Vincent said.

The funeral was not grand, though Junior Ennis deigned to turn up, in order, he said, to honor his parents' and his uncle's long-standing friendship with Big Vin and the Donnelly family, dating back to the good old days. There were elaborate flowers, but a less-than-impressive crowd of mourners. Aurora was in Chicago doing a matinee and an evening and could not travel east. Vincent, who had never admired his father's brains, nor his bravery, nonetheless loved the man who had given him life and a start in the business, and whose career he had taken care of in his later years. He was genuinely bereft as he gave the eulogy after the priest had had his say. Looking out over the sparse crowd, however, he was surprised to see a familiar face, one he would not have expected to encounter. Maggie Hynes, dressed in black but wearing a red rose in one lapel, sat quietly in the front row. More unexpectedly still, she appeared at the gravesite, solemn and unspeaking in the steady drizzle of a late summer afternoon. When Big Vin was finally lowered into the ground and the mourners retreated to their cars, she stepped discretely to Vincent's side.

"I'm so sorry," she said. "I had just begun to process his pension checks and he came in each week to collect them. He seemed like a nice old guy with nothing to do, and he certainly was proud of you."

"You're sweet to come," Vincent said. "Can I buy you a scotch? I could use one. I can catch up with my brother later tonight."

"I'll buy," said Maggie Hynes.

PART THREE

14

LANDMARKS

ON *JULY* 3, 1981, a Friday, two articles appeared in the middle pages of *The New York Times*. The first was headlined "Rare Cancer Seen in 41 Homosexuals." The second proclaimed "New York Stagehands Union Chief Indicted in Pension Fund Fraud." Many lives were about to be snuffed out, but Vincent Donnelly didn't even notice the first article. And perhaps he could not be blamed at that moment. He was about to risk actual jail time, not to mention the wreckage of his marriage.

By this time, the tour of *One More Spring* was a distant memory for Aurora, though it had had its vivid moments. Los Angeles had been a sad and largely fruitless experience. Ethel Waters, now wary of leaving her house and attended by a volunteer nurse from her church, could not come to see Aurora and seemed to have no memory of ever having met her. Steve Allen no longer had a nightly TV show. The movies did not come to call, either. Not a single offer was tendered during her run at the Dorothy Chandler Pavilion.

She took the boys to Alcatraz in San Francisco, and the zoo in San Diego. It was lovely having her days free to be with them, and her nights to herself and her audience. The separation of family life and performing life seemed a gift once there was no home life to compete with either. She missed Vincent, but he was in constant touch, and flew out to see her twice in California, taking the boys to both a Dodgers and a Giants game. They seemed to be living in a dream world of all the attractions spread out over the American landscape. It was a good time.

The highlight of the tour had not been California, however. It was a night in Kansas City when Marius and Jonah had finally come to see her. It wasn't the show that they would have seen in New York; she didn't know they were there and was far from sure she had given it her all. But the two of them stopped by the dressing room, Marius weeping a little in gratitude, and invited her for a quick drink.

"I just want to announce," he intoned, raising a glass of red wine in a local watering hole that was attached to her hotel, "that you've made my life fifty percent better than it otherwise would have been. You alone make me feel like I actually did something, which I wasn't sure I ever could do, and no one but us will ever know, and that's okay, and that's all I've got to say about it."

It was Aurora's time to weep a little, but although it touched her, she quickly realized, as she had in New York, that there was a gulf of distance between them never to be crossed. No one dared mention the night in the West Village, though she could feel each of them trying to gain courage, and then retreating. Had the world become a universe of the unsaid? She was glad to see the two of them, and glad to see her bed in the hotel, alone, that night. Still, real happiness was a hard thing to locate in all of this.

By the time she returned to Larchmont, it was the children who lifted her. Memories of the night with Marius and Jonah clung only a little. Vincent gathered her into his arms and seemed to have gained a kind of courtly demeanor during her absence, the meaning of which was not immediately clear. But over the coming months it began to nag at her that now even her home had been invaded by additional things unsaid, things she had neither the inner strength nor the equilibrium to confront. She recalled a particularly odious expression her father used to use whenever she wanted a hard question explored: Don't stir it, it'll stink.

The decade passed in work. Aurora appeared in a mild flop at the Martin Beck, where Ethel Waters had done *Cabin in the Sky* back in 1940, but her idol's presence could not be detected among the spirits that haunt old theaters. And, for the first time, she accepted a cabaret gig at the Café Carlyle, where she sold out a week's run singing the songs she had learned from Marius Huwiler, the songs Jerry Herman had written for her, and others that touched her. At the first performance she sang "It Might as Well Be Spring," and then choked up as the audience applauded, covering her emotion with a few sips of water. It wasn't spring anymore. She was too old to sing that song. She quickly substituted Waters's "Taking a Chance on Love," which stopped every show, though she was far from sure she had any present connection to its content. She was taking no chances at all, and she knew it. She was a star and treated like a star. But she was a star without a vehicle, and sometimes wondered how she had gotten herself to a place where she was simply waiting—waiting for good material, for something that would excite her, for something that could light a fire. She read novels and plays, looking for a project she might self-start, but nothing appealed to her.

Vincent now had a poker game every Tuesday, which was spent not playing poker, but lying in Maggie Hynes's arms and sharing a few lubricating doses of Johnnie Walker Black along the way. She was fascinated by his family, and how she and Vincent had encountered each other all those years ago, and Vincent was happy to talk, giving her the details of his early life and the lives of his neighbors in the slums and at the lighting factory. He felt liberated by these evenings, and happier to be at home when he found himself there, if somewhat distracted. And Maggie Hynes never asked for more.

Cecelia Austin had become a force to be reckoned with and married a gay civil rights lawyer from New Orleans named Moses de Longpre. Her husband adored her and had his own money. He remodeled a house for her in Hoboken, removing all of the doorsills and widening the doorways so that she could ride her wheelchair around the place without a single barrier. She transferred herself to two walking sticks to move from the chair to her bed or to the walk-in shower that he had caused to be built, and, as her mobility slowly deteriorated, she focused her energy on building Ike Harris Music into a small empire.

By 1980, Ike was contracting half the musicals on Broadway while playing trumpet at the Morosco Theatre for a short-lived enterprise called *Happy New Year*, after spending a year at the St. James working the Hal Prince musical *On the Twentieth Century*. Sometimes, when he got bored of the same score every night, he subbed himself out so that various younger men who were coming up behind him could get a taste of life in the pit. He played for Woody Allen, and he played for Woody Herman. He played record dates and film scores. And yet, when he looked around him, it seemed that everyone he knew, including himself, had reached the middle of life and beyond without having whatever it was they had set out to get. He could not have described himself as unhappy. But he did not have Aurora, and she did not have good enough songs to sing or a show to star in, never mind the lover and husband that she should have had. Cecelia Austin hadn't danced in years, and Moses de Longpre was deeply in love with a woman for whom he had no carnal hunger. As for Vincent Donnelly, Ike could barely think of him at all, and yet, the memory of him still rankled whenever the couple passed through his mind.

Vincent was a stagehand married to a star, which kept him and Aurora from being a real glamour couple. Instead, they were suburban, and she was more often seen at events without Vincent than with him. She hosted charity galas and awards ceremonies. But despite her often solitary appearances, Ike knew more than to approach her. It was a stab in the heart that could do neither of them any good. Everything, he decided, was gradually deteriorating except for the love he felt for her, which followed him around like a spaniel waiting patiently for his attention.

Forty-second Street had by now fallen entirely into the hands of pornographers, drug dealers, and their bosses—the mob. The spectacular theaters that had, back in the day, presented the works of the Gershwin brothers and Eugene O'Neill were, without exception, featuring the letters XXX on marquees that had been cheaply over-clad with lit signs that lacked any kind of grandeur. Within a year, while *Follies* was still running, *Deep Throat* opened around the corner on 49th Street and would spend longer at the World movie theater than *Follies* would last at the Winter Garden.

Ladies emerging from Broadway shows a few blocks away were routinely having silver and gold necklaces ripped from around their necks by muggers waiting quietly in the shadows. The assailants quickly learned which shows left audiences most bedazzled or moved at the final curtain—they were the likeliest marks, the most distracted. Under the marquee at *On Golden Pond* was a mugger's paradise. Some years later the Dustin Hoffman production of *Death of a Salesman* would set the record. Especially after Wednesday matinees, there was a relative fortune to be made. Nothing changed. President Ford's soon-to-be legendary fuck-you to New York was, as far as Ike was concerned, entirely beside the point. The theater district knew how to go to hell all by itself. The Morosco, where Ike was now reporting for duty, was in terrible shape and had been for a long time. The show that was struggling to stay open within its walls was hardly better off.

However, none of this had prepared Ike to read, in the morning paper, that the police had shown up on a Tuesday evening at a modest apartment in the East Thirties, knocked politely, and discovered not only Maggie Hynes but her boss, the head of Local One, about whom the FBI knew only one thing: A lot of the embezzled money had seemed destined for people, real or imagined, who shared Vincent's last name. Vincent and Maggie were both naked under hastily donned silk robes, but quickly dressed and surrendered meekly.

Vincent understood immediately that the consequences would be dire, though it was hard for him to predict just how bad it could get. Even more difficult was his attempt to piece together what had led him to this moment, though he was savvy enough to have some idea of how it might have happened.

The week after Vincent had put his father, Big Vin, in the ground, the old man's retirement check nonetheless arrived at the Local One pension office. Maggie Hynes looked at it quizzically, wondering what mechanism it might be that failed to inform whoever generated such checks when a recipient was deceased. She was about to go to a supervisor about the problem when a much simpler and, to her, more practical idea struck her. She simply endorsed the check over to herself, forging Big Vin's signature, and deposited it in her own account. She had watched her grandmother, the pharmacist's secretary, sign her boss's name for years and never think twice about it. And how would the pension fund or the banks ever notice?

This went on for several months before it occurred to Maggie that there might be other dead stagehands still receiving pensions and, if not, it might be possible to invent some. Computers had not yet come to the pension fund's local offices, which were lined floor to ceiling with file cabinets full of forms and records of every imaginable kind. Altering—or creating—documents and filing them was a simple task. In the two years that followed, Maggie, whose imagination was limited to the accounting side of things, collected as much biographical information as Vincent Donnelly unwittingly gave her—usually in bed with scotch in hand—about his family and his neighbors and the other people who had worked in the lighting factory in Long Island City. He liked to talk, and she was all ears.

With a modest amount of research, she cracked the method by which such names could be inserted into the rank-and-file file, as it was known. Their birth dates, which she also invented, triggered the arrival of more and more checks, all of which she deposited in the multiple bank accounts that she gradually amassed across Manhattan. A remarkable number of these nonexistent stagehands were related, in one way or another, to Vincent Donnelly and bore his name, which would come as a surprise to no one. It was an excellent scheme and might have carried Maggie through retirement and into her own grave, had she not inadvertently stolen a series of checks intended for a nephew of the Ennis clan, whose last name happened to be Donnelly, and who was smart enough to know that checks like these rarely go astray by accident. His mother was an Ennis, after all. And the Ennises knew every game that could be played.

As a relatively young, deeply ambitious district attorney, Robert Morgenthau, who would serve for the rest of the century and beyond, was intrigued by the idea of carrying an embezzling pension fund worker to justice, but much more eager to bring down an actual union boss, especially in the glamorous world of show business. Upon the discovery that so many of the phantom retirees were claimed as relatives of Vincent Donnelly, the case became almost too good to be true, which, in most ways, it was.

Vincent, who had never seen the inside of a jail cell before, had two problems on his hands, and neither was an easy fish to land. He hired a dull, well-placed lawyer named Seth Kuriansky, understanding that when it came to this kind of a fix, the power of the law firm and its interconnectedness to the DA's favor bank was more important than the quality of the lawyer himself. But in the eighteen hours between his arrest and his release, he came to face the fact that, no matter what, he was going to have to confess to Aurora his decade-long liaison with Maggie Hynes. He was also going to have to find a way to prove that the invented part of the Donnelly family was not of his own making and that he'd had no idea what his mistress was up to and never benefited from it, which was true. This second problem was complicated by his understanding that no self-respecting DA was going to let a man in his position off the hook if it could be helped, especially given the delightfully unexpected nature of his capture. And there was the matter of his own private finances, which he did not want anyone to investigate too deeply. He had made a lot of money in a lot of different ways from a lot of different companies that serviced Broadway and the road. Now he would pay; as a Catholic, lapsed or not, these seemed to Vincent to be the wages of sin. He was glad neither parent was around to witness it all.

As for the first problem—the big problem—he had no idea what the outcome would be. He ran through his mind a series of not very credible denials he could issue to Aurora, but he knew Maggie's face would grace the *Daily News* the next morning, as would his own—probably a pair of mug shots—and no amount of talk would ever separate them once that happened. "Thieving Union Boss Trapped in Love Nest." There was no way out.

His wife did not come to pick him up after his bail was paid and he had been arraigned. Seth Kuriansky had his own car parked at the curb and drove Vincent back to Larchmont. He was, if nothing else, a decent chauffer.

Aurora was waiting in the living room, with a martini. She had turned away from brown liquor, a decision she attributed to her mother's fatal attraction to Manhattans, although she knew the day might come. She had exactly one martini each evening, and tonight was no different. She was quietly enraged, but not, perhaps, entirely at her husband.

"Tell me all about it," she said as he entered the room. "Don't leave anything out."

He tried. She sat in icy contained silence. As he stumbled through it, proclaiming his financial innocence and his adulterous guilt, she nodded occasionally, determined not to respond. Finally, he ran out of words. He waited. She looked out the window. The trees were in full midsummer leaf, heavy green things that looked immortal in their solidity and strength. She thought about her first big train trip to Kansas to beg for music lessons from Marius Huwiler, and she thought of autumn, still two months away, when all that green strength would turn out to be an outlandish and insupportable boast, and she thought about spring, two months past, when the pale buds had promised so much more than they could ever actually deliver. Around in circles they had all gone, for sixteen years now.

"You first saw her in a high chair?" she said, finally.

Vincent nodded.

"I was barely sixteen myself," he said, lamely.

She sighed heavily and finished her drink.

"You fell in love with your own spotlight," she said, "and I happened to be the thing you were illuminating—the thing your light fell on. I'm an idiot."

"Not true," Vincent said. "I shined that light on a thousand young women. You were the only one, and I love you as much today as I did then."

"But you needed a whore anyhow," she said, and immediately regretted it. For a brief moment she had regretted turning down Lord Byron's invitation to a one-nighter right before her wedding. Some part of everybody needed a whore, or needed something—a secret, a private place, a life inside of life. There was no explanation for any of it, and she was out of words in any case.

She rose from the sofa and went and got her coat.

"Where are you going?" he asked. Silently, she let herself out of the house. She drove to the train station and caught the express to Grand Central, leaving the car with the keys in it for whoever might want it. She walked across 45th Street and checked into the Hotel Piccadilly, a modest tourist spot adjacent to the Morosco, where no one would know her or take care of her in any special way. *Later,* she thought to herself, *I'll decide if I want to have sex with someone, and I don't even have to wonder about whether I should or shouldn't.* Who could it hurt now? And it might be fun. Or not.

As it turned out, she was exhausted, and in no mood to prowl the streets or sit in a bar making small talk with a hopeful stranger. Instead, she walked to Frankie and Johnnie's for a steak and a salad, then canceled it. She knew she couldn't swallow food. She thought of heading back to Kansas and making herself a guest of Marius and Jonah, just to stay out of the limelight, but then thought better of it. What would they talk about? She considered gathering up both children, pulling them out of their various summer activities—they were teenagers now—and taking them cross-country on an adventure that might encompass all the places she had been to on tour but never really seen, but that, too, seemed part of a foolish reverie. For the first time it struck her as odd that she had no family to turn to. Everyone she knew could be taken in by a sister or brother or elderly parents or a cousin, or someone. But she had no ties at all.

It came over her quite suddenly, like a wave of nausea. No one was waiting to hear what would happen next. Each fantasy, as she ticked them off, was wrapped up in the past. What of the future? Where was she to go, really? She was in no mood to contemplate it. She went back to the hotel, took two pills, and went to sleep. The one person who would have been there for her forever was not someone whose name even crossed her mind.

OLLIE HARRIS TURNED eighty in June, and Ike went to Florida for the party. He had to take a leave from holding down the first trumpet chair at Lena Horne's one-woman show at the Nederlander on 41st Street, and he hated to do it. He loved playing all that Harold Arlen. But Ollie insisted. She had embraced the role of a rich, game old broad, and was now stuffing her condo with New Mexican folk art, wearing oversize turquoise jewelry, and smoking weed. The place smelled to Ike like the barracks back in the days of Poke Belmore, the blue lightbulbs and the Italian prisoners of war tending the marijuana garden.

The party was attended mainly by widows, though there were a few infirm husbands still hanging around, the entire company leathery from the Florida sun. Ollie, the professionally hilarious hostess, kept the champagne and caviar coming, though many of the guests brought their own, more digestible, food in neat Tupperware tubs. Ike found the entire affair depressing even beyond what he had anticipated, and was happy when Missy, who had left Ollie's employ some years earlier, showed up and invited him to breakfast the next morning before having a quick glass of merlot and beating a hasty retreat.

Ike slept badly in the guest room and dreamed of Lil when she was an angry little girl, following in her mother's emotional footsteps. When he awakened, he watched the sunrise, thinking about his daughter, with whom he once shared the most satisfying of friendships. It had begun to drift away when she was at Oberlin, then fell into disrepair as she moved to the West Coast to teach gender studies at the University of Redlands, in part to follow a classical flautist who had gotten a position with the San Bernardino Symphony. What did a twenty-five-year-old girl know about gender studies, he wondered. More than him. And why did San Bernardino have its own orchestra? He felt a pang of guilt that he had not visited. He had only met the flautist once, and, after all, they were fellow musicians. Everything takes more care and feeding than there's time to do, he thought.

Fretfully, he made his way to the Everglades Hotel—one of the last of the grand old high-rise Art Deco Miami Beach extravaganzas still standing—where Missy was staying. Breakfast was served on the roof.

As Ike stepped into the elevator, soft, annoyingly bland Muzak hit his ears and it took him a moment to grasp the tune. It was "Out of Sight, Out of Mind," long forgotten by all, consigned to the heap of indistinguishable aural wallpaper that rolled out with strings and a harp to distract hotel guests from the glacial pace of the ancient elevators. Its only intent was to soothe the savage beast, but by the time he had heard an entire chorus and emerged into the blinding sunlight on the rooftop, he was hyperventilating as if he had walked the whole way up. He stood by himself a moment to regain his composure.

Missy was sitting in a pair of tortoiseshell sunglasses and a sleeveless pale green blouse on the outer deck by the pool, waiting for him. She was now working for a collector named Mitchell Wolfson, who was planning to open an Art Deco museum in Miami Beach a few years down the line and put Missy in charge of it. She was embarking on something, she said, and seemed happy about it.

"What's happened to you?" she asked, as he sat down.

"I'm older," he said. "But I can still eat what I want and have a bourbon before bed, if that's what you mean."

"It's not," she replied. "You're walking around like a dead man."

Ike was silent for a while. Missy drank coffee. She had never been shy about frontal attacks.

"I'm still in love," he said finally. "I'm still in love with the same girl, and it's not you, more's the pity. And it's not with a girl I can have, and I have decided to wait."

"For what?" Missy asked.

"Actually, I didn't decide. I didn't have any options. I thought it would pass. It's never going to pass."

"You're being theatrical," Missy said. "Don't."

Ike shrugged. "I'm in the theater," he said.

"I'm worried about Lil," Missy said, moving on. Her indifference was somehow crushing, even though Ike had no real feelings for her.

"I'm going to see her next week," Ike said. He had no idea that this was his plan until the words came out of his mouth. "I'm worried too, and I'm not even sure why."

"Well," said Missy. "She's as angry as me and as stubborn as you, so how can you not worry?"

IKE PLACED A CALL to his office from his mother's guest room. Cecelia Austin picked up the phone. Ike explained to her that he was going to be gone from Lena Horne for a while longer.

"Family emergency," he said. He had no idea if this was true, but he was letting his mouth do his thinking.

"This is your vacation week," Cecelia said. "You stay away longer than a week, they can replace you, you know that."

"What can I do?" Ike asked. "Try putting in for a medical leave. If I lose the job, I lose it."

"Lena's not gonna like that. You know how she is about trumpet players."

"If she hates me for the rest of my life, I'll get along somehow," Ike said. But he really did regret it. It was a good gig.

Still, the decision was made. The greater good had to be served. He rented a car in South Beach and headed west, toward the other ocean. It was an odd decision, he knew. He wasn't ready to see Lil right away, and he wasn't willing to go home either. Driving seemed to be the best answer. Time to think or time to put off whatever it was he was heading toward. He couldn't say which. He spoke to no one but motel clerks and waitresses in roadside rest stop diners and fast-food joints. He zigzagged from the interstate to local highways and back again. He was determined, but not in a hurry. Missy's words rang in his ear. Walking around like a dead man.

He was getting on and off the highway in search of a small town with a jazz club, but it was not until he found himself a few miles north of Las Cruces, New Mexico, that he found one—more of a juke joint, really—and checked into the flophouse motel next door. He wandered into the club, trumpet case in hand, and put away two quick bourbons—whatever was in the well. He took in the music, which was some kind of an amalgam of western swing and Mexican street band. He had never heard anything like it, really, nor had he ever wanted to. But the chord changes were easy to follow and it was just as easy to see how he might fit into it, so he walked over to the bandstand during a break and asked the bandleader if he could sit in.

"We got no money," the leader said. He was an older man with thinning hair under a costume sombrero, a threadbare cowboy shirt with frayed cuffs, and a bolo tie with one of the metal clips missing. "We pass the hat, and the hat stays empty mostly."

"I don't want your money," Ike said. "I just need to play."

They played until the club filled up and emptied out. Ike couldn't tell if he was playing well or poorly, if he was leading or following. The music came up behind him and lifted him as if he were drugged or drunk, though he was neither. The room had a slight tendency to float. It was just music—a kind he had not played in many years, free of words, of arrangements or routines, a free pass to glory, or so it seemed. He soloed, he comped along behind the others, he bobbed and weaved into and out of it, and, when the police arrived at a little after four in the morning, he was ready to pack it in anyhow. He shook hands all around, put a one-hundred-dollar bill in the tip jar, walked across the concrete past the gas pumps of the shuttered Gulf station that stood between him and his motel, entered his room, and fell into a deep and dreamless sleep.

The next day, he drove back to El Paso, to the airport, and flew to L.A. He wanted to see his daughter.

HE CALLED FROM the Hertz office and an hour and a half later was in a coffee place on the edge of campus, looking at her and realizing that it had been more than a year since they had been face-to-face. She was wraithlike and pale, her round, wide-eyed face dominated by black-framed glasses that gave her the look of a slightly startled bird, curious and a bit puzzled. Even at twenty-five, a few strands of gray hair were beginning to mix into the unruly bun she had piled on top of her head. She had a pencil stuck in there too—a born academic, or at least a convincing one. His heart filled with unexpected joy at seeing her. She was unruly and unsettled and full of life; she would no doubt be equally full of opinions, her quicksilver mind inclined to jump the tracks like a toy train. But she was obviously glad to see him too. They held each other tightly, breaking only reluctantly to sit down.

"I solved the problem of my name," she told him, stirring a mint tea with a wooden popsicle stick. Ike was too old for these places.

"Is that still going on?"

"Not anymore. I did think about it for a long time. When I got here, I thought of calling myself Lillian, which is what the two of you named me after all, but it's just such a hateful name."

"We weren't thinking Lillian," Ike offered lamely.

"People here call me Armstrong," she said.

He was silent, and she didn't seem to mind. He was thinking. Finally, he said, "That was her married name. I mean, as an instructor in gender studies . . . her name was Lil Hardin. She married Louis Armstrong."

"Is there anyone who spent her childhood being called 'Lil' who wouldn't be satisfied with 'Armstrong'?" she asked.

He shrugged. "Probably not," he said.

"Damn straight. Hardin is a bigger problem when it comes to gender studies if you say it and don't spell it. And besides, gender is fluid, so why shouldn't I be Armstrong? You could have named me after him instead of her if you'd been a couple of decades ahead of your time. Mom's worried about you, you know."

"So she told me."

Lil looked him over, cocking her head to one side.

"She said you looked like the walking dead," she said. "Do you feel dead? I do sometimes."

"Well, she was worried about you, too. But I didn't come because of her being worried. I miss you, that's all."

"I think she told me that because she wanted a reliable source to tell her whether you looked like you were dead. She's a very strange person."

"I didn't come three thousand miles to talk about your mother," Ike said. "I miss baseball. I miss whatever it is—whatever genetic material you and I share that I don't share with anyone else."

"There's Grandma Ollie," Lil said.

Ike raised his eyes to the ceiling.

"I get it," Lil said. Then she took a long sip of tea and stirred it again.

"You've always done that, you know, looked up at the ceiling. And I do it too. I realized that I was looking for some explanation from the gods. You too?"

"You believe in God?"

"Gods. Pagan gods. That's the only possible explanation of things."

Now it was Ike's turn to take a beat. It was the first time he'd heard the word *pagan* since Cecelia Austin came back to him after her accident. *What is it,* he wondered, *about these women I seem to need and pagan gods?*

"Explanation of what things?" he asked.

"Look: Any monotheistic religion is, by definition, full of shit," Lil said. "It takes a lot of people just to run the city of Redlands; no one person could do it. And even a lot of people trying their hardest do a terrible, fucked-up job. And running the whole earth? It's ridiculous."

"But God's not a person, isn't that the point?"

"It's idiotic," she said. "The pagan gods, the Hellenic ones, at least, are people—or very much like people. They keep coming down to earth and knocking up women and stealing shit, and turning into hallucinations with snakes and stuff, and blaming innocent bystanders for their feuds with other gods. And then they go back up the mountain and eat and drink wine. People are the chips they move around to get some satisfaction out of each other. It's the best explanation for why our lives are the way they are. 'We're bedeviled by gods.' I said that in a final paper for my religion class in high school, and I got an A. Devil/gods—it was clever, for high school. But I didn't realize it was actually true until college. At the time I was just trying to get an A."

Ike looked at her, full of pride and wonderment. How could he have helped produce this creature?

"Also," she added by way of non sequitur, "The San Bernardino Spirit are taking on Visalia at Fiscalini Field tonight if you want to go to a baseball game."

Ike cleaned up at the Comfort Inn and the two of them drove to the park. They settled into the tiny bandbox of a ballpark with a bag of peanuts and two beers, and toasted the vagaries of their lives, which had brought them to California's Inland Empire by such circuitous routes for a Single A minor league game.

"How much do you know about your origins?" Ike asked her as the San Bernardino pitcher warmed up on the mound. He looked about nineteen. "And how much do you want to know?"

"I think I know the facts," she said. "Mom may have told me more than I wanted to know before I was ready to hear it. The Hotel Astor is gone, right? That's where I was started?"

Ike nodded.

"It's an office tower with a quite awful theater in it called the Minskoff. I played one show there—*King of Hearts*. But I mean . . . why we never married, never were really able to come to grips with what we'd done or how irresponsible we'd been. All of that. Does it matter to you? I think we've been bad parents. Or inattentive ones."

Lil shrugged. "Probably does matter. I don't think I feel like a daughter with parents. I feel like a young person with two older friends who are complicated to get along with because they don't get along with each other, and I'm mad at them sometimes. I have friends who have parents. I have—I don't know what to call you, exactly. Sometime advisers that I love, I guess. But who make me mad. And who owe me something they can't pay anymore because it's too late. I missed that part of life."

The game was lopsided—Visalia had no pitching, which made the distraction of it like a kind of background music, or an occasional musical number that interrupted the plot—the *tonk* of bat on ball and the slapping of the same ball into leather—and the frequent rise of the crowd's delight as ball after ball left the park.

To this underscoring, Ike recounted the journey—a trumpet-playing Odysseus on Otts Oscard's bus, where he first encountered Aurora Shelton, then setting out for home with Missy and the unborn Lil. He described it all—including his ill-fated encounter with the Black pagan dancer Cecelia Austin— but left his feelings out of it. Just the facts. When he finished, he sat in silence for a moment and then said, "Any psychiatrist worth his license would tell me that burdening my daughter with this information is tantamount to child abuse."

"That's silly," Lil shot back. "I'm not a child, for one thing. And it's nice, actually, to get to know at least one of you. Nice if a little late. This is Aphrodite's revenge, of course; you do see that."

"I'm not sure," said Ike, who was expecting any response except this one.

"Aphrodite is the goddess of love, but also of procreation. For some reason, probably some private game or feud or betrayal none of us will ever know anything about, she decided to separate love from procreation directly, one in immediate proximity to the other, for one very god-cursed trumpet-playing sojourner. You. She probably picked you at random, but she must have been really pissed at Hephaestus or somebody. You didn't do anything wrong. You were in the wrong place at the wrong time. And I get to pay some of the price too. And Mom. That's how the gods never solve anything. They just keep going."

Ike was not inclined to ask about Hephaestus, of whom he had never heard. Instead, he asked Lil a question she couldn't possibly answer.

"How does all this end?"

"Well," she said, "the first thing that happens is that Visalia gets the shit kicked out of it for another four innings and ends up in last place again. I've been watching these teams for three years now, and nothing changes. Visalia is just an awful team. Other than that, I think only one thing is clear. You've got to keep playing the trumpet and loving the woman you've been cursed to love and remembering that you have a daughter who loves you very much, and as odd as things are, they are how they are. This isn't like American justice. You don't pay your debt to society and get let off the hook. What the gods arrange goes on forever."

This was intended to be new news, Ike realized, but it was not. It was the one thing he already knew.

"I didn't come all this way to burden you," Ike said. "Quite the opposite. I wanted to know if there was anything that might make your life easier."

"You just made my life easier. We talked. I'd like to meet Aurora Shelton one day," Lil said. "Didn't she win a Tony or something?"

"She did," Ike said. "For *One More Spring.* But she's never had another hit."

"I hope she will," said Lil. "And I hope I meet her. What went wrong with *King of Hearts?* I loved that movie."

By this last question, Ike understood, she meant to say that the conversation about his life and times, his loves and adventures and blunders, had, for the moment, concluded. He felt suddenly as if he might float away, and they watched the last innings of the game in contented silence.

Ike stayed on for two more days, during which he watched her teach class with an astonishing theatricality that warmed him to see. He marveled at her ability to draw connections between ideas and come to conclusions, some of which seemed to him quite brilliant, while others struck him as complete sophistry. He didn't care. What was college if not at least half bullshit? And he was pleased to see that there was a show business gene in there somewhere. She was in her element, but gradually he wanted to be in his—back in an orchestra pit, free to contemplate, between numbers, the meaning of what she had told him about his own life. He didn't believe in Aphrodite any more seriously than he ever had. But in some way that he found both confirming and disconcerting, he believed in his daughter, and vowed to try to call her Armstrong for as long as she wanted to be addressed that way. He didn't think it would be forever, but who knew? He kissed her goodbye with a promise of a plane ticket for her to come to New York when classes were concluded, drove back to L.A., and flew home. The Lena Horne job was gone. But he had a few plans.

AS IT HAPPENED, it was easier for Vincent Donnelly to cop a plea to something he had never done than to fight it out with the DA and potentially lose. His life with Local One was over and done with one way or the other, which didn't mean much to him anymore. He had friends there, he had money hidden away everywhere, and he would be fine. But he was not going to hold down an executive position ever again—the union couldn't afford to have him around. To hell with it. He would be fine.

He had not spoken to Maggie Hynes since the night the two of them had been dragged out of bed together. And while Aurora had never really resettled in the house in Larchmont, she came and went, calculating the pluses and minuses of remaining with her unfaithful and possibly criminal husband. She didn't really think he was a criminal—just a fool for love. Or sex. Or adventure. Or something. It was bewilderingly sad and made her angry all the time. And she knew, though she couldn't say how, that he didn't recognize himself in the man he had become. But in the end, that wasn't her problem. Her immediate problem was that she could no longer keep food down and was beginning to see the outline of her ribs when she got into the shower. She was drawn and pale and couldn't manage to keep her hair colored; it was too much trouble. She did not want to be seen.

On the day of the sentencing, the courtroom was only half full. Reporters were present, though the case had lost some luster over time. Maggie Hynes had already been installed at the Bedford Hills Correctional Facility for Women. Some of Vincent's Local One colleagues were there to lend support. Aurora, her head covered in a shawl, sat apart from them, flanked by the two boys, who had come home from school early for the Thanksgiving break. And Ike Harris sat by himself in the back.

As they all stood for the entrance of the judge, Aurora's eyes met Ike's for the first time in many years, and a look of utter bewilderment came over her face. She gripped the hands of the two boys and stood as if only their support and strength were holding her erect. Ike smiled faintly, which caused her to squeeze her sons' hands tighter. Then they sat, and Vincent was asked to stand and confirm his guilty plea. He was sentenced to two years at Fishkill, but would probably serve no more than six months, which was eventually reduced to three, once the publicity value of his incarceration had lost all currency. He wasn't much of a threat to society. The judge asked Vincent if he had anything to say.

"I do not," he replied in a clear voice. He was not about to express regret for a crime not committed. After he was led away, the room emptied. Ike walked toward Aurora, who took a backward step and then stood her ground.

"What are you doing here?" She asked.

"I wanted to say that I'm sorry."

Aurora inhaled, her nose flaring in anger. Ike knew immediately that he had made things harder, though he was not sure why. He was filled with regret.

"Thank you," she said, ice freezing each word in turn. She did not turn away or move a step. This was on him. He turned and departed.

Aurora had been stunned to see him. She had glimpsed him across the years of course. The district was small, and the business smaller. On the street, in the corridors of one of the half dozen buildings in which the New York theater had headquartered itself for decades, one was bound to see everyone from time to time. She often thought of what a tiny world it was. When she went to the theater, a certain portion of the audience was always made up of her colleagues, and she sometimes wondered what would happen to the economics of the business if people who made theater stopped going to the theater. Would the bottom fall out completely? It was a good question, especially in the early eighties, when most houses that were lucky enough to have a booking were sparsely attended eight times a week, unless Cameron Mackintosh or Andrew Lloyd Webber was involved.

Still, the presence of Ike Harris at her husband's sentencing was obviously not a decision made lightly and had some meaning; he had made an effort to be there. To gloat? To see a long-ago rival receive his comeuppance? To try to open a new chapter on the back of her misfortune? To come back from the dead, as far as she was concerned, to express actual empathy for her situation? It couldn't possibly be that. She spent a sleepless night about it, and then decided to put it from her mind, as it occurred to her that she needed, instead, to make plans for a different life. Her husband was a convict—a circumstance she could never have imagined, despite all she had seen from the time she was a little girl. Shockingly, she had not really considered the reality of it until it happened, though there had been months to prepare. She had behaved like a child and gone about her life as if it simply wasn't going to happen. And the question of how she would conduct herself as a celebrity—at least in the legitimate theater—with Vincent Donnelly for a mate was one she had refused to confront. He had turned out to be not only faithless but a public disgrace, though he maintained his innocence to her with a quiet certitude that seemed entirely sincere. The fact that he told no lies about his life with Maggie Hynes made it clear to her that he was, indeed, telling the truth about the trap he had unwittingly fallen into. After all these years, the fish had caught him.

She made a schedule to visit him, and to spend weekends with both children, who were at two different Connecticut boarding schools, so that each week would be eventful in some way. And she continued to hunt for a project that might stir her passion, though her hope of finding one was dwindling steadily. By now, almost no one was writing the kinds of songs she liked to sing. The entire world of American music had been run over by a revolution driven by electric guitars that left her no place to turn but the past and the cabaret world, where she was always welcome, but where she now declined to appear. It was the place where the gossip about her marriage and her husband would be most animated, and she was not about to face that. Instead, she made the rounds from Fishkill to Connecticut to an empty house in Larchmont and back. She made a definite decision as well, to stop coloring her hair, which meant that, until the gray had fully replaced the ash blond, she did not particularly want to be seen.

To complicate matters, Little Vin took off from boarding school without permission and hitchhiked to Fishkill to see his father. As soon as the school called Aurora to tell her he was missing she knew exactly where he'd gone and headed north to pick him up. She was not angry. He explained that he had knocked one of his classmates to the ground after overhearing a comment about his father and was prepared to do it again. The disciplinary committee did not agree that this was an appropriate thing to have done and put him on probation, so he left. He was tired of the looks he was getting, the gradual way he was being ostracized, the general sense that he, and not his father, had been guilty of anything. He was not having it.

Aurora had no quarrel with anything he had to say—she admired it all except for the hitchhiking. So after a visit with Vincent, they drove to the second boarding school and picked up Gareth, who had been suffering in silence, was in complete denial, and refused to discuss his father, whom he idolized. Aurora was never sure whether she was motivated purely by moral outrage and a need to protect her sons, or whether she simply wanted them home with her. As a trio, they were stronger. The boys enrolled in Larchmont High School and melted into the anonymity that both of them craved. Aurora began to wonder what snobbery or pretension had caused her and Vincent to send them away in the first place.

They dined together at night, off-loading their impressions of the day, and for a moment, at least, it seemed like Aurora had become the mother she never had. They seemed not to have the vaguest idea that she needed them as much or more than they needed her, for which she was deeply grateful. She was content to do very little but look after them, or at least be there if they needed her. Gar's unwillingness to discuss or even acknowledge the situation he found himself in made him the angrier of the two, suffering many of the rebellious impulses of a second son. And Little Vin, who had started the whole transformation of the family by belting a fellow student, suddenly recast himself as the temporary man of the family, keeping his younger brother away from his mother when necessary, and otherwise hewing to his role as a dutiful child to a mother who was suffering in ways he could only partially comprehend. He took it as an act of faith that this was his role, and things remained relatively uneventful.

Then one morning the phone rang.

The voice on the other end was one Aurora had heard only on the local news, and then only once or twice, in recent days.

"It's Joe Papp. Is this Aurora Shelton?"

After a sharp intake of breath, she confirmed that it was. Joseph Papp was, at the time, as important a figure as there was in the American theater, unquestioned boss of Shakespeare in the Park, the Public Theater, and the producer of *A Chorus Line,* which had already spent half a decade at the Shubert with little sign of slowing down. But he was not calling about a show, much to her disappointment.

"You're a public figure," he said. "In part because of your husband, but you just are, and I bet you're doing nothing. Nothing for the American theater! I bet you're afraid to go out of the house!" He admonished her as if through a bullhorn.

"That could be true," she said, not sure what he was talking about.

"I need you," he commanded. "Just like Uncle Sam needs men in the war. Because we're in a war! We're going to stop them from pulling down the Morosco and the Helen Hayes, the Gaiety building, and the Piccadilly Hotel and the Bijou—we need an army—an army of angry, loyal American theater people to fight the bastard developers. To fight the war! I'm conscripting you into this righteous army. There's a meeting at four o'clock downtown at the Public. I need you to be at that meeting. Terrence McNally is writing you a speech. You're the only one of us who has any experience at this kind of thing."

This, in a way, was true. Aurora had, with Vincent's financial assistance and gift for inventive argument, saved three historic buildings in Larchmont—the public library, a nineteenth-century bed-frame factory that had been repurposed as a multistory antique mall, and a carriage house that had become the headquarters of the local historic society. It had been among their happiest activities together before the mess—thwarting developers and preserving the town's local character. Now Joe Papp wanted her.

Aurora had been hearing about the imminent demise of these theaters and the Piccadilly on and off for a decade. Like Vincent's arrest and conviction, it was another thing that had never seemed real.

But the drumbeat had been relaunched by Mayor Ed Koch and had been picked up by *The New York Times*. The theater district could be saved, could be reborn, could be created as a new mecca—if only architect John C. Portman and the various business interests who surrounded him got their way and were allowed to build a massive ugly forty-eight story hotel taking up all of the block between 45th and 46th streets on the west side of Broadway. The Morosco and the Hayes? They were usually empty anyhow, so what difference did it make? They were to be cannon fodder for Broadway's rebirth. The entire scheme seemed absurd to Aurora, and to most everyone else in the business, which always appeared on the verge of extinction in any case.

She had never played these theaters, and the Bijou was too small to be a real Broadway playhouse, anyhow. It featured one-person shows and tiny musical revues. But usually it was dark. The Piccadilly was her home in New York, but surely she could move to the Edison or the Milford Plaza. And, until recently, the likelihood of developers tearing apart the block had seemed remote—too costly, too risky, and why, in the decaying and decrepit theater district, would anyone begin building anything? Let the theaters fall, or not.

But the Gaiety—which had not been a legitimate theatre since the thirties—that was the one that interested her. It was housed in a building that, she knew, had been called for decades "the Black Brill Building." The music industry was unofficially headquartered at the Brill on 49th and Broadway, where music publishers took up residence after fleeing the original Tin Pan Alley's brownstones down on 18th Street just after the Great Depression. Swing was born at the Brill Building. It was the kind of place that Otts Oscard spoke of with reverence. Benny Goodman had an office there, though it was now famous for providing studio space for writers like Carole King and Burt Bacharach. Songs were written, arranged, and plugged into the popular consciousness from the corner of 49th and Broadway. But the Brill building, back in the day, wouldn't rent to Black people. The Gaiety building was where

W. C. Handy and Bert Williams had their offices. And it was where, when she was in New York, Ethel Waters picked up her mail. It was, in fact, a place that Aurora Shelton blessed with a silent prayer every time she walked by—a shrine unbeknownst to all but her. She was aware, of course, that of all the property threatened and now coming under the protection of Joseph Papp, no one else cared about the Gaiety building. But she cared.

And perhaps, she thought, this was something worth fighting for. If she faced them all down in the halls of the Public, down on Lafayette Street, a building that bristled with subversive energy, maybe she could find something more than her routine of family visits and boredom and isolation. Maybe she could learn not to care that her hair was half gray and half blond, that her face was constantly at risk of appearing above some new article in the *News* or the *Post* concerning union corruption, or the grim realities facing the Broadway theater. Maybe she could forget that hers wasn't quite the face it had once been. And maybe she could forget Ike Harris's sympathetic, slightly perplexed eyes meeting hers as he removed his hat and said he was sorry as her husband was being led away. He was not sorry. She was a good enough acting partner to feel the faint, fatal hope that was wafting toward her from his very skin. It made her furious all over again to think about it. She needed to do something, she thought—and here was Joseph Papp, the inevitable unexpected answer. He might be the savior of the hallways once tread by the woman who had made her want to sing.

THE MOST STRIKING thing about the meeting at the Public, however, was not Papp's insatiable energy and need for attention, nor the surprising size of the crowd, many of whom she knew. It was the sight of Antoine Berget. It had lingered on the edge of her consciousness for some time that she had not seen him in the district—but now here he was, ashen, wraithlike, and dead-eyed. For a moment she was not sure it was him at all. He wore a brown fedora that, she could see, covered a scalp on which the hair was gone. He was the model of a dying man; his suit hung on him like a shroud ready to be wrapped around his corpse. She thought back to that early July headline—"Rare Cancer Seen in 41 Homosexuals." That had been seven months earlier.

During most of that time between, Aurora had been preoccupied with her marriage, court dates, legal strategies, and thoughts of revenge, intermingled with her never-ending search for a project to star in. The larger world, as it so often did for her, receded. Now it was in front of her, not staring at her, but avoiding her eyes, as she had turned away from Ike Harris. Antoine Berget saw her, and his spider-leg fingers went to his hat, which he pulled down over his rheumy eyes. And suddenly Aurora knew death was about to be all around her—everywhere.

The "Save the Theaters" movement had grand plans, but no one seemed to understand the implicit irony locked within it. As Times Square succumbed to squalor, to a world of bent needles and used condoms lining the gutter a block away on Eighth Avenue, Papp, Aurora, Celeste Holm, Colleen Dewhurst, and a small army of committed Broadway veterans made public appearances, gave interviews on the radio, and lobbied congressmen and the mayor about the unquantifiable value of the buildings, most especially the Morosco and the Hayes.

To Aurora, who participated in every way that she was asked, the movement was an expression of loss, and a personal nostalgic hardship as she saw the day coming when the wrecking ball would take down the walls of the Gaiety, her own private mecca. But the actual loss was not of brick and mortar. It was not the theaters that needed saving so much as the people who lit up their interiors—the theater makers. And for this, there was no ready answer. They were, some of them, first falling victim to the very pleasures, disreputable and readily available, that were everywhere merchandised all around the district, and then to the consequences of those seductions. Others, stable and settled, simply began to get sick. Who could tell why? None of them, as far as Aurora could see, had acted in any way different from every man and woman she knew. But death began to come calling, morning and evening.

It was, in any case, far too late for whatever landmarking expertise she might have brought to the argument. The buildings in Larchmont had been saved through long and painstaking negotiations, matched by equal doses of courtship and threat. Instead, she found herself on the back of a flatbed truck shouting through a bullhorn, standing next to Papp and Susan Sarandon on a blustery morning in late March, making a last-ditch effort to keep the buildings intact while the wrecking balls hung nearby, looking deceptively inert. When word came that the Supreme Court had lifted the stay and the theaters were to come down, she trooped with the others to the sidewalk in front of the Morosco and set up a barrier of artists, each of whom had agreed to be arrested.

All of this was rehearsed, not only by the actors, for whom rehearsal was a regular part of life, but by law enforcement, which had lined up thirteen police wagons to take away the protestors, and the press, which had cameras and reporters strategically deployed. The ritual of individual defeat and municipal triumph was acted out as it had been through history, but this time on Broadway. Like each of the others, Aurora was arrested while kneeling in place, practicing the classic pose of civil disobedience—she had seen pictures of Mahatma Gandhi and Martin Luther King, Jr., in this crouch—as if this were a matter of life and death. But, of course, there was a very real matter of life and death hiding in plain sight as all of them were loaded into the wagons.

When the bricks began to shatter behind her, and the walls of the Morosco meekly gave way, Aurora thought to herself that now, at least, she and Vincent would each be written down forever in the book of New York miscreants. Guilty as charged. Both sons, guarded by the production stage manager of *One More Spring,* who had become a loyal friend, watched their mother's arrest and departure with pride and delight. They were, in fact, awestruck with admiration, and had missed school for the privilege of witnessing it.

By the first of April there would be nothing but a yawning chasm to be seen on the block between 45th and 46th streets, and Antoine Berget's obituary would appear in the *Times,* on page C-22. He had died at St. Vincent's Hospital, the *Times* reported, of pneumonia. In Aurora's experience, no one had died of pneumonia since the invention of penicillin.

The formless gray bunker that was Portman's hotel rose from the cavity along Broadway, Soviet in style, ugly and threatening, as much a repudiation of glamour as the Hotel Astor, lost a decade earlier, had once been a triumphant expression of it. Broadway, Aurora knew, would never be the same. The street was going the way of the top hat and the boutonnière. The district is dying, she thought, passing from life into memory. AIDS and Portman were signaling the beginning, or perhaps even the middle, of the end.

On the day she returned to the house in Larchmont from her brief incarceration, exhausted and in need of a martini, the boys greeted her with a heroine's dinner, prepared and waiting. They had to keep it warm while she sat in the living room and nursed her cocktail. It was while sitting, glancing around the room in a moment of quiet solitude, that she noticed an envelope on the narrow table in the foyer. Inside was a letter from Ike Harris.

15

Inside Fishkill

MANY YEARS LATER, when Vincent Donnelly was still in possession of just enough of his wits to know that he was losing them, he pinned the blame for his deteriorating condition on the three months he spent at Fishkill. Fishkill, he believed, was where it had all started, his mind warped by the numbing boredom, the repetitive tasks, the terrible and sometimes lethal-smelling food, and the general sense of malaise that overcame him for the first time in his life. Even at their most fractious, when Aurora was coming and going and making no promises about coming back to him for good, he had never found himself so lacking in resources. He was, by nature, a doer, a problem-solver, a steward of light. But whatever innate character or temperament had made him that way simply wilted in the confines of so dark a place.

He came quickly to regret the decision that he and his lawyer, the imagination-free Seth Kuriansky, had arrived at, which was that three months of anything was better than a long, uncertain fight with a district attorney whose thirst for ink was bottomless. Vincent brooded over the decision. He'd always enjoyed a fight, and almost always won them. How could he have allowed himself to think that the Goliath he would have faced was any match for his David? Well, it was too late now. He could scarcely get out of bed. His mind, he later came to believe, actually lost its acuity under these circumstances, like a large animal pacing a small cage until, in utter defeat, it settles on all fours and simply pants for water and air.

After listening to the all but incomprehensible announcements blaring from PA speakers that had no doubt been installed during the Eisenhower years, he wrote to the warden, volunteering to redo the entire sound system at his own expense, replacing it with a state-of-the-art rig that would have been sufficient to please any Broadway audience. In fact, his intention was to get in contact with the Fitzgerald brothers, at that time the business's leading sound wizards, and see if he could get the equipment at cost. But the warden shut him down. It was a state facility and could not be seen to be taking favors from prisoners, lest the prisoner might be perceived as asking favors in return.

The blaring, shocking noise calling him to dinner, to the yard for exercise and assembly, and back to his cell after, began to prey on his nerves. He couldn't understand why anyone would tolerate it.

He was expounding about this to a fellow inmate seated next to him at dinner one night, and the man laughed in his face.

"What are we, Attica?" the man asked. "We riot over an inferior stereo system? Maybe we should go on a mass hunger strike because we think the hollandaise sauce isn't up to snuff. Please, whoever you are, we're not going to take the guards prisoner on account of the loudspeakers."

The man, it turned out, was a minor Ponzi scheme operator called Clemson Mitchell III, who had legally changed his name the day he turned twenty-one and operated his own money management firm in Bronxville until the FBI came to get him.

The two began playing cards, quickly organizing a nightly poker game, which is how Vincent came to believe that the circumstances of his birth, and his rise from the gutter, had somehow put him at a disadvantage when it came time for the world to give him his just reward for achieving the American Dream. He was seized with the idea when Mitchell began to harangue him about it daily over breakfast.

"They gotta punish you," he explained. "They know you're not from their world, and they can't let you live. If you weren't born to it, they're not gonna let you have it—it's as simple as that."

"But everybody thought you were born to it," Vincent replied. "I mean . . . "Clemson Mitchell III?' Wasn't that supposed to protect you like a shield, like your family climbed down the gangplank of the *Mayflower*?"

"They could smell me," Mitchell said. "That was my mistake. Thinking that the name would do it. They won't let you live." The phrase had become his watchcry.

Vincent thought that Mitchell's mistake—whatever his real name was—wasn't that he changed identities, but that he robbed his investors. And yet, there was something in what the man said that appealed to a sense of aggrieved bitterness. His better self resisted, but to no avail. Vincent Donnelly, with no education or manners, with a house in Larchmont, a Broadway star for a wife, a mistress who had tumbled into his bed almost before he asked (whatever her motives), open-door access to the industry's money and power bases—it was bound to make people jealous, and jealous people get angry. Vincent talked about it over every early evening poker game, and it seemed as though he was late to the party. Everyone in the game had long understood the blatant, bastard unfairness of the system. Where had he been all these years? Taking advantage of a world that would one day come to get him.

Vincent brooded about it and felt his outlook changing. None of these minimum-security guys were really to the manor born; they were all ambitious pretenders gone wrong, himself included. Their white-collar crimes had something to do with how hard it had been for them to buy their first shirt with a white collar. It was the sons of bitches—the neighbors, the parents who he saw at school conferences, the bankers, the corporate lawyers, and all the other men who came naturally to the dark wood-paneled offices in which they sat each day who should be in here, he thought. I've done nothing wrong but figure out how to compete with them. He wondered what it would be like to have gone to some elite college and gotten a business school degree. Would it have made him a better man, or simply wasted his time? He opted for the latter opinion. In any case, it had never been an option.

He chewed over his ire each day, ginning up Clemson Mitchell III and being ginned up in return, spinning the entire worldview into a larger and larger ball of yarn, his spare hours gradually employed more by creative anger than by deadening boredom, and even he could feel the tether of logic and clear thinking beginning to come undone. It was deeply pleasurable somehow, the sense of having been misused by the country that had given his parents—his father, anyhow—such hope. There was precious little to enjoy in all the monotony at Fishkill, and one had to find one's satisfactions where one could. Rage provided a modicum of relief. When he emerged from the prison gate a free man, he was also a changed man, a man with no patience for reason, and no time for pretense—a man with a grudge that wouldn't die, even, as he later came to believe, if it was killing his brain.

AURORA HAD LET Ike Harris's letter sit on the narrow table in the foyer for a long time before she opened it. In the weeks since the sentencing, she had paid visits to Vincent, who, it seemed to her, was becoming ever more remote. He was cheered when she brought the boys, but otherwise emotionally immobilized. Yet it was in his absence that she determined she was not going to leave him. It was hard for her to piece together the reasoning for this. True, there was a part of her that loved him still, loved his unruly ambition, his inventive mind, his blunt manner, and his unending confidence. Like her, he had invented himself against all odds, and she loved sharing that. His scent still excited her, and the hair on his forearms when she grabbed him there. She hated him for his idiotic and unnecessary—in her view—need to climb into bed with so obvious a malefactor as Maggie Hynes, or anyone else for that matter, and she did not think she would ever forgive him or would even try. She did not want to be alone. She was not perfect. And she was too old to let herself be courted by anyone else, especially the men who clamor after Broadway stars. It was too hard to sort out their motives, and she would have no energy for it. This was not a clear line of thought, she knew, but a jumble of impulses that added up, somehow, to a conclusion. That was the best she could do. She would make the best of it.

The morning after her fifth visit to Vincent, she received an offer out of the blue—the first serious offer she had ever received to appear in a nonmusical play. New York Rep, the only institutional theater in the city that occupied a Broadway house—the Lyceum—was planning an all-star limited engagement of *Our Town* and wanted her for Mrs. Gibbs. She took the part purely so that she could say two lines: "Come out and smell the heliotrope in the moonlight. Isn't that wonderful?" and "Myrtle Webb! Look at that moon, will you!"

In and of themselves, they were completely innocuous lines, but she felt she understood them better than anyone ever had. In an emotionally straitened little town of all-too-practical men, they were like a song of lost love to her—the virtually unsaid, almost unknowing expression of that connection with the world and all the sensuality that might have been discovered there. Its distance, and the inability of these provincial wives to connect to it, withered them. She thought of her mother, and she knew how to play that.

She read the play over and over and kept stopping at those two tiny moments. They came as the gaggle of wives in the Grover's Corners church choir were wandering home after practice, but what they followed included not only the crabbed complaints of the alcoholic choirmaster exhorting these quotidian singers to raise their voices, but the grinding routine of the men of the town managing the world in a manner that kept things in check, running smoothly and free from poetry. The women, she mused, must have all gone mad, or spent all their energy trying not to. And then, in these two tiny moments, Mrs. Gibbs looked out and smelled the air, and saw the moon: lost hope, carnal knowledge, beauty in the dark—all of it bathing the characters as they walked and yet all of it somehow out of reach. She surmised that no one who had played the role had ever stopped to think about what it all meant. But to her it meant everything. It was a grown woman's expression of "It Might as Well Be Spring," long after spring had come and gone. She longed to tell the older character man playing the choirmaster what she knew of the life of Marius Huwiler, a secretive music man in a straitened little town, but she refrained. The actor had his own process—he didn't need hers.

Toward the end of rehearsal, and with Vincent's release imminent, she felt the time had come to face the envelope that had sat there for so long, and to compose the reply for which Ike Harris was undoubtedly still waiting. Thornton Wilder had something to do with it, she supposed. She spent her days rehearsing a world in which people moved from life to death without ever really understanding anything—or answering anything. The letter, which had been gathering dust for over a month, suddenly seemed like a prop that she was supposed to pick up. So, she picked it up.

Dear Aurora,

Many years ago, you wrote me a letter explaining, or trying to explain, why certain things happened, and why, in your mind at least, it was impossible for us to be together. I have never forgotten it, or the fact that I respected it in its entirety. I won't dwell on my own reaction. I will only say that I have lived by its words, and with its words, ever since. Until yesterday.

Yesterday I broke my own vow to leave you alone—it was an involuntary vow in any case—and I betrayed the command that I had received from you so many years ago—24 years to be exact. Twenty-four years seems like nothing to me now, but as I see it in black and white, I realize that it is a considerable period of time, what we might define as a generation—or an era.

Who knows why we do the things we do? My intention was to wish you well, or so I believe. My intention may have been just the opposite, of course, and I will never know. My motives were entirely honorable, or so I believe. But my motives may have been entirely dishonorable as well, and I will never know. What I do know is that you received my being there as dishonorable, as wishing you ill, or gloating or appearing to admonish you for having made a bad decision, and for all of that additional pain, I am deeply sorry.

I have always been a lousy chess player. I would have made a terrible lawyer. Chess players and lawyers are supposed to imagine every possible reaction to their action before they take one. But all I know how to do is play the trumpet. And for that limitation, I also apologize. I will trouble you no further, and, since I will not communicate by letter again either, I'll take this final opportunity to tell you that I wish you well, that I wish Vincent well, and that I understand, as much as I can understand.

There is no appropriate closing salutation to this letter, so I will simply affix my signature.

Ike

Aurora read the letter twice. It seemed to her that there was no other way to read it other than as a love letter from a vanquished lover, doing his best. She composed three responses, the first sentimental, the second analytical, and the third angry. All of them attempted to explain, in some way or other, why she was staying with her husband, and all three, she felt sure, failed to do so. She burned all three in the fireplace—there was no point in letting any of them survive in any form—and sat down a fourth time. She wrote:

Dear Ike,
Thank you.

Aurora

She sealed it, stamped it, and walked to the post office down the street. The night was warm and dry. The trees were heavy, motionless, and seemed ancient and judgmental, The stars were out, though unlike the comparable evening in *Our Town,* there was no moon at all that she could find. Nor the perfume of lilacs or peonies. Nor anything to stir the heart. Summer had come on, full force. The loveliness of it filled her with a kind of dread, a sense of foreboding, the source of which she could not identify. Quite suddenly she felt distracted and lost, uncertain and a little bewildered. But she dropped the letter in the box and walked back to the house, let herself in, and put herself to bed. The boys had long since retired. Sleep wouldn't come. She took a pill around three A.M. and awoke groggy and in a state at nine. Quickly she rose, dressed, and jogged back to the post office to see if there was a way to retrieve the letter, but the early mail pick-up had gone while she was lost in the haze of a Valium world. Whatever it was she meant to say instead—and she had no earthly idea what it might be—it was now too late.

No one at the Lyceum, where *Our Town* was beginning tech rehearsals, seemed to notice that for the rest of that day she spoke to no one but sat in the second-to-last row, just breathing. No one came to sit by her until almost the end of rehearsal when, during the final break of a twelve-hour day, the company's artistic director, Clayton Monroe, slipped into the row behind her and put a hand gently on her shoulder.

"Has something bad happened?" he asked in a little more than a whisper.

"I think maybe it has," she said. "I don't know."

He sat there, leaving his hand on her for perhaps another minute.

"You'll tell me," he said. "If it needs to be told. You know you're quite magnificent in this play, and in life too."

Then, as if he had embarrassed himself beyond recovery, he slipped out of the row and disappeared.

Aurora sat for another moment and then shook her head. *Men,* she thought. *Men are so incompletely made.*

Opening just after Labor Day, *Our Town* proved something of an unexpected triumph. The play itself, generally mistaken for a sentimental paean to small-town life, was recognized for its clear-eyed examination of the struggling and emotionally unfulfilled world that America had seemed to become. Once regarded as nostalgic, it now seemed prophetically pessimistic, and Aurora found emotional fulfillment in it with each performance. The line about the moon, so innocuous and of so little moment to anyone else, stopped her heart at almost every performance.

Her return to the New York stage was greeted with considerably more fanfare than she expected and, she felt, considerably more than she had earned. Mrs. Gibbs was hardly a leading role. *Perhaps,* she thought, *they're impressed that a musical comedy girl can act at all, and a little is all it takes.* But she tried, in whatever way she could, to recognize that people wanted to see her and thought she was making a fine contribution, emotionally connecting with loss in some way they had not seen before. After every performance, she signed autographs.

She did not hear back from Ike Harris and grew progressively more comfortable with the presence of Vincent, now back in the free world and attending virtually every show. He was there tentatively, she knew—in the theater but not quite of it anymore. He was somehow a changed man, but neither of them could explain what the change was or what it meant, and neither of them tried. Every night he took her to dinner after, they drank a bit too much wine, and then a driver delivered them to Larchmont.

16

ANTIQUES

U*PON HIS RELEASE*, Vincent had determined to take up golf, which is what all of the neighbors seemed to have done, and why not? He was no longer employed, no longer striving to make money, and no longer knew what the hell else to do with himself. Quite quickly, he realized that while he had a natural facility for the game, he hated it with a passion. The links appeared to him as a kind of bilious green landscape from a science-fiction movie. The gentle hum of the golf cart made him want to hit someone, preferably any of the other aging suburbanites bumping along over the grass, whomever they might be. The clubhouse manager put foursomes together at random—four men who had no favorite partners. In the course of a couple of months he golfed with a dozen or so Westchester businessmen. He did not want to be friends with any of them, and none of them seemed particularly welcoming to him. His reputation, no doubt, preceded him.

So, it was not surprising that, driving home from Bonnie Briar Country Club one Sunday, he was minded to take an excursion through Port Chester, sections of which reminded him of his youth in Long Island City, with its rows of redbrick factory buildings, now either abandoned or repurposed as bars, bistros, and retail stores. The town—the most intently working-class place on that side of the county—was somewhere in the middle of a plan for rebirth, which, Vincent concluded, might or might not ever succeed. Like Broadway, it had certainly seen better days. What lay ahead was uncertain.

As he turned back toward Larchmont, cruising slowly through a struggling neighborhood of clapboard houses with largely untended lawns, he saw an old car up on blocks. It was sitting in the driveway of a ranch house that needed paint and new gutters. He immediately recognized the vehicle—a Studebaker with a distinctive bullet nose, meant to imitate an airplane; they had been popular right after the war.

"Late forties," he said aloud to himself. "Maybe fifties." He had bought such a car for his father many years ago, just prior to getting him into the union.

He drove on for a couple of blocks, then braked and pulled over to the curb. He turned off the radio and sat for a few moments, lost in memory and contemplation. Then he made a U-turn and drove back to the old car. He mounted the crumbling brick steps that led to the front door of the ranch house and rang the bell. After a few moments a cliché appeared before him: a beer-bellied man, balding, in a sleeveless T-shirt and stained khakis. There was hair on his shoulders and hair on his arms, and he had not shaved. *Well*, thought Vincent, *it's Sunday.*

"I couldn't help but noticing that beautiful car," Vincent said to the man. "And I wondered if it was for sale."

The man squinted at him. "No sir," he said. "That was my father's car."

Vincent nodded.

"My father had one just like it," Vincent said. "That's what got my attention."

"Sorry," the man said, turning away.

"Wait," Vincent said, stopping him. "That was rude of me, I didn't even introduce myself. Vincent Donnelly."

"Ted O'Horgan," the man said. "Pleased to meet you. But there's a game on TV." Again, he turned. He had not opened the screen door or made any other gesture of invitation, but Vincent was encouraged—two Irishmen. At least there was hope.

"I wonder, Ted . . . I was just wondering. If I fixed it up, if I put it back in shape, would that be possible?"

Ted O'Horgan looked at Vincent with evident suspicion. "I said it's not for sale."

"I don't need to own it," Vincent said, though he was not sure this was true. "I'd just like to restore it. I'd do it at my own expense—just for the fun of it." By this he meant, just to see if I could figure it out. He had no idea how to fix a car.

O'Horgan scratched at his belly through the T-shirt and opened the screen door. But instead of inviting Vincent in, he stepped out on the porch himself, to better observe this stranger. Vincent could feel the man's eyes on him, trying to add things up. Too well dressed for the neighborhood, too old to be trying to build a career in auto restoration, too soft around the edges to have spent a life at blue collar labor, too eager to work for free. It didn't calculate well. Ted O'Horgan was not comfortable, and not a fool.

"Let me get this straight," he said in a vaguely threatening way. "You want to put my father's car back together at your own expense as a way to have fun?"

"Something like that," Vincent said. "I think I need to do something like that."

O'Horgan just stood there, waiting for the punch line. After weighing his options for a moment, Vincent thought, *I better give it to him.*

"I just got out of jail," he said.

O'Horgan said nothing as he stared at this stranger in golf togs claiming to be an ex-con. Instead of speaking, he settled into a threadbare aluminum folding beach chair with faded plaid polyester strapping that looked like it wouldn't hold him. He reached into an old Igloo cooler that was tucked up against the wall of the porch and pulled out two bottles of beer—Miller High Life. He capped both and offered one to Vincent.

"You're dressed too good for that story," he said. "Maybe you better tell me what the hell this is all about. The game on TV ain't likely to be as interesting."

Vincent told him the whole thing—this stranger—about the lighting factory, his immigrant father, his defeated mother who never came to understand that the family had really become successful and died too young, his rise, his fall, Maggie Hynes, his marriage, the boredom of prison, the hated world of golf, the need to find something, anything, that would engage him.

"I'll tell you the truth," he concluded, though he had already been doing so the whole time. "I don't know fuck-all about how to fix a car. But I always could learn anything mechanical, and I think I need to prove to myself that that's still true. One thing I don't need is your money. And however it goes, the car won't be any worse when I give it back to you. Maybe a lot better. If I were you, I'd say yes."

THE CAR WAS towed to a small brick building that Vincent leased on Pearl Street, and the work commenced. O'Horgan, it turned out, was an out-of-work plumber who had grown too large to crawl under sinks and behind toilets. Besides, his joints were too stiff, and his patience too short. It had all begun to slip away after his wife died. He had a nice disability payment from the Korean War, and so, in an unlikely way, had found himself in a situation similar to Vincent's but at a much more modest level. He didn't need to work and had gone to seed under the influence of beer and television. His children were remote. He was not from a class of people who took up golf. And while he had neither the ambition nor the intellect for figuring out a task as complicated as rebuilding an entire automobile, and almost no imagination at all, he did have certain mechanical skills to contribute, given all those years of working with pipes and wrenches. Vincent found him dull but friendly, and useful. Soon they had plunged into the task of re-creating a drivable classic car, something neither of them knew they had the slightest interest in doing a few weeks earlier. It was nothing if not an American tale. The automobile itself had called them to it.

Aurora came by the shop only rarely. Seeing her husband and his beery friend tinkering and banging on things, lit only by bare bulbs strung across the ceiling in an atmosphere smelling of grease and cigarettes, she thought of him as a broken man, and had no idea what the future could possibly hold for him. She kept her own counsel on the subject, however—no point in adding insult to injury.

Vincent, on the other hand, was more content than he had been in years. Freed from the shackles of a desk, a deceptive life of infidelity, a suit and tie, an expectation that he would ever show up anywhere for any purpose at all, he achieved moments of pure bliss rebuilding an ancient carburetor, driving two hundred miles to pick up a restored 1951 water pump that would fit this noble chariot. O'Horgan bolted it into place, and the two of them sat down to bologna and cheese sandwiches while Vincent happily told the story of the fan system he had built out of seven stolen toy boat motors and a bicycle wheel.

The joy of it all was in the variety of things one had to

learn to do. The engine and transmission required one set of intellectual tools, while the window winders needed another, and interior upholstery a third, all unrelated skill sets. Starter motors, brake shoes, radiators all were different, and the level of patience required to learn about them from nothing was enormous. And yet, it could all be discovered. Whatever the task was, someone, somewhere had done it once, which meant it could be done again. The only thing to be subbed out was the painting. Vincent had no patience for spray painting.

They worked through the winter and into the spring. When the car easily took first prize at three antique auto shows in a row, Vincent found himself in demand, and in a new business. He had a sign made for the building and entered into a contract to buy the place. O'Horgan and Donnelly was incorporated and opened shop officially On May 24, 1983, with O'Horgan's father's Studebaker parked out front. It became a landmark, and the business quickly acquired a waiting list of customers; each came bearing an old wreck that could be transformed into a gleaming example of Detroit know-how and ingenuity. Vincent hired two more mechanics.

Two weeks later, he lay in bed with Aurora watching the 1983 Tony Awards on television. It seemed to him to be happening in a galaxy far away.

It was a glamorous affair, though not so much as it had been before it was televised. For Aurora, who had once won one (it was on the piano downstairs), it was an event tinged with nostalgia and a little envy—or perhaps more than a little. For Vincent, theater was rapidly becoming a distant memory, as he forced it from his mind. He wondered how he had allowed himself to grow so far from the tasks that did not involve his hands and his body. True, he had his career path to thank for the house, for the money he had socked away both at home and in various Caribbean banks (all of that was easier to figure out than a hydraulic brake cable), but the show made him sad in a way he had not expected. He was very far from a world where he had once felt he belonged.

It all marched along without incident until the award for best play was announced. The winner was a dark horse called *Torch Song Trilogy,* three long, linked one-acts concerning a Jewish drag queen named Arnold. The audience erupted in a stunning and vocal ovation. It always did, but this felt different. And Vincent knew why.

"The fag play won," he said to Aurora, who was biting her lip.

"Jesus, Vincent," she said as the author, Harvey Fierstein, and his producers mounted the stage to an escalation of appreciation. Something different was happening. But it had not happened yet. There was a palpable tension accompanying the ovation. How was one to talk about this play on national television? And then, there was John Glines, *Torch Song's* originating producer, stepping to the microphone. He made all the usual gestures—to the cast and crew, to the voters, to the playwright, but the speech was loaded. He mentioned by name two early AIDS victims, and thanked "all my brothers and sisters," which could mean only one thing. The air became dry and electric, as if there was none to breathe. The speech was not done.

"Lastly and most importantly," Glines said, "I want to thank the one person who believed, who followed the dream from the very beginning, who never said 'You're crazy it can't be done.' I refer to my partner and my lover, Lawrence Lane."

In the scattered applause and sense of shock that immediately followed—it was nothing like the ovation that had greeted the announcement of the play's win—Vincent said, quietly, "Holy shit."

"Holy shit is right," Aurora said. "He did it. He actually said it."

"I meant," Vincent said, "Holy shit—he's got a lot of nerve. On CBS. He should be ashamed of himself."

Aurora looked at him for a moment in stunned silence. She was not good at this kind of discussion. She had no experience of it. She had grown up backing out of rooms where adults were in dispute. She had walked out on him once, and now she did not know what else to do. She got out of bed and left the room, heading down the stairs.

"What?" Vincent demanded. "You know what this will do for ratings?"

For a long time, she sat in the living room, with a brandy, and then another. She did not want to leave the house or be dramatic. She walked out on the porch. There was no smell of heliotrope in the moonlight, only darkness and the sound of light rain on the porch rooftop. She was filled with a terrible sense of foreboding, so much so that at a certain point Vincent was forgotten. It was only the darkness of the world itself that surrounded her.

17

THE SCOURGE

THE TWO MOST beautiful notes Ike Harris ever played were a B and a G. This was in the spring of 1984. They were the last two notes of the first act of *Sunday in the Park with George,* and Ike only got to share them with a French horn because when the show moved from off-Broadway to the Booth, a theater he had never played before, he got to expand the orchestra slightly. He expanded it to include himself. Much about the show—to the degree that he could sense what was going on above him on the stage, was confusing to him. It didn't seem to have a story like other shows—not really—and instead it proceeded through an uninterrupted series of fractious arguments, concluding with one of the most beautiful and harmonious pieces of music he had ever had the privilege to play. And when the act ended with only the two players ascending from the B to the G, followed by a bed of other instruments coming up beneath them, holding the chord that brought the curtain down, he began to weep, tears running down his cheeks and onto his mouthpiece. It was all he could do to hold his embouchure without wobbling. At home, he would play the two notes repeatedly each morning, and they seemed to present no particular challenge. But in the theater, at the end of that crazily beautiful piece of music after an hour and fifteen minutes of human disputation, they were hard to control, as was his emotional state. Some undefined longing overcame him, and he took most of intermission by himself, sitting on a stool in an isolated area of the musician's robing room under the stage, just breathing.

The show played into the fall of '85, and he never got it completely under control. There were days where he was relatively numb to it, but then it would come and get him again. He began to hate the G when he was playing the B, and to fear it. Some days he thought he wouldn't reach it, and, on occasion, he sat the moment out altogether, leaving them to the horn player, who did not seem to have the same reaction at all, and merely played them without effort before letting herself into the alley for a smoke. For Ike, the entire experience seemed to be some sort of test that he was barely passing. He turned sixty on a two-show Wednesday and gave a pair of flawless performances, after which he took himself to Joe Allen for a cocktail with Cecelia Austin and Moses de Longpre. By the time he got back to his apartment he was numb with alcohol.

When the show finally closed, Ike was unaccountably depressed. He had been looking forward to getting away from it, but now that it had vanished, it seemed to him to have taken the toll of a tumultuous love affair. *Good riddance,* he thought—*but where is she? A show is not like a woman,* he reasoned. *When it's gone it's gone—not run off with another lover, but gone out of this world, vanished, as ephemeral as love itself.*

Ollie died in her sleep on New Year's Eve or day, sometime between 1985 and 1986—no one could establish the exact moment of death with any certainty. Ike flew to Miami, where Lil picked him up. They had, by now, become familiar friends. Missy met them at the funeral home. They were, Ike realized, all that was left of the dream that Dr. Albert Horowitz had brought to America in 1924—three souls in an unfamiliar and characterless Florida burial parlor. Ollie had a large social circle, many of whom crowded into the hastily arranged service, but Ike did not know any of them. His mother died a local celebrity, a woman with a salon of friends and acolytes who would now have to find a new queen bee to hover around, for as long as any of them lasted. Snowbirds.

There was, at Ike's insistence, no rabbi present. There had been no room in any of their lives for practicing Judaism in any real sense. Besides, both Ike and Lil were drawn to the pagans and the existentialists, and Missy, to whom Ollie's Florida home had been left, had no beliefs left at all. Ike made a brief tribute to the woman who had raised him as if he was already a man, bought him his first trumpet, taught him the value of following his heart, and lived as if each day might be her last. He tipped his hat to his real father, whom he did not remember well, and Count Palaffi, whom he remembered with a mix of affection and disrespect. He was lucky to have spent his life, he said, around unconventional people, and for that there was no one to thank but Ollie Harris. She had chosen to be laid to rest in Florida, which Ike found neither more nor less baffling than any other decision she had ever made. In death, as in life, she was a hard woman to understand. As her coffin was lowered into a grave surrounded by coconut palms and agave plants, he looked around and took Lil's hand, then Missy's. *I better find another show,* he thought. *Otherwise I might float away and never be seen again.*

IN EARLY 1987, Aurora Shelton played two weeks at the Carlyle mainly for the purpose of making a live recording. Although the record business was about to go into a tailspin and the Great American Songbook had become a niche market at best, a producer named Arthur Fordin had approached her with the idea, and she warmed to it quickly. It gave her the opportunity to revisit old musical friends and try to make a few new ones.

There were old tunes she had never heard before, and she kept hoping to find a contemporary one to fall in love with, from a show—or from somewhere—that she had missed. Fordin, with heavy-lidded eyes and a baleful look, a coffee addict and a loner, was tireless in uncovering material she might want to explore. She imagined that he never slept but spent all twenty-four hours in a day searching for songs, categorizing them in his mind, and filing them away in the deepest well of a memory bank she had ever encountered. He needed to listen only once and the song was there forever. There was nothing she could name that he didn't know, and it occurred to her that these kinds of savants lived in every world, and that she was lucky to have found one in hers.

He lived in a brownstone in Brooklyn, and had bought the adjacent one to house his voluminous collection of sheet music, Playbills, 78 rpm recordings, and posters. He was a madman by most definitions, a man with no personal life at all that she could determine. And all this despite his having been born and reared in rural Arkansas. *How does such a thing happen?* she wondered. They get here somehow, by plane and train and bus. And they find their way to Times Square eventually. And, of course, it did not take her long to realize that she was thinking about herself. Whatever this community was, she had joined it decades before. They were all in this, whatever it was, together.

In a month's time she had rehearsed two dozen standards

that were performance ready. Then, three days before the engagement was to begin, Fordin played her something new that she loved.

It was a song by a woman named Djanga Kimball, of whom she had never heard. It was a subtle, careful, and utterly heartbreaking dissection of a marriage fallen prey to silence called "The House at the End of the Road." It was knowing in some way that she found frightening, and tender, not judgmental, and she had to sing it. That need hadn't exhibited itself in her in a very long time. While waiting for Fordin to try to locate Djanga Kimball in person and try to get her together with Aurora, he and his performer had only one dispute, and it seemed like a small one. Fordin suggested that Ike Harris sit in on trumpet, because he thought the concerts wanted a player who always kept in period and could switch from the forties to the seventies on a dime. But this was not something Aurora was willing to do. When he asked her why not, she sat silently for a moment and then said, "A million reasons."

Fordin's eyebrows went up and he opened his mouth to speak, then shut it again.

"Find me a reed player," Aurora suggested. "An oboe who can double on English horn."

And that was the end of that.

Djanga Kimball was elusive—forever touring through the lesser folk clubs and the cabaret world, appearing at the occasional international festival, and never available. Her manager was no help, and neither was her music publishing company. In the end, Aurora sang the song as she heard it, and it landed at each performance with a hush.

The shows went well, and the recording was mixed in the spring. She attended a release party at the Rainbow Room that she had to pay for herself, but it was a satisfying evening. Vincent toasted her; the boys—now young men—flew in from across the country. She drank far too much champagne.

As she sat on the bed brushing her hair out afterward, Vincent reached over and stroked her bare back—something between a caress and a kindly pat, she couldn't quite tell which. She turned to him too suddenly and he pulled his hand away.

"Vincent," She said. "You know that song—'The House at the End of the Road'? Don't make that our house."

He sat up as if a bullet had whizzed by his ear .

"What?" he asked. "What's this?"

"I haven't touched you in a long time," she said.

"Don't think I haven't noticed."

"It's the Tony Awards," she said.

He looked at her, completely at sea. "That's what you were thinking about? CBS and the ratings?"

"Ratings?" she asked angrily. "What are you talking about ratings?"

"Me? I don't know. It's not about me. What am I supposed to be thinking, if you don't mind my asking? I made a crack about that guy and CBS and what it would do to the ratings, and you decided never to have sex with me again? That doesn't seem to be the most rational of all possible choices."

"You're right, you're right," she said. "You know what? I'm too drunk to talk about it logically. I shouldn't have brought it up. But I miss you and I feel like one of us just isn't here. I suppose it's me."

She was nursing a headache the next morning over a late cup of coffee in the breakfast nook after Vincent had left for the car shop when the phone rang. The number was unfamiliar, from an area code she only vaguely recognized and could not place. She struggled with whether to pick it up or not—there were more than a few crazy Aurora Shelton fans out in the world—but something made her reach for it. On the other end of the line was Jonah Kingston.

Marius Huwiler had suspected there was something wrong in the early summer. He'd caught a summer cold that lingered too long, and then had a bout of diarrhea that he mistook for food poisoning. But it plagued him for more than a week and never entirely abated. When, just after Labor Day, his mouth erupted with a series of sores that made it difficult to eat, it could be ignored no longer. Jonah took him to a doctor in nearby Manhattan, Kansas, where no one knew either of them. It was impossible to reckon with the bizarre truth that, while Marius was worried about what the doctor would tell him, his concern was equally for the possible discovery it could lead to about who he was—and who Jonah was to him. He did not want his doctor in Junction City to know anything yet. Maybe, though he was beginning to feel certain this wasn't true, there would be nothing to know. Maybe life would just go on.

A week later he knew that it was not to be. Instead, he was going to die soon.

Aurora arrived two days later.

The disease was rampaging through Times Square, chewing up large sections of Chelsea and the East and West Village, leaving a wide swath of horror and despair like a filthy oil slick that would stain the streets and make them impassable for generations. But Junction City, Kansas? This was not something Aurora had given the slightest thought to. And Marius Huwiler, the most virtually married of married men—how was it possible? Jonah brought her to the house, which seemed remarkably unchanged. Marius was in the piano room, seated atilt, his backside tucked into one corner of an oversize chair that served to emphasize how small he had become. He rose and approached her but stopped short of touching her.

"No one knows what it means, really," he said. "I'm afraid to touch anyone. But if I could hold you I would do it forever."

There was nothing to do but ignore his warning. She wrapped her arms about him delicately, as if she were holding a baby, or a Ming vase. She placed her hand behind his neck, supported his head, and just stood there. They were silent for what seemed like a very long time and then he began to weep quietly, a resigned, dignified sound, as if he was too fearful of what it might mean if he really broke down. When he grew quiet, she released him, and he sat again. She looked around for Jonah, but he had gone.

"Don't mind him," said Marius. "He's like Julie Jordan in *Carousel*."

Aurora looked at him uncomprehending.

"Quieter and deeper than a well. And he'll never tell you nothing, either."

"Maybe it's not as bad—" Aurora began, but he held up his hand to silence her.

"Let's not start that," he said. "Tell me about Broadway."

Jonah reappeared with a tray and three glasses of iced tea.

But what could she tell him about Broadway? That it was in a state of triage? That she had not been able to find a new work to interest her in years? That half her Café Carlyle fan club had disappeared into early graves? What possible news could she deliver?

"There's nothing on the street that remotely compares to *The Pajama Game*," she said. "There's no world left where that kind of carefree atmosphere exists. It's like we're all in the army now. And taking heavy losses."

"And you're the army nurse," said Marius. "Listen—if I can still play, will you sing?"

They did, and Jonah was an appreciative audience of one.

The next night he called Toni Landry, who arrived after a dinner that Aurora had cooked, and the entire performance was repeated. Toni, after a few years of widowhood, had found a lover who actually liked music, a wide, bespectacled woman named Elise van Epps, who had retired after thirty years as the hospital administrator at Junction City Memorial. *What a strange world,* Aurora thought as she looked at these two women, each with a shock of white hair.

"There's a song," said Elise van Epps after Aurora had run through her current repertoire, "that I wonder if you know. It's from that musical about Fiorello LaGuardia. A young man took me to see it in a tent in Cleveland one night. This was back when I would still see young men. Back in the days of shows in tents."

"*Fiorello!*" said Marius. He turned to a sheet music cabinet adjacent to the piano and immediately located the vocal selection book.

"There are two really good comedy songs in that show," he said.

"This wasn't a comedy song," said Elise. "It was called 'When Did I Fall in Love?' or at least I think it was."

Aurora had sung it in her cabaret act years earlier. Marius stumbled through it—he was no sight reader—and Aurora sang to Toni Landry and Elise van Epps as they held hands on the sofa. It was a song of middle-aged surprise, a realization that love had happened somehow, but not in a single moment, or not one that could be recalled. Yet, somehow it was here, and it was not going away.

Midway through the song she realized that it would be sensible to change the final "him" to a "her," but otherwise she left the words unaltered. It was a command performance, and she understood that nothing else need be sung that night.

Carrying her coffee onto the porch the next morning she

passed the doorway to the music room—site of the previous night's revels—and confronted an alarming sight. Marius was on all fours, in his pajamas and robe, his head lodged in the low cabinet where once, in 1954, she had discovered the *SEX PSYCHOLOGY* booklet that he had squirreled away and forgotten. The carpet was littered with old magazines, paperback books, and vinyl record albums, and the cabinet was virtually empty.

"Marius?" she said uncertainly.

He backed violently out of the cabinet as if he'd been caught out at something, banging his head as he turned to her, a sheepish look on his face. It was a move worthy of Dick Van Dyke on TV, but she didn't smile.

"I don't sleep anymore," he said. "And I know I've got something for you."

She took a step down into the room and waited for him to explain.

"Go have your coffee," he said. "If I can find it, I'll bring it to you."

She settled on the screen porch pretending to read the paper and wondering what, exactly, was going on. She'd read about some AIDS victims displaying signs of dementia, but nothing the previous evening had suggested that Marius was having any neurological issues—at least not yet. She was pondering going to find Jonah to ask him about this odd behavior when Marius appeared at the porch door clutching an ancient oversize magazine—the kind that had disappeared with the last weekly issue of *LIFE*. His face was drenched in sweat; his hair, which was now thinned to a fine scatter, stood up on his head giving him the look of an old, not very well Tintin. He stepped down to her and held out the magazine. It was an issue of *Collier's*, from 1946.

"Early this morning," he said, "about three or three-thirty,

I had an idea. At least in my head I did. It was something I remembered, and I felt that if I had remembered it accurately, it might be useful to you. And when the sun came up, I wondered if I really still had the piece that gave me the idea, somewhere. And I did."

He handed her the crumbling publication, which was flaking at the edges, its color plates faded to an almost uniform gray wash.

"It's called 'Speak for Yourself.' Read it."

Aurora took the magazine gingerly and opened it to the contents page. "Speak for Yourself" was a short story by someone called Morris Shapiro, of whom she had never heard. As she started to read, Marius took her coffee cup into the kitchen, moving slowly, as if a vigorous expression of himself might somehow debilitate him, and brought her a fresh cup.

"Speak for Yourself" was a period romance, but an unusual one. A mother expecting her son home from the Pacific is, instead, paid a visit by a young, local enlisted man, a sergeant, with news that her son has been declared a casualty of the war. In her stunned numbness, the mother begs the young man to leave her house, but then, thinking better of it, asks him to return each day, at least for a few days. In the ensuing weeks, as her husband grows distant and remote at the vanishing of his only heir, the mother finds herself drawn to the young sergeant, and, over time, her interest in him grows from the maternal to the romantic. Somehow, in the mood of desperate loss and loneliness, underpinned by the unlikely virtuosity of Shapiro's writing, this does not seem as strange as it might, despite the difference in their ages. The sergeant is twenty years her junior, but as good as his word about returning. And while he seems to be doing it innocently, the tension—over time—grows palpable. He brings her flowers. He drives her to church. And then, most unexpectedly, she kisses him.

He leaves her, tasting her lips, and in a state of complete confusion returns to his home where, much to the reader's surprise, his wife awaits him. Even more surprising, the young sergeant confesses it all, and sits down to see what will happen. The wife listens and then leaves the house. She's gone until late that night when she returns and lets herself in quietly. She finds her husband where she left him: at the kitchen table, smoking.

"I want you to go," she says to him.

"I'm not surprised," he says.

"No," she says, "You misunderstand me."

He looks up at her.

"I'll be a mother one day and be as wrapped up in a child as that woman must have been. Must still be. She must feel the pride of his accomplishments and her own in helping to create such a person, and to support him and lose him must be terrible beyond anything I can imagine. I don't want to lose my child, but I want to know that it would be that tragic for me if I did."

The sergeant waits, not sure what she is suggesting.

"I want you to go to her," she says. "Give her what she needs, for one night. And then come back to me, and we'll never speak about it again."

The sergeant stands up. But the reader never finds out if he goes to the woman or not.

There the story came to an end. Aurora read it a second time, moved, puzzled, feeling like she had been let into a private world that she did not understand the meaning or purpose of. Why had Marius Huwiler, of all people, facing the end of his days, forced this obscure wartime fiction on her? And yet, she felt sure it was not a random thing.

By the time she looked up from a second reading he was standing in the doorway. He had combed his hair and shaved, and although he was still in his bathrobe, he looked an elegant invalid, a man of refinement, fading away.

She put the magazine down on a glass table in front of her and looked up at him.

"It's strangely touching," she said.

"I won't live to see it," he replied, "but it's your next show. It's a role. It's you. I saved it all these years and had no idea why. Maybe I was waiting for you to be old enough."

THE COPYRIGHT HAD gone unrenewed and had long since expired. Morris Shapiro had disappeared, like so many talented, unfulfilled American short story writers in the era of *Look* and *Collier's* and *Story Magazine* and *The Saturday Evening Post,* into the mists of time. His achievements were not even ephemera; they were utterly invisible. This was not the kind of material that Aurora pictured for a Broadway musical, especially not a vehicle for herself. And yet, Broadway had changed, and she couldn't get the damn thing out of her mind. The story itself, she reasoned, was a middle act. It would need an introductory section about mother and son. It would need a resolution, a denouement after the tryst—or non-tryst . . . well, there had to be a tryst. And what of the young sergeant's wife? She would need her own story, her own reasons. It would need a conclusion that would satisfy instead of merely tantalize. And suddenly she realized she was turning it into theater in her head and couldn't stop. She made a copy of the story at the local Staples in Junction City. Perhaps, she thought, it's only the second copy still extant on the globe. On the day she left for New York she promised Marius that she would return every two months, sooner if needed. Her husband, she swore, would cover his medical expenses, since he was, of course, not covered under Jonah's veterans plan.

"You're going to finance my demise?" he asked her, raising his eyebrows, as if daring her to respond.

She was stopped by this. Then she remembered how he had spoken to her all those years ago in the music room at school, when he had told her that her singing was like a machine, and she had cried, and then learned to sing. He had been blunt, but not insulting.

"That's right," she said to him. "I'm going to finance your demise. And be present for it."

When she boarded the plane that would take her to Dallas–Fort Worth on her way back to the city, she was thinking about sound textures and melodic style. She was thinking about music as different from Jerry Herman and even Stephen Sondheim as Mozart was from Joni Mitchell. She was thinking about how she was going to finally locate Djanga Kimball. Djanga Kimball was going to figure all of this out.

Vincent picked her up at JFK.

"That poor man is dying," she said to him on the way home. "My first and only real teacher. I told him we'd pay whatever it cost. Of course, his partner's insurance doesn't cover anything. Thank you, U.S. military."

"I've been thinking about all of that," Vincent said. "I want you back. Even if it means I have to think. I'm not much of a that-kind-of thinker."

"I want to hear about that," she said. "But the other thing is . . . he gave me a show. It's confusing. He's going to die, and he gave me a show."

VINCENT DONNELLY SETTLED into a comfortable state of gripesmanship at the antique car shop. Over the course of the year, he and his employees, who had become as close to confidantes as employees can, had spent almost as much time assailing American society, hypocrisy, entitlement, and the self-delusion of democracy as they had rebuilding cars, though their reputation for care and consistency in the latter trade was unchallenged. They took their time. They charged astronomical prices. They came to know DeSotos, Nash Ramblers, and Impalas in every detail. They had even rebuilt a couple of Edsels, and these, like the memory of any bright-eyed dream that had crash-landed, like his wife's debut in *Nowhere to Go But Up* (in a year when the Edsel was actually being manufactured), filled Vincent's heart up. Nothing was so touching as a glamorous dream dashed.

But as much as they admired these examples of automotive genius, they decried the country that had produced them—it was a rich man's paradise, a source of unending tax burdens, a place where, in the land of the free, no man could really be free. Vincent enjoyed their calumny, the more extravagant the better, and joined in with a certain lightness of touch. The place had been good to him, overall, and to some degree he was indulging in what he considered harmless sport.

They had a '68 red Pontiac Tempest up on the lift during a lunch break one afternoon when the subject of Aurora's increased absences came up almost casually. Ted O'Horgan, who had known Vincent the longest, and whose father's car was still parked glamorously out front, inquired almost casually, though he had become more mischievous as the shop had gained a place in the world and he, himself, had begun to earn enough extra money to fix up the ranch house.

"You're still married?" he tweaked Vincent. "Because we only see the missus now in months with no "R" in them, and then only once in a while. I hope you're not lonely. Looks like she's off living the glamorous life."

"As a matter of fact," said Vincent, "she's off nursing a sick friend." Aurora was paying her third visit to Marius and Jonah, helping sort out some ramping that needed to go into the house in Junction City to accommodate a wheelchair. Vincent never complained about the expense.

"The old music teacher," replied O'Horgan, who knew the story well.

"A music teacher?" asked the youngest of the workers, an Italian kid named Marco Di Natale. He was the only one still spry enough to get himself underneath a dashboard when wiring needed replacing (mice chewed up the insulation, usually), and they'd hired him for just such purposes. "Tell me he don't have AIDS. Them music teachers—"

"As a matter of fact, he does," said Vincent. "He does."

"Jesus," said Di Natale. "Your wife's out in fuckin' Kansas takin' care of some fudgepacker who packed the wrong fudge? In Kansas? Who could he fuck in Kansas?"

The men laughed, all except Vincent, though he could not claim to be entirely surprised by their response.

"You better not touch her when she gets back," said a brake shoe guy named Hoskins. "You touch her, you could be a dead man. You know what the worst part about getting AIDS is?"

The others looked at him expectantly.

"Convincing your parents you're a Haitian."

The four men roared. Vincent looked at them darkly.

"You're talking about my wife," he said.

"Fuck we are," said Di Natale. "We're talkin' about a guy so unlucky he's not only a fudgepacker, he's a fudgepacker in Kansas. Fags everywhere, I guess. That's what you get when America turns to shit. Even Reagan can't fix it."

"Reagan can't fix anything," Vincent said, "and you can't fix anything except an ignition switch. Why don't you just get the fuck out of my shop?"

"Me?" Di Natale asked in disbelief. "What the fuck you talkin' about, boss? I only said—"

"You only said *boss*," Vincent said. "And that's right. I'm your boss. But not anymore. Just get out."

"What?!"

"Vincent, think twice," said O'Horgan. "He's a good kid. He's no different than any American kid. Besides, we're just talking. What harm does it do?"

Vincent looked them over one by one: O'Horgan, di Natale, Hoskins, and a faded lounge lizard with a pencil moustache named Teddy Dominick, who was an ex-con like Vincent and never opened his mouth.

"Lunch is over," said Vincent, somewhat ambivalently. Di Natale didn't move, and Vincent made no move toward him. Instead, he gestured toward the Pontiac.

"Fucker's got a cracked engine block from a blown head gasket," he said. Somebody get on the phone and find me a replacement."

Vincent didn't go in the next day. He had not slept, but, between fitful attempts, picked off 120 pages of a book he was reading about World War I. *The Lost Generation*. Other people's catastrophes—those he could handle. But there was something in that phrase—*The Lost Generation*—that was too obvious for irony. In the morning, he read the obituary pages in the *Times*. Two deaths he could discern were from AIDS, though neither said so in so many words. He spoke to Aurora on the phone but mentioned nothing about the previous day. Marius was physically comfortable but furious that he could no longer walk more than a few steps without losing his balance. Something had gotten into his brain, and his lungs no longer kept him supplied with enough air to go far anyhow. It was not a good situation. Vincent showered and dressed, and, bleary-eyed, took himself to the Larchmont Public Library where he asked to see anything they had on the epidemic. The librarian looked at him strangely and led him to a couple of science magazines in the reading room, but he couldn't read them.

Vincent was a self-taught man—not even an autodidact, for he dealt in life, without realizing it, only through primary sources. He read history for amusement, but when he wanted to learn anything for himself, he could only do it by going to people. He'd had no formal education since he walked out of the schoolhouse in Queens at age fourteen and into the factory. After the library he picked up a sandwich from the local deli, and then went home and took a fitful nap. When darkness set in he got into the car and drove to New York, parking in a lot on Greenwich Street just off Seventh Avenue South. St. Vincent's Hospital was up the block, but he didn't go there. Instead, he began to walk down Bleecker toward MacDougal, looking for bars. Bars full of men.

He had not gotten very far—only to Thompson Street—when it became clear to him that he would stand out like a sore thumb in a gay bar even if he could identify one. The street was crowded, and he saw many men walking together. He took mental notes on what they were wearing and checked against his own body type and age—he was no longer young, not particularly slim, though his body suggested power, and he could lift a radiator out of a Plymouth with no trouble at all.

Nothing to be done about it now. He would just have to learn whatever he could looking the way he always did. Although the sun had gone down, and the streets were artificially lit up, Vincent hoped the bars would be darker, and that the dim light might help him learn something.

For a couple of hours, he dipped in and out of different places and had a drink in each. There was a dreary drag performer in one place and a clutch of cross-dressers in another, a muscle bar where he actually feared he could not compete, and quite a few neighborhood places, but collectively they taught him little. The tone was subdued, grim, joyless—conviviality had vanished from this race of men. At the end of a bar downstairs on MacDougal a kid was sitting in a flannel shirt and jeans, looking for all the world like a lost hiker who'd stepped off the Appalachian Trail and, as if by magic, found himself in the West Village. Vincent stood behind the kid, who was drinking a Michelob and crying softly to himself.

How much do I want to know? Vincent asked himself. But indecision was not a strong point of his temperament.

"Tell me about it," he said into the kid's ear, leaning in quickly. The kid looked around, surprised and a little frightened. He looked Vincent up and down.

"Get this kid another beer," Vincent said to the bartender. "And gin for me. Beefeater on the rocks."

The kid nodded slightly and looked down at the bar. Then he began to weep again. The bartender brought the drinks, and Vincent took a slug.

"For God's sake, tell me about it," he said. "No matter what it is, I don't know anything about it, you'll probably never see me again, so whaddaya got to lose? Just fuckin' get it off your chest."

The kid looked at him pitiably and put his hand on Vincent's shoulder. He took a deep shuddering breath.

"It's the Mets," the kid said sarcastically. "The Mets can't even beat the goddamn Cubs, and that's why I'm crying. You satisfied? Now leave me the fuck alone."

As his eyes adjusted to the light, Vincent could now see the kid was delicate featured and beautiful, beardless, with plucked eyebrows and deep brown eyes. He was a bit drunk, too.

"It ain't the Mets," Vincent said. "You're being ridiculous. I'm sorry, but you are."

"Oh, no," the kid said, steadying his voice. "The Mets,

Leonard Cohen, those first chords when Porgy comes into Catfish Row on his goat cart—everything makes me cry."

Vincent thought for a moment about what he had gotten himself into. Then he plunged forward—this was, after all, what he had come for.

"You're not crying about Porgy and his goat cart," he said. He had once been a follow-spot operator on a tour of *Porgy and Bess*, and remembered the tribulations of traveling with a goat. They could not be toilet trained, for starters.

The kid looked up at him and tipped his beer bottle slightly.

"Thanks for the beer, mister," he said. "But you're not my type."

"I'm not your type," Vincent repeated. "Of course I'm not your type. For chrissakes, I'm not even a real homosexual."

"What?" the kid asked. "Not what?"

"You need food," Vincent said. "Let me buy you dinner. I don't want to have sex with you. I got a wife and two kids."

"That never stopped anyone," the kid said.

"Well, it's gonna stop me," Vincent said. "So pull yourself together and let me get some food in you. I promise you it's the only thing I'm gonna try to put in your mouth. Scout's honor."

The kid stared at Vincent, and his face twisted up as if he was doing an impression of thinking hard.

"You're right," he said finally. "You're not a homosexual."

After a burger and fries they went to St. Vincent's. The kid, whose name—at least for the moment—was Bobby Saturn, after Freddie Mercury—had three friends in various states of decline. The nursing staff was efficiently brusque. Bobby introduced Vincent as a friend; no one seemed to be surprised. The atmosphere of melancholy was like nothing Vincent had ever experienced. He'd never been in a war, but here he was at the front. At the end of the visit the two of them sat in the little park where Seventh crosses Greenwich on a much-defaced bench. In the distance, over the Hudson, a lightning storm lit up the sky.

"I don't know what to do," Vincent said.

"You don't know what to do," Bobby said, on the edge of tears again.

"Well," said Vincent, "for one thing, you need some kind of mood elevator, but you can't risk turning into a junkie. And I don't suppose you've actually been tested because you're too goddamn scared. On the other hand, what I really want to do is bring you to my auto repair shop and somehow integrate you into the staff. Then I could bring one of them here and make them learn something about this world you live in, and then, little by little, I could save the world and cause people to understand each other, and you would be sainted, as my mother would say if she were here to say it, and I would be God. But the problem is if I actually did bring you to the car shop, they'd just fucking kill you. So I don't know what the fuck to do."

They sat in silence and watched the lightning show. Finally, Bobby asked, almost intimidated, "You're a car repair guy?"

"It's a long story, kid. I was a stagehand."

"Ugh," said Bobby, "bigots in their own world."

"That's right," Vincent said. "I ran the union. Before they put me in jail."

"This is going too fast for me," Bobby said, and it began to rain.

"Never mind," Vincent said. "Let's get you home."

He sprang from the park bench and leapt for a vacant cab knowing that, in a moment, when it began to teem, there would be none to be found. He dropped Bobby Saturn at a walk-up in Alphabet City and kept the cab back to the garage near St. Vincent's. By then the storm had passed, and he drove home with the windows wide open, the cool air washed clean by the storm. It would have been too much to ask for the stars to come out. *I wonder*, he thought, *who the fuck Leonard Cohen is.*

IKE HARRIS HAD his first heart attack while playing a killer Billy Byers lick in Cy Coleman's jazz musical *City of Angels.* He was three notes—a half and two quarters—from the trumpet shake at the climax when his chest was seized as if someone had thrown a straitjacket around him and hung him upside down. His balls seized up and shrunk into his groin. He felt like he would shit himself. He was suddenly blind. Somehow he managed the last three notes, including the shake, thinking that, if he was dying, it was a good way to go. It was a hell of a lick.

But he didn't go. Instead, he tapped the second trumpet player on the shoulder, pointed to his part, and stumbled toward the rickety stairway at the back of the pit. When he reached the top of it, he looked back, and it occurred to him that—though he could barely see—this was how he had first encountered a Broadway theater, back in 1940 when he'd climbed into the pit of the Ethel Barrymore and looked around at the empty house for the first time before a performance of *Pal Joey.* Being a man of the theater he understood that this, too, was a perfect setting for his death. Then he tumbled down the stairs and landed on his back under the stage.

When he awoke, he was in a room at Roosevelt Hospital, and a small bald man was sitting next to him reading the *Post* through impossibly large black-rimmed glasses. Ike stirred in bed. There were tubes all around and inside him. The little bald man looked at him and patted his wrist.

"Sid Lupowitz," he said. "How ya feeling?"

Ike felt like shit. For a moment he thought he was dead, for where but in the afterlife was he likely to be reunited with his annoying old army buddy, the composer of *Nowhere to Go But Up*? But looking around, he discovered that his own condition—tethered to a hospital bed by half-inch hoses—combined with what the years had done to Sid Lupowitz, and probably to himself as well, suggested otherwise. This was not heaven, nor, as a good pagan might have believed, the land of Osiris and his Forty-Two Judges, but the West Side of Manhattan, somewhere north of the theater district. Ike exhaled and coughed, which caused a machine above his left shoulder to bleat piteously.

"Sid?" he asked, though the word barely came out. "What are you doing here?"

"I'm retired," Sid said, though this hardly seemed an adequate explanation.

The truth is the two had almost reencountered each other three years earlier at the Lyceum on the opening night of Aurora Shelton's celebrated return to the musical theater, *Other Voices,* the musical adaptation of Morris Shapiro's short story "Speak for Yourself," which had, in a tangled and unsatisfactory way, reunited Ike with the woman he had loved for all those years.

AURORA AND VINCENT had caught up with Djanga Kimball at a little club in Piermont, New York, called the Turning Point, where she was performing with a cellist and a bass player. She appeared to be somewhat under forty, a beautiful mixed-race woman with a shock of African hair and Asian eyes, her skin too pale to miss that there was some Caucasian ancestry in her DNA as well, yet brown enough to mark her as a brown person too. She was an entertainer, and her fans loved her, underground though the whole scene may have been. When Vincent and Aurora—who were the oldest couple in the crowd by a generation—visited with her in the cramped dressing room after her set, it was impossible not to notice that she had a tiny hearing aid in each ear, which struck Aurora as odd for a person who had chosen to make a life in music. In all the time Aurora was to spend with her over the next several years, Djanga Kimball never once mentioned them, and Aurora never grew close enough to her personally to ask. The hearing aids were just one more oddity in the stack of peculiarities surrounding her, beginning with her name, which was real.

The Turning Point was informal enough a club so that no one was guarding the dressing room, and Aurora simply knocked, and entered with Vincent trailing, when bidden. Djanga looked up from the room's only chair and seemed puzzled to be confronting older strangers rather than friends. Aurora introduced herself and Vincent and said, after complimenting Djanga and the other players on their set, "I don't suppose you have any idea who I am."

"I do," said Djanga, "on two counts. You recorded one of my songs. And you were in a Broadway show once that was written by my music professor."

"Music professor?" Aurora asked.

"I took composition and harmony classes with Professor Lupowitz at Queens College," she said. "Sid Lupowitz. He was like a crazy man, but he taught me a lot. I was going to be a classical composer once."

Djanga Kimball, who originally hailed from outside Houston, had seen a total of two Broadway shows in her life—*A Chorus Line,* on tour in Dallas, and, strangely, a quick flop called *70, Girls, 70* which her professor had urged on her before either of them knew much about it. Sid was an admirer of

John Kander, with whom Sid used to compete for dance-arranging jobs back in the late fifties. Kander had had quite a career, but this one was not a high point, although Djanga vaguely remembered enjoying the music.

"Well, get ready," Vincent said to her. "Because now you're going to have to write one." He thrust the short story onto the shallow shelf in front of the dressing room mirror and left his card. Aurora had written her phone number on the front page of the photocopy.

"I know you have another set," Aurora said. "So we'll let you prepare. But please—read it when you can. We can go on an adventure together. It might be fun. Or as the stage manager in *Our Town* says, 'Once in a thousand times it's interesting.'"

Djanga Kimball looked at Aurora with surprise, stood, and glanced over at the photocopied pages of Collier's.

"That's it?" she asked.

"That's it," said Aurora. "I love your music and lyrics. I love your songs—and I want to sing a whole score written by you, and I'm a pretty determined person, and that's it."

Djanga nodded quietly and took each of them by a hand, very Zen, very noncommittal. She did not acknowledge that they'd left anything with her, or expected anything, or even knew that this was more than a visit from a couple of adoring fans.

"Thank you for coming to see me," she said.

It was not easy for Djanga Kimball to write a musical—she'd never written an intentionally theatrical song in her life. And since there was no playwright attached, the entire storyline seemed a little uncertain. She had called Aurora a couple of days after their meeting at the Turning Point, and they had gotten together for scattered days, limited by Djanga's touring schedule. At their fifth meeting, she told Aurora that she did not believe that the two of them had the skills or the tools to write their own Broadway musical.

"I've now been a professional long enough to know when something isn't professional," she said. "In my world, there are far more amateurs than not. I'm willing to learn how to do something I don't know how to do, but I'm not willing to be an amateur."

Aurora nodded. There was obvious wisdom here. "We need a producer," she said. "Someone who puts together shows for a living."

"I don't even know that much," Djanga said. "What does a producer do?"

"No one knows," said Aurora. "But we need one."

Aurora considered her options as Djanga set off for a northwestern swing through Missoula, Portland, and Mendocino. Thinking about Djanga out on the road, Aurora grew nostalgic for her days on Otts Oscard's bus with the Debutantes. A lot of water under the bridge. Her options for producers were limited, although any number of them might have answered the call. But Broadway shows weren't happening the way they used to when *One More Spring* had gone to Boston for four weeks at the Colonial Theatre—they were emerging from nonprofit theaters around the country, guided by commercial producers in partnership with artistic directors at these places, who built shows little by little, doing readings, then workshops, then small productions, before earning their way onto Broadway. It was a completely different method and model, and Aurora didn't really understand it. Nor did she know anyone at those faraway places. She was a performer, and had never birthed her own show, or even guided one. She was aware that the final results were often different from old-fashioned musicals too. Tired businessmen had moved on to some other form of entertainment. Shows were often smaller and more intimate than they had been, which was one of the things that made Aurora believe that Marius was being prescient in hanging on to this issue of *Collier's* for almost half a century. This was going to be a small show, a show with a uniquely intimate feel, and Aurora needed to find someone experienced to whom she could convey the kind of inchoate original vision that danced in her head before she drifted off to sleep each night.

Three days after Djanga left, she picked up the phone and called Joseph Papp.

She hadn't talked to him since the day they spent on the back of the flatbed that was parked across from the Morosco—the day that theater and its neighbors died. The whole event was almost a distant memory to her, though she had cared passionately at the time. Papp told her to come to the Public, down on Lafayette Street, right away. This was not what she'd expected, but he was an impulsive man, so she got in the car and drove to the East Village.

His office was cluttered with manuscripts and books, contracts, and yellow pads full of handwritten notes. He greeted her brusquely and moved a stack of Playbills off the chair across from his desk. There was no time for pleasantries.

"So," he said, "what are you selling today?" His accent barely betrayed a Brooklyn youth, but the cadence of his voice retained the harsh edge of Lithuania. He talked fast and sounded like he meant whatever it was he was trying to say.

She was prepared for this and thrust the short story into his hands. By now she had dozens of copies.

He seemed unsurprised and began to read immediately. Aurora looked around the office, staggered by the achievement it chronicled, from a framed reprint of Brooks Atkinson's review of Papp's first free production of *The Taming of the Shrew* to posters for *Hair, The Normal Heart*, and, of course, *A Chorus Line*. There were photos of George C. Scott and Colleen Dewhurst, James Earl Jones and Michael Bennett. A hardcover copy of *For Colored Girls* lay atop the stack of Playbills he had moved out of the way. Aurora suddenly felt like the most ridiculous of pretenders, like a little girl who had snuck into a world-renowned jewelry store after hours. She was sitting across from a giant, who was reading a forgotten short story from more than four decades ago, published in a magazine that hadn't existed since the fifties. Yet there he was, absorbed in what she had handed him. From time to time his lips moved and his eyes darted. She waited. Finally, he turned the last page and handed it back to her. He looked off into the middle distance and thought for a moment. Then his gaze shifted, and he looked her in the eye.

"The abundant mysteries of the human heart," he said. "You might say the normal heart."

"That's right," said Aurora. "A small musical with a composer I've fallen in love with, but I'm not a producer, I don't have a playwright to work with, I don't know what the hell I'm doing really, I just . . . need a show. And this is it."

"And you want me to take it on?" Papp asked. "It's a promising piece."

"Yes!" she said. "Would you?"

"No," he said. "The abundant mysteries of the human heart? Not for me. I mean Shakespeare, yes, of course. But me? I'm David Rabe and Larry Kramer and all of that clatter and shouting. *Hair*, yes, *Julius Caesar* with an all-Black cast, anything that says 'Go fuck yourself' in a new way."

Aurora was startled but unbowed. "*A Chorus Line*?" she said. "'What I Did for Love'?"

"That's different," said Papp. "Michael Bennett is a genius, and you don't say no to geniuses."

Then he gestured around the room.

"Besides," he said, "it pays for everything else. It pays for my life. And, of course, it's brilliant, which doesn't hurt. Though I'm no fan of that song, to tell the truth."

"Sentimental."

They sat in silence for a moment. Then Papp said, "I see the dilemma. You've done two important things on Broadway, and we're not discussing all those guest shots on TV shows and movie roles that no doubt kept you busy and working, plus your life at the Carlyle—I respect all of that, and it's a life well spent so far, but two important things on Broadway."

"That's right," Aurora said.

"One was produced by Antoine Berget, and he's gone."

"The first victim I knew," she said.

Papp stared at her.

"My son is ill," he said. "I don't like to talk about it. Abundant mysteries."

Aurora nodded. "The man who gave me the story is dying," she said. "My first singing teacher, in Kansas. I don't like to talk about it either. But I feel like I'm in a race against time."

"Who isn't?"

She did not respond.

"*Our Town*—that was New York Rep, no?"

"I don't think they do much new work," she said.

"But he has," Papp said. "Clayton Monroe. Before he took over New York Rep he had years developing plays and playwrights off-Broadway—even musicals. And what were half of them about? Love not war. People not ideas. Beautiful, the best of them. I'm a clatterer, he's a weeper. The abundant mysteries of the human heart—that's his corner. I'd only fuck this thing up. And besides, I'm not all that long for this world myself. Don't tell anyone."

"What?" Aurora said, her breath suddenly gone. He was not an old man.

"I didn't say it and you didn't hear it," Papp said. "Not

AIDS. Something else. Maybe I'll beat it and live forever. Who knows? Please . . . why the fuck did I even tell you?"

"I don't know," she said.

"Race against time." He gestured to the pages in her hand. "Something about that story. Loosed my tongue, like Shakespeare said. I don't know. Composure isn't exactly my strong point. Please, take it to Clayton Monroe."

A READABLE FIRST draft of *Other Voices* was completed in October 1988, and Aurora, with Clayton Monroe's blessing, arranged to take a small company of actors by plane to Junction City to do a performance for Marius and Jonah. By this point Marius was bedridden.

Monroe had warmed to the idea of the story at once, and found a playwright named Luke Saarinen. Saarinen had written a couple of failed off-Broadway shows before decamping to television land where he had spent a miserable but profitable decade writing episodes of any one-hour drama that would hire him. He was a craftsman and a nostalgia buff, with a seemingly bottomless collection of swing band music, and was thrilled to get his hands on something from the war years, which he glimpsed through the gauzy haze of someone who had obviously not been there at the time. His agents were dismayed that he wanted to spend an all-but-commission-free year writing a musical, but they were powerless to stop him. Efficiently he structured a book, spotted the song opportunities, wrote dummy versions of what they ought to say, and handed them over to Djanga, who suddenly found the score easy to handle, especially with the guidance of a music director named Don Pippin, who was decades her senior and had been doing the job for a very long time.

"Veterans and rookies," said Clayton Monroe when he insisted on hiring Pippin to help organize Djanga's thinking. "Winning teams are made up of veterans and rookies."

Clayton Monroe was, perhaps, the very last of the gentleman producers: from an old New York family, Princeton educated and so gentle voiced that he often commanded a room by uttering a few words so close to inaudible that a hush fell around him. Despite his mild manner, he did not back down, did not do work that he did not want to do, and fought like a strangely civilized jungle beast for the work he believed in. He believed *Our Town* to be the greatest American play, and he believed that Aurora Shelton was probably the finest Mrs. Gibbs of all time, in a production that he was proud to have presented. He also believed that "Speak for Yourself" was the greatest piece of undiscovered underlying material that he had ever been presented with, for the very reason that Joseph Papp had turned it down: The hearts it portrayed were as fragile as his own, and as fiercely protected—until they no longer could be. And that, in his mind, was what made it worth doing. Its heroine's heart came undone in a way that he knew his never would. He had never had a partner or lover, and he knew that he would die without ever experiencing true intimacy. On some days, he was at peace with it.

He did not, in the end, have the emotional fortitude to accompany Aurora and the cast to Kansas. The presence of disease made him pathologically unstable, and he was quite a hypochondriac himself. So, he sent the little performing army on its way and stayed home to interview potential directors for the piece, to present two or three of them to Aurora, Djanga, and Luke when they returned.

The house in Junction City now had a series of ramps leading to the front and side doors, but Marius was no longer able to ride the wheelchair very often. He was in his bed, which had been moved to the music room. He would never venture upstairs again. Eight actors, Vincent and Aurora, Djanga, and Luke Saarinen arrived on a Tuesday afternoon and set up the room for the reading, which took place that evening. Jonah Kingston, now quite fat, and bald as an eagle's egg, had adopted a thick set of black-rimmed eyeglasses that gave him the look of a curious hoot owl. He sat by Marius's bed and held his hand. Vincent seated himself on the other side of the bed. They were the only audience. Don Pippin, whom Marius was looking forward to meeting, had stayed back in New York, where he was working to salvage an unsalvageable Jule Styne musical based on *The Red Shoes*.

Djanga sat at the piano. Luke read stage directions, and in the intimacy of Marius Huwiler's sickroom, it could be said, *Other Voices* was born.

About halfway through act one, Marius began to weep quietly. Jonah patted his hand, to no avail, and eventually Aurora stopped in the middle of a song.

"Marius?" she asked. "Can we help?"

Marius took two deep breaths that seemed to hold back his emotion. But his voice was barely audible, and it took all he had to speak.

"Go back to the beginning of the song," he said, "and don't stop for me. I'm doing the best I can."

She nodded, but he held up one finger. There was something to add.

"Once I told you," he said, "that a song could say three things about you at once, do you remember?"

Again she nodded, thinking about the music room at school.

"Sad, angry, and blue," he said. "It was an idea I improvised on the spur of the moment. I didn't know it would come true. Now sing."

The show had quality. The music was good; it was moving,

subtly shifting closer and further from the world of swing and the big bands—the world of Otts Oscard, in fact. And Aurora knew that she would find herself in it in a way that she hadn't quite yet, except for those fleeting moments as Mrs. Gibbs. Her heart was a mess, celebrating the value of the piece and what it might mean back in New York even as it was torn apart by the sight of Marius Huwiler, reduced almost to ashes, lying in bed in front of her. A part of her felt triumphant and a different part was consumed with despair, salted with gratitude for this story that Marius had kept for her all these years. She had never spent a more bewildering evening. She had her hands on a hit show and was losing the mentor and friend who was responsible. As they reached the finale, Marius shifted in his bed and sat up straighter, seeming for the first time that evening to be, in fact, unmoved by the piece and alert to his own feelings.

"For a Midwestern music teacher," he began softly, "to hear this—to be allowed into this—it's, I just can't say what it means. I'm very, very grateful. But that's not what I want to say."

He breathed heavily for a moment, trying to gather himself together, trying to find a way to communicate something under the surface, trying to bring it up. Aurora moved to the bed.

"Wanting," he said. "This story—I didn't know what it was about really."

He spoke slowly, but with a heroic determination, and he was not to be silenced, though the assembled group had to wait as he expended and regathered his strength.

"About wanting and losing," he said, "and wanting, and, you see, when I was young, I wanted so much, so many people, so many young men I saw and so much that I could imagine, wanting a world I didn't have, wanting people, wanting some kind of ecstasy."

He stopped. He looked at Jonah and took three sharp intakes of breath.

"But I was really never wanted. I never got to be any part of that world of the wanted until tonight. And I was never wanted in the way I wanted to be wanted until . . ."

He clasped Jonah's hand.

"And yet," he almost whispered after another long pause, "we just keep wanting. Or I do, or did, and I think, because I got so little of what I wanted for so long . . . I just kept wanting. And that doesn't seem unreasonable to me in a fair world—it's just a condition of life, like the people in this story who begin wanting again just when they think that their wanting days are over, or ought to be, and, well, all that wanting has killed me."

Possibly he was done. Aurora, who held his left hand as Jonah clutched his right, leaned over to kiss his cheek, but he stopped her with a spider-leg forefinger.

"And before I go, here I am, past wanting—I can't enjoy anything, food, drink, certainly not sex. All that wanting has led to no more wanting. And the irony of it isn't lost on me. So, thank you for coming. I didn't know I could ever enjoy anything anymore until tonight. And you are all wonderful."

There was a silence in the room so profound that Aurora could hear eight or nine kinds of breathing. Private thoughts were careening through the air, and Aurora could feel them bouncing against her skin. She should have been remembering the music room, that airless moment when Marius first put his hand on her abdomen. But she was not. She was thinking of the night—a week after Vincent had begun to court her—when Ike Harris kissed her in the vestibule of her walk-up apartment in Hell's Kitchen, how they pressed into each other through heavy overcoats and layers of wine and cognac, hungry and wanting, and somehow doomed to miss the moment. Had she ever felt that kind of desire again? Had she ever lost an opportunity like that? Her reverie was interrupted by Marius, who had rolled sideways in the bed and taken Jonah by his shoulders.

"I'm sorry," Marius said, making something of a public confession. "I'm just so sorry. So blue and scared and angry . . . and sorry."

A week later he was gone. Aurora had stayed on, sending everyone, including Vincent, home. She had held his hand, and kept his face cool with compresses, and seen the light go out, helped Jonah with the arrangements, and gone with him to scatter the ashes from the overpass over Milford Lake, at Jonah's insistence, though he would not explain why. As they walked away, she worked up the courage to ask him: "Can you tell me what he meant? If you want to. Wanting more and it killed him. Hearing that must have killed you."

"One day I'll explain it," Jonah said.

"When you come to New York for the opening," Aurora said, letting him off the hook.

"When I come to New York," he said, "I'll explain it."

But he did not explain it. Two days after Aurora went back to New York, Jonah Kingston got a small stepladder out of the basement and put it in the back seat of the car. He drove back to the overpass, arriving a little after two in the morning. The area was deserted and breezy. He pulled the car up on the curb of the overpass, got the ladder out of the back seat, and set it up by the bridge railing. He was too ungainly now to get over the railing without it. But quite easily he climbed up the three steps, felt the breeze on his cheeks for the last time, and, without hesitation, plummeted forward, toward the water where the ashes had settled the week before.

PART FOUR

18

THE TRUTH

WHEN IKE HARRIS emerged from the stage door of the Hilton Theatre on a spring evening in 2005, the light stunned him. It always did now. It was after eleven o'clock, and he'd been in the building since noon, playing the matinee and evening shows of a painfully unhappy musical called *Chitty Chitty Bang Bang*. During the fifteen years that had elapsed since the final performance of *Other Voices,* the musical that had reacquainted him with Aurora Shelton, he had played and managed orchestras for twenty-eight Broadway shows, some hits, some flops, none as dispiriting as this one. And over that period, everything had changed. His beloved thirteen blocks, from 41st Street to 53rd, had been subject to a war, an invasion, a salvation, a ruination. In this now prosperous and blazingly lit district, tourists thronged the streets. At that moment there were no fewer than four musicals playing that recycled the hit songs of rock artists from the Beach Boys to Elvis Presley and John Lennon.

He had played many fractious, unworkable shows before, but they had all failed almost immediately and released their unhappy prisoners to whatever vagabond life could be scraped together next. But *Chitty Chitty Bang Bang* seemed destined for a run, despite the grumblings of critics and native New York audiences, and especially the company itself, which seemed to express a collective sense of apology at every curtain call. Ike felt lucky to be hidden away in the pit of this gargantuan theater, which had been fashioned from two disused 42nd Street playhouses that had been joined together by the tearing down of the walls between them, not that long after the porno revolution had moved to the Internet. It was a new world altogether.

It was, he supposed, the logical outcome of the day almost a quarter of a century earlier when the Morosco, the Helen Hayes, and the Bijou had been bulldozed to make way for the Portman Hotel, which had since been taken over by the Marriott chain and renamed the Marquis. All the way up Broadway, from the appalling cacophony of design on 42nd Street itself—now featuring a McDonald's and a branch of Madame Tussauds Wax Museum—to the FAO Schwarz branch on 45th to the crazily anachronistic style of the new marquee of the Broadway Theatre, at the north end of the district, there was virtually nothing for which he could feel affection, other than the theaters themselves. Every night they pumped a kind of lifeblood from within, and he watched it spill out onto the streets as it had back in the days of *Pal Joey,* though the population had most certainly changed. They no longer dressed, they no longer hailed from New York, and in many cases, they no longer spoke his language. Was this what age was supposed to mean—a life determined only by memory, by longing for an earlier, more graceful or familiar time? Or was he simply the cliché he'd feared becoming? Sometimes he pondered this as his eyes darted around, looking for a familiar sign or symbol. *When I get to heaven,* he thought, *surely there will be a man painted on a wall advertising Camel cigarettes; real smoke will come out of his mouth, and I'll be happy at last.*

He had become the first trumpet player in *Other Voices* all those years ago entirely because of his past—but not because of his past with Aurora. As it happened—and he knew only some of the story—Djanga Kimball had turned to Don Pippin for advice about how to best achieve the sound of wartime America, sliced through a contemporary songwriter's sensibility, and Pippin had only one name to offer: Charlie Vodery. Vodery was older now, and could be caustic and impatient, but he also knew the territory better than anyone. He had, after all, run the best band ("They called it 'the best colored band' back then," Pippin said unapologetically) in the army.

For Vodery and Djanga, it was an immediate love affair, a Black grandfather and a mixed-race granddaughter who saw the world across the decades through one pair of eyes and whose ears heard music in all the same ways. Vodery wrote orchestrations of Djanga's score that made her feel giddy when she read through them. She could only imagine what hearing them played live would be like. Vodery and Pippin squabbled a bit about who the best players might be for these contemporary-retro charts but were agreed on one point—Ike Harris had to play first trumpet.

By the time Aurora heard about this, Ike had been hired as both contractor and player. She was not happy. Was it too late to change?

Vodery looked at her through slightly rheumy eyes. His goatee, no longer stylish, was scraggly and gray.

"He doesn't have to play," Vodery said to her. "I can just take my charts and go home. I've written lots of arrangements that never got played. There's other orchestrators out there—good ones, too. I'm long past retirement age. I don't have to work—my life is all figured out. So, nobody ever has to hear this orchestration, and we can part friends. But if the charts are gonna be played, Ike Harris is gonna play the first trumpet part. But like I said, it's up to you, or the producer or somebody. It's not up to me."

For Ike, the sitzprobe—that first meeting of the acting company and the orchestra—took him all the way back to *Nowhere to Go But Up.* He sat in his chair after a morning rehearsal with just the band and waited for the acting company to troop in after the lunch hour. This time, of course, he knew who was coming. Aurora entered as part of the pack, somewhere in the middle. She looked his way and nodded. He nodded back. That was it, until the first break. The score was quite breathtaking, and when she sang, it was impossible not to believe every word that came out of her mouth. Yet he hesitated to approach her—to compliment her or greet her—as the musicians and actors milled around, taking their contractually provided fifteen minutes off. She, on the other hand, walked up to him directly, and put a hand on his shoulder.

"Ike," she said.

"You sound great," he replied.

"I think I owe you an apology."

"I don't know if you do or you don't," Ike said.

"That letter . . ."

"I started the whole thing," he said. "I don't know what I was thinking."

"I didn't know what I was thinking, believe me," she said. "I still don't."

"Well, that makes two of us," said Ike. "It was a long time ago. I'm as surprised to be here as you are surprised to see me, but we're neither of us young, and I think we will need to simply do our jobs. You'll act and sing; I'll play the trumpet. And since this is an extraordinarily promising show, we may be working together for a long time. I'll do my best."

"I'll do the same," said Aurora. "But I just wanted to say

that it's good to see you. Uncomfortable, of course, but it is good to see you."

They stood for a moment, not knowing how to draw this encounter to an end. A handshake seemed foolish. Ike dove his head in quickly and tried to kiss her cheek but missed it and kissed the air near it. She smiled at him but made no attempt to return the errant kiss.

"I do love you, you know," she said, though she'd had no plan to say it. It sounded the way it had always sounded. And then it was time to rehearse again. Aphrodite had a mordent sense of humor, Ike observed to himself.

Now, fourteen years had passed since the closing of *Other Voices,* and when Ike arrived back at the apartment after his two-show day at *Chitty Chitty Bang Bang,* there was a voice-mail from Aurora Shelton.

They met at the upstairs bar at Sardi's the next evening. Normally, Ike didn't drink before going to work, but he figured a single bourbon wouldn't kill him—and he was unaccountably nervous. It seemed preposterous that at this late date he would await this woman in a bar with a sense of anticipation and mystery. Still, waiting for a beautiful woman in a bar—there was no feeling quite like it. He needed the drink. He also had a feeling he had never had before, and it saddened him. If he clammed a note—or a dozen notes—at *Chitty Chitty Bang Bang*—no one in today's audience would notice, and he wouldn't care. He was turning the implications of this over in his mind when he saw Aurora come up the stairs and make a U-turn toward him at the corner of the bar.

"Manhattan," she said to the bartender, who greeted her by name.

She gave Ike a proper hug, one that felt more like gratitude than anything else, and thanked him for meeting her.

"The thing is," she said. "I don't know who else to talk to, and I don't want to tell the kids."

"I think I'm flattered," Ike said. "What's up?"

The bartender delivered her drink, and Aurora lifted it toward Ike's glass in a quick toast, after which she took down half of it in a single gulp. Then she spent a moment catching her breath.

"Last Monday," she said finally, "they honored Vincent at that Actors Fund Gala."

"I know," Ike said. "I contracted that band. He made a lovely speech. I saw you at the table there."

Aurora nodded but didn't respond.

"When it was all over," she said after a somewhat less impressive pull at her drink, "we were driving home. At least I thought we were driving home. I closed my eyes for a bit—I don't think I dropped off, but I wasn't concentrating—and when I opened them again, we were halfway across the 59th Street Bridge, heading into Queens. We live in Larchmont."

"I know you don't live in Queens."

"I said, 'Vincent, where are we going?' and he said, 'Home.' But he didn't sound like himself, and there was no way to get off the bridge, and when we got on the other side, he drove through Long Island City, and down some street I had never been on before and parked the car."

"Jesus," was all Ike could manage.

"At first I thought maybe he was drunk, or had some surprise in store for me, but, no, it wasn't that at all. He thought he was home. The house he grew up in, only it wasn't there anymore, of course, and he got very disoriented. I swear to God, Ike, I thought I was in a movie. Not that I was acting in one but that I had found myself in some other story, not mine."

"Aurora," Ike said. "I'm so sorry. It's a pathetic response, but I don't know what to say. What did you do?"

"I don't even know. I think I started to talk to him like he was a small child, I don't even know why. I tried to explain that this wasn't our home, and that I would enjoy it so much if he would let me drive, and he nodded, very docile, very confused, and I didn't know whether to go to the emergency room someplace or what, and so somehow, I don't even know how, I found myself getting back to Larchmont, and somewhere on the drive, he started to return to himself. Started to apologize and try to explain, but he couldn't, of course, and then he was very quiet, and finally he said, 'What happened?' and I told him I didn't know."

"Have you seen a doctor? Had an MRI or whatever?"

"He won't let me do anything," Aurora said. "He seems fine. It's like it never happened. He won't hear of me talking to the kids about it, and I didn't actually know where to turn, but I kept thinking of you, in the courtroom, trying to express some kind of concern, and I just called you. Because I had to call someone. Do I just wait and see? I can't force him to the hospital—he seems fine."

Ike sipped at his drink, suspecting it would have been better not to have had one. But he didn't leave drinks unfinished. He looked at Aurora. At seventy, she carried invincibility and frailty side by side in the palm of her hand. And yet the fear in her was palpable, and she had come to him. His instinct to empathy and his sense of ego left him all but breathless. Putting his faith in the alcohol to make him not only wise but bold, he spoke.

"You need to see your doctor," he said. "You need to consult with someone he'll refer you to—a cognitive guy or a neurologist or someone: There's someone in the profession who has heard of this before. I know these things seem like dreams while they are going on, but there are answers to be had. He won't help you look, so you have to look for yourself."

"I know. I do. But I'm afraid to start."

"I'll help you look," Ike said. "If you'll let me."

"I have to think about that."

Ike nodded and drained the remains of his drink. "I have to play a show," he said. "Not a very good show."

"I've seen it," Aurora said, not committing to an opinion.

"Whether you let me help or not," Ike said. "You have to keep me informed. That's only fair. You called me, I want to help, but you can't leave me in the dark about this—I'm concerned for you, for him, for everyone. Promise me that, at least—that you will keep me posted."

Aurora nodded.

"I do love you, you know," he said, echoing the words he had heard back in the day.

Ike played a miserable show. And while the audience may or may not have noticed, the conductor, a young associate named Stan Tucker, did.

"You all right?" he asked Ike after the exit music.

"I'm fine," Ike said, but he was not. He'd had a bourbon, he had Aurora's presence hovering around him all night, he was unfocused and resentful that he had to play. He was not himself.

"I know it's delicate," said Stan, "but I gotta ask, because, you know, the heart thing, the age thing . . ."

"I had a heart attack," Ike said. "It was more than ten years ago. I take my medication, I do my exercises, I'm fine. And yes, I'm almost eighty, and if that's a problem for you, you can call the union. Don't forget, I hired you, not the other way around."

"Ike, I'm sorry," Stan said, but Ike was already heading for the stairs at the back of the pit, his trumpet in his hand. Even before he got out of the building, he was having trouble justifying that speech. The poor little pisher was trying to express concern. Why rage at the guy? Ike did not go home. He went back to Sardi's and woke up Sid Lupowitz with his cellphone.

"Come down here," he said. "I gotta talk to someone."

Sid was plagued by boredom. Unretiring by nature, he had precious little to do, having long since divorced the chorus dancer and never finding anyone else who could tolerate large doses of him. As Ike regained his strength, he found Sid a good companion, principally for nostalgic reasons. Sid had lost none of his bristling arrogance or certainty, but he was company, and he remembered everything and everyone, going right back to Poke Belmore and the barracks. Ike also knew he wouldn't mind being awakened if, in fact, he ever slept. He was at Sardi's in fifteen minutes. Ike had already had one bourbon and was nursing a second. It was a lot of bourbon for a man his age and size.

"Who do you think came to see me this evening?" he asked Sid, who ordered a seltzer with an extra glass of ice and two wedges of lime on the side. He would continually mix the proportions between the two glasses as the conversation wore on. This was standard procedure.

"Well," Sid said as he poured seltzer water over frozen water trying to achieve exactly what blend no man could say, "if you're drinking alone at midnight after playing your guts out for two and a half hours at age eighty—"

"I'm seventy-nine," Ike said.

"For another month," Sid conceded. "I'd say it was Aurora Shelton."

"Well," Ike said, "that's why I called you. Because you'd know."

"I vas dere, Sharlie," said Sid, quoting an obscure comic named Baron Münchhausen, now remembered by absolutely no one but himself.

"I suppose you were."

Sid lifted a single ice cube out of his drink and returned it to the glass of ice.

"Look," he said, "I saw you spinning around in circles over her in Philly back in 1960, and by then you had already been long gone for years. I knew you were doomed the minute I saw you watching her. And that trumpet solo—you think that was Charlie Vodery's idea? That was me, baby, that was me. I know how to make love, even if I'm doing it for someone else. Call me Cyrano de Bushwick."

Ike took another sip. "If you're so smart, why ain't you rich?"

"My personality," said Sid, unapologetically. "Look, John Kander and I worked side by side as dance arrangers and rehearsal pianists in the fifties, and I write a tune just as good as he does every time out, but he's wealthy and famous with his own brownstone, and I'm a retired composition teacher living in a studio apartment. Why? I'll tell you why—he's the nicest fucking guy in the world, plus talented, that's why. And I'm an asshole plus talented. Those are the breaks. Maybe it pays to come from the Midwest."

"So, what do I do?" Ike asked, uninterested in contesting Sid's characterization of himself vis à vis John Kander.

"Take it from an asshole," Sid said, pouring the last of the seltzer onto the last of the ice. "Tell everyone the truth, that's the only thing that's worth anything."

"But," Ike said, "tell what to whom? Aurora Shelton is still married—she's not going to run off with an eighty-year-old trumpet player. So what do I tell her? What do I tell anyone? You're so good at making love, how about just making me feel like I'm not spinning out of control?"

"That's exactly what you're doing," Sid said. "Spinning out of control. Seen it a million times. That's why there's literature."

"This is not supposed to be the way things are for people our age, Sid, really. We're all supposed to be dead and resting."

"There is no *supposed to*," Sid replied. "If there was you would have married Aurora Shelton in 1957 and by now you would have fucked her almost ten thousand times and it wouldn't be so special anymore."

"Sid, really," Ike said.

"That would have been your life," Sid added, "And I'd be Steve Sondheim."

He looked toward the bartender, who was hoping to close up as soon as her last two customers settled their bill.

"Dear," he said. "Could I get another glass of seltzer, another glass of ice, and two more slices of lime?"

VINCENT DONNELLY came to grips with what had happened a few days after the incident, but said nothing about it for almost a week. The truth was this was not the first time he had gotten lost. There had been two other occasions, but he had been alone. His disorientation had passed. He had figured out where he was and made his way back. He had told no one.

Almost no one. The second time it happened, he awakened the next morning full of fear that he was losing his mental grip on the world, and there was a question he had never been able to answer, one that he felt he wanted to settle before it was too late. He made a phone call and booked a round trip to Cincinnati, where he was met at the airport by Cappy Casparian. They drove to the Skyline Chili place on Third and Philly—technically they were in Kentucky.

Sliding into a booth, Cappy told Vincent he looked good. Vincent nodded. He didn't feel good.

"I'm losing it," he told Cappy.

"Unlikely," said Cappy. "You got your hair; you got no gut. Look at me—I'm an old man all of a sudden. I look like a hairless Vietnamese potbellied pig."

Vincent nodded again. The waitress, preternaturally friendly, took their order and brought Cappy a Coke with ice, which he promptly sent back. Vincent explained the situation as he saw it.

"If I'm going to lose my mind," he said at the end, "which seems likely, I'd like to know one thing. What's your poker secret? I've been watching you at the table on and off for decades, and I've never seen a thing. If you were doing anything against Hoyle, I'd have seen it. You're not."

"If I tell you," Cappy said, "you'll start doing it yourself. I can't have that."

"Please," Vincent pleaded. "I don't think I can ever play again."

"We'll see," said Cappy. "Come to the game tonight. Only one thing. You gotta play—at least a few hands."

Cappy Casparian had a weekly game. Vincent sat in; within an hour he was broke. The cards were just confusing enough to him so that he never knew if he should stay in or fold, and it didn't seem to matter. He backed away from the table and watched his friend, who, for once, had a losing night. Afterward, they went back to the Casparian house, where Cappy's longtime girlfriend had made up the guest room. Vincent sat over a scotch as Cappy poured a caffeine-free Coke into a glass.

"My friend," he said to Vincent, "you are correct. I'm the doctor, you're the patient, and my prescription is that you are never to play poker again, and that's all I have to say about it. Something seems to have slipped in you. Your brain is off the leash. I won't lie."

Vincent sat silently and took two short sips from his drink.

"So then," he said, finally, "how do you do it? You see I can't steal it, it's no risk for you, and I need to know."

"It's very simple," Cappy said. "I'm a good actor."

"A good actor?"

"I'm good at one thing—well, really two. At any poker table, no matter if it's all my friends or a roomful of strangers, it takes me about ten minutes to figure out who the dullest, least imaginative, dumbest guy in the room is. And my mission is only to appear to be dumber, more unreliable, and noisier than that guy. And I can—I'm a good actor. So first I detect, and then I act."

"I'm not sure I get it," Vincent said.

"The room loosens up. No matter who the big threat in the room is, it can't possibly be me—I'm an idiot—a fool. So, they start to concentrate on each other, looking for the most dangerous enemy. And the more they do, the dopier I get. And the dopier I get, the less they take me seriously. And the less they take me seriously, the more I win."

"That's it?"

"That's it," Cappy said. "Victory hard-won by stupidity. It's a foolproof formula, as long as you're not actually stupid."

"It's like always having the follow spot in the wrong place," said Vincent.

"It's not like that," Cappy replied. "It is that. Misdirection. Ask any amateur magician."

"It doesn't work with horse racing," Vincent said.

"Horses are not distractible," Cappy said. "That's recreation. Make money with men."

Vincent slept poorly, wondering if what Cappy had told him was the whole truth. For so many years the company of men—regular men—had been his respite from the artistic temperament of theater people. And now he was being told that the key to poker was acting. Perhaps it was. Perhaps there was no escaping one's fate. Take a job in a lighting factory at fourteen and somehow, you've already shaken hands with the devil. Without meaning to, he had spent his whole life with performers, and even married one. It seemed an earth-shattering revelation to him in the dark. But it didn't matter in the end. By the time he had gotten back from Cincinnati he wasn't sure he could explain it to anybody.

AURORA HAD BEEN waiting patiently for him to say something, wondering if he even remembered the trip across the bridge to Queens. There was a courtly distance between them, mutually respected. Then, on a Thursday evening, a week after he got back from Cincinnati, he said to her, just as she was about to settle down for a drink, "Come, take a walk with me."

There was a pond across the road, and a narrow dirt path that led a circle around it. The sun was dying, and it was chilly, but not yet unpleasantly so. They suited up in denim show jackets with *Other Voices* logos on the back and set out. For a while they walked in silence. When they reached the halfway point of the perimeter path Vincent finally spoke.

"I made an appointment," he said. "I'm going to have them look at my brain. You know why, of course."

"I do," said Aurora.

"The scan won't hurt me," he said, "but the results might. But something is wrong—I know that. I wanted you to know that I know."

"Thank you," Aurora said. "Even that lifts a great weight."

"There two things I think about all the time," Vincent said. "One is that this is a fish I may not be able to catch, and there has never been such a fish in all of my life so far, since the first one I caught back in Breezy Point when I was a kid. Never, not one."

Aurora was overfamiliar with this well-worn family metaphor and not charmed to hear it dragged out on such an alarming occasion, but she held in her annoyance as best she could.

Vincent had his ways, such as they were. And he wasn't likely to mention prison and Maggie Hynes—the big fish in his life that had gotten away. There was an agreed-upon news blackout about that one.

"I'm sorry," she said. "We all have those. Sometimes, though, I think, through the years, there have been fish you didn't even see."

"Is it a 'through the years' conversation? I wasn't expecting that."

"No," said Aurora. "I'm sorry. I'm trying to picture what you're going through and it just came out. It's not about me—I get that."

"It's okay," Vincent said. "In fact, that's what the second thing is about. Through the years, you know?"

They walked.

"I've behaved like an asshole sometimes," Vincent said finally. "And I don't particularly want to go into detail."

"Please don't."

"But through it all, since that first or second performance at the Winter Garden where I followed you with the light, I've been in love with you, and that's never changed. I just never thought a working-class guy could have you, or any of this, and that's still true. If my life's gonna be over soon, or I'm gonna lose my mind, I have to convince myself that I can have it, and that I do have it already—if I do. I want to know if you love me, or have ever loved me, or will still love me. Also because I feel like I am about to become a huge burden—I thought we had been through 'for better, for worse,' already but I don't think so now. Not yet, not the biggest part of it."

"Vincent, you swept me off my feet," she said. "And of course, I'm there for you—rain or shine."

"One thing I know," Vincent said, "even though I did terrible things that you did not do—at least I don't think you did, and now I don't care if you did—you did have a crush on Ike Harris at one time . . ."

"I never had a crush on Ike Harris," Aurora said, and it occurred to her that she was skating near the edge. A chill went through her as she spoke; she was not a liar, quite. *Crush* was not a word she could ever apply to her feelings for Ike Harris, and therefore she was on the right side of the law. But an old feeling rose in her, and she puzzled over a question that sometimes plagued her on sleepless nights, as Vincent breathed heavily in the bed next to her. Since the day she had told her parents that she was going to be a counselor at a Christian summer camp in Kansas, had she ever really told the whole truth, plainly and clearly? About anything? And the answer she gave herself was always the same: onstage she did. Mrs. Gibbs was the truth. The bereaved, hungry mother in *Other Voices* had been the truth. "It Might as Well Be Spring" was the truth. She told the truth when she was impersonating other people, which was, in itself, a kind of lie. As herself, if she had a self, she was not sure. Perhaps the world demanded half truths and well-constructed evasions, perhaps it was the only way to get from one end of life to the other. The stage made things easier, clearer, better. This was why, she believed, she'd had whatever success had come to her: Bathed in a spotlight she could tell the truth to a thousand people in an audience who could never quite bring themselves to tell it to one another or themselves.

They turned the curve across from the house and began a second circumnavigation of the pond. It was almost dark.

"There was a moment," Aurora said, "when I might have actually run off with Djanga Kimball, if she had asked. I really wanted to touch her. But we're both straight. Rare in this business. That was an odd time."

"I'd have paid to see the pictures," Vincent said,

"Vincent," Aurora said now, as the pond began to catch the glassy rays of the day's final sun, "I'll take care of you if that's what it comes down to, and I won't regret a thing about it. We've had a good life and I'd like it to continue, and I'd like a martini."

Compromises, she thought. *Who knows what I mean? Certainly not me.*

They turned back toward the house.

"I've raised a lot of money for the Actors Fund," Vincent said. "They have some very good facilities, residential facilities, and if it comes to that, you shouldn't hesitate."

"Vincent, don't be ridiculous," she said. "I said I wanted a drink, not to cry in my beer. You're going to be fine."

"I know I will," he said.

There was no truth in anything now.

19

The Cigar Box

VINCENT'S SLOW, tortuous decline was an exhausting trial for Aurora, and who can ever know what it was for Vincent himself? Many days he wasn't sure of anything, except that it could only go in one direction. For a long time, he was almost himself. He harped on the welcoming atmosphere of the Actors Fund facilities that he visited, which he seemed almost to look forward to entering at the appropriate moment. He drove, while he still could, to the local tobacconist in Larchmont, bought a modest box of cigars, and dumped the contents on the way home. Over the course of years, he placed small things in it to take with him when the day came—bits of memorabilia, most of it his, some of it Aurora's. He grew attached to the box and its contents for no reason at all that she could fathom, but she never objected. This was his business, and the meaning of his business became more and more difficult to discern over time.

He began to shower every other day instead of every day, with the explanation that the soap lasted longer that way.

"And, you see," he said to her, "I have always measured time by how often I have to open the box on a new cake of soap. I feel like if the soap wears down twice as slowly, maybe I will too. It's nonsense, but I do it anyhow."

From time to time he harangued Aurora about the time he'd spent in prison, blaming his deteriorating condition on having had his brain frozen by the deadly routine of convict life. At one point he told her that he was going to find Seth Kuriansky, the terrible lawyer, and give him a piece of his mind, "although," he said, "I don't have much of a piece to give, thanks to him and his fucking jail. I can't afford to give away any."

Sometime in 2011, it became clear to Aurora that she could no longer let him out of the house on his own, that he could not drive anymore, and that he was never completely present in the moment—those lucid periods where he sounded almost like himself, where he could discuss politics and theater and auto mechanics with some clarity, had evaporated slowly, like the water sloshed onto a swimming pool deck on a hot day, until there was no moisture left, only a hard, hot, impermeable surface. Aurora had not worked in two years, forgoing even the Carlyle gigs, and appearing only at occasional charity galas. Within the industry everyone knew what she was up to and up against. She herself was a kind of prisoner in Larchmont. From time to time, simply as a matter of hearing a friendly voice, she told herself, she would put in a call to Ike Harris.

Ike had made the determination to give up playing at the end of the *Chitty Chitty Bang Bang* run. It was an inglorious way to go out. But although he never played another performance as hapless and full of error as the one he played on the night of his preshow cocktail with Aurora, he was still going downhill. His teeth were giving him trouble, which only made him think of the rainy afternoon all those years ago when he had presided over the sudden collapse of Tommy Ladnier in a Harlem walk-up. He had, of course, escaped the straitened circumstances of his early idol's life, but Ladnier's sucked-in, haunted face visited him from time to time when he missed a note, and he couldn't help but notice the overly polite deference with which the rest of the band had begun to treat him. He was not a fool; he knew he was being invited out, by the gods, by the world, by the band—by his teeth.

The week before they closed, he took Stan Tucker aside between the matinee and the evening on a Wednesday and told him.

"I want to apologize," he said. "I blew up at you for no reason, at least no reason you had anything to do with, and there is no excuse for a member of the band to do that. If I hadn't been the contractor, you probably would have called the union, but you didn't, and I'm grateful for that. I just want to tell you I've made a decision that I'm not going to play another show."

Stan began to object, but Ike held up a hand sternly.

"I wouldn't hire me," Ike said. "I'm not a good enough trumpet player for a good, conscientious contractor to hire. And I am a good, conscientious contractor. Of course, it's painful to say it, and let's just say that I took out some of those emotions on you, and I apologize."

The pit was empty except for the two of them. They looked at each other and then, completely to Ike's surprise, Stan threw his arms around Ike and held him, like a son holds an elderly father. The two men had never touched each other before, not so much as a handshake.

Who knows, Ike thought, as they awkwardly disengaged. *Maybe he thinks he's now a part of history. Not likely any history anyone will ever hear about, but it still felt good.*

"I'm sorry, Ike," Stan said. "And I'm honored that you told me, of all people."

"Sometimes it happens that way," Ike said. And his career as a player was suddenly over.

It seemed, perhaps, that he was a small part of history after all, for as soon as his retirement from playing had become known, Lil flew in to see him—she was between jobs, having moved from women's studies to women's health to women's gerontology—and it was while she was sitting in the breakfast room drinking coffee that the phone rang. She picked it up and handed it to Ike. He looked at her and saw, really for the first time, that his daughter was now more than middle-aged. She wore reading glasses and a loose burgundy cardigan as she sat among scattered sections of the *Times,* and might, for all the world, have been his sister. It took him a moment to clear that thought out of his mind, by which time he had been connected to Clayton Monroe, producer of *Other Voices* and now the chairman of the Tony Awards Administration Committee.

"Ike," he said. "You doing all right?"

"I've never been better," Ike said, suddenly worried that he had made some fatal error for which he was about to be punished by the authorities.

"You're about to be even better," Monroe said. "I'm deputized to tell you that you've just won a special Tony for lifetime achievement."

Ike was silent. His mind scattered. It was as if someone he liked and respected had told him the date of his funeral was all set. But, of course, it was well intended—a cheerful, congratulatory call. Still, he couldn't speak.

"Ike?" Monroe said, a little uncertainly. "You okay? You're winning a Tony Award."

"But," Ike said, "will that make for good television?"

It was not intended to be televised but was presented during a commercial break. Still, Ike bought a new tuxedo—Bond Clothing Store was no more, though a restaurant around the corner had been named in its honor, and he had to go to Brooks Brothers. He bought a ticket for Lil and asked Missy to attend, but she no longer left New Mexico, where she had long since retired.

He then wrote a brief note to Clayton Monroe requesting that the award be presented to him by Aurora Shelton.

When the time came, he stood in the wings of Radio City Music Hall, where he had occasionally contracted orchestras and played in the holiday show, and listened to the litany of his accomplishments. Aurora sounded like she meant to immortalize him, but the list struck Ike as something that no one could possibly be interested in. He had worked on 141 Broadway shows, tours, out-of-town casualties, and special events, playing the trumpet in over a hundred of them, yet no one outside the industry had ever heard of him. When he heard his name, he entered, took the silver disc mounted on an ebony base, and walked into Aurora's embrace, where he received the first real, meaningful kiss he had gotten from her in forty-five years. The force of it took him by surprise, and for a moment he couldn't speak at all. Had she intended it? Was it impulsive? What did it mean?

His discombobulation touched the crowd, but for all the wrong reasons. There he was, a little old man, hero to the industry, unknown to the public, finally getting his recognition after all these decades of plowing the fields. As he stepped to the microphone, pulling himself together, he thought, *Bless their hearts—if that's what six thousand people want to think, let them think it. This is show business, after all.*

He thanked the usual suspects, the Broadway League and the American Theatre Wing, his longtime associate Cecelia Austin, who was watching on TV from North Carolina, and his daughter for putting up with him and going to ball games with him when she was a girl. Then he took a breath and offered a last bit of gratitude.

"Most especially," he said, "I'd like to thank Aurora Shelton. I played her first show, which ran a week, and her most recent one, which won the Tony. So, from my perspective, in terms of my own career, she's my good-luck charm, and it's very encouraging."

And then he was gone, and the show went on.

He did not go to the ball afterward. He was too old for afterparties, he reasoned, although he did not sleep either. The next morning, Lil looked over the breakfast table at him and, when she had his attention, raised her eyebrows dramatically.

"So?" she asked. "The hug, the kiss? Inquiring minds want to know."

"Everybody's in show business," Ike said. 'Let's leave it at that."

"But—the woman you love," she said.

"Honey, this is not the kind of thing one discusses with one's daughter."

"I'm fifty-one years old," Lil said. "I work in hospice now. I don't think you can shock me."

"What makes me crazy," Ike said, "is that Aphrodite drops in so infrequently, but won't ever leave you alone. It's like she's a drummer on some far-off, never-ending tour of *Miss Saigon* who calls to complain about once every five years. Why can't she stay in the city and invite Aurora and me to lunch and straighten all this out? You're fifty-one, that makes me eighty-two. You want to know the truth, Ms. Hospice? I haven't had a real erection in a decade, maybe more, but I still dream of her. And in my dreams . . ."

"You dream?"

"Not really every night, but always the same dream. I'm standing in a beautiful music store—a little boutique store, like it's in the West Village or someplace. And the wall is lined with trumpets. All the trumpets I could ever want. And I see the one I've never been able to afford and it's just sitting there mounted on the wall and it's for sale, like all the others, and there's no reason why I can't have it—I have the money, the trumpet's right there on the wall . . . but as I reach for it, Aurora Shelton comes in the front door. I turn and she walks into my arms, and I hold her, and all the trumpets are gone, and I'm happy, and suddenly I realize it's a dream. But I tell myself if I hold her hard enough, if I don't let go, maybe I can carry her from the dream world to the real world, and when I wake up, she'll be with me."

"That never works," said Lil. "I've had that dream."

"No, it does not," said Ike. "But last night she kissed me."

"No erection," said Lil.

"Don't get fresh."

Ike never asked Aurora about the kiss, and she never volunteered any information about it either. They continued to talk from time to time, as Vincent's condition gradually deteriorated, and Ike maintained his work schedule, racking up multiple contracts in each season, even as the bands got smaller, the sound became more electrified, and the nature of the shows themselves marched relentlessly to different, more contemporary beats. Broadway stayed behind the times, but it no longer hid from rock. There was no point in denying the value of the national music. He found himself hiring players half a century younger than himself, and soon had dozens on his list. They played in bands that sometimes required no more than a rhythm section and a couple of extra guitars. But the work—and the workload—never seemed to change.

During this period, sometime after 2011, Aurora realized that, without meaning to, she had retired. Her life consisted primarily of taking care of Vincent, who had become ever more erratic. He rarely spoke, though he could when he wanted to, and was generally docile, with occasional outbursts so fiery that they reminded her of her father, which triggered a lever of fear that was always somewhere within her, waiting to be thrown.

In his shifts from indolent distraction to fierce and sometimes physical threats, he had become, she realized, both of her parents at once. She tried to banish that thought, and another less kindly one: She believed, to her shame, that on the day of her parents' fiery auto crash she had been freed of the terror, the mortification, and the paralyzing sense of responsibility to them forever. Now, when she least expected it, it was back. And her skills for coping were surprisingly more primitive than she would have expected, given the decades that had passed and the experience that had been gained.

Yet here was Vincent, descending the stairs almost shouting, pointing a finger at her, and demanding, "Where is it? What the hell have you done with it?"

She looked up to see her husband, a three-day scraggle of whiskers on his cheeks, his white hair tossed in all directions, wearing a bathrobe over long pants and slippers. She was surprised only to be unsurprised. How had she let it come to this?

She rose from the sofa, where she had been nursing a small Manhattan, and tried her best to be motherly, which sometimes worked on these occasions.

"What, honey?" she asked. "Where is what?"

"The box! The goddamn cigar box! Have you hidden it somewhere?"

She moved to him and tried to take his arm as he descended to ground level, but he batted it away angrily.

"Don't touch me!"

Her hands moved back and upward reflexively, as if she had been told to raise them by a cop or a street mugger with a cheap pistol. *This is my husband,* she told herself. *He doesn't mean any of this. He's in there somewhere, but neither of us can find him.*

Vincent stormed past her and into the garage, which was now kept locked from the outside so that he could not wander off. Once he was safely out of sight, she began to climb the stairs, snorting with anger and not a little afraid. She was ticking off in her mind the tools that were out there—a bow saw, a hammer, anything that might have been used to harm her in an obvious way had long since been locked up. Screwdriver? Crowbar? She wasn't sure.

She let herself into his bedroom—he now slept in what had once been Little Vin's room—and went to the bottom drawer of the bureau. The cigar box was in its usual place, nestled in an old bath towel, swaddled like a newborn. She took it from its place and was about to start down when a thought occurred to her. She turned and went into her own bedroom, the one they had shared for thirty years. The bureau had been torn apart. Her clothes were scattered across the bed and on the floor; the drawers were flipped on their sides, cast across the room. Vincent had ransacked the wrong room.

How did I not hear this? she wondered. She recalled a scuffling sound from above but realized that it was not an unfamiliar phenomenon in the house anymore. Vincent stormed around, doing one thing and another up there, and sometimes she felt like the tortured souls in *Long Day's Journey into Night,* trying not to hear Mary Tyrone stumbling through the upper story in a morphine haze. But nothing like this had ever happened before. She considered cleaning up the mess but decided to wait. She took the box, which she had vowed never to look in, back down the stairs and into the garage.

Vincent had the hood of the car up and was staring at the engine, as if he had plans for it, though what they might have been was impossible to say. His temper had cooled, and he was humming softly—a tune she could not discern. She moved to him carefully, never knowing what might come next.

"The box," she said. "Here it is."

He looked up from the engine and stared at her in obvious confusion. Just the attempt to focus, to recognize why it was that she was standing there holding his precious collection of whatever was in there broke her heart. There was so little of him left.

"My box," he said.

"You were looking for it," she said.

"Was I?"

"You were. At least that's what you said."

He held out his hands to her, and she placed the box in them. He held it and tears began to course down his face, which caused her to begin to cry as well. He put the box on the car radiator and moved to her, clung to her like a bewildered child. She could feel the wracking sobs shaking his entire body. She held on for dear life, knowing that he was doing the same thing. Finally the shaking stopped; the wail he had been emitting at regular intervals slowed, then ceased. He pulled himself back from her and looked at her, his hands on her shoulders. She could see from his eyes that he was not 100 percent sure of her identity. He looked and looked, and finally he spoke.

"I want to go home," he said.

"Vincent, you are home. This is our house."

"Not this home," he said. "I don't know where I am."

"You're home," she said, "in the garage. This is your car. There's your box, I'm your wife. Aurora."

Vincent shook his head. His eyes refocused, and Aurora could see a lucidity there that sometimes reappeared, as if the tracks had been repaired, just for a moment.

"The Actors Fund Home," he said. "I can't stand to see you like this anymore. Please. Take me to the Actors Fund Home."

—

AURORA CAME HOME to an empty house. Little Vin and Gar had helped with the move, but then she asked them to go. They had shows to work anyhow. She wanted to walk in the front door alone. She wanted her autonomy, at least for a moment. She put her purse on the table in the foyer and walked through each room. In the den she picked up a cachepot with a begonia in it that needed a trim. She carried it through the rest of the ground floor, then put it in the kitchen sink. She went up the stairs and inspected the master bedroom—it was now her bedroom, forever after—and then the children's rooms. The place was familiar, welcoming, cold and empty. She knew that she and Vincent would never set foot in it together again. That reality would have to wait until she was prepared to face it.

She went back down to the kitchen and dealt with the begonia, replacing it in the den looking sprucer than it had. Really, there was nothing else that needed doing, so she made herself a Manhattan. She toasted her mother, Beatrice, and Djanga Kimball, the two women who, through no fault of their own, had provided such scant solidarity. She thought she owed it to Ike Harris to let him know that Vincent had been moved, but it seemed disrespectful to her marriage and her husband, and so that, too, would have to wait. She went to the piano, where pictures of both kids at various ages shared space with the two Tony Awards.

20

GREEN-WOOD

WHEN *VINCENT HAD* been at the Actors Fund home for six months she faced the reality that he wasn't coming home anymore. His wardrobe had been the first thing to go, donated to the Larchmont Goodwill. The personal articles were next—the pills, hairbrushes, extra cans of shaving cream and unused cologne, bottles of which he bought in quantity. They went into a trash bin one night late, when Aurora couldn't sleep. Old contracts and memos were next—a couple of file drawers that had lived in the basement for decades. The house was mostly purged of the things she could no longer stand to confront. And yet it remained, in some ineffable way, Vincent's house, their house. Having disposed of the last of it, she lay back in bed for a few minutes to reassure herself that the house was really empty, really hers. Then she reached for the phone and called Ike Harris.

"Meet me tomorrow," he said when she told him they needed to speak. "I'm at the Gershwin, but meet me on the corner of 50th, by the subway station next to the Winter Garden. I have a lunch break at two."

Lil looked up at him quizzically from her perch by the window. She had moved in to take care of him, though he needed no caring for, and had taken a job at St. Luke's Roosevelt, heading up the hospice program. Ike suspected it was about free rent as much as anything else, as much as he loved her.

"Aphrodite business," he said.

"And you're meeting outside the Winter Garden." She almost smirked. "Clever."

"You have to do what you can," he said.

JUST AFTER TWO Aurora and Ike began to walk east, through throngs of tourists speaking multiple languages who were still pouring into the theater for a matinee of *Mamma Mia!*

"There used to be a perfectly nice streetwalker named Fanta on this corner," Ike said.

"She named herself after an orange drink?" Aurora asked.

"That's not the point," Ike said. "Look what we've come through. And look at the landscape. It's another planet. I can remember true glamour in the forties. And true hell in the seventies. Now what fresh hell is this?"

"Dorothy Parker," said Aurora. "No one remembers Dorothy Parker. Listen, Ike, I know why we're walking here, and I appreciate the nostalgia, in a way, but I've got to tell you: I've moved Vincent into an Actors Fund Home where they can take care of him. So, I'm not feeling very nostalgic, about that, or about anything else. I just wanted to talk."

Ike took her hand.

"No one's taken my hand in a very long time," she said.

"I mean only concern and affection," Ike said. "I'm sorry. You must be going through hell."

"Someday I'll tell you. It's full of surprises."

"I'm sorry," Ike said again, wondering if there were any more powerless words than these in the whole language.

They walked in silence, crossing Seventh Avenue and heading east, out of the district.

"Are we really going to take this walk?" Aurora asked.

"Only if you want to," Ike replied.

"I don't know what I want," Aurora said. "Does it seem to you sometimes that we've been sleeping together for fifty years?"

Ike contemplated revealing Sid Lupowitz's calculation of their would-be encounters had that been the case but demurred. Indelicacy had its place, and this was not it.

"Aurora," he said, "we don't have to walk. We can go to the Warwick and have tea, or a drink. It's just down the block."

She clutched his hand, not affectionately, but as if he had suggested committing murder.

"Please, no," she said. "Let's walk. Talk to me. Tell me something. Something about Broadway."

"What the hell do I know about Broadway anymore?"

"The glamour part. When I was a little girl. When you were here, and I was dreaming about coming here. When did you first see Broadway?"

"Is that why you wanted to see me?"

"I think I just want to get away from today and yesterday for a little bit," she said. "Just a little vacation from it. Does that make you feel used? I'm sorry if it does."

"Not at all," said Ike, though he wasn't quite sure how it made him feel. Mainly he felt lucky to be in her presence, whatever her motives might have been. Her misery was a sad opportunity, but he had to admit to himself that it was an opportunity, nonetheless.

He told her the story of Henry Vesey, the piano player at *Pal Joey*. Even as he told it, it seemed to grow more remote, to the point where he wasn't even sure it had ever happened. But she began to relax as he talked. He told her about the war and

Poke Belmore and the blue lightbulbs. He reminded her that she had wandered into the tent where he was practicing when she was a little girl, and she actually giggled.

"Sometimes I think I remember that," she said, "and sometimes I think I've just heard about it and think I remember it. I have lots of those kinds of memories."

He told her anything he could think of, some it no doubt invented, none of it painful. When they reached Second Avenue, where L'Amèrique had once stood, she was ready to go home. She thanked him and asked if he would put her in a cab to Grand Central.

"No, no," Ike said. "Watch this."

He took out his cellphone and tapped it repeatedly. This was beyond anything that Aurora understood. Within a couple of minutes, a black sedan pulled up beside them, and Ike opened the door.

"He'll take you home," Ike said.

"To Larchmont?" she asked.

"I already told him," Ike said, holding up the cellphone and waving it at her proudly. "Progress," he said, "one way or the other. And goodbye forever to Fanta the streetwalker, may she rest comfortably wherever she is."

He leaned down and kissed her softly, and then watched as the car headed east on 50th toward the FDR Drive.

The next time he saw her, as it happened, was also the last time he played the trumpet in public. It was another sad opportunity. On a blistering late July afternoon, in an apartment on 106th and Riverside, Charlie Vodery exhaled for the last time, as his wife and three children hovered around his bed. He had been on heavy doses of morphine for days and had passed the time erratically tapping out rhythms with his fingers on the bedcovers, in a pattern that seemed at times to resemble "Take the 'A' Train" and at other times to be Bessie Smith's "Gimme a Pigfoot," according to his wife, suddenly a widow. And then, he was gone.

Sid Lupowitz delivered the news to Ike, and also the instructions that went with it.

"He wanted a jazz funeral, but in Brooklyn—at Green-Wood," Sid told him over the phone. "He said if it was good enough for Bernstein . . . some of the Ellington guys are planning on being there, and you should brush up on 'Didn't He Ramble.' The rest you can fake. How's your teeth?"

It was humid and threatening on the day of Charlie Vodery's funeral. The family and friends followed the coffin through the labyrinth of Green-Wood Cemetery, trailed by two dozen musicians playing Vodery's arrangement of Ellington's "Black and Tan Fantasy," which was, in turn, a reworking of Chopin's funeral march. Ike Harris was honored, self-conscious about being one of the only white men in the band, and sweating profusely through his orchestra pit suit in the heavy, unforgiving air. On several occasions he thought he would have to drop out, to sit down, to quit. But that was not an option, he told himself. This was Vodery.

He unbuttoned his jacket at the gravesite, and someone offered him a white folding chair, which he took gratefully. When the coffin had been lowered and the last words had been spoken, the crowd turned back, and the band rose as one and launched into "Didn't He Ramble," which Ike had been woodshedding for three days in the apartment, much to Lil's annoyance. He had insisted on going to the funeral alone, promising that when he returned, she would never have to hear the damn song again—but he was going to play it right at least the one time it mattered. Now, he thought at certain moments, he might blow his heart out, but he reasoned, as he had during his first heart attack, this would not be the worst way to go out, except for distracting attention from the proper corpse. No, it wouldn't do. Vodery had to have his day.

When the band reached the curb on the corner at Hamilton Avenue and Sam Naples Road he felt a hand on his elbow and lowered the trumpet from his lip. Aurora, whom he had not seen before, was standing at his side, holding him lightly.

"Don't be too big a hero," she said. "He knows you loved him."

"He wrote that damn trumpet solo," Ike said. "The one where you were packing your suitcase. It could break your heart."

"What are you talking about?" Aurora asked.

"Nothing," Ike said. "Could you take me to the emergency room?"

He had a pacemaker installed the next afternoon. In a day or two he felt better.

Aurora checked up on him for a few days after that, and then they retreated to their customary corners. *As long as Vincent Donnelly was alive,* he thought, this is *what I have to do. And what makes me think that when he goes, I'll be here to see it? After all, I'm the oldest.* He put the trumpet in the coat closet on the shelf above the wooden dowel that held the hangers. As he climbed down from the footstool he now needed in order to reach the shelf, he wondered briefly if he'd see it again.

It did not pay to be preoccupied with such thoughts, he told himself, and he went back to work. He had *The Addams Family.* He had *How the Grinch Stole Christmas.* Revivals of *Gypsy* and *Anything Goes* he got, of course. Somehow, he landed *Passing Strange,* with its outré semi-rock band. This led to a revival of *Hair. Bloody Bloody Andrew Jackson* he had, although he didn't understand a single thing about it. Sitting in the back of the Newman Theater at the Public during a run-through he said, aloud, “I kind of like it—I just don’t understand what the hell it is.” There was no one sitting next to him. And he realized for the first time that he was beginning to talk to himself. And then came the new eighties jukebox musical at the Winter Garden.

21

Can You Fix This?

Ike Harris stood for a moment in the aisle of the Winter Garden, watching Vincent Donnelly's ghost merging with the innumerable others who inhabited the place, some for a century or more. Tino Flores, the Cuban music director, had already slipped a phone from its holster and dialed 911. The others stood frozen on the spot, except for Ike, who got back down on his knees and put a hand on Vincent's brow, offering a silent benediction in the name of some religion—he could never have said which one—to his lifelong rival.

Vincent's fist, which he had been shaking threateningly at Ike moments earlier, loosened slightly, and Ike could see that there was blood there too—that whatever was in Vincent's hand had lacerated his palm and fingers as he clutched at it. Moments before, Vincent, very much alive if completely demented, had shouted at Ike.

"Can you fix this? I'm supposed to be the one who can fix anything! But I can't fix this!"

Now Ike wanted to know what it was that Vincent thought he might be able to fix; gently he prised the dead man's fingers open. Inside the fist was a shard-like piece of shellac, the shattered center of a 78 rpm record, like the ones Ike had grown up with. The label was torn and now bloodstained. Ike took it from Vincent's hand and, as unassumingly as possible, slipped it into his own pocket.

He called Aurora and told her that an ambulance was on its way. When the paramedics arrived and he determined that they were taking Vincent to Lenox Hill Hospital, he called again to update her.

"Don't drive yourself," he said. "I'm sending a car."

"Do you think . . . ?" her voice trailed off.

"I think it's trouble," Ike said. "But what do I know? I'm a trumpet player." It was an old excuse that had worn out its welcome, and it wasn't even true anymore.

He beat her to the hospital by almost an hour. Vincent was in an operating room or someplace—you never knew what happened to people—hopeless cases or otherwise—once those double doors closed. Aurora entered the ER waiting area, her complexion paler than Ike had ever seen it. She had put on no makeup and wore a knit cardigan under a raincoat. He could see, for the first time really, that he was confronting and comforting an old woman. And he knew, in that instant, that she was looking at an old man. She took both of his hands, but did not want to be embraced or kissed. She wanted only to sit down. Around them various family groups huddled in chairs and sofas, reading, tapping on phones, some of the children scribbling in workbooks or coloring books. The murmuring chatter surrounding them was in at least three languages that Ike could detect: Spanish, Mandarin, and some Indian dialect that he could not identify. Aurora didn't speak, didn't pick up a magazine, didn't glance at the TV set on the wall or acknowledge its ceaseless prattle. She sat very still, awaiting the inevitable. She did not have to wait long.

Within a quarter of an hour a doctor in green scrubs entered and went directly to her—she was the only possible wife of Vincent Donnelly in the room.

"I'm sorry," he said, as she rose to meet him. He also was Indian, but with only a trace of an accent. Aurora nodded.

"Can I see him?" she asked.

"Come with me," said the doctor.

"Aurora," Ike said as she turned to follow the doctor. She stopped and looked back at him.

"I'm so sorry," he said.

"I have to go see my husband," she replied.

She turned back and followed the doctor, who was by now several paces ahead of her.

THE FUNERAL WAS scheduled for almost a week later. During the intervening days, Aurora had been in Larchmont with the boys, both of whom were on running shows, and trekked dutifully between Times Square and the suburbs each day so that they could comfort their mother. They were company, but not much comfort. Aurora, fueled by the Manhattans she used to watch her mother consume with such passion, felt almost like she was in competition with her. She shuttlecocked between rage and guilt, unable to settle in any one room, or on any one mood or point of view. She haunted the place. Then she looked at the empty glass that she was about to refill.

The only imprint left was Ike Harris. She had scrubbed him from her soul decades ago, then let him back in. No one was to blame for this but her, unless you could count Charlie Vodery, who had insisted on hiring him for the pit band of *Other Voices*. But how could Vodery be blamed? It was her own failing, or need, or something. And then, on the other hand, she wondered, particularly in the dark, on one of several sleepless nights, if she wasn't grateful? How could such a thing even be contemplated after fifty-one years of marriage? She went downstairs and made herself another drink. Sleep had to come some time.

On the eve of Vincent Donnelly's funeral, Ike was sitting across from Lil in his kitchen nursing a bourbon. He was doing everything he could to interpret the lacquered shard he had discovered in Vincent's hand. The song title and artist could not be discerned, but the matrix number was visible, and, with the use of a magnifying glass, Lil had been able to decode and write down the series of numbers and letters that identified it. Ike recognized the design pattern of the label, which was white, and featured the capital letter *L* just above the matrix ID: P29031Y.

"That's a rare label," he said. "'Liberty Music Shop.' They struggled along using the Brunswick recording studio during the forties. Liberty sold the records out of the store and by mail. I played a date with some band for that label not long after the war—I don't remember who. I wonder how he got it."

The Internet revealed the crucial information: Liberty Music Shop's record number L-310, Matrix P29031Y was a recording of Ethel Waters singing "Taking a Chance on Love," recorded with the Martin Beck Theatre Orchestra, led by Max Meth.

"I knew Max Meth too," Ike said. "Miserable son of a bitch."

Lil was tapping away at her laptop keys but looked up at this observation.

"A long time ago," Ike said, feeling invited to talk, "there used to be a record store on 45th Street between Fifth and Sixth. Not Liberty, they were on Madison. It was a very strange place—the walls were lined from floor to ceiling with old records—LPs, but also 78s, each in a plain cardboard sleeve with the matrix number written on it in pen. It was run by a little guy with a fringe of black hair around his head. He wore half glasses on a string and a white shirt and a bow tie. Feinstein? Epstein? Something like that. And he was a savant. If you slipped a cardboard sleeve out from any place in the shop and told him the matrix number, he would tell you the name of the song, the artist, and the label. There must have been ten thousand records in there, and you couldn't stump him. He was a magician. He was the Internet before the Internet, and it was a hell of a lot more fun. He was an actual living person, with a living brain—a very peculiar one. He hated to sell a record. And if he only had one copy, he wouldn't sell it. He would make you an acetate copy with a white label with the title typed out on an old Remington that he kept on the counter. I bought one once—Walter Huston singing 'September Song,' with 'The Scars' on the B side. Acetates didn't last that long, but if you wore it out, you could always go back, and he'd sell you a replacement. Half price."

Ike took a long pull from the bourbon beside him and looked out the window. It was starting to rain. Lil tapped her keyboard and looked up.

"You can get Ethel Waters singing 'You Had It Coming' on Bluebird from eBay," she said. "Fourteen ninety-five. Not the typed-up one on the Remington—the original."

"Seems like a shame," Ike said. "It was more fun when it wasn't so simple. Where's the hunt? Where's the little guy with the half glasses and the parlor trick?"

He paused and thought for a moment. "What about "Taking a Chance on Love?"

"Always a good idea," Lil said.

"Don't be a smartass. The record not the idea."

Lil tapped the keyboard.

"That must be a rare one," she said. "On Liberty Music Shop? It's being offered at four hundred dollars."

"Buy it," Ike said.

THE FOLLOWING DAY was the funeral, a big affair attended by union members from across the city. Even a couple of younger members of the Ennis family were there, dispatched, no doubt, by one of the patriarchs. By the time Ike arrived at St. Malachy's, accompanied by Lil, he knew quite a lot about that shattered record.

This was hardly the moment to have such thoughts, he told himself, but perhaps if he waited. Anything else would be worse than misplaced honesty—it would be dancing on Vincent Donnelly's grave. But whatever the shard of shellac meant, maybe it would help him, save him even. But of course Aurora would immediately identify that part of him that was glad Vincent was gone. It was her blessing and curse to be able to do. It was what made her an artist who could become other people onstage, who could see the truth, ingest it like cigarette smoke, and speak it as she exhaled. She had seen the center of him: She would know what he was after. Still, he was hopeful for the first time in years, and there was no moral dimension to it at all. Who was he to Vincent Donnelly or Vincent Donnelly to him? This scavenger piece of his soul that wanted only what it wanted would not stay quiet either. In the turmoil there was only one thing to do: put his faith in the talisman that he had been gifted from a dead man's fist.

Ike had arrived at St. Malachy's at the last minute, so as to sit in the back and not upset the widow, but he was not the last one in the door. Just as the service was beginning a middle-aged woman with artificially red hair covered with a black scarf knelt in the aisle, crossed herself, and slid in beside him. She nodded pleasantly. He had never met Maggie Hynes, and never would. She was wrapped in a black trench coat, wore sunglasses, and was doing her best to be invisible; as soon as the service ended, she rose, crossed herself again, and slipped out as unobtrusively as she had arrived, unrecognized and unknown, though she had spent most of the service wiping her eyes and anxiously threading a handkerchief through her fingers. Where she went from the church no one would ever know.

Aurora was in the front row, flanked by her two sons; Djanga Kimball sat behind them. It was the first time Ike had seen the composer since the closing-night party of *Other Voices*. She had spent the intervening years making her own albums, winning Grammys, and touring. She was, in fact, the biggest celebrity in the place, and looked well.

He sat through the funeral dry-eyed, in a state of confusion. Afterward, he met Aurora out front on 49th Street. They had not seen each other since the hospital, and she received his unspoken condolences without comment. He hugged her, but could feel her body stiffen slightly, and he let her go.

Then the two boys were there—Little Vin and Gareth, both looking sturdy and well fed at forty-eight and fifty—to help her into the car that would carry them to the cemetery. There was a reception in Larchmont—Catholics didn't sit shiva; the Irish usually had wakes before the funeral, but Ike was dubious that there had been one. Ike went back to the apartment. He was determined to put things in place.

FOR THE NEXT THREE or four months, Aurora subsisted mainly on Manhattans and saltines spread with peanut butter. There was an occasional omelet, and there were summer tomatoes. Little Vin and Gar visited but quickly tired of her long silences, and even more of her occasional rambles through the past, which were seldom coherent enough to be interesting. They worried for her and tried gently to move her away from her diet of grief, alcohol, and recrimination, or whatever it was. This might have continued indefinitely had she not set off to get some cash one afternoon in early June and crashed headlong into the drive-up window of the Chase branch in Larchmont. Alarms shrieked all around her and she found herself almost unable to breathe. Her head had slapped against the windshield, and a splitting headache enveloped her, but she seemed otherwise unharmed.

As the police cars arrived her first concern was not for her injuries, if any, but whether she could pass a sobriety test, and the ensuing bad publicity that might follow. She could not. At the police station she called Little Vin, who picked up his cell.

"I drove into the bank," she said.

He seemed puzzled.

"No, I mean I really drove into the bank."

"Mom?"

"I'm at the police station in Larchmont waiting to be booked. First call someone from the Ennis's or someplace and keep it out of the papers. Then come get me, with a lawyer."

Her license was revoked permanently, and she paid a fine and consented to enter a rehabilitation hospital voluntarily, agreeing not to leave the state until her treatment was complete. She spent the night in Larchmont with the two boys. At dinner, as she nursed what was putatively to be a last bourbon and sweet vermouth, while Gareth pestered her to have a few bites of chicken and some salad, Little Vin pushed back his chair and looked at her.

"Ma," he said, using a term he employed only when things were serious. "I need you to listen to me."

"I'm listening," she said. But she held her glass between them—scant protection, but it was all she had.

"Gar and I talked this over," Little Vin said as Gareth lowered his head toward his plate and scooped up a spoonful of mashed potatoes.

"Here's what we think. Retirement doesn't suit you. Being a widow doesn't suit you. I know it's hard, but they just don't suit you. Unless, of course, you want to sit around this place and drink yourself to death, which is a definite alternative."

"Jesus, Vinny!" she said, but the words did not come out all that smoothly.

"Lemme finish," Little Vin said. "The point is, if that's your choice, at least you can't drive. And me and Gar will take care of you no matter what. But from our point of view, it's a shitty choice, a stupid choice. But it's your choice. So go to the place, get yourself straightened out, and we'll talk."

"Is this your idea of an intervention?" she asked, stifling a laugh.

"Intervention, my ass," Little Vin said. "We're not asking you to do anything. We think your life is lousy, and you should just make up your mind and tell us what you want to do with it. It's not our life—it's your life."

"That's all we wanted to say," added Gar, putting down his silverware and pulling on a can of Schlitz.

"Fair enough," Aurora said. "And you said it."

"That," said Gar, "and we love you of course. Whatever happens. We love you."

She did think about it. The boys were supposed to take her to Treatment Alternatives in White Plains at nine, but she rose before the sun, packed a light bag, and quietly called a cab, which took her to JFK. Using a passport for identification—the license was gone—she bought a ticket to Albuquerque via Denver. As had so often happened in her life, the moment had come to flee. She would have preferred a long train ride, but it was too dangerous. There would be too many opportunities for her to be picked off. She dialed Little Vin from the plane before it took off, awakening him.

"I'm on a plane," she said. "You're not to worry about me

or come after me. I've done enough damage for the moment. I'm going to bleach this out of me."

"Mom. You can't get on a plane," Little Vin said. "You're confined to the state."

"We're moving down the runway," she said, "and they're making me turn the phone off." She snapped it shut.

The arid, beautiful orange rock all around struck her as a model of breathtaking austerity, just what she was seeking. The city itself held no appeal at all. But she took a cab to a hotel, looked at a map provided by the front desk, and located a moderately remote town with a motel in it at the edge of the Navajo lands. After spending one night in town, she got as much cash as she could from the ATM in the lobby and took a cab to the little town of Grants, checked in to the motel, and called the Native Hearts Hotline to offer herself as a volunteer in the afternoons. She did not know, and would never find out, that Missy Cozzens, retired art consultant, mother of Ike Harris's daughter, had been in Santa Fe for just over a decade, doyenne of her own social circle, as far from Broadway as she could get.

After a restless night's sleep, thirsty for alcohol and suffering from a blistering headache, Aurora rose with the sun and began to explore the area behind the motel. By nine, she had found what she was looking for—a secluded flat rock plateau, slightly up the mountain toward the Acoma Reservation, surrounded by barren orange hills and distant mesas. She went back to the patio behind her room and dragged the shredding aluminum lounge chair, which was covered in polyester tubing, out to her hideout, slathered her arms and legs with sunblock, and lay down to suffer.

For three months, hoping the boys would have enough sense to collect the mail and pay the bills, she walked out each morning in the sun, applied the sunblock, and challenged the heat to drive her back indoors, which it never succeeded in doing. While she began in a bathing suit, she realized after two or three days that she would not meet another human being up there, and took to the discipline of lying completely naked, trying her best not to observe her own body, of which, in her mind there was nothing left to be proud. She wore the darkest sunglasses she could and alternated between looking at the spectacular orange mountains, the sere roadways, and the empty fields and cacti, and keeping her eyes closed. For the first week she experienced vicious symptoms of alcohol withdrawal, shaking uncontrollably, battling headaches and cramps. But during the second week they abated, and by the first of July, she found herself dozing whenever she felt the need. The racket in her brain slowed, and she allowed herself no new thoughts, focused as she was on purging the old ones.

Each afternoon she returned to the room and dressed, and was picked up by a Native Hearts van, which took her to the hotline's quarters in a low, one-story adobe-style mini-mall in what there was of downtown Grants. She had completed her two-day training course after her second week in town, when the shakes had abated, and now she settled into a chair at a phone bank for an eight-hour shift and waited for trouble. It was never long in coming. There was domestic violence, unwanted pregnancies, threatened suicides and homicides, tales of gender confusion and bankruptcy, physical battles with repo men and runaways—young teens mostly, who had gotten themselves in too deep and wanted to come home, or go somewhere else. And alcohol. Always there was alcohol, or some other, even more pernicious substance.

She mastered the art of listening to how bad it could get. It had never been that bad for her. She had a list of recommendations, a roster of lawyers, phone numbers to call, clinics to visit, language choices to use with parents who were balled up in some inarticulate state of rage and fear, and children, the same. She remained anonymous. She used her own experiences only in an abstract way, but she continued to think of herself as an actress, with a role to play. She listened well and spoke as judiciously as she could.

She worked late into the night and baked herself clean in the morning. She began to walk for an hour, then two. She did not drink. She ate green and red chile and drank water, and, sometimes, sugarless iced tea. Once a week she called home. And late at night, when she turned off the light, she sometimes comforted herself with a vibrator that she and Djanga had found on West 4th Street years before.

As the weather began to change, she could no longer stay out all morning. Months had gone by and the high desert was beginning to be invaded by a chill wind. On the mesa that served as home to the Acoma people snow had begun to fall, sometimes in and around blinding bouts of cold sunlight. Aurora bundled up one Saturday determined not to be bested by the elements, but the feeling of stasis in the heat was gone. She realized that she had stopped thinking so much about Vincent, stopped thinking about Broadway, stopped puzzling over Ike Harris and the intrusions that, earlier that spring, still had the power to send her adrenaline into a state of chaos. She had made not the slightest attempt to do any of this. Time, heat, sun, and other people's troubles had done it for her. She had not had a drink in three and a half months and no longer craved one. It was time to go home.

IKE HARRIS KNEW she was gone, but not her whereabouts. He had humbled himself to call her agent, who was cagey and not helpful. Some time away, he said, after the loss of her beloved husband. More than understandable. That was it. In late summer, some six months after Vincent's funeral, he wrote her a simple letter, telling her that he had something that belonged to her, and he wanted to return it to its proper place. He was no more specific than that, and, for a time, received no reply.

She saw the letter when she returned. It was now October, the fall foliage had taken over the suburbs, and Ike was opening two new shows, one on Broadway and one at the Public down on Lafayette Street. The show at the Winter Garden had blown up in a flurry of legal tangles, and the Winter Garden was unexpectedly without a booking, which was rarely true.

Ike's focus had shifted. There was a revival of *Follies* that had made some noise in Los Angeles, and a couple of wealthy board members of the Ahmanson Theatre out there, where it was playing, thought it deserved to be seen in New York, and damn the costs. It would improve the West Coast theater's profile to have a run on Broadway. The Winter Garden was its natural home. It had been written for the Winter Garden. Aurora Shelton, Ike was convinced, should be playing Hattie Walker, the aged Ziegfeld star who sings "Broadway Baby" about a third of the way in.

Ike called the show's New York manager to make the suggestion and got hired to contract the orchestra.

"But," asked the manager, who had been a child when the original *Follies* had played the Winter Garden, "what's with Aurora Shelton? Why do you care?"

"She'd be great," Ike said. "And audiences will want to see her."

"We're mostly bringing the L.A. cast, but thanks for the suggestion," said the manager, barely stifling a yawn. "I'll pass it on to the powers that be."

When Aurora read Ike's letter she was not inclined to respond by post. She called him.

"You're very mysterious," she said.

"I could say the same. Where have you been for the last six months?"

"Pilgrimage," she said. "It's a beautiful day. Can you meet me in the park by the Bethesda Fountain? It'll take me about an hour."

He was waiting for her, carrying a brown shopping bag Lil had salvaged from the recycling bin. It was sturdy. He sat on the curved granite along the edge of the fountain, staring across at the benches on which old men and women were also sitting, taking in the clean autumn air. Younger couples were all around them. Dogs strained at leashes or slept in the sun. It was, in fact, as beautiful a day as was likely to be encountered in New York City.

Aurora, striding with the energy of the newly sober and committed, approached, and Ike stood. Then they both moved to one of the benches that surrounded the fountain, and, after a few unrevealing pleasantries, he told her that he needed to describe to her Vincent's last moments. He did not want to rekindle, or instigate a painful conversation, but he felt she needed to hear it, and, besides, he had a question. She nodded gravely.

It was the first time she'd heard it from an eyewitness, or at least one who would speak in detail. She sat quietly, visualizing the scene, moved but not agitated. It seemed to her, quite suddenly, that it had happened a long time ago.

Ike reached into the paper bag and extracted the sad remains of that particular copy of Liberty Music Shop L-310, Matrix P29031Y. She took it in her hand and turned it over, and then over again.

"The cigar box," she said. "This was what was in the cigar box."

"Not the only thing," Ike said. "But the only thing he was holding in his fist. He seemed to think that I had something to do with it."

"You had nothing to do with it," she said, "and you had everything to do with it."

And with that statement she launched into the story—the first time she had ever spoken it out loud, more than half a century after it had occurred, of how she came to possess this particular shard of shellac, rescued from her father's violent assault on her mother's sustaining possessions, and why, and who she—Aurora—really was, and who she was afraid she had become. At the very least, she had had a near brush with turning into Beatrice, and once was enough. Ike listened without moving. When she was done, she sat contemplating for a moment, and then concluded, "So the present, for me, has always only been the past. That, and the next job. And those have been scarce."

Ike let this pass. It was not something he could respond to coherently, or, perhaps, at all. Finally, he spoke.

"That, what I just gave you, that has always belonged to you. But I bought you a present, just in case."

He reached again into the bag and removed the relatively pristine copy of "Taking a Chance on Love" that Lil had discovered on eBay. It had been shipped in a thick brown cardboard sleeve with the matrix number written on the side in pen.

"I have nothing to play it on," he said, "and you probably don't either. But here it is. Some things can be saved."

She looked at the record in something approaching disbelief. Then she found her voice.

"Put it back in the bag," she said. "I want to hug you and I don't want to break it again."

"You didn't break it the first time," he said. And he slipped it back in the paper bag.

She gave him a proper hug, and then pulled away and looked at him as a new thought occurred to her.

"That place on 45th Street can't still be there," she said. "With that idiot savant."

He laughed. "Long gone," he said. "But the Internet . . ."

She nodded. They sat in silence for a long time. Then he handed her the bag.

"You don't know what this means to me," she said. "Or perhaps you do."

Ike took her hand, and then removed it.

"He came down the aisle," Ike said. "And he said to me, almost like it was an accusation, 'I can't fix this, maybe you can fix it. Can you fix it?' Or something like that. What does that mean? Nobody can fix a broken 78."

Aurora's eyes withdrew. She was thinking. She began to nod quietly to herself as Ike waited.

"He was afraid of you," she said.

Ike touched his chest with his hand, a silent expression of disbelief. As far as he knew, he had never inspired fear in any man.

"All I needed my whole life," Aurora said, "was the spotlight and the music. He could only give me the spotlight. He could fix anything; from the time he was a little boy. But he couldn't fix that. He couldn't make music."

He sat silently by her. There didn't seem to be any need to respond. Finally she spoke again.

"I was on the run," she said. "And I knew where I was running. I couldn't risk anyone who might run in some other direction—wherever the music took you. I didn't know it would take you to the same place I was going. How could I know that? And then, when I did, it was too late. You see? And so I did what I did, to avoid trouble. And you've been trouble to me ever since."

Ike nodded.

"The gods do that," he said. "We don't have much say."

22

FOLLIES

"THEY WANT ME for *Follies,*" She said. "To sing 'Broadway Baby.'"

"I told them they should," Ike said.

They were sitting in a coffee shop on Ninth Avenue near 44th Street, where they had taken to meeting once a week for a sandwich and tea. It was not the kind of a place where a Tony-winning Broadway actress went, which was why she liked it.

"I don't think I can do eight a week anymore," She said.

"Go to the gym. Or do whatever you have to do. Why should your public be denied?"

"I should be singing 'I'm Still Here,' but they're bringing some retired sitcom babe from the California production whose autobiography matches the character. All those sitcoms I could never get. She got 'em."

"Luck of the draw," Ike said. "'Better 'Broadway Baby.' It's who you are anyway."

"That's what they want," she said.

She told him that she had gone on the Internet and purchased a phonograph that could play 78 rpm records, but she had yet to listen to the record he had given her.

"It's a Silvertone record player," she said. "The kind they used to sell at Sears. I thought you might like to listen with me."

He wondered briefly if she had set this up. The malt shop. *Our Town*. Suddenly they were sixteen years old and maybe trying to say bigger things, but maybe not. He tried to drive this thought from his mind, though he remembered well that *Our Town* had, in fact, been one of her scattered triumphs on Broadway. He nodded, not too eagerly, he hoped, at the suggestion.

"I would like that very much."

He had never seen the inside of the house in Larchmont, though he had once driven by it in a fit of thwarted passion. He could not remember exactly when. The house was now spare and a bit forlorn, like a place in transition from one inhabitant to another but in no particular rush. She had been back for a couple of months, but had taken no trouble with the place, which she had begun to regard as a nest she would abandon when the weather turned cold.

The hedges needed pruning and the leaves had been left on the lawn and had sunk to the bottom of the pool, which was yet to be covered for winter. Tufts of wild grasses grew from the edges of the driveway. Inside, there was the vague odor of disuse, of air that had not moved.

She made tea. He plugged in the Silvertone, which, unlike any modern piece of sound equipment, had only an on/off switch and no options for adjustments, links to other equipment, or choices of any kind that needed to be made. It was simplicity itself—a thing of beauty. She emerged from the kitchen and set a tray on the coffee table in the living room that also held the phonograph. As she poured, and he directed her to add a lump of sugar but no milk to his cup, she said, "God, I hate tea." But she took some anyhow.

He placed the tone arm on the record, and, through a steady hiss of surface noise, Max Meth and the Martin Beck

Theatre Orchestra took up the gentle swing of Vernon Duke's melody, and then there was Ethel Waters. Aurora had not heard her voice in years. They sat in silence.

"Here I go again," she sang. "I hear those trumpets blow again . . ."

When the recording ended. Aurora put down her cup and nodded.

"That's it," she said. "That's the entire and whole reason that I did everything I did."

Ike stood and put the tone arm back at the outer edge of the record so it would play again.

"Dance with me," he said.

They danced in the living room, two old people who had grown up with this music, made by people long dead and mostly forgotten, and as he held her he realized that the steps they were doing were also antiques. She followed him lightly, easily, and with evident pleasure. She was a much better dancer than he, but a good partner. She didn't show off. They moved around the room in unobserved grace for almost three minutes. Then the music ended and they stood still as the needle of the Silvertone phonograph swung back and forth in the groves around the label, making a rhythmic hiss, a rocking pulse that caused them to remain pressed against each other. He held her face in his hands and, as if some long-suppressed liquid joy bubbled up inside of him, he kissed her, a real kiss. He had been waiting fifty-four years.

"Come upstairs," she said.

He followed her into the bedroom as she closed the blinds and began to undress.

"Aurora," he said haltingly, as she slipped into bed. "I have to explain something. After all these years . . . I'm not. It's been a long time since—"

"You can't fuck me," she said, turning on her side and

looking at him. It was, she thought, the first time she had said the word out loud within another's earshot, possibly ever. She liked the sound of it.

He watched her, naked under the covers, only her head and shoulders visible.

"I can't," he said.

"There are other places to start," she said. "Come to bed."

TWO NIGHTS LATER, as Ike was cleaning up the dishes from his solitary dinner in the apartment, Lil let herself in and went to his bedroom. She reemerged moments later, put away her coat and the scarf she had been using to shield her hair from the pelting rain, and went to the liquor cabinet for a brandy.

"It fucking sucks out there," she said.

She sat in the living room and waited for Ike to wipe down the counters and join her.

"What did you bring me?" he asked.

"I talked to a doctor today at hospice. I told them how old you were, your heart history, your drug regimen, and everything else."

"Five pills in the morning, nine at bedtime," Ike interrupted.

"They said you should try a quarter of a Viagra and see what happens. Those pills are hard to cut up. By the time I got done I was lucky to have a quarter—the other three quarters were pulverized."

Ike looked at her in disbelief. "You're talking to some doctor about your father's erectile dysfunction?"

Lil shrugged.

"We're dating," she said.

This took Ike by surprise. He did not inquire about the doctor's gender.

"Jewish?" he asked.

"That's very old-school," Lil replied. "The new models are much more diverse. Caribbean, this one. Went to Harvard."

Ike nodded skeptically.

"She's a doctor!" Lil said. "Every father wants his daughter to marry a Jewish doctor. But it's the twenty-first century. Besides, you and I have no secrets."

"And we're not keeping them from anyone else, apparently," said Ike. "I could see my own doctor."

"But you never will," Lil replied. "Look, you've loved this woman all your life. What else matters?"

"My privacy?"

"Doesn't compare. Not remotely. I left the quarter of a pill on your night table. I'm going to see Mom for a few days—they're letting me off work, unpaid. I'll be back in a week. Tell me nothing. And you're welcome."

It felt like a mechanical exercise that might drain all the romance out of a life that had been lived in ardent, poetic hope. But on the other hand, what was a ninety-year-old man to do? He called Aurora and asked if she would join him for dinner at the adequate Italian restaurant down the block that night. It was the fifth time they had spoken in forty-eight hours.

They tried. The first time was chaotic and strange, a plundering of good intentions for a confusing outcome. But, Ike noted, it was the first orgasm he had achieved in over a decade. Then they lay side by side and talked, talked as if the only proper result of such an intimate experience, however botched, was to confess things.

"I was not a very good parent," she said.

"We have that in common," Ike said, not trying to make her feel better. These were the facts.

Ike relayed the story of his ill-advised liaison with Missy, the night that ruined his chances with Aurora but gave him the daughter he hadn't wanted but came to love as deeply as he had ever loved anyone except the woman who was now in his bed. He told her of his night with Cee-Cee Austin and its disastrous results, and his lifelong sense of guilt over what had followed.

"It must have been quite a night though," Aurora commented, taking his hand in the darkened bedroom.

He rolled toward her and said, "Nothing to what this night can still be."

And then they really made love, delicately, slowly, each feeling the rhythms, the needs, the desires of the other. They took time and they took account of each other just long enough for them to gradually become one. Ike and Aurora improvised as if they were playing a suite of increasingly difficult and joyful piano pieces for four hands.

After, Aurora lay almost quiet, her hips rocking slightly and quietly against him as he slept. He was suddenly absent and took a portion of the room with him. She was in a strange place, one where she had never been, and contented herself that he was nearby if she needed him. She could hardly begrudge him his sudden unconsciousness, his heavy breathing, or his apparent physical and emotional absence from what had just occurred. A part of her was as content as a napping tabby cat in a ray of light on a windowsill, but she was lonely too, and waited for him to awaken.

When he did, he did not feel well. His head and his gut ached, and his teeth felt loose in his mouth, as if his gums had retracted and left them on their own. His heartbeat felt regular enough, but each beat resonated at his temples, and the consequent pain alarmed him. But he kept silent. In the morning, he rose and brought her coffee, feeling not much better. He felt so ill, in fact, that it was hard for him to appreciate the momentousness of what had happened. Still, he kept it from her. There was no chance that he was going to rob her of whatever joy remained with her at what they had done. They made plans for dinner.

Ike took himself off to his doctor on Park and 73rd.

The doctor, who had been treating him for more than a decade now, was calmly horrified. He steepled his fingers under his chin and looked at Ike with the kind of gravity that was usually reserved for terminal patients receiving the news for the first time or fifth graders who had gotten a C- in arithmetic.

"Ike," he said. "You're on three blood pressure medications, you have a pacemaker, your kidney function is marginal, and you take medication for arrhythmia, cholesterol, and your blood sugar.

Ike nodded.

"You might have dropped dead on the spot."

"I thought of that," Ike said. "But I threw caution to the wind." He did not mention Lil's new doctor girlfriend. What good would it have done? And the doctor did not ask him the source of the Viagra, for the same reason.

"I thought of all of that," Ike said, "but I thought, on the other hand, if I were to die in such a manner, it would not be a terrible way to die. And at my age, I may not have my pick of ways to die, so . . ." He trailed off.

The doctor nodded. "You're ninety," he said. "And have some consideration for the girl."

Ike nodded. "She's not a girl," Ike replied. "She's almost eighty, and we're in love."

"Well, then," the doctor said, "even more so. Call me at dinnertime tonight if the symptoms don't abate. And Ike? Don't do it again."

He had reached an age where telling anyone anything was

not so difficult, so, feeling better over dinner, he explained the situation to Aurora, who was sympathetic and just short of amused.

"My hero," she said. "You risked your life for me."

"To have you," Ike corrected her. "Entirely selfish. And I'd do it again."

"Uh-uh," she said. "Let's not lose each other yet. There are other things we can do."

That evening, after they discussed the possibility of her putting the Larchmont house on the market and moving into what Ike continued to call "Ollie's apartment," though it had been his now for more than two decades, he went through the library in the den until he found the Dickens novel he had been hunting. When Lil returned from Santa Fe, he showed a page to her and asked if she could find a place to have it transcribed and printed in a nice decorative calligraphy. The next day, when she picked it up and brought it to him on a fine cardboard stock, he looked it over with satisfaction and put it in the mail to Aurora with no note attached:

> There once lived, in a sequestered part of the county of Devonshire, one Mr. Godfrey Nickleby: a worthy gentleman, who, taking it into his head rather late in life that he must get married, and not being young enough or rich enough to aspire to the hand of a lady of fortune, had wedded an old flame out of attachment, who in her turn had taken him for the same reason. Thus two people who cannot afford to play cards for money, sometimes sit down to a quiet game for love.

He waited five days for a reply, knowing that this was a game they would play, and that neither was going to call the other in the meantime. In the Saturday mail there was an equally florid and thick-looking envelope from Aurora. When he opened it, he discovered that she had handwritten on the front of a handmade paper card one simple sentence: "It has to be hotter than that."

He opened the card. Inside was a beautiful reproduction of a Georgia O'Keefe's painting: the interior of a white lily, its yellow pistil nestled in the folds of the flower itself, needing attention.

23

THE WINTER GARDEN

THEY QUICKLY DISCOVERED that the infirmities of old age had been inflicted on both about equally. It had been years, perhaps decades, since either could remember proper nouns, and they were grateful for having figured out how to use their phones for help. Neither could sleep through the night. Aurora frequently began sentences that she neglected to finish as if she had lost interest in them at the halfway mark; Ike tended to mutter the ends of his sentences more than once, checking to see if they had arrived at the proper destination. And, of course, there was the small but annoying matter of his speaking his thoughts aloud without meaning to. Some mornings she would sit on the edge of the bed so stiff that she was unable to reach down and put on her own shoes. On these occasions he would get to his knees and fit them around her feet, which, for some reason he could never divine, gave him enormous pleasure.

But despite everything that had changed, they were both surprised at how vividly they each remembered their first sightings of each other, on Otts Oscard's bus, and before that in the tent where Ike had been playing by himself. They were sure this had really happened, at least on good days.

"What was it, do you think," she asked him as they lay in the bedroom of Ollie's apartment, "What was it that you noticed so intently on the bus? I can't imagine there was anything particularly vivid about me. I was a terrified kid."

"Your forearms and wrists," he said without hesitation. "It was late summer, but warm, and your arms were bare in a print dress. You must have got on the bus like a wood sprite or something. You have to remember we were a bunch of rum-dums stuck in a tenth-rate territory band with nothing to look forward to. I pulled my arm off the armrest so that you could use it. I just wanted to be in visual contact with perfection. The slenderest wrists, the lankiest, palest forearms. I don't know. The grace of them, I guess. I wasn't thinking of you as a woman, or a date—you were only a little more than a kid. I think I was admiring the bravery of your getting on that bus. Of course, I had no idea what you'd already been through. But the bravery of it—it was all in your forearms. Such a frail body pushing out into the world. I almost passed out."

She leaned over and turned on the bedside lamp. In the shadow it cast on the covers she held her arms up for them both to examine.

"A rare cooperative mystery," she said. "They are actually the only part of me that has not really changed."

It was true. They were lean and pale, as shapely and unblemished as a baby doe's trembling legs. Ike took a wrist in each hand lightly.

"Still there," he said.

"Watch them," she said.

She kicked off the bed cover. Ike was transfixed as she slipped her right hand into her panties and found herself with her fingers. With the other she pulled aside the top of her nightgown and crooked her forearm under her left breast, taking the nipple of the right breast between a thumb and forefinger.

"Help me," she said.

He lowered his mouth to the other breast and fed there, putting his hand on top of hers inside her panties, where he pressed her gently as she worked, until she said, in a whisper, "Put your fingers inside me."

He slipped into her, and he felt just how alive and young she was there, as if there was at least one more thing that had never been touched by the years. He almost held his breath as her hips began to rock back and forth, and she started to keen, an irregular, open-throated sound like an animal so unguarded that she must feel the forest belongs entirely to her.

When she came, she placed her left hand on top of his, sandwiching his hand between hers, holding it steady, and they lay still for a long time.

"The fountain of youth," she said, finally.

As he watched her fall into repose again, it came over him that while he was not able to share in her moment of ecstasy, the state of bliss that followed was entirely his. He watched her and was all but overwhelmed by a visceral sense of charmed contentment that he hoped would go on forever. But eventually, he spoke.

"Now let me ask you something."

She rolled on her side toward him.

"On the same bus," he said. "A month or two later. You chased me away. You had those death gratuity papers and I said something, I don't remember what, and you chased me off the bus. Maybe you don't remember."

"I remember," she said. "I remember even when I try not to remember. It was very wicked and unforgivable."

"Making me leave? It was nothing. You were upset."

"No. That was nothing. Only the why of it."

"Whatever it was, you're forgiven, believe me."

"Not so easily," she said. She paused for a moment, as if whatever she had to say had been bottled up inside her mouth for a very long time. "I didn't want another father," she said, finally. "I had just—at least I believed I had just engineered the end of my father, and my mother had paid a terrible price, but I was free. I had been trying for years to get free. And I didn't want another father. I was an orphan. And in some awful way, I liked it. I didn't know that you were never going to be my father. I didn't know anything. But I was free. And ashamed of the way it felt, and furious."

He took her hand.

"Absolution," he said, and he meant it, though he couldn't help thinking that the pagans might not be comfortable with the idea.

Later, after he rubbed her shoulders and fed her a brandy, he watched her sleep. He could watch her forever, he believed. But it wasn't to be. Eventually he, too, drifted off, destination unknown.

Lil had found an apartment in the West Sixties with her doctor, and Aurora had Little Vin and Gar organize a Local One crew to move her to Ike's place at the Alwyn Court. It was no longer Ollie's apartment, she declared. The Winter Garden was only seven blocks to the south, which would be convenient. The producers from California, seeking publicity, were all too happy to arrange a post-performance senior citizen wedding after the opening, and while Ike would have preferred, for that one evening, to contract the Martin Beck Theatre Orchestra, that theater had been renamed in honor of the caricaturist Al Hirschfeld, and the current band was an augmented rock aggregation with a lot of extra brass and reeds. At least *Follies* called for a traditional Broadway orchestra, and Ike was assembling the best.

One morning, lying in the bed that had once been the rowdy playpen of Ollie Harris and Count Willie Palaffi, Aurora said to Ike, "Let's take a train to Kansas. See where Otts Osgard's bus was parked when I sat down next to you.

Ike took a sip of the morning coffee he had brought to them, as he did each morning. There was no point in getting dressed before the first cup had been had.

He understood that trains had always been Aurora's preferred mode of transportation, that they were romantic and lonely and promising. All good things. But there was simply no way he could survive an overnight trip in an Amtrak roomette—struggling down the rocking and rolling corridor for his two *A.M.* and five *A.M.* pees alone would likely result in a fractured hip.

"Look," he said finally. "We can do better than Kansas. I know a place where there's a lot of trains."

ZURICH IN EARLY June looked to them both like the most elaborate movie set ever constructed—it put anything by Disney, animated or otherwise, to shame. Despite the city's daunting reputation as a banking and business capital, its lake was a sapphire blue that seemed like it belonged in the Caribbean; the bridges and cathedrals, lit by thousands of single bulbs by night, created the reassuring sense that one was in heaven without even having to die first. Vincent, Aurora pointed out with a little sadness, would have been impressed by the lights.

"We're taking our honeymoon before the wedding," she said. "I hope you realize that."

"Always eat dessert first, you never know what's going to happen," Ike replied.

Unsurprisingly perhaps, Franz Carl Weber's internationally famous toy emporium no longer featured the elaborate electric train sets that Count Willie had introduced to Ike back when he was fourteen, before the war. The toy world—like the real one—had simply moved on. The store was not even in the same location. When Ike expressed his disappointment to one of the immaculately uniformed clerks—he had brought his fiancée across the ocean specifically to enjoy the trains, after all—the clerk reassured him that there was a Franz Carl Weber Museum not far away, where he and the lady could see all the trains they desired.

The museum was yet another wonderland—six stories of old toys and advertisements for same, dating back to the beginning of the twentieth century. Aurora moved from one train exhibit to another taking imaginary journeys through alpine tunnels, running along rivers and lakes, through impressive model cities and past Lilliputian vineyards and farms. The reassuring hum and click of the trains on the tracks, the pointed detail of the locomotives and passenger cars, all lighted and featuring seating and sleeping quarters that could be glimpsed through tiny windows, left her with a serenity she had rarely known. She took Ike's arm and circulated once, twice, and a third time before she was ready to go.

A week later, they arrived in Paris, where they ate in small unassuming bistros. Le Cave de la Heure d'Or had disappeared, but Ike realized that he did not miss it. He had discovered his taste for nostalgia had evaporated somewhere along the line. He had all he wanted, really.

By the time they made their way to London, Ike had one last surprise. The tiny theater known as the Menier Chocolate Factory, located in the old factory building, was presenting a pocket-sized revival of *One More Spring.*

"It holds up pretty well," she said. "On the other hand, if it's old enough to revive, is that the same thing as being at your own funeral?"

"Not you," said Ike. "Not even me."

They posed for pictures with the current cast, and at a pub party afterward, held in her honor, Aurora sang both of the Jerry Herman songs to wild applause. She got quite happily drunk, for the first time since her return from the Southwest and stayed in bed all the next day.

When it was time to return home, they took the *Queen Elizabeth II,* one of its few remaining transatlantic voyages, setting their watches back one hour a day until they arrived at the Hudson River piers. They had been gone almost two months.

Rehearsals for *Follies* began, and when Aurora came home from rehearsal each evening, Ike prepared a light supper for the two of them. Aurora sometimes took a glass of wine, but not often. Ike nursed a bourbon before dinner, another at the table, and a small one at bedtime, which was frequently forgotten before the lights were turned out. The weather grew colder, and rain pelted down outside the windows on the many evenings they made love in their way.

Tech rehearsals began in earnest on a Tuesday, and for the first week, Ike needed to supply only a pianist and drummer. During the last four days, the entire orchestra was required, and Aurora reveled in singing once again with that old-time Broadway sound. She was a sensation. Ike watched from the wings.

Ike Harris spent December 8—his last day—sitting in row F at the Winter Garden watching the *Follies* final tech rehearsal, listening to his musicians and waiting for Aurora's big moment, after which she came out into the house and sat by his side in costume, holding hands until she was needed again. In the show, she was trailed by a chorine who played the ghost of her younger self. It was unnerving in a way—the young actress looked just enough like Aurora had when she performed

"Out of Sight, Out of Mind" on this same stage to give Ike a kind of double vision. She seemed a genuine alter ego, dressed in sepulchral gray and decorated with rhinestones that caught the light and sent it reflecting out into the empty house. Ike watched this young woman with curiosity. She was of no interest to him at all, whatever the resemblance. He and Aurora were together, and although he could remember her looking that way, he much preferred her now, and would have been happier to keep the ghosts where they belonged: permanently at bay. He did not ask who was running follow spot number two.

The final run-through ended just before midnight, and it was getting on toward one in the morning by the time Aurora had given up her microphone, changed into street clothes, and gotten a final set of notes from the production team. She and Ike, without discussion, went to the diner on 44th and Ninth and shared a grilled cheese sandwich and a bowl of chicken soup. The first preview was less than twenty-four hours away. They hardly discussed it. Aurora was tired, and there was little left to say about the show itself.

"Do you think we'll run?" she asked.

"You'll run as long as you'll run," Ike said. "It's a good show, but everything closes eventually."

A week later, they were to be married between a matinee and an evening performance, and provide supper for the cast, crew, Lil, Little Vin, Gar, and a few others. There was to be no minister or civil servant present—they would simply say their vows, and that would be enough. They couldn't see the point of official documents. That was the plan—a simple one.

They let themselves into the apartment at about two-thirty, undressed, and got into bed. Ten minutes later, she was happily asleep.

As he looked at her, he could see, across the room through

the bedroom window, that the snow had begun to fall, a January storm in December that swirled through the city. He reached for the glass on his bed table and drained the last dregs of his bourbon just before turning out the light.

He too drifted off, letting his mind float happily as more and more details returned to him about the brief, frantic week he had spent in the pit during the run of *Nowhere to Go But Up,* when he serenaded Aurora Shelton from below with his Harmon mute and his sixteen-bar solo that had been written by either Sid Lupowitz or Charlie Vodery—now he would never know which—and how Vincent Donnelly must have looked down upon the scene from above, trapping Aurora in his lamp, how two men ardently used every tool they had mastered to woo this unsuspecting young songbird as if they, too, were birds, gliding along the placid surface of a lake toward the potential of a lifelong fellow traveler who waited patiently in the reeds. Nothing goes as planned, he concluded, but everything goes. *Still,* he thought, *it's enough. It's enough for a lifetime, and more than so many have had.*

He awakened as if from a bad dream just before four. Something had gotten him up, yet no dream materialized in his mind. He looked over at Aurora, and his heart filled up in some way he had never felt before; quite unexpectedly, he felt himself falling. His head began to spin. He imagined himself in the pit of the Winter Garden again playing that solo during which he had fallen the first time, fallen so deeply that there was no other path for his life to take except to be near this woman who now he could be with, forever. He heard her voice trail off in that song, as he timed his trumpet entrance to dovetail with it seamlessly, so that they could, in that moment, be one voice emerging from two instruments, from two mouths.

Then he saw, clearly and for the first time, his father, whom he barely remembered, falling in the middle of Fifth Avenue, his own head spinning as the pavement rose up to meet him, the great doctor helpless in the face of his own body's declaration that there were some matters even a doctor could not mend. He saw his father's arm hit the pavement and the glass of his wristwatch shatter on the street. And there was Tommy Ladnier, falling, pitching forward onto a grooved and gritty unwashed floor in a Harlem apartment. He breathed as deeply as he could, which was not as deeply as he wanted to, and, for a moment, Vincent Donnelly was training a follow spot on Aurora, falling through his own beam of light.

He looked over at Aurora now and saw a double exposure, the woman he had loved at eighteen in the seat of a bus before he knew that he loved her, and the woman of seventy-six, whose breathing rose and fell in a steady, undulating beat, like the bolero he had once played in the original production of *Follies*. Her hair, silver in the dim light that reflected off the snow outside the window, was plaited at each side of her head; the braids fell against her collarbone.

He understood that Vincent Donnelly had had no more free will in the matter than he, for the light around her made it impossible not to fall. And so, Vincent had—fallen in the aisle, spilling blood on the back of a seat, a seat that tens of thousands of people had occupied over so many, many years, and in which each of them had, at some point, also fallen, fallen hopelessly for whatever story was on the stage that night in that theater that was his place of work and his only church. Tens of thousands more would follow, falling one by one, in the communal dark. He was soon to be married, that was the plan, but tonight his heart continued to fill as he watched her breathe, and he was falling. Falling away. And falling.

ACKNOWLEDGMENTS

This book was inaugurated by my friendship with Red Press, longtime music contractor and immortal number one reed player of the Encores! Orchestra for the *Encores!* series at New York City Center. I'm indebted to him for many reasons, not the least of which is the gift of his unpublished memoir of his early years in the army and playing with Big Bands. All the rest, as Maria Irene Fornes once said, I made up. My thanks to Rob Fisher for introducing me to Red in the first place and giving me my initial education into how a Broadway orchestra functions. Rob Berman taught me more and was kind enough to read an earlier draft of the manuscript and make valuable suggestions. Several other readers also read the work as it moved along and offered counsel and encouragement. Al Sayers, longtime head electrician at the St, James Theatre on Broadway, taught me everything I know about being a spotlight operator. Paul Libin coached me on theater union politics. My agents, first Becky Sweren and then Robin Straus were helpful in many ways, and I'm indebted to Robin especially for the title. Copy Editor Michelle Daniel, designer Edwin Vazquez, and especially the legendary Broadway poster designer Fraver, who created the dust jacket cover, all contributed tremendous work and wonderful support, and I wouldn't have found the first two without the willingness of Benjamin Dreyer to lend a hand. My son Josh gave me his optimistic definition of his fishing experience as a boy, and finally, my daughter Anna Daisy and my wife Linda were wonderful sounding boards; Linda read countless drafts without complaint and with much wisdom. I could have not arrived at this point without the support of them all.

JV
Little Deer Isle,
Maine, 2023

About the Author

Jack Viertel began his professional career playing National bottleneck steel guitar behind Bonnie Raitt, Son House, and The Pointer Sisters. He soon graduated to the theater world, where he spent seven years as a critic, two as the dramaturg for the Mark Taper Forum, and the succeeding three decades as Creative Director/ Senior Vice President of Jujamcyn Theaters, which owns and operates five Broadway theaters. In that capacity he worked with myriad artists including August Wilson, Tony Kushner, David Henry Hwang, Maury Yeston, Cy Coleman, Stephen Sondheim, George C. Wolfe, Jerry Zaks and many others. For two of those decades (2001-2021) he was also the Artistic Director of New York City Center's *Encores!* series, producing 65 musical revivals. On Broadway he produced the Patti Lupone revival of GYPSY and conceived the long running *Smokey Joe's Café*, the critically acclaimed *After Midnight* and served as the dramaturg for *Hairspray*, *Dear Evan Hansen*, and *The Outsiders*. The musical and movie *The Prom* were developed from his original concept. He taught musical theater at NYU Tisch School of the Arts for a decade and is the author of the New York Times bestseller *The Secret Life of The American Musical*. He lives with his wife Linda in Tarrytown, New York and Little Deer Isle, Maine.

www.ingramcontent.com/pod-product-compliance
Lightning Source LLC
Chambersburg PA
CBHW060551310726
48982CB00008B/1083/J
* 9 7 9 8 9 8 9 3 9 6 7 0 2 *